CW01660692

JEN EVE TAYLOR

Rebel Rebel

First published by Blue Jay Way Publishing 2023

First edition

ISBN: 978-1-916944-01-5

This book was professionally typeset on Reedsy.
Find out more at reedsy.com

For all the Jesses out there.
You're worth more than you think.

Contents

Playlist

To listen to the songs that accompany the thoughts, feelings and soul of these characters and their adventures, you can listen to the Rebel Rebel playlist.

These are tunes that encompass all the big emotions of this novel, that can only really be felt through music, and life; the two forever interwoven, at least in my mind.

It follows an arc, like any good adventure does, the songs placed in an order that makes narrative and musical sense, so I would recommend listening to it in order.

But who am I to tell you what to do? Break the rules, if you want.

www.jenevetaylor.com/playlist

Chapter 1

I noticed her the moment she arrived.

Written across her back in silver sequins were two words: 'Rebel Rebel'.

She liked Bowie.

She liked Bowie enough to wear him.

She wore a beret perched on her blonde bob, which somehow didn't look at all pretentious. She seemed to know everyone, making her way around the party holding a glass of red wine, which felt risky given she was wearing a white boiler suit, but it was pristine. I would have spilled wine down my front long before.

The crowd that night was more artsy than usual. There were so many parties in those days, it's a wonder we got any work done. They were mostly your friends, I just tagged along, pretending I was part of something. That's how we worked. You were the outgoing guy with the friends, and I was the girlfriend.

You scrunched up your nose as we walked in, while my eyes darted around the room. People were lounging on blue sofas or chatting in small conspiratorial groups. Others were congregating in the kitchen, as was standard at house parties. They were all dressed differently too; colourful, or in all black.

They looked so trendy.

You'd found the guy who invited us and were talking to him about something sports related. The music was buzzing slightly as Blink-182 blasted out of the speakers just that bit too loudly, so that people had to shout to be heard over it. Everyone had gone through a phase of listening to them in early high school and I wondered if it was already far enough past that time be considered nostalgic.

My concentration shifted erratically between my shoes and her – the blonde. I'd never met anyone else my age who was still stuck on Bowie. I was probably looking at her too much, for too long. I never have any idea how my actions look to the outside. Eventually she looked at me. I went to look away, but she held my gaze, then smiled. My stomach felt suddenly empty. I smiled back.

'Who's that?' The words came out of my mouth before I could stop them. I realised I'd interrupted your conversation and you were both staring at me.

'Who's... who?' you asked.

'Uh... her...' I said, looking at her.

'What, Astrid?' asked your friend.

'I guess.'

'She's been away for a bit, took some time off. I heard she was back in Berlin, doing some modelling and DJing in a club.'

'She... What?'

'Yeah. It sounded pretty cool. She's always very busy, does a lot of different things.'

All I had done over the summer was read books and go on walks.

People were getting louder, drunker, more brash. I stood around for a bit longer, then went to get another drink before heading outside for some fresh air. It wasn't until I got out the door and my eyes adjusted to the dark that I noticed she was out there on her own, smoking a cigarette, a leather jacket draped across her shoulders. Her eyes found me. She pulled out a silver cigarette case and flipped it open, gesturing it in my direction.

I shook my head. 'No thanks, it's cool and all, but I'm not so keen on the higher-chance-of-death factor.'

I heard the words as they came out of my mouth. That wasn't how I wanted to come across. She took a drag and stared at me for a few moments. The hairs on the back of my neck prickled.

'We're all going to die,' she said after exhaling a cloud of smoke through her delicate lips. Her voice was deep and smooth. She continued holding the cigarette case out to me.

Normally I would say no. I should have said no, but I was drawn to her, leaning against that wall, all leather jacket and Doc Martens. I glanced down, running the toe of my ballet flat over some of the dying grass in the garden, buying time. I looked back up, shrugged, and took one. She handed me the lighter, eyes still on me. I took it, struggled to light the damn thing, finally succeeded, and then breathed in, shallow. Very shallow. After another moment, she nodded and rested her head back on the brick wall.

'I've decided not to die,' she said. I noticed she had a very slight accent, something European.

'What?'

'I'm just not going to. It's such a bore.'

'Ok,' I said. 'That sounds like a good plan. I won't either.'

She looked at me. It felt like her blue eyes were gazing into my soul.

'Oh no, you will,' she said, the hint of a smile on her face.

'Well then...' A thought came into my head, too good to let it go. I threw out a couple of lines from Bowie's song 'My Death', ending with the part about drinking to life and the passing time. Then I held up my glass.

I hoped she wouldn't be the type of person to emblazon words on her back without them being important to her. That gaze stayed on me until finally, she replied in turn, with the line about death amongst the flowers.

She knew. She held up her glass, and I met it with mine.

'A fan,' she said just before we took a sip of our drinks.

'Avid,' I responded, after. 'You know he didn't write that though, right?' The words tumbled out of my mouth once again before I could stop them. 'I mean... Of course you know. I dunno, maybe you know. It's just...' My face felt hot and my collar, tight.

'It was originally by Brel?'

I exhaled. 'Yes.'

'You think a lot, don't you?'

'Um... yeah, I guess so...'

She nodded. 'All the best people do.' I looked at her, wondering if I'd heard right and she had referred to me as one of the 'best people'. She continued to speak, hardly even pausing to dwell on it like I had. 'My mum went into labour with me right after she was at a Bowie concert. I was weeks early. She used to joke that I was so into Bowie that I decided I had to come out immediately. Probably fits. I've been well into him ever since.'

I didn't have a cool story, I just liked him.

Silence fell between us and I wondered what I might say, if I could think of anything interesting enough to break it with.

'So, are you a first year?' she asked, making it seem so easy.

'No, it's my second. You?'

'A bit of both, I guess. I started last year, did a semester, deferred. Wasn't the right time, you know?'

I didn't know. I thought people just went to university after school. But I nodded along, anyway.

'You seem to know everyone though,' I said.

'I met a few last year, knew a few from elsewhere, make friends fast, I guess.'

I didn't make friends fast. I didn't make friends at all.

'What are you studying?' I asked her.

'Philosophy and music'

She was studying philosophy. Of course she was studying philosophy. Maybe this was the life I might have had if I'd studied philosophy. I could be the one telling people at parties, and they would look at me knowingly, aware that I was a thinker.

'I love philosophy.'

'Do you study it too? I haven't seen you in class.'

'Oh, no. I don't.' I hesitated. 'I do... economics.'

'Oh. Not economics and philosophy?'

'No.'

The thought hadn't even crossed my mind. Philosophy seemed like a hobby, not something to waste university fees on.

'I write though, on the side,' I said quickly. 'I've been writing for the uni paper.'

I'd only written one article about the food on campus, but I figured it had to count for something.

'Oh, that's cool,' she said. 'Next time I've got a gig you should come and write about it. I'm always up for some free press. I'll hook you up with tickets.'

'Oh wow. Yeah, sounds great.'

'All right.' She held out her hand to shake mine, an oddly formal gesture. Once I'd caught on to what was happening, I held out my hand too, and we shook them together. Then she stubbed her cigarette against the wall, walked over to the door, opened it, and disappeared inside.

I exhaled a long breath. Then I copied her move with the cigarette and headed back to the party.

When I got inside, you knew.

'Have you been... smoking?' you asked, looking at me with narrow eyes.

'No...'

'Well you stink of smoke.'

'I was just outside, I don't know, it must have got in my hair.'

My collar started to feel tight again.

'You'd better not have been smoking. Those things will kill you. And besides, it's disgusting.'

'We're all going to die...' I offered, emulating what I thought was nonchalance, but probably just came across as rather pathetic.

You rolled your eyes and walked away. It was a night of being walked away from. I wanted to walk away from myself too.

Chapter 2

The first time you ever spoke to me, back in sixth form, came as a complete shock. Partly because there was a boy talking to me and partly because *anyone* was talking to me. People mostly seemed to ignore me. I was the quiet kid who didn't speak in class and spent my lunchtimes in the library reading. The loneliness of school had felt eternal.

That day, I was sitting out on the grass, my back against the wall in the school quadrangle and for some reason, you decided to approach me and ask what I was reading. I nearly dropped the book.

'Oh, it's *The Stranger* by Camus,' I said, once I'd regained composure.

'Are you reading it in French?' you asked, as if that was a perfectly normal thing.

'No, I can't read French.'

'Oh, I see. Well, are you reading it for English class?'

'No, just for fun.'

'And is it fun?'

You sat down next to me and took the book out of my hand. You had short, sandy-coloured hair and even when you were sitting, it was obvious you were tall.

'Hey!' I tried to grab it back but failed. You flicked through it.

'Well? Is it?'

'Not really. It's supposed to be this great classic, but I don't know... It just seems very... white male.'

'And that's bad?'

'There's just so much of it around, it's kind of boring.'

'Fair enough.'

I couldn't tell whether you were being genuine or dismissive. I also couldn't tell if you were making fun of me. I thought there might be some big joke about talking to me. Maybe someone had dared you to do it. But I reminded myself that we were all new, and no one knew me yet.

You said you had to get to debating practice, but that you hoped to see me again. It turned out we caught the same bus home, and we started to sit together and discuss books. One day you brought one in for me to read – Kerouac. Another white male. I brought you Margaret Atwood, which you seemed to like more than I liked Kerouac. But I said I loved Kerouac. It was worth it to see you smile.

We started hanging out more, which both excited and terrified me. I wanted you to see me as more than a bus friend who talked books.

I used to listen to the other girls talking amongst themselves. They spoke so much about boys, but I'd hardly spoken to any, having just come from an all-girls' school. I'd spent most of high school begging my parents to let me change schools – I'd felt so alone and was sure somewhere else would be better. But when it finally happened for sixth form, being around boys in a new co-ed environment was so foreign to me. The girls all passed around magazines that instructed on things like 'How to please your man' and 'How to get the guy to notice you'. I wasn't part of the sharing circle, so I would save up my pocket money and buy them after school, reading them from cover to cover. I thought the articles were terribly written, and that I could do a much better job, but of course I had no idea about how to make a man happy. I tried to say all the right things when I talked to you, tried to like the same things you did. I wanted to be the girl you wanted to be with. I thought maybe I was being too over-the-top, too obvious, but you called me mysterious and said you never knew what I was thinking. I loved that.

Then it happened. Our first kiss was behind the wall in the courtyard at school, where no one could see. I felt slightly ill whenever I saw you, the excitement making it feel like something was doing somersaults in my stomach. I hoped you were feeling the same, though I think you were too cool to show it a lot of the time. We never officially discussed being together, we just sort of were. Being your girlfriend seemed to give me a space in the world that I'd never had. Your friends talked to me, even the girls at school started talking to me. I would go to watch you in your debating tournaments, feeling so proud as you bore down upon your opponents. I found it exhilarating to watch you. You were so composed, so authoritative. I loved being associated with you. I felt real for the first time I could remember.

I kept waiting for it to end, for you to grow tired of me, but it never happened. We started planning where we would go to university. Together.

You had it all worked out; you knew exactly where you wanted to go to study law, ready to go into your family's business when the time came. I had always known I wanted to go to university, so much that it didn't feel like a decision to go, it was just what was going to happen. I dreamed of being a professional businesswoman, going to work in a high-rise building in London every day, wearing smart clothes and sitting in an office, doing something important. That felt like success.

The uni you chose hadn't been my first choice of university; I'd wanted to stay nearer home and go to the same uni my mum had. But I remembered only too well the never-ending years of nothingness before I met you, and I couldn't go back to that. Mum would understand; I was making my own way, choosing my own path.

I'd pulled up the course list to see what I could study. There was no way I was choosing law. I wasn't smart enough for a start, and the idea of arguing in a public forum was terrifying. Eventually I settled on economics. It seemed like a good degree, and Dad was an accountant.

I'd never been sure exactly what I wanted to do. How was anyone supposed to know their life's calling at eighteen? Some people seemed to... I wonder if, fast forward twenty years, they'd still be with those careers? I doubt that whatever fits at eighteen is likely to fit forever. So, I decided to study something that would set me up with a good career and then figure the rest out later. Economics it was. Dad seemed proud when I told him.

We'd decided to live in the student halls for the first year. I couldn't help picturing high school all over again, thrown together with hundreds of people who didn't want to know me. But it would surely be different this time, I had you.

I was filled with anticipation at the thought of going off to uni. I thought you would drive us both and we would listen to music – perhaps I'd make a road trip CD. I often had pictures of things in my head that were so far removed from reality that I had to remember to manage my expectations. In reality, all our things wouldn't fit in your car and in reality, it made more sense for my parents to drive me and in reality, they wouldn't want to listen to any CD I'd made, anyway.

I'd had to arrive early because it was the only time my parents could find to drive me. I sat quietly in the back of the car while they argued over which way to go, which exit to take. The drive seemed so long, and I felt slightly nauseous the whole way, staring out the window and hoping I wasn't going to throw up.

When we arrived, we piled my things into my room, which didn't take long as I didn't have much stuff. The room itself contained only a bed, a desk, an uncomfortable looking plastic chair, and a wardrobe. The faded orange curtains hanging over the window were frayed at the bottom. Even with my things in it, it looked so empty.

My parents were meant to be heading straight back home again, but I suddenly wished they would stay, even just for a bit longer.

'Do you maybe want to get some lunch?' I asked them, before they could leave.

'Oh no, honey, we should get going now.' Mum had that smile on her face that didn't reach her eyes and I knew she couldn't be argued with.

'Or a coffee?' I tried again. 'I'm sure we could grab a quick coffee somewhere? It won't take long.'

Dad looked at his watch, then they looked at each other and back to me. They stood awkwardly in my doorway, neither in, nor out, of my room.

'No, I don't think we can,' he said, after they appeared to have had a whole conversation with their eyes. 'We don't want to be caught out on the road when it gets dark.'

It wouldn't be dark for hours.

'Yes, you know what those roads are like at night, and your father's eyes aren't what they used to be.' This was something Mum said, though I had no idea why. He didn't wear glasses and for all intents and purposes, he seemed to be able to see things fine. But she always worried.

'You'll be fine, sweetie,' she said. 'I'm sure you'll make new friends in no time. And Robert will be here soon.'

She gave me a hug. I supposed she was right; you would be arriving soon. Things might be different this time. No, they would *have* to be. I could do this.

I kissed my parents goodbye. As mum was leaving, she turned back around and reached out to hold my arm.

'You will be ok, won't you?' she said in a soft, strained voice, her eyes searching my face.

I put on a smile. I didn't want to worry her even more. I'd work it out. I'd be ok, somehow.

'Yeah, Mum. Don't worry about it. I'm fine. You get home.'

She patted me on the arm, and they left to drive back. I realised that I was happy for them to leave, really. I suddenly didn't want them spending too long in my new space, it felt as if they could somehow rub off on it. I wanted to make a clean break.

But still, as I sat on the bed after they'd gone, I couldn't stop the tears starting to prickle at the corners of my eyes. I felt so alone. I didn't know what to do. There were people around, other early birds unpacking and chatting, but I already felt like I was on the outside – plunged back into the loneliness of high school before I met you. I went to bed early and cried myself to sleep in the tiny room with barren walls. The walls were painted the colour that all soul-less rooms are painted – magnolia. It all felt so foreign, I felt so small. I woke up sometime in the night and couldn't work out where I was. I couldn't even work out which way up the room was. The walls felt like the ceiling and the ceiling felt like the floor. I tried to move my head, to sit up, but the world was spinning. I closed my eyes and willed it all to melt away. I pictured myself in a completely white room filled with light, with no furniture, just me sitting in the middle. I kept my eyes closed and eventually I must have fallen back to sleep. When I woke up in the morning, everything was back where it should be.

That day I went to the shops to pick up a few things. I found a record store and stopped in to see if they had any posters. I got a Franz Ferdinand one that was still kicking around from their second album, which had come out the year before. I also managed to find a Killers poster. They didn't have any Bowie ones, probably because he hadn't put an album out for years and it felt like everyone else had forgotten about him. I also got a soft toy elephant to keep me company. I named him Hoover.

The following night I slept better knowing I had reference points to look at on my walls. I didn't feel any less alone, but I felt comforted by having Hoover to hug. I felt proud of myself. I'd been resourceful and had done my best to solve a problem. When the second night passed with less distress, I felt like I had succeeded.

I still hadn't really spoken to anyone, aside from a passing 'hello' in the corridors. They seemed nice enough, but I had shuffled back into the safety of my room before much more conversation could be had. How was I supposed to make conversation with people I didn't know? I was just trying to work through one thing at a time.

You turned up on the third day. I was sitting in my room, and I glanced out the window. I thought I saw you in the courtyard, though surely you would have told me if you'd arrived... But it looked like you, so I decided to venture down casually, as if I were heading somewhere else. I found you chatting to some people. I walked up and you smiled and put your arm around me.

'There she is,' you said. 'Hey everyone, this is Jess.'

I smiled as they all said hi. It was going to be all right.

Chapter 3

I'd spent so long looking forward to going to university, but the memories of it have faded over time. It was just one long, never-ending stream of things I didn't care much about. Even with people around constantly, there were days when I felt more alone than ever before. I didn't feel like anyone really knew me.

I'd realised quite quickly that I didn't fit in with the other economics kids. I guess I'd thought that a shared interest would mean we'd have something in common, but they actually *liked* maths and numbers. I had a brain for patterns and things making sense, sure, but it was only going to be a job, right? Economics was hardly my life's calling.

You, however, had no problems fitting in with your fellow law students. I don't think you ever really understood what it felt like to always be on the outside – to want to hide in the background and not talk to anyone. You never got why I often wanted to skip lectures and avoid it altogether...

'Don't you have class this morning?' you asked with your head leaning through my doorway, a smile on your face. That morning, I was sitting on my bed with the door open, watching *Veronica Mars*. I hadn't been allowed to watch much TV growing up, and there were so many shows I'd missed, that other people seemed to know and they would make references I didn't get. People had connected their computers to the uni network, and there were so many TV series and movies just waiting to be copied over and watched. I'd already made my way through *The OC* and was up to date on *One Tree Hill*.

'Umm yeah, I was thinking I might just go to my tutorial later.'

'You're not going to the lecture?' You were looking over at the timetable pinned up on my wall.

'I... wasn't going to...'

'Don't be silly, come on. I have one too, we can go together. I'll drive.'

I weighed up the options: stay with Kristen Bell as she fights crime with her friends or spend time with you but have to sit through a boring lecture. You were right, of course. I grabbed my things and shut my door behind me.

Some of my classes took attendance, but others didn't. Lectures felt huge and impersonal, and I struggled to really learn anything from them. I tried to go to them all at first, but as the year progressed, I found there were some I could miss and it would still be ok. It seemed different for you; Law was a bit more full on. But I could get away with sleeping in and missing my 9 a.m. lectures.

I imagined how angry my parents would be if they knew I had chosen to stay in bed over going to class. Part of me felt a thrill for making my own decision and not doing what was expected of me. Then, of course, the guilt would set in, and I'd diligently go to all my classes for a week before getting lazy again and missing a couple more. It was an adjustment, I guess.

But even despite all my ambivalence about my course and

the lectures, the novelty of being at university never wore off. I loved the place itself – the buildings, the feeling of walking around them, and knowing that I was setting myself up for my future. Sometimes I just wandered around the campus in awe that I was there, that I'd made it.

We moved out of dorms after first year. We got a five-bedroom house with three of our friends. It was an upgrade to blue curtains from the horrible faded and frayed orange curtains we'd had before, but the walls were still magnolia.

The others we moved in with were nice enough. There was Lauren, the one girl in your group of law friends. She was short, typically pretty and had glistening long hair. When she smiled, she looked dopey and apologetic. But the rest of the time, she had a permanently angry face – the sides of her lips were down-turned at resting, and for a long time I thought she hated me. I liked her, though. I imagined really *truly* being her friend, but I wasn't sure what we'd talk about. She wanted to go into women's rights law, and she always asked me if I had experienced any sexual harassment lately. I would shake my head and the conversation would end. I fantasised about making something up one day so that we could bond. Once, in first year, she'd invited me to her book club along with some other girls. I went, and we all sat too close to each other to fit in her dorm room, while she passed out sweet berry cider in small plastic cups. I was too nervous to take in anybody's name. I hadn't even been able to get through the book. It was Germaine Greer and while I wanted to be the type of person who reads Germaine Greer, I found out I wasn't. I never got invited back.

Then there were the boys: Matt and Ethan. They were grammar school boys with immaculate hair. I didn't understand a lot of what they said but I laughed at their jokes with an open mouth, like they did. They talked about law, complained a lot about something called 'torts', and used words like 'fungible'. The four of you got along well and our house felt full. I just never felt particularly part of it.

Near the end of first year, I came across a sign saying that the uni newspaper was looking for new recruits. I wanted to get involved, but I had no experience. I sat on the thought for a few days, before mentioning it to you one night after dinner. I told you about a silly dream I had of being a writer. I was ready for you to say that it was a ridiculous idea, that I wouldn't be good enough. I heard my mother's voice in my head too, telling me that I had no experience and nothing interesting to say. But I was surprised when you said you thought it was a great idea and told me I should do it. I felt such a rush of love for you, glimpsing myself through the eyes of someone who believed in me. It gave me the confidence to think that maybe they wouldn't laugh me out of the room.

The next day I walked in and asked whether they had anything I could do at the paper. The person I spoke to was a tall guy with long, thin limbs.

'Can you write?' he asked in a thick northern accent, as he was folding a stack of newspapers. 'We need a new writer, one of ours finished last term so we're a man down.'

'I think so,' I answered.

'Great, well, why not get out there and write something and we'll see if that's your role. Sound good?'

I nodded. It sounded very good. I couldn't believe he'd asked me to write, I thought I'd start with a much smaller role. Almost as soon as the excitement hit me, so did fear. I had no idea how to come up with ideas, I wasn't that kind of person.

Some people seemed to be able to generate ideas on the spot – you certainly did, I watched you debate with just a handful of words written down on palm cards. But that just wasn't me. I couldn't imagine why I ever thought it would be, I guess I was hoping they'd tell me what they wanted me to write.

I grabbed a copy of the paper on the way out so I could see what kind of articles they usually printed. There was a section on general campus news, a gig review of a concert that had happened in the quadrangle outside the library, some stuff about the NUS – the national student union… I had no idea what I could write about. But then, somewhat serendipitously, I was handed a flyer while I was walking between classes. Apparently, there was a vegetarian crisis in the campus café. People were up in arms about the limited vegetarian options, and a group of students were boycotting the café until they expanded their menu. I felt like an undercover reporter as I checked out the food and surreptitiously took photos with the digital camera my parents had got me for Christmas. I figured I needed to get some quotes from people who were unhappy about the menu but was scared about the idea of just walking up to strangers and talking to them. I tried giving myself a pep talk: 'Come on Jess, you idiot, you're at university, it's time to challenge yourself…'

I managed to start some casual discussions with people, asking what they thought about the menu. I put together an article, complete with photos of the sandwiches and one of someone I spoke to who had agreed to go on the record, looking disgruntled outside the café.

I was nervous about showing the people at the paper my work, of course. What if it wasn't what they were looking for? What if they laughed at me? What if they told me I couldn't write? I printed out my article and left it sitting on the edge of my desk for a couple of days while I stared at it out of the corner of my eye and wondered if I was doing the right thing. But I'd told you I was submitting something, so I knew I couldn't back out.

Eventually, I emailed it to the people at the newspaper. I got a quick response; they wanted me to drop by to discuss it. My hands felt clammy as I walked back into their office. To my surprise, when the tall guy greeted me he said they were publishing it in the next week's edition. There were a few tweaks, but it was a 'good piece of journalism', he said. And, more than that, they wanted more, regular, submissions from me. He told me his name was Oliver, and we shook hands as I left.

I walked home smiling. I'd heard that some people peaked in high school, but others came into their own at university – maybe this would be my time.

Chapter 4

It was a while before I saw Astrid again, after that first party. Her presence had been burned into my mind and I couldn't shake the memory of it. I'd been going to all the parties, wondering if she would be there. I'd figured that we ran in quite different circles, but our paths had crossed once, and I hoped they would again. I walked through nondescript living rooms, searching for a sign of her amongst the partygoers. Each time it became apparent she wasn't there, I passed the time drinking and watching the people around me. I started to notice what everyone was wearing, how they behaved and how they were received.

An idea grew in my mind until one day, I found myself wandering the shops, looking for something slightly different to what I usually wore. There were bright patterned shirts, long tartan coats and studded belts. I ran my hands over the different textures but felt overwhelmed by their boldness. In the end, I picked out some chunky black boots, and a fake leather jacket. Back in my room, I pulled a couple of crushed sun dresses out of the back of my wardrobe that my mum had bought me, but I'd never worn. For some reason, I had packed them on a whim when I left for uni. And thick black tights. Always tights. I wasn't about to get my legs out.

The first time you saw my new outfit, you looked at me in a strange way.

'You look different...' you said. 'I don't think I've seen you in anything other than jeans.'

I shrugged, trying nonchalance on for size once again, and said I felt like a change. In that moment, part of me loved the way my new look made me feel – like I might stand out a little more. Although when we got to the party, I felt like a child who had raided her older sister's wardrobe. I immediately wanted to leave. I was sure everyone's eyes were on me, and that they knew I was an imposter.

When I finally convinced you to leave and go home, I went straight to my room, slipped out of my new outfit, and stuffed the clothes right at the back of my wardrobe. I lingered in the bathroom that night after brushing my teeth and looked in the mirror, deep into the eyes staring back. After a while I stopped recognising my own reflection. Like saying a word so many times in a row that it stops making sense. I wondered what she had seen when she saw me, what she had thought when she'd spoken to me. I couldn't imagine she would have thought anything. I wasn't anything. I was just a combination of features messily put together. Just a girl with mousy hair.

By the next weekend I'd convinced myself to try again. I dug the dress and the leather jacket out of the back of the wardrobe. When you came to get me to leave for the party, you didn't say anything about how I looked. I fought down the tightness spreading across my chest. We went to the party, and I managed to stay longer. I'd set myself a challenge and was determined to win. I was starting to feel more natural in my new look.

But then one night at another party, it all got too much again.

I suddenly felt ridiculous – what on earth did I think I was doing? I'd got caught up in some strange fantasy I'd made up in my head, wanting to be friends with someone I didn't even know. I was acting crazy. I needed a breath of air. I burst out the back door of the house, my head spinning. I heard voices to the right and looked over.

Of all the people who could have been standing there, it was her. She was leaning against the wall, with a boy in tight black jeans and a leather jacket standing in front of her. They were laughing, her head thrown back. His hand held the front of her jacket. I felt like I had disrupted something sacred. She turned to look at me.

'Hey, it's you,' she said. 'The writer.'

'Hi,' I said, shifting my weight so I was resting on one leg, trying to look casual. *The writer.* I was glad that was what she'd remembered of me.

'I haven't... seen you for a while,' I said offhandedly, trying to make it sound like I'd only just happened to notice.

She pushed the boy gently away. When he didn't move, she put out her foot and pushed his leg. He shrugged and wandered over to another group of people further down the garden who were sitting around a big wooden picnic table.

'I've been away,' she said.

'Oh.'

She pulled out her silver cigarette case again and took one out, stopping to offer me one. This time I took one without hesitation. It smelled sweet, kind of like toothpaste. She must have noticed me smelling it, as she said 'Menthol' when she held out the lighter. As if that was meant to be some form of explanation.

'Oh,' I said. 'Cool.'

We stood in silence, the voices from the nearby group floating towards us.

'Been anywhere nice?' I asked eventually.

'Oh, I was in Hungary, doing a bit of work. Needed a break, you know? The ruin bars in Budapest are incredible. I went to a rave in one of the baths. It was magic.'

I took what was becoming my signature shallow drag of the cigarette (menthol), hoping she didn't notice that I wasn't breathing it in properly. But I reckoned that I was at least cutting my risk of cancer from lung, throat and mouth, to just mouth.

'Have you ever been to Budapest?' she asked.

I shook my head. I'd hardly been anywhere.

'I haven't travelled as much as I might like,' I replied.

'You must. Travel is the most important thing there is, don't you think? It's the only time we step out of our tiny corners of the world and see things for what they really are. Putting ourselves in situations we would never usually encounter, with people who are different from us... well... that's the meaning of life, I think. Don't you?'

I had no idea. The thought of going somewhere new scared me, especially somewhere that didn't speak my language. But I wanted to understand the meaning of life.

'Eastern Europe is fab,' she continued, seemingly unaware of my lack of response. 'I just love it. The Nordic countries too. You must get there one day.'

I nodded. 'I will.'

She took a final drag on her cigarette, kicked herself off the wall and dropped the butt before putting it out with her foot. She went to walk away.

'I've been thinking about it,' I said quickly, and she stopped to half-turn back towards me. 'I know what you said but... I've decided that I'm really not going to die either.'

She fixed those eyes on me, and I immediately felt stupid for saying it. Why would she remember a conversation she'd had with some random at a party? It had been so long ago, and she'd done so much since then. Eventually her face softened, and she nodded.

'Maybe, maybe,' she said as she turned again to head inside.

'I'm Jess,' I offered, not wanting to let her slip away again, to lose her to months of wondering...

She stopped, turned around and smiled at me – that smile that could light up a room. I felt like I had managed to do something right.

'All right then, Jess the writer. Here.'

She took a mobile phone out of her pocket and tossed it to me. Miraculously I caught it. Was she asking me for my number? I looked at her and she nodded towards it. I typed my number in, before closing the gap between us to hand it back.

'See you around then,' she said as she pocketed it and walked inside.

She now knew my name.

Chapter 5

I didn't hear from Astrid for weeks. I had almost convinced myself that she had been making fun of me by asking for my number. Maybe she and her cool friends were sitting at a party somewhere and laughing together over glasses of red wine at how stupid I was.

But then one day, to my complete surprise, I received a message from her.

Gig tonight at the Phoenix Bar. Got your name on the door and a +1.

It felt like frogs were leaping around in my stomach as I tried to work out if she was expecting me to review her gig. I hadn't even floated the idea of covering live music with the paper, and there wasn't time to check with them first. I tried to think how you would handle the situation, and I came up with the idea of pretending it was all sorted, then somehow persuading Oliver to print the review. An uneasy excitement started to rise within me. Could I do that?

I asked you if you wanted to come with me to the gig – I had a '+1' after all.

'Um... it doesn't really sound like my thing,' you'd said, and I appreciated your honesty. 'You go, though. Have some fun. I'll probably just hang out with the guys.'

'Yeah, of course, no worries. I'll probably just go for a bit anyway...'

I don't know why I said that, I had every intention of staying until the end. I'd bought some black eyeliner and eyeshadow. Astrid wore it, but I never had. I found a website that explained how to do it, and I decided to try it out. It took me three goes to put the eyeliner on steadily, and even then, it was uneven. Her lines were always perfect. My eyeliner came with a 'blending brush' so I smoothed the edges of the lines, giving it what was apparently called a 'smoky' look. I hardly recognised myself. My eyes felt lost amongst the blackness.

But I knew I was pretending to play the part of the music journalist and I needed to look convincing. I didn't want you to see me, so I was glad that you headed out with Matt and Ethan before I started to get ready. I wasn't prepared for what you might say about how I looked. I needed to stay in my own head. I needed to stay in control.

I was 'the writer', like she had said I was. I repeated the word over and over to myself, trying to convince myself to believe it.

I took a small black notebook with me that I had purchased weeks before but hadn't found a worthy use for yet. . I also took my camera. I got there early. I got everywhere early. When I walked in, Astrid was standing near the bar chatting with a few people I didn't recognise. I felt my heart start to race as my mind rushed through options of what I should do. I could loiter at the other end of the bar and maybe get a drink. I could walk swiftly past into the other room and pretend I hadn't seen her. Or I could go and say hi. All three options seemed daunting. I decided to get a drink and went and stood at the bar, wondering what to order. I didn't have a go-to drink, but red wine seemed a good choice and I noticed it was what she was drinking. So I ordered a house red. When I turned around, I saw that she'd noticed me and was waving me over. I paid and walked over to her.

'Guys, this is the writer I was telling you about.'

They all turned to me.

'Hi, I'm Jess.' I smiled and nodded as they told me their names, none of which settled in my head. I was far too preoccupied with keeping my nerves under control.

'I'm on in about an hour,' she said. 'So glad you could make it!' She reached out and squeezed my arm.

We all stood together for a while, as Astrid told us about the gigs she'd played on her recent trip away. She said she'd brought back some new songs that she'd written, that she was planning to play for us all. I made a mental note to write about that detail in my review. She excused herself after a while to go and get ready for her set, and one of the girls suggested that the four of us take a seat. I excused myself to go to the bathroom, where I ran into Astrid. She was splashing water up her arms and across her neck. She laughed when she saw me.

'It gets hot under the lights up there, this helps me to get in the zone!'

'Makes sense,' I said, setting my glass of wine down on the bench beside the sink and checking my hair in the mirror, while Astrid dried her arms with some paper towel.

'I'm so glad you could make it,' she said, and gave me a hug. 'Well, I'd better go set up! I'll see you out there!'

'Good luck!' I said. 'And thanks for the invite!'

I quickly went to the toilet, before heading back out. There wasn't any room next to the group of people I'd met, so I settled into an empty seat at the side of the room. It wasn't a huge room, but it felt warm and homely. There were heavy red curtains around the sides, blocking the windows to outside. She'd finished setting up by the time I found my spot, and there was a keyboard and a guitar onstage.

I wasn't sure what to expect from her gig. I had no idea what kind of music she was into, other than Bowie of course, and I realised I didn't even know what instrument she played. She took her place onstage, behind the keyboard, accompanied by the exuberant applause and cheers of the audience. The first atmospheric notes she played hushed the crowd immediately. After a few chords, she started singing, weaving a melody above the keyboard backing. I couldn't take my eyes off her, she was so engaging to watch. It was as if her voice was running through me, and then out into the people around me and back. We were all connected in that moment. I had goosebumps. It felt like the first time I was really experiencing music; like I was part of something bigger than just me.

Her music was a mix of everything. I heard 80s vibes coming through, some soaring Bowie-like choruses, hints of classical piano, elements of psychedelia, parts of it even sounded quite electronic. Then some way into her set, she got up from the keyboard, and grabbed the guitar. The keyboard notes she'd been playing somehow continued by themselves, and she played the guitar over the top of it. I'd never seen someone playing multiple instruments live before. I had no idea how she'd done it.

As far as I could tell, she was playing all originals. Then near the end, she started playing a song that made me shiver and after a few moments I realised she was doing a cover of 'The Man Who Sold the World'. I had forgotten about that song, I realised I hadn't heard it for ages. I usually hated covers of songs I loved, but her version breathed a whole new life into it. I felt tears prickling at the corners of my eyes as she sang it, feeling so much emotion coming through her performance. I looked around and could see that other people also had eyes glistening with tears.

Her set went on for about an hour and I didn't want it to end. The applause when she finished was huge.

A DJ took over after Astrid's set ended, and as she packed up her things onstage, the room turned into a dance floor. I went to the bathroom again, then to get myself another drink. I found her at the bar, surrounded by a group of people. I hovered nearby, eventually getting the chance to tell her how much I'd enjoyed her set. She thanked me again, graciously, then said, 'Shall we go dance?'

We ended up dancing for hours, taking it in turns to request music that made us smile. The other people she knew dropped off one by one, but she and I stayed. I felt compelled to stay much longer than I usually would have, I didn't want to miss a moment. Her song choices were eclectic – from demanding the DJ play 'Albatross' by Fleetwood Mac (an odd song to dance to), to 'Golden Skans' by the Klaxons, and the ultra-groovy 'Electric Feel' by MGMT. Somehow, whether she'd picked a dancey number or something more esoteric, they all seemed to perfectly fit the vibe of the night. We had some crossovers in songs we asked for, most obviously, Bowie songs. But I diverted many of my turns to choose the music back to her, the pressure to get it right feeling too much.

'Don't you think that listening to songs you love feels like being stabbed in the heart?' she asked, her arms weaving, stretching up above her head.

'What?' I replied, over the voice of Freddie Mercury.

'Right here,' she reached out and took my hand, placing it on her chest. 'Like it's all too much. And you feel like you're about to explode. Like everything else stops existing in that moment and it drags you down into its spiral, and it's like you'll never feel anything else ever again.'

I thought I knew what she meant. I'd felt like that when she had played her set earlier that night. I felt like it when I listened to 'Life On Mars' or even 'While My Guitar Gently Weeps'. Sometimes it felt like the musicians had seen deep into my soul, pulled out my heart, only to throw it back at me to pick up. All my darkest thoughts, all my deepest emotions were laid bare when I heard those songs, emotions I was otherwise too scared to allow myself to feel.

I nodded, my hand still on her chest, her heart beating beneath my fingers.

She spun across to the other side of the room, and the moment passed.

The DJ started playing 'Forever Young' by Alphaville and Astrid shouted at him to turn it up as she spun across the dancefloor, eyes closed.

***

The next day, I had to start writing my review, knowing I would somehow need to find a way to convince the newspaper they wanted to print it. My head was pounding from too many wines, too much loud music, and too little sleep, but I was still on a high from the night before. When I got up to get a glass of water and some Paracetamol, my legs hurt from dancing. When I tried to brush my teeth, I found out my neck hurt too. I had vague recollections of head-banging to that Scandinavian band it took me way too long to recall the name of (it came back to me later, as I was making a coffee: The Hives). What had possessed me to tell her I was a writer? I'd only had one article published and I had no idea what I was doing. I tried writing about the venue and the audience, then I got on to writing about her performance: *Each song left you wanting more. It was as if she had been tasked with holding onto the hearts of everyone in the room and we trusted her not to throw them away...*

I wrote it, printed it out, then paced around my room. I didn't want to send it, but what would she think of me if there was no review? I would have been going along under false pretences. She was relying on me, and I didn't want to let her down. I sat on my bed and started to read through it, which only made me doubt my ability to string a sentence together. It was terrible, every single word of it. At that moment, you came into my room and found me in a state.

'Is this about the review of last night? Where is it?' you asked.

'It's not... I'm not sure if it's ready.'

You walked over to my laptop. I had the email open, with the piece I'd written and some pictures attached. You leaned over, looking at my computer. The email was brief and you couldn't see what I'd written in the attached article, but I still felt like I was on show. Then – and I can't believe you did this – you reached out and touched the mouse. I heard a click, followed by the noise it makes when an email is sent. My stomach dropped.

'What did you just do?!' I said as I rushed over to you.

'Jess, you had it there ready to send. You were just getting yourself worked up. It'll be fine.'

'But how do you know if it'll be fine? I should have checked it again. I wasn't ready! What if—'

You grabbed me and pulled me into your arms.

'Jess, you're getting out of control,' you said, as if it was so obvious, so easy, so logical. And it *was* easy for you to say – you had that easy confidence in everything you did. But I didn't. I knew I wasn't a writer. That first piece I'd sent had been a fluke. They would read my review and laugh me out of the paper. I knew it. And Astrid would find out that I had lied about being a writer.

'You're still going on in your head, aren't you?' Your voice cut into my thoughts.

'What?'

'I know you, you silly over-thinker.' You pushed me out slightly so that we were looking at each other's faces, and you moved your hands to the sides of my head, smoothing down my hair. 'You would worry about it for days and then might not even send it. Now you have nothing to worry about. It's out of your hands.'

I blinked. You were right in some sense; there was certainly nothing I could do now.

'I would have sent it...' I said, though you looked at me with a raised eyebrow. 'I just... was thinking about it. I don't even know if they'll want it...'

'Well, there's only one way to find out, isn't there? In the meantime, let's go eat.'

I breathed out a nervous sigh and nodded.

'OK. Um... thanks.'

'You're welcome.' You smiled and kissed the top of my head. 'See, I know what you need, even if you don't.'

I managed a smile. You were probably right.

And indeed, it turned out you were right. The newspaper

published my review the following week. I cringed at some of the things I'd written, but overall, I actually felt a sense of pride, seeing it there in the paper with my name on it, alongside the pictures I'd taken of Astrid on stage. I wondered whether she'd seen it. The edition had been distributed around campus, but I wasn't sure if she would have known to look for it. Eventually, I decided to message her. I rewrote the message so many times, finally settling on trying to sound relaxed and jokey.

Seen the uni paper? Made you famous :p

It didn't take long for her to reply.

You are an absolute gem! Drinks tonight with my fave writer to celebrate? X

She was being too kind, it was such a small deal, a one-pager in the university newspaper. But it was a Friday night, and I had no plans. I was hardly going to say no anyway. You had a 'boy's night' playing poker at our place, and you seemed happy for me to be going out and doing my own thing rather than hanging around. The spontaneity excited me. Was I going to become someone who was spontaneous? Anything felt possible.

Chapter 6

We met in the rain, under the streetlights. I had an umbrella keeping me somewhat dry while I waited for Astrid to arrive. I was early, as per usual. She had told me to meet her on a particular street corner close to a bar that had just opened. I'd never heard of it, but apparently you could only find it using a set of coordinates.

She arrived, looking as cool as ever, wearing a leather jacket, which I was sure wouldn't be warm enough, as it had really started to get cold. She also had a scarf, though. I had my big puffy and unflattering coat on, attempting to stay warm. As soon as she reached me, she gave me a huge hug. We walked through puddles shimmering in the moonlight towards a nondescript wooden door, which was illuminated by a single light.

Astrid looked at me and shrugged.

'I guess this is it?' she said, taking a moment to look up and down the street from where we were standing.

'I suppose so,' I replied. 'But how do we get in? Maybe it's not open yet. Perhaps we should...'

Before I could suggest going somewhere else, she knocked on the door. It was a confidence I wouldn't have had, to just knock on a random door, even if I did have a set of coordinates.

The whole thing felt slightly preposterous, and if it were just me, I would have felt silly and probably just waited for someone else to arrive, or even chosen somewhere else to go. But moments later, the door opened with a heavy clunking sound, and a suited man ushered us in, down a staircase and to another heavy door. I could hear faint music coming from behind it. He smiled at us before turning a big round handle and pulling at the door with his body weight.

Jazz music burst out at us, along with the chattering of voices and a rush of warm air. I followed Astrid inside and we hung our coats up by the door, as it closed again behind us. The floor was a white and black tiled checkerboard pattern, which we crossed as we headed to the bar. The staff were straight out of *The Great Gatsby* – button up shirts, braces, some wore waistcoats. I loved that era. It all felt so romantic. Astrid ordered us a bottle of red wine and two glasses, and we went and sat down at a table in the corner by what appeared to be a charcuterie bar. In the other corner, a live jazz band was playing. The bartender came over to put a bowl of popcorn on our table. I noticed he winked at Astrid as he left. She just smiled back.

I looked around, taking in the incredible scene, feeling like I was in a movie. People at the table next to us were drinking what I assumed was beer, concealed in brown paper bags that were decorated with a black lightning bolt. It was all very in keeping with the prohibition theme, and the symbol made me think of Bowie. I noticed Astrid was smiling at me and I realised I was acting like a tourist, while she seemed so relaxed, as if she belonged there.

'It's perfect, isn't it?' she said as she held her wine glass out. 'Cheers.'

I quickly picked mine up and touched the side of it to hers. I tried to bring my attention closer in, concentrating on her and letting the rest fade into the background.

'How did you even know about this place?' I asked her.

'Didn't you see the posters around uni about it? They've been advertising for months leading up to opening, just posting the coordinates with no other information. It was pretty clever, really. People love a bit of a mystery and a feeling of exclusivity. They've certainly managed that, I think.'

I shook my head, having not noticed any posters. I was glad she had, though.

'Yeah, it's pretty special being here,' I replied. 'It feels like we're somewhere else.'

'Exactly. Escapism.'

I had been slightly worried I wouldn't be able to keep up with her – that she would know so much more about all things music and culture. And of course, she did. But I didn't feel like I was falling behind, she made it feel like my opinions really mattered and were, perhaps, interesting. It didn't take long before we started talking about Bowie. I may not have known much about music, or instruments, but when I liked something, I tended to obsess over it. And I could certainly hold my own in a conversation about Bowie.

'He just makes me feel like I can be me, you know?' Astrid said. 'That all my flaws and faults are just part of life, and I can make something of that.'

I wanted to agree, but I wasn't sure I felt that way about myself. If Astrid even had any flaws, I was sure she'd be able to make something of them, but mine were terrible things that I needed to try and hide away. I doubted anyone would ever want to speak to me again if they knew some of the stupid things I had thought and done. But I nodded anyway and took a sip of my drink.

'I think I always found solace in that fact that he made being different trendy,' she continued. 'I live to be different. I couldn't think of anything more boring than being... well... boring, could you?'

I shook my head and replied. 'No, definitely not.' But I felt suddenly like a complete imposter, being in Astrid's company and talking about Bowie like we all might be kindred spirits. I knew from the first time I saw Astrid that she was special. She was interesting and different, just like Bowie. But I wasn't any of those things. How long could I keep up the act? How long would it take her to find out who I really was? How boring and unimportant I was in comparison to her...

'So, what about you? How come you're so into him?' she asked me.

It was a simple question but I'd never really thought about why I liked Bowie; I just did. His music had been an escape in times when I'd felt so lonely, so alone... it was something to hold onto as a beacon of hope.

'I guess I just love his music and... I like how he can be anyone, you know? Whoever he wants to be... Not just who everyone expects him to be. As soon as people start to understand what he's doing, he veers off in a completely different direction, always keeping them guessing.'

'Yeah, so ground-breaking, isn't he? Though it's been so long since he's had a new persona. I miss them. Who's been your favourite?'

'Can I say Jareth?'

She laughed. 'Cheeky, but I'll allow it. Gosh I must have watched that movie ten thousand times.'

'Oh yes. Me too. I so wanted to be Sarah.'

'I wanted to be Bowie.'

That didn't surprise me at all.

'I've always wanted to get a Bowie tattoo, something to remind me that he's there, that I've always got a link to him.'

'Oh, yeah, that would be really cool,' I'd said, meaning that it would be cool for her to get one. There was no way I'd get a tattoo, though I guess part of me secretly wished that I was the kind of person who could get a tattoo.

'You should get one too,' she'd said.

I don't know what came over me – the wine (which I was feeling by then, as at some point she'd gone and got us a second bottle, which we were powering through), or wanting to impress her, or just being swept up in the moment, but I found myself nodding, then meeting her glass when she held it up to cheers. I knew that you thought tattoos were trashy, and that my parents thought they were for 'bums and outcasts', but for the first time in my life, I allowed myself the thought that maybe getting a tattoo wouldn't be the worst thing in the world.

'So, what other music do you like, other than Bowie?' She asked me, and I scrambled through the depths of my mind to say some that she would think were cool. It was as if the name of every band had suddenly disappeared from my mind, and I couldn't think of any. I started with the obvious: 'The Beatles,' (to which she replied 'of course'), then a few more came to me: 'Franz Ferdinand, The Arctic Monkeys, and... I love Bright Eyes. They're one of my favourites.'

'Oh yeah, I know them,' she said. 'I like some of their songs.'

She'd nodded at each name as I said them, and I felt relieved that I'd chosen bands that seemed to meet her approval. Ever since I'd first met Astrid, I'd been so desperate to impress her, to persuade her that I was worth her time. I suppose I'd been selfish in a way – I'd sought her out then tried to endear myself to her. But now I'd spent more time talking to her, I saw how genuinely interested in me and attentive she was, and her kindness made me feel bad that I wasn't being entirely truthful. I was only pretending that I was like her – calling myself a writer, dressing in my new clothes with black eyeliner, trying to seem cool... Was I taking advantage of her? Perhaps if we became friends, that wouldn't matter.

After we'd finished talking tattoos and musicians who weren't Bowie, she smiled at me before getting up and indicating for me to 'wait there'. She disappeared through the tables and past the jazz band, leaving me still sitting at the table. I wasn't sure where she was going until I saw her at the bar, which made me realise our glasses were empty. I saw her talking to the bartender who had served us. They talked for what seemed like an age, and I watched them through the dark glow of the bar, laughing and touching each other's arm. Perhaps they were flirting. Eventually she came back with two glasses of something golden-brown, with a single block of ice in each and something tucked under her arm.

'My favourite!' she said as she sat back down. Did she mean me? Was I her favourite? She put one of the glasses down in front of me and I laughed inwardly at my stupidity. Of course she didn't mean me, she meant whatever drink was now sitting in front of me. Another bottle of wine came out from under her arm, and she put it down on the table.

'Let me know what you think of it,' she said, indicating the glass of golden liquid. I didn't know what it was, but I smiled and took a sip. It tasted like smoke and something akin to vinegar. I tried not to cough as it burned my throat and the back of my nose.

'Good, isn't it? Laphroaig. I think it's the best one for sure.'

I looked it up later and found out it was a single malt whisky, from Scotland. I took another sip, more prepared the second time. I braced my throat to close off the passage to my nose as much as possible, so it didn't hit me there. It was... tolerable.

'Thank you,' I said. 'It's lovely.'

She clapped her hands together. 'I'm so glad you love it too!'

I'd never drunk whisky before, though I know you and your friends occasionally got a bottle for your poker nights. I usually just drank wine or cider... Drinking whisky felt so refined.

The bartender I'd seen Astrid speaking to suddenly appeared behind her, putting his hand gently on her shoulder. Astrid just leaned back in her chair to look at him, a slight smile on her face.

'Are you ladies enjoying your whisky?' he asked, looking mainly at Astrid.

'Oh, yes,' I replied, my brain jumping in before I could stop myself speaking. Astrid just nodded, still smiling. I made a note to myself to try and hold back a bit; I needed to be more like Astrid and play it cool, not always leap in with the first thing that came to mind.

He looked at me, as if only just noticing I was there.

'Hi,' he said. 'I'm Adrien.' He held out his hand for me to shake, which I did.

He then leant over, moving his face near Astrid's, and whispered something in her ear. I wondered if they already knew each other. Her eyes sparkled and she nodded and looked at her watch. He walked away.

I had no idea what had just happened, but she didn't say anything about it and so neither did I. She did however tell me that our Laphroaigs were courtesy of 'our' new friend, which took me a little while to process – that a bartender would buy someone a drink. Or maybe he could just get away with pouring two and not registering them in the system.

We started on the bottle of wine, and I thought I should tell her just how much I'd enjoyed her gig.

'How do you do it?' I asked her, to which she cocked her head to the side and scrunched up her brow. I clarified – 'I mean... how do you get up there in front of a whole lot of people and perform? You're so brave.'

'How do I?' she looked at me while I took a drink of my wine. 'How do I not?'

I must have looked puzzled then, because she shook her head and leant forward onto the table.

'Come on, you know what it's like... sharing your art with people you love... with anyone, for that matter... well, there's no greater feeling in the world, is there? I couldn't imagine not wanting to chase that feeling.'

'Umm...' I said, trying to think of a time I'd ever shared 'art' with anyone. Maybe when I was young and came home from school with a finger painting or something to show my parents... which they probably put on the fridge out of obligation to pretend it was a masterpiece. But I learned quickly that I didn't have any talent for art. Or music. The closest I'd got to it was dancing, but that was different. And I was hardly 'a dancer', not anymore anyway. I wondered whether I should pretend I knew what she was talking about, or confess to not being an artist.

'It just burns up inside you if you don't let it out,' she continued. 'And the feeling of... what is it... what do you call it...? Fulfilment. That's it. There's nothing more fulfilling than sharing your art with people who get it. It's addictive, isn't it?'

She looked at me expectantly.

'I uh...' I took another sip of my drink. 'I don't... I'm not really an artist, so I don't think I really know what you mean. I don't share anything with anyone. I've got nothing to share.'

'Don't be silly, you have your writing!'

I laughed. As if me writing an occasional article could be considered art. I couldn't tell if she was patronising me or not. But I realised she wasn't laughing. She wasn't making fun of me, she was serious. I must have talked it up way more than it actually was.

'Oh, I don't really think that counts.'

'Of course it does. One art is not greater than another art. We all create. We're all artists.'

'Oh, I'm definitely not. I can't draw to save myself.'

'Come on, you of all people should know that art isn't purely limited to drawing. And that's such a classic writer mentality to always doubt your own worth. Creativity exists in everything we do, it's what makes us human. Take cooking, for example.'

'Cooking is art? Oh, I guess cake decorating might be.'

'Well, yes, but not only that. Cooking is the process of putting raw materials together and creating something from it. You know how at school they used cooking as an example of the scientific method in everyday life?'

'Oh, yeah. I remember that.'

'Well they neglected to mention that it's also a form of

creating. But it is.'

The way I cooked didn't feel particularly artistic, but I took her point. Perhaps there were more forms of art than I realised, maybe I'd got it all wrong. It was certainly a nice thought that creativity could be hiding in parts of my life I hadn't considered.

The bar was starting to empty. The band had finished and were packing up. The sound system had taken over providing a much quieter 1920s-themed backing track while things were winding down. As we were reaching the end of our wine, I noticed her looking over to the other side of the bar as I was telling her about something. I wondered where her attention had gone and presumed I was just being boring. But then I noticed she seemed to be seeking out the gaze of the bartender, who nodded at her. Then she looked back at me. She had a way of smiling that was somehow mischievous and reassuring all at once.

'How do you feel about a little adventure?' she said.

'Sure,' I replied, the wine and whisky evidently spurring me on.

We finished our glasses of wine, then she beckoned for me to get up and follow her. We walked towards the entrance, and I wondered if we were going to leave. But before we reached it, we were met by the bartender, who ushered us quickly into a door to the left.

The room we entered had a low ceiling and the interior was all made of wood.

'Through here,' he said, and we went into another even smaller room.

There were big brown leather chairs around the room, and he indicated for us to sit. I felt like I'd stepped through a portal into another world.

He started pouring three glasses. I was so alert to the sound of the bottle opening and the liquid splashing into the glass. He turned around and handed one to each of us and sat down next to Astrid. I must have looked confused because he laughed.

'We come in here to chill and drink after everyone leaves. This is the whisky and cigar room.'

'Bars have whisky and cigar rooms?' I asked, amazed.

He laughed, but not unkindly. 'Not usually, but you know, the prohibition theme and all... the owners wanted to do it properly. People can come and entertain business clients here. We also have a cellar on the other side of the entrance with floor to ceiling gold cabinets where our regulars can keep bottles of the good stuff for when they're in.'

I stared at him, then realised my mouth was open, so I shut it. I just thought bars were bars, I didn't know they had secrets. How did I end up here? I looked over at Astrid, who was looking right back at me, with that smile. Astrid. She was why.

The other bar staff made their way in to join us, in dribs and drabs. It felt like a secret men's club that we had snuck into. It was something I previously could only have dreamed of being part of, and yet there I was, right in the middle of it all. Soft Jazz music played through speakers in the wall as someone opened a box of cigars and passed it around. I'd long since abandoned the idea of saying no to things when I was with Astrid, so I took one too. Once I'd selected it, she got up and came over to me, holding out her hand to take it. I handed it over, wondering what she was doing, until I saw the lighter in her hand. She stood next to me, her tall form slightly hunched in the low ceilinged room, lighting my cigar before handing it back and returning to her chair. I thanked her, then looked at the cigar I was holding, wondering what to do next. I knew I was meant to smoke it, of course, it just suddenly felt a little overwhelming.

'Have you ever smoked a cigar, Little Mouse?' Astrid asked, and I realised she was talking to me.

'No, I haven't, actually,' I said, the alcohol helping me to say it in a way that I think sounded like I just hadn't got around to it yet.

'You don't inhale, you just draw it into your mouth, hold it there for a bit, then breathe it out. You don't want it in your lungs, you just taste it.'

Little did she know how I'd been previously smoking the cigarettes she'd given me.

I did what she said and got a mouthful of smoke, which tasted somehow more intense than cigarettes – big and smoky, like the whisky they kept pouring.

'I'm going to get in trouble for this,' I said after my first go, then started giggling and couldn't stop.

'Why?' Adrien the bartender asked once I'd got myself back under control.

'Oh, my boyfriend hates it. He thinks it's disgusting. Not that I agree, of course,' I added quickly.

'Classic,' said Adrien. 'He sounds useless. Get rid of him, I say. Only fun people allowed!'

They all clapped and cheered at that, which made me feel slightly self-conscious. Astrid joined in too.

'I don't think I knew you had a boyfriend,' Astrid said, once they'd quietened down. 'You haven't really mentioned him.'

'Haven't I?' I replied, then realised she was probably right.

I don't know why I hadn't really talked about you. For some reason, talking about having a boyfriend felt out of place.

The bartenders started talking again, taking the focus off me, which I was grateful for. They were all uni students, studying interesting things like politics and sociology. I tried to stay engaged in their conversations, but I didn't know a lot about international affairs. I just enjoyed sitting back in my chair and taking it all in.

It must have been around 3 a.m. by the time we left. My voice had become husky, and Astrid said I sounded sexy. I felt on top of the world.

'So... did you know those bartenders?' I asked, as we left.

'Nope, just met them tonight while I was getting our drinks.'

Of course she did.

'Did you have a good night?' she asked, linking her arm through mine. She knew the answer, but it was sweet that she'd asked. I nodded.

When we parted ways, she hugged me and handed me something, saying, 'You might want these,' before disappearing off into the night. I looked down and it was a pack of gum. I put two in my mouth as I took the night bus home.

You were still up playing cards with Matt and Ethan when I got home. You'd clearly been drinking all night too.

'Did you fall in a fire?' you asked when I came over to say hi.

'Yeah, I did, actually,' I replied, and the others laughed, which caught me by surprise. I felt light until I saw your unimpressed face.

'I was just around people who were smoking,' I said, and then added, 'So gross,' for effect.

'Really disgusting,' you replied as you played two Aces.

I excused myself and went to get ready for bed. As I showered in the early hours of the morning after a night out with my incredible new friend, my heart felt full.

Chapter 7

It was a ritual that on Sundays I had to call my mother. It was a condition of going away to uni that we spoke every week. I never had much to tell her about, and she would mostly just say the same things.

'How's Robert?' was always the first thing she asked.

'He's fine.'

'He's such a nice boy. You know, by the time I was your age, your father had already proposed to me.'

'I know, Mum.'

I sat on the edge of my bed, stretching my neck from side to side as I held the phone to my ear.

'I just want you to be happy.'

'I know, Mum. I am.' I tried to change the topic. 'Uni is going well. Classes are interesting. We're learning about the history of economic thought, which I'm quite enjoying. It's about—'

'That's good, dear. Your father wants to know if you and Robert might drive down for a weekend soon? He could use some help fixing up the shed. I don't know why he insists on doing it himself as he'll put his back out at this rate. But sometimes there's just no reasoning with him, once he gets his mind set on something.'

I could hear her clattering around the house while she spoke.

'Yeah, I guess we could. I'll have to see when he's free.'

'You know you're always welcome, it would be so lovely to see you both.' She then let out a big sigh before continuing. 'I'm so much happier knowing you've got Robert there with you. I don't know how all those other parents can handle allowing their daughters to go to university completely on their own. I'd be a bundle of nerves knowing you had no one looking after you. You're very lucky to have Robert, you know.'

I stopped myself from pointing out she was generally quite a 'bundle of nerves' anyway, because although it made me roll my eyes to keep hearing it, I knew she was right. I knew how much of a reassurance it was for them knowing I wasn't on my own, that I had you to look out for me and make sure everything was ok.

'Yep, Mum, you don't need to worry, I'm all good.'

'And are you making sure you're eating right? We think about you every night when we have dinner. We worry whether you're eating enough.'

I fought down my annoyance that my parents thought I couldn't work out how to feed myself.

'Mum, I know how to eat! I'm fine!'

'Make sure you're getting enough protein and iron, otherwise you'll get sick. And eat veggies with every meal. I know you don't like them very much, but they're important.'

I was perfectly happy eating vegetables; I had been for as long as I could remember. But she seemed to still be holding onto something from when I was a child. I bit my lip to stop myself snapping at her. It wouldn't achieve anything, and she only got defensive when I got annoyed. Thankfully, she moved onto another topic of conversation before I could answer.

'You know your Aunt Pauline is having no end of troubles with this wedding,' Mum went on. Her sister was getting remarried, to someone she'd been with for a few years, but Mum had never really accepted her decision to get a divorce from her first husband. 'Why she ever left your Uncle Dan is beyond me, making those poor children grow up without a proper family... And now she and this new man are having to get married in some strange church that will accept people who have been divorced... It all seems more trouble than it's worth, if you ask me. Imagine not being allowed in your own Church! Who knows what the service will be like!'

'Well, at least she's happy, I suppose,' I said, as I had many times before whenever the conversation had come up. Mum just scoffed in response.

'Well, I'd better go, these dishes won't wash themselves,' she said.

'Ok Mum. Bye then. Talk soon.'

'Bye bye.'

I flopped back on the bed, exhausted. Mum had been a teacher but had left it all behind back when I was eight. She ended up helping at the local library here and there after that, but I think part of her always missed teaching. I suppose I became her major project after that, in lieu of having a classroom of children to teach and shape.

She would often say things to me like, 'I just want what's best for you' and 'I don't know where I would be without your father'. She'd been delighted when I first told her about you. You were tall and confident, and from a good family – you ticked all the boxes.

'He's going places,' she'd said. 'Make sure you hold on to him, no matter what.'

I knew how much she wanted me to get married and start a family. Sometimes I wondered if that would make up for the ways I'd managed to disappoint her... But it was fine, that was what I wanted, too. I wanted to be with you, to be safe, to know what my future would look like. I needed to make sure I didn't end up alone. I couldn't think of anything worse.

Shortly after I got off the phone with Mum, you came in to tell me that we were going to head out for dinner. It was our Sunday night 'family' meal, where the five of us went out together, to the nearest fast-food joint – we weren't picky, and it was nice and cheap. You boys all ordered triple cheeseburgers and I had no idea how you got your mouths around them or could handle the oil dripping through your fingers. I couldn't watch. Lauren got a fish burger —she said it was the most sustainable option on the menu— and I ate some chicken nuggets as I listened to you all talk about your week ahead of law lectures. I didn't mind, but I was starting to realise I was finding your conversations increasingly boring. My mind was somewhere else.

***

A few days later, Astrid texted me saying she wanted to go to some pub that evening, was I free? Of course I was free.

The pub was nestled in a side street, just off the main road, up three steps and behind glass panelled, wooden doors. I realised when we got there that I'd walked past it before, but had thought it was closed. The blinds were always drawn, and I never saw anyone go inside. There was a name painted on the front, but it was so faded that it was hard to make out the words. When we arrived that evening though, the blinds were raised, and the lights were switched on. Inside it was minimally decorated, mostly brown with wooden furniture, floors and bar, but by the entrance, a Jukebox flashed in neon.

'I didn't know this place was actually a pub,' I said as we sat by the bar. 'Have you been here before?'

Astrid just smiled and waved at the bartender, who saw and made her way over. I remembered once being taught in a creative writing class to 'show, don't tell', which sprung to mind when I thought of Astrid – if she could answer my question with an action, she wouldn't say a word.

'Hi, love,' the bartender said to Astrid when she reached us. 'Red wine?'

'A bottle thanks, Ada!' Astrid replied, and flashed that smile.

'Well, that answers my question then,' I said, as Ada went off to the other end of the bar to get our wine. 'Is there anyone you don't know?'

'Nope, no one,' she replied with a smile, which had us both laughing by the time a bottle of wine and two glasses were handed across the bar to us. Astrid opened it and filled both glasses almost to the top.

'To... Fridays?' she said, holding her glass up.

'Works for me!' I replied, trying not to spill it as I moved my glass to meet hers.

'So how come you know Ada?' I asked.

'Oh, just been here a few times. I like the jukebox. Actually...' She trailed off as she got up and went over to it, standing in front of it, resting on one hip as she scrolled through the music. I watched as her face lit up, and she selected something, before coming back to me.

'The Strokes,' I said, as the first notes of 'You Only Live Once' started playing.

'You got it,' she replied with a smile.

As we sat and talked, I noticed she had plasters on two of the fingers on her left hand. When there was a gap in conversation, I decided to ask her about it, hoping she didn't think I was prying.

'Astrid,' I said, tentatively.

'Yeah...?'

'Why do you have... are they Spiderman plasters? On your fingers?'

'Oh, that,' she said, holding her hand up to look at them. I noticed they stretched over the tips of two of her middle fingers. I wondered if she'd cut herself. 'Yeah. I've been practicing for a gig. Evidently haven't played enough bass lately, they're rather ripped and bloody.'

'Woah, that sounds painful! Are you ok?'

'It's all in the name of music, and what a cruel mistress she is.'

'But why Spiderman?' I asked.

'Well, they seem to allow me to still play while I'm wearing them. Plastic coating, or something, I think. Regular plasters are a bit shit. And these cushion my fingers a bit, so it doesn't hurt so much and I can keep going. Otherwise I'd have to wait for them to heal before I could play again. And you know what they say – practice until you need plasters then practice until they fall off. I realise it's all a bit silly. Lord, what fools these mortals be, I suppose.'

'Is that... Shakespeare?'

'Yes, I think it is.'

I laughed, marvelling at her throwing Shakespeare into regular conversation at a pub.

At some point we got another bottle of wine, and by the time we'd polished off the two of them, Astrid reached over and held my arm, a cheeky look in her eyes.

'Shall we go on an adventure?' she asked. 'This place feels too dull for us tonight. And we're getting into the part of the night where something means everything... Who knows what's just around the corner?'

I marvelled at her spontaneity and trust that we would somehow find an adventure. Her remark that a pub was somehow beneath us gave me a weird feeling that I could only describe as a 'thrill'. What could we possibly find that was more exciting, without having a plan? Part of me was saying to stay where we were, not to go gallivanting around the streets at night with this near stranger. But she wasn't really a stranger anymore; I felt like I could trust her, that I could actually call her a friend. And she certainly hadn't let me down yet – she'd never taken me anywhere unsafe, and with her, I felt like my presence was always welcome.

And so, I found myself nodding my head and grinning, my heart starting to race in anticipation.

We left the pub and I tried to keep up with Astrid as she ran across the road, beckoning for me to follow. After a few drinks I felt surprisingly daring, but I still looked carefully both ways before I crossed after her, usually preferring to cross only when there was a little green man telling me it was safe. We walked down the road for a little while until we came to a small park with a solitary bench in the middle. She steered me towards it, and we sat down. She pulled out a hip flask, taking a swig then passing it to me. I'd never known someone who carried around a hip flask. Hers was silver, like her cigarette case. It had an 'A' etched on one side. I reached out to take it off her and had a cautious sip. It tasted like an alcoholic syrupy coffee.

'What on earth is this?' I asked.

'Do you like it?'

'Sort of...'

'It's Coffee Patron.'

'Patron? What's that?'

'Tequila. But this one's coffee flavoured.'

I shrugged and took another sip. I didn't love it, but it was certainly better than regular tequila.

'So what were you thinking?' I asked her after we'd sat for a few moments.

'The universe will bring us something,' she replied. 'It always does. You just gotta trust it.'

There was a weird feeling in the air that night. We'd already had the run of Halloween, Guy Fawkes and Diwali and it was now starting to turn into winter. The period before Christmas always felt somewhat unsettled to me.

A loud bang nearby startled us, as over our heads showered the glittery fractals of fireworks. She looked at me and grinned.

'I guess someone's got some left over,' I said, taking another sip from the flask.

'And here is our gift! Told you something would come to us!' She grabbed my hand and pulled me up before leading me in the direction of the fireworks. One, two, three more erupted above us, creating a beacon for us to follow. We weaved through the streets, trying to find the source. I tried to tell her it was probably just some random people, but without saying anything, she smiled and led on. My hand felt warm and safe in hers.

Eventually we started to hear the unmistakable rabble of a party. We rounded the corner and there, in a small park next to a row of houses, a group of about fifteen people were gathered around, chatting, laughing and letting off fireworks. To my surprise, Astrid, pulling me along with her, just walked straight over. Nothing seemed off-limits to her. I was worried they'd ask who we were and get angry at us for being there, but they didn't.

The party seemed to be held by the people whose flat was next to the little park, which was really just a patch of grass on a corner with a few benches in it. People were milling around in and outside the flat, and spilling out into the park. There were bins filled with ice and drinks and Astrid walked over and fished us out two beers. I couldn't believe how natural she was. I was terrified. She must have noticed because she put her arm around me.

'It's fine, I promise.'

'Do you know these people?' I asked.

'Not yet...'

I took a deep breath and went to have a sip of my beer before realising the top was still on it.

'Hey, how are we...' I trailed off before finishing, as I'd looked at Astrid and saw that she had got out her keys, which had a bottle opener on the keyring. She opened hers before reaching for mine.

When she handed it back to me, I took a big mouthful, feeling the cold flowing into my body, calming me slightly. As she put her keys away, I stood with my eyes closed for a few moments, deeply inhaling and exhaling. I was cool, I was calm. I must have paused for longer than intended because when I opened my eyes, I saw Astrid had left my side. She was a few feet away, already in deep discussion with two guys. I took a few more breaths before tentatively making my way over.

'Jess!' she said, when I reached them. 'Guys, you simply must meet Jess!'

'Hi,' I said, unsure quite what was going on.

'Hi,' they both said back to me, and we all clinked our bottles together. Astrid introduced them as Ben and James, and I marvelled at how she already had their names memorised. I made a conscious effort to do the same. It turned out that they had just published the first copy of an independent magazine they'd been working on. It was launch day and they were celebrating, hence the party and fireworks. They didn't seem at all bothered that we had crashed it and were standing there drinking their beer.

'Jess writes, don't you?' She said, putting her arm around me and pulling me close before turning back to them. 'You should get her to write something for your next edition.'

I choked on my beer and tried to protest that no, I wasn't very good. But Ben was already saying he'd love for me to submit something for the next one, and James was nodding along.

'We're dying for some short stories or poems or anything really!'

My words caught in my throat, but Astrid was there to help me out.

'She'd love to! She also writes these amazing music reviews!'

'No, I...' but before I'd managed to get out my sentence, Ben handed me a business card, which had the name of the publication on it: *'The Relativity Cadenza'*. It also had their names and email addresses.

'Cool name,' I said, finally finding my voice again once I

had something else to focus on.

'Thanks,' said James. 'It's an obscure Beatles reference – from their movie *Help.*'

'Oh, cool. I've never seen it.' I replied.

'It's pretty ridiculous,' said Astrid, 'but I love it. We'll have to watch it together sometime.'

They asked Astrid if she had anything to submit for the next issue and she said she probably had some art or a poem she could send them. They were eager to give her a business card too.

The party didn't seem real. I couldn't believe that we had just walked in and were now somehow part of it. Astrid said she was going to grab us some more drinks and disappeared for a while. I got talking with a couple of girls who were also at my uni. They were both studying something arts related. They seemed nice enough. Then Astrid came running up to me and whispered in my ear, 'We're going on an adventure.'

'I thought we were already on one,' I said.

'No, a *proper* one!' Her eyes gleamed.

I didn't know what that meant, but of course I was going with her. A small group of us left the party. A couple of them had rucksacks. They spoke in hushed, conspiratorial tones. I had no idea what was going on. We crossed the road and went down the street. We were a couple of blocks away when the first of our party stopped at a wall at the end of a dark dead-end road. I looked around to see why we'd stopped and was amazed to see Ben climbing on top of a car, then somehow, he scrambled up the side of a one-storey building that had a flat roof. Once he was on the roof, he turned, knelt, and reached a hand down as another of the group climbed onto the car and scrambled up the wall, grabbing his hand to be pulled up to join him. My jaw dropped, and I immediately felt chilled and sweaty all at once. Surely, they weren't expecting me to get up there... I watched another go up. Then it was Astrid's turn. She smiled at me. A daring smile which said, 'Will you follow?'

It was like the cigarette all over again.

She got up on the car, then just like the others, jumped up to grab the hand of the person who had gone up before her, and disappeared onto the roof. She reappeared, standing triumphantly on top of the wall, looking down at me with hands on hips. She used her head to beckon me in her direction.

'I... I can't...' I stammered. How was I supposed to make my body do that? I felt a familiar ache in my back at the very thought of it and had a sudden reminder of a past warning that I must protect it. There was no way I was strong enough to scale a wall. Plus, I was wearing a dress! Though I had put my thick fleece-lined tights on, since the weather was getting colder. James was the only one still down on the pavement with me, and he came over and put his arm around my shoulders.

'It'll be fine,' he said, surprisingly reassuringly. 'Here, let me help you.'

He took my hand before I could protest and led me to the car, which I followed him up onto, taking back my hand to use it to climb up ungracefully on all fours. Once I was standing beside him on the car roof, he bent down and laced his fingers together.

'Here, I'll give you a boost.'

I looked around, then up at the faces looking down. They were all peering over, waiting for me.

I looked back at James, this random guy who was ready to boost me up onto a strange building. He was looking at me expectantly, and it struck me how ridiculous and unbelievable this whole situation was. It was dark, but I still felt conspicuous. I started to hear my heart pounding in my ears, and I made the decision to give in to it. I couldn't believe I was giving in to it. I grabbed the skirt of my dress and twisted the fabric, so it went tight, before tucking it into the waistband of my tights, making sure it couldn't hinder me.

'Put your foot in my hands.'

I did as he asked.

'On the count of three.'

'Ok... wait, on or after?'

'On.'

And before I could back out, he started to count. And on three, he boosted my leg, I jumped, and upwards I went. I felt hands grab me and suddenly my top half was over the top of the wall, and I was pulled up onto the roof. I stood up and Astrid immediately pulled me into her arms and hugged me.

We went along the rooftop, before coming to a ladder fixed on a wall, which went up to another level. One after another, we went up the ladder, and up another storey, to another flat rooftop. The ladder was much easier to scale than the wall had been, and as I felt the wind playing with my hair while I climbed, I felt a smile rise from deep within me. I no longer felt so scared. The feeling had been taken over by the realisation that this was the most exciting thing I'd done, possibly ever. We stopped when we came to a white wall that was looking out onto the main road out of the city. Where we were standing was somewhat obscured by the facade of the adjoining building. The guys pulled out a big, folded piece of paper, which turned out to be a stencil with the name of their magazine on it. They fixed it to the wall with some sort of adhesive, then started spray painting the words *'The Relativity Cadenza'* onto the wall high enough to be seen by passing cars.

I was standing above the world, the wind in my hair, having just conquered a wall. I was no longer the same little old, worried, me. I was something else, something stronger, something better. I felt liberated, and so alive.

Astrid was trying to get my attention. When I looked over, I noticed she had a tin of spray paint in her hand that she must have taken from one of the rucksacks.

'So we'll never forget, and the world will know,' she announced, and started to spray the roof beneath our feet. In great big black letters:

A + J

I took the spray can from her and shook it like she had. I'd never used spray paint before, but it was easy enough, though I managed to get paint on my fingers as I pushed the nozzle down. I painted a lightning bolt below our initials. For Bowie.

I felt immortal.

Chapter 8

'What do you want with that boring lawyer?'

Astrid's voice came from where she was lying on my bed, her head hanging off the side, down towards the floor. Her legs were up against the wall, stretching towards the ceiling. Just spending time together and enjoying each other's company felt like a sign of real friendship.

That day, a few weeks on from the rooftop, I was trying to finish writing an article and Astrid was distracting me. I was writing about the bar/speakeasy that she'd taken me to, which I thought I might send to the guys at *The Relativity Cadenza.*

'Maybe he'll get you out of trouble one day,' I replied.

She snorted and tried to throw a book at me. You two hadn't really spent any time together, though you'd sort of met in passing here and there, as she and I started to hang out more. I wasn't intentionally keeping you separate, but I may have been a little bit nervous about whether you'd get along.

'You said you wanted to ask me something,' I mentioned.

When she messaged me to ask if she could come over, I had immediately said yes. Then I'd looked around my room and realised it was a complete mess – clothes all over the floor, bed unmade, my desk covered in books and papers, dirty glasses and a bowl… I had no idea how I had amassed so many things. My mother would have been on at me to tidy it long before, and maybe part of me had been rebelling against that. I hurriedly straightened it all up and threw a load of washing on. I didn't want to come across like a total slob. I wasn't, it was just hard to keep on top of things all the time.

'Right, yeah… So, Arcade Fire are playing in London in a few weeks.' She'd given me their first album and I had listened to it a few times. She'd been eager to know what I'd thought. I'd liked it. 'Wanna go for the weekend? I got two tickets when they went on sale and need to find someone to come. We can stay with my sister so accommodation will be free. Could be fun.'

I didn't know she had a sister. In fact, I didn't know much about her family – we hadn't really discussed our families; there were plenty more interesting things to talk about. I guess I'd sort of pictured her as being an only child.

The prospect of a weekend in London with Astrid sounded exciting. I would never have contemplated going to London for the weekend to see a band, but suddenly, I could think of nothing else I'd rather do.

'Yeah, wow, that would be great! I'd love to come,' I said.

That was when you appeared at my door.

'Oh, hi!' I said, once I noticed you standing there.

'Hi,' you answered, looking at Astrid.

'Oh, I'm so sorry,' I said quickly, realising you two had never properly met. 'Robert, you remember Astrid? Astrid, this is Robert.'

'Hi,' you said.

'So nice to meet you,' said Astrid, and she held out her hand without moving from where she was lying upside down on my bed, stretching it out above her.

You hesitated for a moment, looking slightly confused, then walked over and put your hand out to awkwardly shake her upside-down hand. The handshake seemed to go on for longer than I was expecting, with the two of you holding a weird amount of eye contact.

'Astrid just asked if I wanted to go see Arcade Fire with her in London,' I said, not sure what the vibe in the room was.

'Nice,' you'd said, and just stood there, still shaking Astrid's hand.

'So... What are you up to?' I asked.

You took your eyes off Astrid and looked back to me, finally breaking the handshake.

'A bunch of us are going for a drive out to one of those campsites where we can light a fire, since it's so cold out. Do you want to come? Both of you, I guess.'

I looked at Astrid to see what she thought.

'Sure, why not,' she said. 'I've not got anything else on.'

I wasn't sure who would be going, which would usually have bothered me, but if Astrid was there, I knew we'd have fun. While I felt uncomfortable being in a group of people that I didn't know, she was wonderfully relaxed about such situations. And I think some of that rubbed off on me when I was by her side. I did have to finish my article though, so I put my notebook in my bag.

You drove the three of us out of the city, where suburban streets met industrial area, which eventually gave way to woodland. I sat in the front of your car while you drove, with Astrid in the back. I asked what she wanted to listen to, turning the radio to Radio 6, which had a man with an annoying voice talking very quickly. A few moments later, after rummaging around in her bag, she handed me a CD. It was Arcade Fire. I put it on. You looked over to me when it started, your brow crinkled, but you didn't say anything.

When we got there, someone had already turned up their car speakers so there was music, and a couple of people were busying themselves with getting a fire going. It had been so cold and grey, and the February malaise had penetrated deep into my bones. But once the fire was going, I felt like it was thawing me out as it crackled and popped over the music. Someone had brought marshmallows and we sat and toasted them. The stickiness of the balls of sugar clinging to the end of the stick bothered me, but I managed to eat one carefully without touching it with my hands.

I took a seat by the fire as the sun went down and pulled out my notebook, determined to finish the last of my article.

'My writer,' Astrid called out to me as I sat and wrote, while she danced around the fire to the music. 'Perhaps one day you'll immortalise me in the pages of a book.'

You'd laughed, making us both look over.

'What?' you'd said. 'What is there to write about anything at our age anyway? It's not like we've done anything worth reading about.'

'Ah, Robert,' she'd said as she jumped up to balance on a log, one foot touching down in front of the other. 'I think you'll find that everyone's worth writing about. Maybe even you...'

I laughed, although you did not. I knew I wasn't special, there wouldn't be books written about me, but I had somehow managed to carve out my place as the writer. It felt good thinking I could be part of something bigger.

As always, Astrid was in her element that day, even though

she didn't know anyone. I always struggled to focus on more than a couple of people at a time, and I could never think of what to say. But she seemed so at ease making conversation with anyone.

It was getting cold and dark, and I was grateful for the fire. It felt like one of those truly perfect moments, out in the wilderness with a group of people, and for once I didn't feel on the outside because I had Astrid and she was there because of me. We were Astrid and Jess.

You came and sat with me for a bit as I finished up my article. You asked if I was cold and then put your arm around me. I smiled and snuggled against you, feeling suddenly warm and safe. I tried to concentrate on what I was writing, but I was distracted by Astrid dancing around in the flickering light of the fire.

We stayed out late that night, lying on the grass and staring at the stars. I thought about how all the stars continued to shine so long after they'd burnt out.

Chapter 9

A few weeks before our trip to London, Astrid called me, her voice sounding quick and excited.

'Jess!' she'd said after I said hello, the sound of her voice helping me relax.

I hated talking on the phone, but it seemed less stressful when I knew it was her calling. Usually when it rang, I would just stare at it as it buzzed. I preferred to let whoever it was leave a message, and then I would at least have the time for adequate preparation before replying.

'Bright Eyes are playing on the Friday night. In North London!' she said.

'Oh, I love them!'

'I know.'

I had listened to their song 'Lover I Don't Have to Love' on repeat in high school. It had been a gritty escape from reality. I fantasised about being the singer and having a secret life of debauchery. I imagined being desired, and not having to care about anything or anyone. I listened to it on headphones, late at night in the dark, when I felt like I was the only one still awake in the world. That song had taken me to places far away from my own reality.

'How do you feel about stacking gigs?' she asked.

'I feel incredible.'

'Great. I'll get us tickets.'

When I hung up, my stomach felt jittery. I couldn't believe that she had found out that a band I loved just happened to be playing the day after Arcade Fire. I wondered how things could pan out so perfectly. Everything always seemed to just fall into place with her.

***

We got the train to London on the Thursday – the night that Arcade Fire were due to play. She'd arranged for us to stay with her sister, Sofia. Sofia was younger by three years and lived in east London where the rent was low and where all the interesting people lived. She worked in a pub, having dropped out of her design degree after a week. This seemed to annoy Astrid, she'd rolled her eyes when she told me that Sofia had 'given up', but she said it was fine, as long as Sof was doing something with her life. Astrid herself had deferred her degree, as well as started late at uni – I'd been surprised to find out she was actually two years older than me and was twenty-two.

We dumped our things at the flat, which Sofia shared with her girlfriend, Elle. I hadn't realised Sofia was a lesbian until Astrid mentioned it a few days before we left. I don't think I'd ever properly met anyone who was gay; it wasn't really accepted in the institutions I grew up in. I had mostly been told that it was a sin, but I'd always struggled to get onboard with that way of thinking. In fact, that was part of what had pushed me away from the church in the first place. I couldn't see how anyone loving someone else could be considered a sin. But I have to admit I felt—and I hope this is an ok thing to say—quite excited to be meeting, and in fact staying with, a lesbian couple. I was feeling more and more drawn to people who bucked social norms and lived outside the arbitrary limits society tried to impose.

Their flat was above a shop that sold old computer parts. The blue front door sat next to the shopfront, and it led to a narrow corridor with stairs leading up to the flat, which was split over two levels. The first thing I noticed as we filed through their hallway and into their open plan kitchen/living room, was that there were a whole lot of pots and pans filled with water sitting in the sink and on the bench.

'Sof,' Astrid said once we'd all gone through to the living room.

'Yeah, Sis?' Sofia had replied once she'd closed the door behind us and followed us in, lifting herself up so she was sitting on the bench, next to a frying pan.

'Why are you collecting cookware?'

'Oh, these?' She said, waving her hand in the direction of the lines of pots. 'They're soaking. We're going through a phase of burning food onto pans. I suspect it will pass. Beers? Elle?' She looked at Elle, who just looked straight back at her, without moving. Then she pointed at the fridge. 'Beers? Elle?'

Elle sighed, rolled her eyes and shook her head, before going to their tiny bar fridge, opening it and kneeling in front of it, disappearing behind the door for a moment to look inside.

'Well, we've got... two lagers, and half a bottle of the cheapest white wine the offie had. Shall we go to Barney's?'

'To Barney's!' Sofia exclaimed, launching herself off the counter. 'Big Sis will pay, won't you, darling Astie?' she called, as she made her way back out the front door, before leaning back through to say to Astrid, 'You did just get back from one of your trips, after all.'

I looked at Astrid, standing there so cool and composed, and wondered how someone with such a chaotic energy could be related to her. She just sighed and said to me, 'Well, she is giving us somewhere to stay, I guess. Let's find out who Barney is...'

We followed Sofia and Elle down to the corner of their street and into a pub called The Red Lion. Apparently Barney was the owner, though he didn't seem to be around.

Sofia and Elle were both very high energy, chattering excitedly all the time with hardly a moment to breathe. I found it all a bit overwhelming, and very difficult to join in the conversation, so I mostly just stayed quiet. Astrid must have noticed I was feeling a bit out of it, as she leaned over at one point and squeezed my hand. We stood out on the street outside the pub, holding our beers while the two of them smoked. Astrid and I didn't generally smoke in the daylight, so we just sipped at our beers while they had cigarette after cigarette. We didn't do that, either. We usually just had one, for effect, and to see what happened during that time; something usually did – a conversation would start with someone new, or an adventure would appear. If not, we'd go for another drink. Astrid said that cigarettes were only for street corners, while waiting for someone, or for meeting people in smoking areas. And only ever at night time. I liked that there were rules to it. Eventually, after two beers, we all parted ways; for them to go to the bar where Sofia worked, and for us to go off to grab some dinner before heading to the gig.

Arcade Fire were playing at a beautiful old theatre in Brixton, south London, called the Brixton Academy. We'd got there early enough to ensure spots at the front.

'I'm too tall to be up this close, really,' she said as we stood there, waiting for it to start and clutching our plastic cups of slowly warming beer. 'But I think if you know all the words then people don't mind too much. They know you need to be at the front.'

She wasn't a giant by any stretch, but she'd said she was closing in on six feet tall, and she certainly looked it from my vantage point at 5'5". It didn't seem like her to be self-conscious about something like that, but once she'd mentioned it, I noticed she was taller than a lot of the people standing behind us. I wondered if someone had once said something to her about it.

There was a look of pure joy on Astrid's face as soon as the band came onstage, and she put her hand on her chest, above her heart, at the first chords they played. She was at her happiest when she was surrounded by music. During some songs she closed her eyes, singing along, her hands on her heart or above her head. It was easy to get swept up in the moment with her around.

Astrid had told me that there was a defining sound of bands from Montreal. She called it the 'endless oppression of winter'. She said it made them all sound like they were fighting against an unbeatable oppressor – the weather – and that all the music that came out of there had a similar quality. I felt it that night. I felt like I was part of an uprising. When we all sang together, it felt like we could win against anything, singing along with the lyrics at the top of our lungs. I had tears in my eyes, overwhelmed by the fact that this was now my life.

The set finished with a cover of 'Guns of Brixton' by The Clash. It sounded like a protest sea shanty. The lead singer sang it through a megaphone, and everyone clapped along, joining in with the chorus, us all singing it in unison. It gave me goosebumps.

When it ended, we filed out of the venue and onto the streets of Brixton, where everyone continued to sing as we made our way onto tubes and buses. We'd promised Sofia that we would head to her work after the gig. She worked in a karaoke bar in Soho, which pretty much sounded like my idea of hell, but Astrid assured me that she hated karaoke even more than I did.

'Oh, really?' I asked when she'd told me. 'I thought you might like it – you love singing and performing.'

'Yes,' she'd said and scrunched up her nose. 'But karaoke is neither of those things. It's just an excuse for drunk people to pretend they can sing, whilst wailing incredibly off-key to songs that should probably not be attempted by anyone.'

'Oh? Like what?'

'Bohemian Rhapsody.'

I'd laughed at that, thinking that surely no one would think they should attempt to sing that song, especially if they couldn't sing.

We got off at Tottenham Court Road station, which Astrid told me was the deepest station in London. Everyone at the bar was drunk when we got there, even, it appeared, those who were working. The karaoke had started, it was rowdy, and we were tired. I think we'd already given and received all the love we could that night.

'I *hate* this,' Astrid said through gritted teeth, as someone started attempting 'I Will Survive'. She shook her head then went off to the bar to get us both a double vodka, fresh lime, and soda. When she returned, we stood against a wall by a neon pink Hello Kitty sign. It felt so different from where we'd just come from. We both drank quickly.

We had just about finished our drinks when the unmistakable first line of Bohemian Rhapsody started being part sung, part shouted through a microphone.

'Oh, hell no,' Astrid said, finishing the last of her drink immediately. She nodded at me to do the same, and I followed suit. We went to say bye to Sofia, but she was standing on the bar pouring a clear spirit straight into some guy's mouth.

We left without saying anything and made our way back to the flat, where we pretty much went straight to bed. Astrid was sleeping on the sofa upstairs in the living room, and I was sleeping in a weird little alcove that was tucked away in the landing under the stairs at the back of the house, downstairs where the bedroom was. It was sort of obscured unless you knew to look for it, and they called it their 'guest bedroom', but it wasn't much more than a glorified broom cupboard. I felt like Harry Potter. I only just fit in it and had to lie slightly curled up on my side to fit. Astrid would have been far too tall to fit in at all. I told myself it was fine for a couple of nights.

I wasn't exactly sleeping well; I never could in new places anyway, but sometime during the night I was woken up by what sounded like a party happening upstairs. Not long after the music, loud talking and singing started, someone pulled the door open and appeared in the alcove, nearly standing on my leg. The light filtered down from the stairway and when my eyes had adjusted, I realised it was Astrid's sister.

'Who are you? Why are you in my flat?' she asked, somewhat aggressively, hands on hips.

'I'm... Jess...' I sat up and tried to get my bearings. Her eyes wouldn't sit still, they darted around, not settling on anything.

'I'm Astrid's friend. We're staying this weekend.'

'Oh,' she said, then walked out and thumped back up the stairs.

I forced my eyes closed and put my fingers in my ears, desperate to try and get some sleep, but I don't think I slept anymore that night.

The next morning, I got a text message from Astrid:

You awake? I'm in their bedroom X

I got up, opened the door, and shuffled out of the 'guest bedroom', peering up the stairs to see empty bottles strewn about the place and abandoned on the stairs and what I hoped was just red wine on the walls. I tiptoed across and into the room Astrid was in, closing the door behind me and climbing into bed with her.

'Hey, Little Mouse, you ok?'

I nodded, noticing she'd called me 'Little Mouse' again. I wondered if it was a nickname she'd made for me, or if she called other people that, too. I found myself hoping for the former. It seemed somehow sweet coming from her, and I found I quite liked it.

'Are you?' I asked her. 'What happened?'

'They came home around three. Sof had invited the last few people from the bar back here. They were on acid. They jumped on me, then blasted the music and started raving in the living room. I sat up with them for a bit, but they were all over the place, seeing all sorts of weird things that obviously weren't there. One guy spent quite a long period of time curled up in the corner of the room sucking his thumb... I checked to see if he was ok and he seemed to be physically fine, but he was on a completely different plane. It was all a bit scary to watch, to be honest. After a little while I escaped down here and locked the door. I don't think they would have realised I left, they were so out of it.'

I hadn't met anyone on drugs before. The thought scared me slightly.

'Sofia came into the "guest room" and didn't know who I was or why I was there. She looked... strange,' I said.

'Sounds about right. She was very confused why I was here too. Kept asking if mum was here.' She half-laughed. 'Hey, how do you feel about maybe getting a hotel room for tonight? Near the venue? I just got paid from last week's gig, should just about cover it.'

I nodded, quickly. I didn't really feel like facing another night of chaos.

'I'm sorry for all this...' she said, lying on her back and staring at the ceiling as she spoke.

It wasn't like Astrid to apologise. It was strange to see her so vulnerable. This wasn't the Astrid who breezed effortlessly through parties, this was someone who felt let down by her little sister. I could see the hurt in her eyes. I vowed in that moment to never let her down, I didn't ever want her to be upset on my account. I rolled over and put my arms around her.

'It's ok,' I said. 'I'm sure it will make for a great story one day.'

She smiled. 'Promise me you'll write about it? Make it all seem worthwhile in some way?'

'Of course I will.'

Astrid found a laptop in the bedroom, sticking out from under a pile of clothes, which turned out to be Elle's and wasn't password protected. Astrid used it to find and book a room in a hotel just around the corner from where the gig was that night. When we told Sofia we were leaving, we said I had a friend we were going to stay with.

'Change of plans,' Astrid said, giving her a hug as if nothing was wrong. 'But thanks for having us.'

Sofia seemed disappointed and told us there was a huge party that night at the bar that we simply mustn't miss. We made our apologies for not being able to make it and left. We did laugh about it once we were safely out, but it was still fresh, and I know Astrid couldn't shake the worry—and perhaps also embarrassment—of seeing her sister like that.

We got to the gig early again, to make sure we were at the front, at Astrid's insistence. The support act was just starting as we arrived, so we went to grab a couple of drinks before making our way to the front to watch their set and get a good spot. The band was fine, but I didn't know any of their music so it all sounded mostly the same to me. I was just enjoying being at a gig in London, with my best friend.

As we were waiting for Bright Eyes to start, I mentioned to Astrid how lucky it was that she'd found out about our two bands playing on consecutive nights. I asked her how she'd come across the fact that Bright Eyes were playing.

'I went looking for gigs in London that we could go to tonight. Arcade Fire was my band. I know you like them, but you don't really know them. I wanted to try and get you a band you loved too.'

'Oh, wow, did you? I guess I thought you just happened to hear about it.'

'No, I spent a while searching through gig lists before I found it. I think if you want something, it rarely works out if you just hope for it.'

'Well, thanks. It's amazing!'

She excused herself to go to the bathroom and then to get us each another beer before they started. My heart was in my throat as I stood there waiting for Bright Eyes to play. I was so jittery that I almost dropped the beer that Astrid handed me when she returned. She got back just in time, as the audience started cheering and the band came out onto the stage. I couldn't believe I was in the same room as Conor Oberst. I had listened to his voice so many times and now here he was, in front of me.

The vibe was so different from the previous night. Astrid called Bright Eyes 'chaotic folk music'. I kept waiting for them to play my song. They played a few songs I loved but I hadn't listened to the album they were touring yet and as the gig went on, I started to worry that they weren't going to play my song at all. Surely they were just saving it for the end, I thought. They couldn't not play it. But my heart sank when they all said 'Thank you,' and 'Goodbye,' and left the stage. I looked over to Astrid and she mouthed 'encore' at me, restoring my hope. They came back on stage and played a song from the new album, and I figured mine would be next. Then they moved on to a really old one. I waited for them to play a third, but then Conor thanked us, and they walked off stage.

As the lights came up, Astrid turned to me.

'They didn't play it, did they?'

'No,' I said, and my voice sounded more disappointed than I had intended it to.

'Come on, let's go get drunk,' she said as she linked her arm through mine, and we made our way out along with everyone else. No one was singing this time as we left the venue. I felt deflated.

We went to a nearby pub, and it didn't take long to start feeling a bit better – Astrid always had a way of sweeping me up in her energy and enthusiasm. The pub was dark, there was a DJ playing loud music, and we were dancing. As we were standing in the middle of the dancefloor, my glass slipped from my hand. It shattered into thousands of pieces. It was busy and loud and I'm not entirely sure anyone noticed, but I was horrified as I stared at it all spread out on the floor. I felt like such an idiot. I had no idea how it had happened. I couldn't even manage to hold onto my glass. I was so useless. Astrid grabbed me gently by the shoulders and steered me away from the crime scene, kissed me on the cheek and went and got me another drink. Someone came to clean it up, and we pretended we knew nothing about it. She had turned my moment of shame into a secret feeling of camaraderie between us.

That night in the bed we were sharing in the hotel, she thanked me for a memorable trip and for coming with her.

But it felt like my turn to apologise.

'What for?' she asked.

'For dragging you along tonight.'

'But you didn't drag me, I suggested it.'

'But you only found the gig because I like them. I don't even know why I like them.'

I felt like I'd failed her. She didn't say anything for a moment as we lay there in the dark, the only sounds coming from the cars driving past outside.

'I do,' she said, finally.

'You do?'

'Yeah. Well, correct me if I'm wrong, but he's a poet, isn't he? A writer. His lyrics... they take you on a journey. And that's you. That's what you connect with. And he gives you a moment outside of yourself. The music isn't bad, but it's more... Dylan than Bowie.'

'I haven't listened to a lot of Dylan,' I replied.

'I mean... you should, of course. But I'm not sure he'll grab you in quite the same way. There isn't quite the same level of despondency that you crave.'

I craved despondency? I didn't even know what that meant. I just knew I was drawn to the music and the sentiment. I felt the bed move next to me, creaking slightly as she got up and went over to her bag to rummage around in it. She came back and put her hand on my arm, feeling for my hand, before passing me an earphone. She'd got her iPod out. I put it in my ear, assuming she'd done the same with the other one and the unmistakeable first sounds of the song I'd been waiting for all night, my song, started playing. We lay there in the dark, and as Conor started singing 'Lover I Don't Have to Love', she reached out for my hand and held two of my fingers with two of hers.

Chapter 10

I was still on a high from our trip to London as I sat on Astrid's sofa in her tiny flat the following Friday. She lived in a bedsit, with the bed backing onto the sofa we were sitting on, and the kitchen stretching around one side of the whole room. It was small and eccentric, but had started to feel like home to me. I felt so safe and happy there, and I'd got to know its quirks – I knew to avoid where the corner of the bed frame jumps out to bite you (her words) and where to make sure not to trip over the cords coming out in all directions from the limited number of power points in the flat, all of which had double adapters on top of double adapters. I loved feeling so much at home in someone else's space. Astrid was going through a phase of loving margaritas and was in the kitchen area making us some.

'Aren't they just everything you want in one glass?' she'd said, the first time she handed me one. 'Plus, they're almost entirely alcohol.'

I could certainly taste that. I didn't know if I really liked the bitterness and strength of the drink, or the way it partially mixed with the salt balanced on the rim. But if Astrid liked them, I was going to like them too. And it wasn't so bad; by the time I'd made it to the end of my first glass, I could start to feel it in my head, and it didn't seem so harsh anymore. Nothing did.

While she was in the kitchen, her phone rang, announced by the tinny sound of her 'Friday I'm in Love' ringtone. It was sitting on the coffee table in front of me.

'Will you get that for me?' she called out over the sound of her shaking the spirits with ice in the cocktail shaker.

Answer her phone? I was paralysed with fear every time my own phone rang; how was I going to answer Astrid's? But she'd asked me to do it, I couldn't just stare at it and let it ring out. So I picked it up, took a deep breath and answered.

'Hello, Astrid's phone... uh... this is Jess speaking.'

I winced at how awkward I sounded.

'Hi Jess,' came the reply in that strange, compressed voice you hear through the phone. 'It's Sofia... Astrid's sister. I think we've met.'

Relief came over me as I realised it wasn't some new person that I was going to need to get the measure of.

'Oh, hi! How are you?'

'Fine thanks, you?'

'Yes, I'm well thanks. Astrid is just pouring us some drinks. She should only be a sec.'

As if on cue, she walked over and put the two glasses down on the table.

'Here she is,' I told Sofia as I handed the phone to Astrid and mouthed 'Your sister'.

Something passed across her face – a slight frown and a narrowing of her eyes. She took the phone from me.

'Hi.'

'Fine.'

A pause.

‘This Saturday? As in tomorrow? Can’t. I’m going away.’

I didn’t know she was going away, she hadn’t even mentioned it. I felt hurt that she hadn’t told me and wondered why she’d kept it a secret.

Another pause. Astrid put her hand on her hip and shook her head, looking annoyed.

‘Maybe.’

Another pause.

‘K. Bye.’

She hung up, put the phone down on the table and picked up the two glasses, handing one to me.

‘Cheers!’ she said with a big smile, as we clinked our glasses together. ‘Oh! Music!’

She went and picked a vinyl to put on: *A Funeral*, by Arcade Fire, to remind us of the wonderful gig we’d been to.

I didn’t think I’d imagined the tension in her voice during her conversation with her sister, nor the sharp tone, but I wasn’t sure whether to acknowledge it. I also wanted to know where she was going away to. It wasn’t like she had to tell me everything, but I just thought that was a detail she might have mentioned. Two margaritas in, it seemed necessary to bring it up.

‘So... How’s Sofia?’

She shrugged.

I persevered. ‘Seemed frosty...’

‘She wanted to know if she could come and stay tomorrow.’

‘And you’re going away?’

‘Of course not. I just don’t want her staying here. Not last minute, like I’ve got no other plans. And she just expects I’ll say yes. No way. Especially after that night we stayed with her... No respect whatsoever.’

'Don't you just... put up with these things for family? Or something?'

She sighed and shook her head.

'You wouldn't understand. You're lucky – you don't have a sister.'

I wondered whether to say anything. It was so rarely relevant, and just brought people down if I ever mentioned it. Plus, the ensuing looks of pity were more than I could take, so I generally preferred not to say it. But for once, it seemed weirder to keep it to myself.

'Well, actually... I did. Once.'

She laughed, one of those sort of constricted laughs that comes out when the person is unsure of what the joke is, but wants to play along. I just shrugged.

'Wait... what? What do you mean?' She was clearly confused. It was understandable. I'd only ever really given her the impression that I was an only child.

'She was my twin. We were seven when she died. She had been sick for some time, so we'd been expecting it.'

'I'm not sure what to say. God, I'm so sorry, Jess. What was her name?'

'Emily.'

'And you've lived your whole life since, with this hanging over you.'

I'd never thought of it as 'hanging over' me.

'How did you even comprehend it at that age?' she asked.

'I don't know, but I knew what it meant... death. I guess we'd all lived with the possibility of it for a while. I remember asking my mum if I could die for her so she could stay.' It suddenly sounded morbid to say that out loud and I instantly regretted it.

'Sorry, that sounds really weird.' I said quickly. 'I just... I guess my mum and dad seemed so sad and lost at the idea of losing her that I thought maybe if I could be the one to go instead, then they wouldn't have to be sad... I don't know if that makes any sense.'

'Absolutely. Like the Kate Bush song.'

'Kate Bush?'

'Yeah, you know that song?' She started singing, a haunting melody with lyrics about wanting to make a deal with God to swap places. I noticed I had goosebumps appearing on my arms. I had, in fact, prayed to God to bring her back and take me instead. Looking back, I thought I was mad for doing it, but suddenly I felt seen and understood. 'I don't think I know that song,' I said, my voice catching in my throat.

'Hang on, one sec,' she said, getting up, 'I think I've got it...'

She went over to where the record player was and as soon as her back was turned, I wiped away the tears that had just escaped my eyes and fallen down my cheek, and hoped she hadn't seen them. I had no idea why I was crying; it was ridiculous. Emily had died well over a decade ago. Astrid rifled through her record collection whilst humming to herself, picked one out and put it on. The song came on immediately, it must have been the first track. It was as haunting from the very first notes as Astrid's rendition, and the goosebumps came back again.

'Ohhh, it's beautiful,' I said as she came and sat back down next to me. We were silent as the song played and I listened to the words and let the music, and the wild and free sound of Kate's voice wash over me. I suddenly felt less alone. It seemed like she got it.

'It's so spot on,' I said as the song was ending.

She nodded. 'There's a song for everything. With music, you never need to feel alone for long. See, you're not the only one to have that thought. It's not weird.'

'I guess not.'

'But you know, if it had been you instead of her, people would have been sad that you were gone.'

I shook my head. 'I didn't see it like that. I didn't think anyone noticed me much. And I don't think they would have missed me like they missed Emily.'

'Sounds lonely. Did you have any support?'

I shrugged. 'Not really, I guess. My parents tried, at least I think they did, but I'm not sure they ever truly got over it themselves. Though how could they?'

'What about you?'

'Get over it? No. But I'm fine. It was different for me. I was young. I didn't feel like I'd let her down, but I think maybe they did. They got stuck on thinking about what they could have done differently.'

'Can I ask what happened?'

'Cancer.'

'Ah. But that wasn't their fault...'

'No. But I think they'll always wonder if there was more they could have done. If they'd only caught it earlier, chosen a different treatment... There's always something. And there's a lot of the blame game when it comes to cancer.'

'Must have been so rough. How come you're only telling me this now?'

'Yeah... Sorry to drop it all on you now, it's just not exactly the first thing I open with. And there's rarely a good moment to say "Oh, hey, so my sister's dead..." It happened so long ago. I just try to get on with things.'

'And...' she paused and bit her lip, casting her eyes down for a second. She looked back up at me with a slight smile on her face, and added: 'You wanted to make a point?'

I suddenly realised how my timing must have come across: that she shouldn't complain about her sister because mine was dead. What a horrible thing to do. How could I be so dismissive of her feelings?

'Oh, gosh,' I stammered. 'I'm sorry, I—

'Don't worry about it,' she cut in, while shaking her head and smiling. 'And certainly don't apologise, it was a good point to make, Little Mouse, and needed. I wouldn't wish my sister to be dead by any stretch, but I don't really understand why I have to do things for her if she's going to be generally rubbish to me. She's just not someone I really want to spend my time with. Why should we automatically get along, just because we were birthed by the same person?'

It made sense. I only really had my parents and there was some sort of obligation to them because they had brought me up.

'Honestly, do whatever you like, ignore me. It's certainly not up to me to tell you how to be with her. I guess I'd just say that... you might be sad if she wasn't here.' I looked down at the glass in my hands. 'All I know is that my sister not being around made everyone sad...'

She put her hand on mine.

'Hey,' she said, 'you both mattered. You're no less important than she was. And I want you to remember that.'

I looked up at her, smiled, and said, 'Thanks.'

'Come on,' she said, rubbing my arm affectionately. 'Let's have another drink.'

She took my empty glass and got up. But before she reached the kitchen, she paused and turned back. 'Thank you, Little Mouse.'

'For what?'

'For trusting me enough to share that with me. And for pulling me back down to earth.'

'But not too much, I hope.'

She laughed. 'No, not too much.'

Chapter 11

I couldn't believe we were hurtling through second year. After a brief trip home for a pre-exam holiday, we were all back and trying to study for exams, which was pretty much my idea of hell. I wasn't good at tests at all. Give me a task and let me go away and think about it and carefully put my words together and I'll be fine. But I buckle under the pressure of exams. In addition, my study tactics were apparently rubbish and nothing stayed in my head. You had this way of reading something and somehow having it memorised. You called it a 'photographic memory', which I was sure wasn't actually a thing (you assured me it was), but I tried to keep reminding myself that I couldn't compare the level of studying I needed to yours. Or anyone else's, for that matter, otherwise I'd drive myself mad. But the thought did tend to hang around in my head: why did my success seem to take so much more work than everyone else's?

I'd started to wonder what we were going to do for living arrangements for our third year. The obvious thing was just to stay where we were, but I had this dream of us moving out and living with Astrid. The lease was coming up on her little flat, and the landlord wanted it back to do it up and sell it. It certainly needed work done; the hot tap in the bathroom kept falling off the wall and Astrid was forever repairing it with super glue, the kitchen taps often dripped, which required a nifty rubber band fix she'd come up with, and Astrid said the carpet underneath her rugs was horrible. She'd painted over what were apparently discoloured walls with fun, bright colours, making every wall a 'feature wall', but she was in the process of painting them back to everyone's favourite colour (good old magnolia) before she had to hand back her keys.

I also had an idea that maybe she could move into one of the rooms in our house. We'd originally all got a room each so we had our own spaces to study in, but I slept in your room quite often anyway, so I thought maybe I could move in there permanently, and Astrid could have my room. But I hadn't mentioned anything, I wasn't sure which was the most likely of all the seemingly unlikely scenarios – convincing you to leave your friends, or convincing Astrid to join them.

I had been trying to think of the best way to bring up our plans for the following year. I decided to start with Astrid, to see what she was thinking. But first, I wanted to work out what she actually thought of you all. Between the time we all went out to the campsite together and lit the fire, to the times she'd bumped into you when she was around at our place, she must have formed some opinion. Though if she did, so far, she'd kept it to herself. So one evening at hers, over a bottle of red wine and the empowering tunes of Blondie, I asked her what she thought of you, and the group in general.

She'd laughed first, then said, 'Oh, you're serious!'

'Well, yeah,' I'd replied, not sure what the joke was.

'Well, they're not exactly our people, are they?'

That made me think for a moment. *Our people.* I wondered what that meant. Sure, the friends of Astrid's I'd met were more artistic, I guess they had different priorities and views on things and the conversations were more creative and less about law, but I wondered how she'd so quickly come to that decision. She'd met the others a couple of times, here and there, but surely it wasn't enough to have such a strong idea of what they were like.

'You probably just haven't spent enough time with them,' I said, for some reason feeling like I needed to come to their defence, though I wasn't sure why.

'Little Mouse, I knew from the moment I saw them. You can tell immediately, you know? Whether you're going to gel with someone or not. And Robert and his crew are just not... my people.'

I hadn't realised she was also talking about you when she'd made the comment. Surely she didn't dislike you? I wasn't sure what to say.

'I mean...' she continued, realising I'd been caught off guard by her assessment, '...it's totally fine for you to hang out with them all, obviously, and I don't have anything against seeing them here and there, they're fine, they're nice enough. But I'm hardly going to start hanging out with them. They're just not my kin. Surely you get that. Do you even like them?' I went to open my mouth, about to jump to your defence, but she quickly added, 'The others, I mean. Lauren and Ethan and them. Do you hang out with them one on one? As friends?'

'Well, no, I suppose I don't. But I guess I can't quite understand how you can make a call on them so quickly. You've hardly spent any time with them.'

'It's a vibe. I can tell pretty much as soon as I meet someone whether they'll get me or not. It's totally fine if they don't, not everyone has to like me, I probably won't like them either.

You can't please everyone.'

I couldn't bear the idea of people not liking me. I knew I couldn't be friends with everyone, but I didn't want them to not like me, the idea of it made me feel lonely. But perhaps having you and now Astrid too, meant I didn't have to worry quite so much about people like Lauren, Ethan and Matt... I decided after that conversation that Astrid moving into the flat seemed unlikely. But I was sure she hadn't meant that she didn't like you, so I was still hoping maybe you'd come around to the idea of living in a bit of a smaller flat, maybe with just the three of us...

I was psyching myself up to bring it up with you, but before I could, you brought it up first. I remember standing in the kitchen at the time, washing the dishes when you said it:

'I'm thinking of doing a year abroad next year.'

I stopped, staring down at the yellow rubber gloves, the soapy water swirling around them. I must have misheard.

'What...?' I looked over at you where you were sitting at the kitchen table, but you were looking down at the paper you were reading.

'I just thought I might try something else for a year,' you said, turning the page before finally looking up at me. 'It gets a bit boring here, doesn't it?'

I still didn't really understand what you were saying.

'What do you mean?'

'I think it will be good for me.'

'Good for you...' I rolled the words over my tongue. They hung in the air for a moment as I tried to process what you were saying. My immediate thought was that I had done something wrong, and this was your way of breaking up with me.

'I don't understand,' I managed eventually. 'We only came here because you wanted to and now you're telling me you're leaving?'

'Don't be like that. You like it here, don't you?'

'Of course I do, but that doesn't mean this isn't a shock.'

'Why does it matter anyway?'

I couldn't work out what you meant. Why does it matter? Why *wouldn't* it matter to me? My boyfriend was planning on leaving me for an entire year. Wasn't that a big deal?

'I was thinking of doing third year in America.'

'Isn't this something we should discuss together?'

'Come on, Jess. We are our own people; we can make our own decisions. It will be good for my career. They say people who study abroad for a year end up in higher paying jobs, even straight out of uni. It will help set up our future – you want that, don't you? It's only one year, nothing's going to change, I think we can manage to spend a year apart. You're not seriously going to try and hold me back, are you?'

'No! Of course not. It's just...' I wavered slightly and you cut in before I could work out how to phrase my thoughts.

'Hey, hey, come on.' You got up walked over to me, smoothing my hair with your hands. 'Don't be one of *those girls.*'

'No, no, I'm not.' I didn't know who 'those girls' were, but I was certain I didn't want to be one. 'I just don't understand why—'

'Look, I can't talk to you if you're going to be like this,' you said, breaking away from me and striding over to where your car keys were. 'I'm going to head out for a bit. We can talk later once you've calmed down.'

And before I could get my head around any of it, you left.

I didn't see you until the next day. You'd left to go somewhere in your car and when you got back, you'd gone to bed without coming to see me. I don't think I got any sleep that night. I just kept going over and over in my mind wondering what I had done wrong. What had I done to make you want to leave? The next day, I went through the motions of going to uni, trying to distract myself, but I was in a daze, and constantly on the verge of tears. You were already out of the house by the time I'd got up, so I still hadn't seen you. I was so worried about what was going to happen. You deciding to leave me felt like the world was ending. I tried to view it in isolation – that you just wanted this experience, that it had nothing to do with me. But all I could see was us breaking up, and me being alone again. I knew I had to do anything I could to avoid that, the thought of it happening paralysed me. I finally saw you again after class the next day when we'd both got home.

'Are we going to talk about this?' I asked over dinner. It was just the two of us in the kitchen again, I don't know where the others were.

'Is there anything to talk about? I'm only going away for a year. You can make a big deal out of it, but I'd rather you didn't.'

'Do you want me to come with you?' I'd asked.

'Why would you do that?'

'I dunno. I just thought—'

'I'll be back in a year. We're not so dependent on each other that we can't survive a year apart. It would be worrying if we couldn't.'

We went around and around in circles talking about it that evening. I knew I was probably being too clingy, but I didn't want you to leave. Our life was good, things felt like they were slotting into place. I had you, I had university, and now I had Astrid too. For the first time in my life, it seemed like it was all going well; I felt happy and I even had hope for the future. I tried to persuade you to stay, but the more I begged, the more you pulled away. Ultimately, I knew I had to let it go, I wasn't getting anywhere trying to change your mind. I realised I had to let you go and hope that you came back.

I wondered what would have happened if I had been the one who wanted to do a year abroad. I certainly wouldn't want you to tell me I couldn't do something I wanted to, but I was sure that I would have at least discussed it with you first. Maybe that was something I needed to work on – being more independent. And you were right, it was only going to be a year. Perhaps it was doable if it was just for a year. Then we'd be back on track. I could do it. I would have to.

I was glad at least that going away for a year meant that you wanted to travel too. It was something that had taken up a fair bit of space in my mind since I'd first met Astrid and she'd mentioned Budapest and later Paris, Berlin and all the adventures she'd had. I'd decided I wanted to experience more of the world and although I'd mentioned the idea of it to you in passing, I wasn't sure how keen you were. But now I finally knew, and there was some comfort in that knowledge. There was part of you that was looking for adventure too.

I sent Astrid a message.

Need a drink asap. Wine bar @ 5?

At the bar, one we'd been meaning to check out for a while, I told her everything. Through tears and mouthfuls of red wine, I recounted it all, while she listened intently. I'd tried to convince myself it was ok – that I was ok with it – but when

I said it out loud it all felt so fresh again. She put her arms around me and stroked my hair.

'He's a dick, Mouse.'

'He's not...'

'Of course he is, if he treats you like this.'

'It's ok,' I said as I wiped my eyes with the back of my hand. Astrid rummaged around in her bag and pulled out a small packet of tissues, handing me one. I was a mess. I wiped my eyes, the black of my eyeliner patterning streaks across the white surface, then blew my nose with it. 'Thanks. I mean... he's allowed to go away. People go on years abroad all the time. We'll survive being apart. It's just a bit of a shock, that's all. I can't help feeling... that everything's falling apart...'

'Ah, perhaps,' she said, reaching up to wipe some eyeliner off my cheek that had evidently smudged. 'But that's just life; constantly thinking the world is going to end but then all that happens is new beginnings. Actually... speaking of new beginnings, I've just had the most wicked idea.'

'Yeah?' I said, blowing my nose again.

'Let's move in together!'

My heart leapt into my throat. I could hardly believe she'd been the one to suggest it, I hadn't needed to say anything.

'Yes! Oh my gosh!' I replied quickly. 'Are you sure you want to?'

'Of course I do! Why not? I've gotta get out of my place soon anyway, let's find somewhere together. I know we'll have the most fabulous time. We'll share so many pots of tea and drink all the wine in the world and have lots of parties. What do you say? Silver lining?'

Silver lining? More like a solid gold cloud, I thought.

'Yes! Absolutely!' I gushed. 'I'm in!'

'Well, we'd better drink to that, I think.'

We held our glasses up and touched them together. The day had turned from being so terrible, into having so much hope.

'It's going to be just you and me, Mouse, together at last! What fun!'

The wine kept coming, and we kept clinking our glasses together. There seemed to be so many things to cheers to, and I found myself getting excited about the next year. I felt the familiar comforting buzz of alcohol and of being around Astrid, and I almost forgot about how upset I had been just hours before.

I busied myself with planning for it all. I wanted to show you that I could succeed without you, that I wasn't dependent on you, and that I could perhaps even thrive whilst you were gone. I wanted you to see that I was relaxed, not crazy or desperate or any of the other things I didn't want to be.

Astrid and I found a place to live. After viewing so many terrible flats, we finally found the one. We knew we had to have it as soon as we saw it, so we immediately put in an offer and Astrid covered the upfront deposit needed to secure it for the year. She knew I felt uncomfortable asking my parents for extra money and she said she'd just been paid for some modelling work she'd done, and that the deposit from her previous flat would cover a large chunk of it anyway.

The flat was everything I could have hoped for. It was spread across two floors, with slightly steep, crooked stairs between them. The top floor had two equally sized small bedrooms and a bathroom, while the bottom floor had the living room which contained a small dining table by the window, and a kitchen opening off to the side. It even had access to a fairly compact garden space out the back, which Astrid said would be perfect for parties and reading in the afternoon sun.

It was an upgrade to cream coloured curtains, which seemed like an improvement on all my previous living spaces. It made it feel crisp and fresh. The walls, of course, were magnolia.

We agreed to move in early, during the uni holidays. That suited me just fine.

Chapter 12

I was dreading the summer holidays. I knew it would be our last time together before you left. I had somehow got through exams, even though my mind was elsewhere. I had no idea how I managed to pass them.

You and I packed up and went back home to Hampshire to spend the holidays with our parents. Astrid was leaving for Europe; she said she had to go to her Mum's house in Germany first, then was going on to her Dad's apartment in Paris. I realised how little I knew about her family, I guess I'd never thought to ask. So when she'd told me her summer holiday plans one day while she was over at mine, I thought I'd ask a bit more about them.

'Oh, so your parents are divorced?' I said after she'd told me they lived apart.

'Um... no, not really,' she'd replied, and didn't offer up any more information. I figured she didn't want to talk about it and so I left it.

You had packed all your things into your car, and we'd moved out of the house. I hugged Matt, Ethan and Lauren goodbye. We all said that we'd catch up after the holidays, but I had very little intention of doing so. I didn't need them, and I revelled in the knowledge that I could leave them all behind.

I was moving on to greater things. I understood now why Astrid had said they weren't *our people*. I realised I'd been so preoccupied with trying to make them like me, that I hadn't taken a moment to think if I even liked them.

You drove us home with a car so full it was hard to see through the back window. With each mile, I felt heavier, like we were moving closer to the end. We were stopping at my parents' place first, and you planned on staying with us for a few days before heading on to yours.

Before I went to uni, I'd never been away from home for a prolonged period, and every time I came back it felt more and more strange. Each time highlighted how different I was from the person who used to inhabit that bedroom. And every time I got back in it, it felt like I regressed. Somehow, I managed to turn back into my teenage self, and everything my parents did annoyed me. You weren't like that though, while I was increasingly dreading those trips home, you always looked forward to them. You were really close with your family, though. I liked that feeling of being part of a group when we visited them.

As we pulled up to my house, I saw movement in the front window, and mum's face appeared, looking out onto the street. Moment later, she opened the front door and stood in the doorway, watching us as we got out of the car and grabbed some of our things.

'How was the trip?' she asked. 'How was the traffic? It can get quite busy this time of year.'

'Hi, Mum.' I hugged her. 'Yes, the traffic was fine.'

'Hi, Mrs Wight,' you said, as you walked up behind me.

'Hello Robert,' she said, as you kissed her on the cheek. 'Traffic ok?'

'Yes, we didn't have any problems. We left early.'

'Good, good. Come in. I've put the kettle on.'

Inside, you took our bags to our rooms. Separate rooms, of course. Mum wouldn't dare let us share. You always stayed down the hall in the guest room and I moved back into my childhood bedroom.

We all settled into the living room as Mum poured us cups of tea. She'd brought out the set with pink and yellow flowers on it, which used to be her mother's. They were pretty, but the cups were so small that it didn't feel like there was ever enough tea in them.

'I was just saying to your father that you'll get to meet our new minister tomorrow, wasn't I, Phil?' Mum said as she handed out the cups to each of us.

'Yes, darling,' Dad replied.

'Oh, he's lovely. We weren't sure at first, were we? Bit young, I thought. But he's turned out to be very good. He gave a wonderful sermon last week about being grateful for what we have and sending our prayers to those poor children in Africa.'

'That sounds great, Mum,' I said, already finished half of my tea.

An unwritten rule of staying at my parents' place was of course going to church. When I was little, I got to go to Sunday school instead, which was a lot more fun. I had some good memories from that time. That was where I'd met my best friend, Claire. She was small and pretty, and all the adults loved her. I wanted to be just like her.

'Would Claire do this?' My mother would ask, any time I didn't want to eat my vegetables, or was in trouble for something.

Sometimes I thought she might, other times probably not, but either way, it just seemed easier to try and be more like Claire. I hated when my parents were unhappy with me; I hated letting them down. Then Claire's family moved away to America and once again, I had no one. Sunday school no longer felt like my safe space to look forward to each week, and I'd struggled to find many friends at all after that.

But of course, I'd met you at college. You were from a religious family too, which pleased my mother. When we moved away to uni, she asked you to make sure we kept going to church. I think we meant to do it, but things got in the way and we never did. Also, the older I got, the more conflicted I felt about religion. I know my parents found solace in the idea that God was looking after my sister after she died, but I couldn't work out why he had taken her at all... Surely that wasn't fair. People at church often used to tell us that 'everything happens for a reason', which seemed to comfort my parents, but it really bothered me. She hadn't deserved it, and any God who thought a child needed to die didn't sound like one I liked very much.

I didn't think about Emily often, but I felt her presence when I was at home. Her ballet shoes hung above the mantelpiece, and I would sometimes touch them when I walked past. Emily and I had taken up dancing together before she got ill. Matching little tutus and pink satin shoes, Christmas concerts and our hair in buns. She had really loved it, but I think I did it mostly because she did. When she died, I kept dancing. Mum had been a dancer when she was young too, and I enjoyed doing something that had been so important to her. And to Emily. I wanted to make Mum proud, and dancing seemed to do that.

When I was about ten, my parents took me to see the Bolshoi Ballet perform *Swan Lake* and I was transfixed. The elegance and grace of it was beyond anything I'd ever seen. I was mesmerised. In the car on the way home, I was chattering excitedly about it.

'I've decided,' I announced to my parents, 'that I'm going to be a famous ballerina and I will play the Swan Princess when I grow up.'

Mum had laughed. 'Honey, that's a lovely dream, but dancing is hard. It takes a lot of dedication and hard work and only the very best actually make it. It's not an easy life, and you don't want that. Keep working hard at it, but it's much better to keep it just as a hobby; that way you won't end up hating it.'

I cried that night when I went to bed, my dream having been shattered.

Mum had tried to be a professional dancer when she was young, but she never quite made it. She always told me how gruelling the training was, how much of a toll it took on her body. Her feet were slightly misshapen, which she said was due to spending so much time in ballet shoes whilst they were growing. I did it a fair amount too, but I don't think I'd done anywhere near as much as she had.

She was probably right. Professional dancing wasn't for me. There was no way I was good enough, anyway. Emily had a natural talent for it, but I don't think I did. But I did keep dancing, taking lessons after school and doing shows and competitions on weekends; sometimes solo, sometimes in a group.

That is, until the accident. Until the moment when my leap and twist that was supposed to be caught, wasn't. They called it a 'stress fracture'. Apparently the constant back bends and leaps had caused underlying damage, and the fall was the final straw that literally broke my back. The doctor had suggested that perhaps my core wasn't strong enough, or my form might have been incorrect, and I was so angry at myself for causing it due to not being a good enough dancer. Or at least exacerbating it. It took months to recover from the injury, and I spent a lot of time lying in bed, dosed up on painkillers that only just seemed to take the edge off – I got to miss a whole lot of school though, which felt like a silver lining. But they were long, dark days. Trying to find a way to face the reality that I could no longer dance, that I could no longer make my mum proud. I didn't know who I was without it. I felt like I'd let Emily down too, I was supposed to keep dancing because she couldn't... And I'd ruined that, just like I ruined everything. Mum kept saying I might be able to build back up to it, but it never properly healed. I never danced again.

I tried not to think about it too often but whenever I felt pain in my back (which happened more often than I might like), it felt like I was right back there, lying in that bed, desperately wishing to heal... I felt like I'd suppressed it well when we'd climbed up that wall at the magazine launch party, but even then, my mind had flicked back to that familiar place and the things that I had lost.

I felt like I had a place when I danced. I was so shy and unconfident in most areas of my life, but when I was dancing it was just me and my body and the music. It was the only time when I felt truly present. Hours could pass by and I wouldn't notice them.

Emily had been the fun, bubbly one. I used to make her

speak to people first and hide behind her for a while before I spoke to them. She didn't mind, she was in her element with new people. After she died, I used to pretend to myself that I was Emily when I first met people. I suppose that wasn't a very healthy coping mechanism, but we all find our own ways of surviving.

My parents still referred to her in the present tense, as if she was off somewhere else, like holiday camp or at a friend's place; she wasn't gone, she was just *not here right now*. Perhaps it was a refusal, even years on, to accept that she was gone. I suppose it was strange, but I was used to it. You handled it all well too. It always amazed me how you just fitted in and didn't make a big deal about these things. I was so grateful to have you in my life, that you could put up with my strange family.

Sometimes I'd imagine what it would be like if Emily was still alive. Would we have gone to uni together? Would I still have followed you? Would she and I have lived together and been the best of friends or would we not get along, like Astrid and Sofia? I had so many scenarios I would play out in my head. There was one where we were best friends and one where we were estranged. And there was one where I killed her... Sometimes, I would imagine standing above her with a knife, before plunging it into her chest. I don't know why, and I would never dare tell anyone about it. My thoughts often went quite dark. But most often I would just think of what it would be like if she were still here. We weren't identical twins, but we looked similar enough. Would we look alike as adults? I sometimes obsessed about these scenarios when I was alone, wondering how the balance of nature vs. nurture might have played out.

I always got a strange recurring dream when I stayed at my parent's place. It involved me being asleep in a bunk bed, on the bottom bunk. In my dream, I'd wake up and part of me was missing. An arm, an ear, or sometimes my whole lower body... it would just be gone. Then I'd look up, and there was a hole in the mattress above me and someone was peering down through it at me. I'd feel both terror and reassurance at seeing them. Then I'd wake up.

Chapter 13

After you left to go to your parents' place, I felt so alone in that house. My parents seemed tolerable when you were there, and you would rub my shoulders in the evening while Mum and Dad watched TV and we sat reading, melting away my stress. But after you'd gone home, I started to notice all their strange habits and Mum's comments started to wear me down. I counted down the days until you were due to pick me up to go stay with your family, even though I knew it meant that it was almost time for you to leave.

Your family were so different from mine. There was you three boys and your mum and dad – all lawyers, of course. Your older brothers were either married or engaged, and it gave me a glimpse of what my future might look like.

To be perfectly honest, your family kind of overwhelmed me. I tried to fit in, but I often felt left behind. I never told you this, but I always felt a bit sorry for your mum. She seemed to do a lot of the work around the house, while the four of you would play strategy board games or have heated discussions about world issues. She would join in here or there, but I could tell she wasn't really part of the team. Maybe I was reading too much into it and maybe she enjoyed her role in the family. It just felt quite different from my parents, who seemed to do absolutely everything together. I would always go and help your mum out in the kitchen when I was visiting.

I think I got on well with your sister-in-law, Esmé, and your other brother's fiancé, Caroline. It felt a bit like a girls' club. We'd sit and chat while watching you boys throw a ball around the garden, or we would listen to your debates as we sat in the living room. You'd ask us for topics to discuss and I suggested a couple, but they were never chosen.

Sometimes I thought I might like to get more involved in what you boys were doing, but the activities felt a bit beyond me. I once asked if I should join in with a game you were playing, but you just smiled and put your arms around me and said: 'No, no, you wouldn't enjoy this. You're perfect just how you are.' That made me smile.

You were the youngest, and I suppose the quietest of your brothers. I know you tried hard to keep up. You'd get so tired after a day with your family; I suppose intellectual stimulation will do that. And you were all so competitive. It exhausted me just watching. I don't know how you did it, but I was impressed that you could.

That summer, two days before you were due to leave for America, we were all sitting around the dinner table. Your father was talking about your future in the family law firm, when he said: 'And I have decided that there will be a spot for *you* at the firm once you graduate, too.'

I looked up from my meal, wondering who he was talking about, and saw that everyone was looking at me. Even then, it took me a moment to realise he was talking to me. I froze, wondering what I was supposed to do.

'Oh, me?' I managed to say, after what felt like hours of all their eyes on me.

'Well, yes,' he replied in his big, loud voice.

You nudged me under the table from where you were sitting across from me. I looked at you, and you raised your eyebrows.

'But... I'm not a lawyer,' I said, feeling very confused.

Everyone was quiet for a moment, then your father started laughing, and then they all did too. I wasn't sure what was happening, but I smiled along.

'No, dear,' your mother added as she leaned over towards me, so I could hear her over the last of the laughing. 'We thought you'd be at home in the finance department. Put your Economics degree to good work.'

'Oh, I see.' I replied slowly. I didn't like being put on the spot at the best of times. I just couldn't think how to respond. Eventually you came to my rescue.

'Thanks, Dad, that's so good of you. We're very grateful. Aren't we, Jess?'

With a deep breath, I finally found my feet.

'Oh, yes. Of course. Thank you very much for the offer. That's very kind.'

Your father just looked at me for a moment and I worried I'd said something wrong. Then he bellowed to the room: 'A toast! Welcome to the firm, Jess!'

And everyone raised their glasses and repeated, 'Welcome, Jess.'

I put a smile on my face and made sure I held it there. I was grateful, I really was. It could be the office dream I'd always imagined for myself. But something about it being decided for me felt uncomfortable. I guess I had wanted to set myself up, find my own place to work. But I also knew how competitive the job market was. It would probably be incredibly difficult to get a job on my own, especially in London, where I dreamed of living and where the firm's offices were also located. I could obviously use all the help I could get, a foot in the door. I didn't want you all to think I was ungrateful, because I really wasn't. It was an offer anyone would be silly not to accept.

I thought I recovered from the immediate shock of it all well, but you brought it up again later that night when we were getting ready for bed. In your house we were allowed to share a room, and I had been rubbing your shoulders, as was customary for our time at yours when I shifted into the supporting role.

'Why are you being so weird about the job?'

'Am I?'

'Very.'

'I'm sorry, I don't mean to be. It's just...' I trailed off, I didn't know what I was trying to say. I hadn't formed any of the thoughts fully in my head, let alone been able to put them into words. 'I guess I just thought maybe I'd find my own thing, make my own way...'

You turned around and looked at me. Your brow was scrunched as you shook your head.

'Don't be silly. They're being very generous taking you on, and you should really be grateful for that.'

'I am! Of course I am! I've said thank you.' I was starting to feel tired; I was so unprepared to have this conversation. 'But—'

'No buts, this will be great for us.'

You always sounded menacing when we fought. I didn't even know what I felt about it all yet, I just wanted some time to think about it. But there was no point in arguing, I didn't have any words to say.

After a moment, you softened and held your arms out. I

leaned into you, and you wrapped your arms around me. You kissed my head and stroked my hair, and I felt safe in your arms.

'I know it was a shock,' you said, your voice sounding much gentler, 'but it will be brilliant for us. One day you'll be part of this family, and this opportunity is exactly what we need. Just give it a few days to sink in and then you'll see it's great. This is our future, right here laid out before us.'

I felt horrified that my surprise might have come across as ungrateful. You were probably right; it was a great opportunity for us. I just needed time to let it sink in.

***

It was still only part-way through the summer holiday, but you'd decided to go to America early, to get set up for the year. It fit in with me, because I was also heading back early to move in with Astrid, but it made our last bits of time together feel so fleeting. You were going to stay with your uncle at first, until term started, when you'd be moving into uni accommodation, where you'd actually be sharing a *room* with a stranger. The thought absolutely horrified me, but you seemed fine with it.

We'd had a lovely time together in those days before you flew, but the night before you left, I cried. I just couldn't picture my life without you, it loomed like a big grey smudge on the horizon; I couldn't picture how my future would play out. I honestly didn't know how I was going to get through a year without you. I was so scared I would lose you entirely.

'There's no need for that,' you'd said, wiping a tear from my cheek. 'I'll be back in a year. A year is nothing.'

They say it's easier to leave than to be left behind.

I mostly tried to pretend it didn't bother me, you leaving, but I couldn't stop playing over and over in my mind how I had sacrificed the dreams I'd had of going to the university Mum had, in order to be with you. And now you were leaving without a second thought. But then I'd get annoyed at myself for overreacting. You were right, it was only a year and then you'd be back. But I was still hung up on wishing you'd talked to me about it first.

The day that you left came far too quickly. I went with you and your parents to the airport. We had a rushed goodbye, and it didn't feel like enough. It was almost as if I could feel the physical separation deepen as your plane left Heathrow and put ever increasing distance between us. I felt the bond between us stretching, the further away you went.

You said you'd call when you landed, but I didn't hear from you that day. I sent you a message, then another one, saying I missed you and hoped you'd had a good journey. But there was no reply. I couldn't help myself; I searched your flight on the internet, picturing your plane going down over the ocean and you, there amongst it all, watching your life flash before your eyes as the plane spiralled downward... But the flight tracking webpage said it had landed.

The next day, I still hadn't heard from you. Eventually, I called your mobile using the phone on the table by the front door at my parent's place. I tried not to think about how much a phone call to America would cost and just hoped they wouldn't notice it on their phone bill at the end of the month. I looked at the time zones and just picked a time I thought you would be most likely to answer.

'Hello?'

The sound of your voice filled me with relief.

'Hi, it's me.'

I'm not sure why I felt the need to specify it was 'me' calling.

'I know, hi.'

'How are you?'

'Yeah, good. What's up?'

'I just wanted to check you got there safely.'

'Yeah, of course I did. You weren't worrying, were you?'

'Oh… no… It's just that you said you'd call, and when you hadn't answered my messages…'

'I've been busy, Jess. I haven't worked out a phone plan yet, I only just arrived. And time zones are tricky.'

I stopped myself pointing out that sending me a quick email from your laptop wouldn't require the sender and receiver to both be available at the same time, nor did it require a phone plan. I was mostly just relieved to hear you; to know you were still alive.

'Yeah, yeah of course. How is it?'

You filled me in on your flight and then arrival, going to your uncle's place, who you hadn't seen for a few years. It did sound like you were busy. And you seemed to be having a good time, which made me happy to hear. Before we hung up, you said you loved me, and I realised none of it mattered; the lack of messages or calls or replies. You were safe, we were good, everything was fine. But I still missed you.

After a final week spent moping around my parent's house, it came time for them to drive me back. We took the same route we had two years before, when they drove me to uni the first time… It felt like going backward.

Chapter 14

Astrid was already in the flat by the time I got there – she'd moved in a couple of days before me. I knocked on the door of the flat, our flat, for some reason feeling nervous. My parents decided to stay standing in the street by their car, peering over. It wasn't long before Astrid came rushing out the door and immediately threw her arms around me.

'You're here! I missed you!' she said, and every muscle in my body relaxed. After letting me out of the hug, she looked over at mum and dad. 'Are these your parents?'

'Oh, yeah.'

She waved at them, and they waved back, but they didn't move.

'Mum, Dad, do you want to come say hi?' I called to them, wondering why they were being so awkward.

They walked over and seemed rather surprised when Astrid hugged them both; we weren't a particularly physically affectionate family, so I think it caught them off guard.

'Come in, come in!' she said. 'I'll put the kettle on.'

She walked inside without waiting for a reply. I don't think they'd been planning to stay, but I guess they felt obliged to follow, so they filed in through the front door. I smiled to myself at the fact that Astrid could make even my parents change their plans.

She made us all tea and then regaled us with stories of her summer. Germany had been a bit of a bore, she'd said. Her mum lived in the North, just outside of Münster, apparently, which I'd heard of but couldn't quite place geographically, or say anything about. She said it was nice enough, but 'nothing special'.

'Closer to Amsterdam than anywhere cool in Germany, like Berlin,' she'd said, but I thought anywhere in Europe was a cool place to be from. I wondered if one day she might take me there, show me where she'd grown up. I could meet her mum and maybe her dad too? I realised once again that I didn't know much about her family. I wondered if her parents would be more like the chaotic Sofia, or the cool, creative Astrid.

Apparently her time spent in Paris during the holiday had been more fun, though. She said she had played a sort of residency in a café/bar near her dad's place, doing an acoustic set each Sunday. She'd also caught up with some friends and been to lots of parties. I shifted slightly in my seat when she said that, wondering how my parents would react to the idea of partying. They'd never let me go to the few I was ever invited to as a teenager, but when I looked at them, they were smiling.

'Have you ever been to Paris?' she asked my parents as she poured milk into our cups of tea.

'We have been there once, when I was a lot younger,' Mum replied, looking fondly over at Dad. 'I loved it.' she added, which surprised me. She didn't very often comment on loving things. She even seemed somehow wistful as she'd said it, which was an expression I'd not often seen on her.

'Yes! I love it too,' Astrid said, clapping her hands together.

'It's such a magic place. There's such a feeling of expanse in that city, not to mention the regal buildings and so many beautiful parks; even the children's playgrounds have statues in the middle. And I find the sunlight is just different there. I went for lots of walks out around the Louvre while I was there, which felt pretty special. I always think that walking along those white paths by the ponds feels like walking on the surface of ice cream.'

Mum was nodding along, a big smile on her face.

When Astrid asked how my holidays had been, I wasn't sure how to answer. I had no way to follow on from her adventures, my holiday was nothing compared with Paris.

'It was quite quiet,' I settled for. 'We... had a nice time. Some nice local walks, some nice meals...'

'Hampshire is no Paris, I'm sure,' added Mum, still smiling. 'I think Jessica was probably quite bored hanging out with us oldies.'

I blushed. It felt odd hearing my mother speaking for me. I wasn't aware I'd given them the impression that I was bored, and I hated to think that I had.

My parents looked so out of place sitting there in the living room with Astrid; two completely polarised parts of my life suddenly thrown in together. After we'd finished our tea, I went to get my things from the car. Astrid came out and grabbed some things too, and my parents brought in the last of it. Before long, our living room was full and the car was empty, and it was time to say goodbye. I walked my parents out to the car and when we got there, Mum hugged me.

'It's so nice to see you've got a lovely friend to look after you,' she said.

'Thanks Mum,' I replied.

Astrid then came out to say goodbye to them too, all smiles.

'Thank you for looking after Jess for us,' my mum said to her when she'd reached the car, and I was mortified. Mum often thanked you for taking good care of me, but it felt like a step too far for her to be saying it to Astrid. Like she was doing them a favour by being my friend. My cheeks felt hot, and I didn't know how to react.

Astrid laughed lightly, and then hugged my mum.

'Thanks for having a lovely daughter who puts up with me!' she said, then hugged my dad too. He looked surprised again, but not unpleasantly.

As Astrid and I watched them drive off, waving from where we stood on the footpath, she had her arm around my shoulders.

Astrid seemed to realise quite quickly that I wasn't entirely myself when I arrived. I guess I was still coming to terms with you being gone. I'd sent you quite a few emails, but whenever you replied, you sounded distracted and distant. Astrid left me to go and have a shower and when she returned, I was still sitting on the sofa, staring off into space. She came marching over and knelt in front of me, putting her hands on my shoulders.

'We're heading out.'

'Where to?'

'I don't know. But we need to get you out of your head. This isn't helping anyone.'

She got up, pulled on her Doc Martins, and grabbed the keys to her car.

'We need to get outside. I know where we can go,' she said as we drove.

She asked me to pick a CD from the big wallet that lived

under the front seat in her car. It was bursting at the seams, with burned CDs shoved in wherever there was room. I chose the one that had 'Pop music is dead' scrawled across the front in thick black marker in her unmistakeable handwriting and was surprised to find it was mostly quite poppy music; Duran Duran, Spandau Ballet, A-ha, The Buggles.

'Geez Jess,' Astrid said, taking a glance at me, a worried look on her face. 'Even 'Video Killed the Radio Star' isn't making you smile. This is serious. All right, maybe we need to shout it out... get out the CD with 'Fuck it all' on the front.'

I picked up the CD wallet again and found the one she was referring to. I swapped it for the other one in the disc slot. The first song came on and it was Linkin Park. I must have looked surprised, because when she looked at me again, her face had turned into a cheeky smile.

'What, I can't have had an angsty teen phase?

And despite myself, I laughed. And indeed, I shouted along. Because I too, had had an angsty teen phase, hidden inside the walls of my bedroom, so my parents didn't find out what I'd been listening to.

After some time of shouting at the top of our lungs together, we ended up at a park on the side of a hill that overlooked the city. We got out of the car and as we walked, the evening sun stretched out our shadows and made us look like giants. The fresh air felt nice on my face. She was right, it felt good to get out. We played on the swings then climbed up a tower in the middle of the park which stood high above the city. She took my hand, and we entwined our fingers. Perhaps I would be ok. With her by my side, I could do this.

'I know you're sad about Robert leaving. But we only need us, Little Mouse. Look at all this stretching ahead of us. Our future. Our city. Our year.'

I smiled and nodded, so grateful for her.

'Our kingdom,' I added.

She put her arm around me and pulled me in close.

I wasn't alone, it would be ok.

***

'To the year of Astrid and Jess!' she exclaimed, tequila shot held high. We'd gone back to the pub we went to on the night we crashed the magazine launch party. Astrid had been making friends, and we'd already amassed a crowd around us. They all had tequila shots too.

'To Astrid and Jess,' they all cheered.

That night I felt on top of the world, alongside Astrid.

'Fuck boyfriends!' she said.

'Fuck boyfriends!' we all cheered and drank another shot.

How could I ever be alone when surrounded by so many people? This must be what Astrid felt like all the time.

The two of us stumbled home in the early hours of the morning, arm in arm, singing at the top of our lungs. Astrid had started singing 'Zombie', by The Cranberries, and I joined in. I was singing the tune along with her, and then she switched and started singing a harmony. Listening to our voices melding together gave me goosebumps.

'You can sing, Little Mouse!' she said as she grabbed my head with both hands and kissed my cheek.

'No, I can't,' I protested.

'Yes! You can! Keep singing!'

I had to admit it sounded nice, us singing together. One thing I had learned from singing at church, and then choir practice at school, was how to hold a tune even if someone else was singing a harmony.

'How have you kept this from me for so long? Why do you never sing?' Astrid asked.

'Because I'm not any good!'

'Aah,' she said. 'You've had the creativity shame moment, haven't you.'

'The what?'

'Creativity shame. The time when, probably when you were young, someone said your art isn't good, or a teacher or parent put you down about something you'd created. And for bonus points, it might have happened in front of other people, like your whole class. It makes you feel like you should hide your art away or stop creating altogether. I bet you any "non creative" adult will have had one. It's what makes people think they're "not creative people", which, quite frankly, is a travesty.'

I tried to think of something, but I was drawing a blank. I doubted I had ever been creative enough to have had such a thing.

'You will have one, I'm sure. It's probably buried down deep. No child is born thinking "I shouldn't let anyone hear me sing", someone will have said it to you. It will come back to you, I'm sure. Then you can let it go and we can sing together some time. Properly! Promise me?' She held out her pinkie finger towards me.

I smiled, the influence of alcohol inhibiting my natural overwhelming desire to find a way to say no. I wasn't the type of person who wanted the spotlight, but at that moment I felt I could do anything with Astrid beside me. I reached out and took her pinkie with mine. She didn't let go, so we walked with them still linked.

'I've known you for a whole year and it's only now he's gone that the real you suddenly comes out! It's fabulous to see this side of you!'

I wasn't sure if this was the 'real Jess', singing in the street, but it was nice to let loose for a night without fear of judgement. I knew what you would have thought if you'd seen us that night, singing loudly while walking down the street holding hands, not a care in the world. You wouldn't have been impressed. You would have told us to be quiet so as not to disturb anyone.

By the time we'd got back to the house, Astrid's words about the 'creativity shame' moment had brought up a memory for me. I'm not sure I would have thought of it otherwise, but alcohol seems to have a way of tapping into your subconscious and allowing things you've tried to forget to swim up higher.

She poured us two whiskies and we sat on her couch. I hadn't had whisky since that night when we'd first gone out together to the prohibition bar. I still didn't love it, but Astrid did, and I liked the idea of drinking it with her so that went a long way.

'Ok so, I think I remember something that might be a 'creativity shame' thing,' I said, and she leaned in closer, linking her fingers together to rest under her chin. 'Not long after my sister died, my new school was putting on a Christmas play. We were singing "The First Noel" and mum had taught me a harmony line to sing. She was a bit annoyed that our music teacher hadn't taught us one, but I don't know, we were seven-year-old kids. I'm not sure if we really understood harmony.'

'*You* clearly did, she taught you it,' Astrid interjected.

'Oh, yeah, true. Well, I somehow got up the courage to ask the teacher if I could sing the harmony. They handed me a microphone and made me sing my part over the top of everyone else.'

'Weird behaviour,' she said, taking a sip of her whisky as I nodded and paused slightly to collect my thoughts, the memory feeling unsettling in my head.

'I was terrified, I hadn't expected to be given a microphone. Everyone would be able to hear me loudly over the top... Anyway, I pushed through somehow and sang it while everyone sang through the song again. Afterwards, they took the mic back off me. I thought I'd sung it quite well, but my teacher said, in front of everyone: "No, I don't think that will work. Just sing the line I taught you like everyone else." And the other kids all laughed at me. Quite a few teased me for 'singing out of tune', which I'm sure I wasn't, it was just that I was singing something different. No one really wanted to talk to me after that, you know how kids are at that age...'

'Yep well, that definitely meets the requirements.' She put down her whisky, leaned over and hugged me. 'See, that would have been enough to make you think you shouldn't put yourself out there again. It's self-preservation in a way.'

'Yeah, you're right. I guess I convinced myself that I just hadn't sung it right enough...'

'Yeah, well, hearing you tonight, I think that's unlikely. So weird of the teacher though, a harmony obviously isn't a solo...'

I shook my head, for once feeling sorry for the little girl that had been in that moment, rather than blaming her. 'I used to dance as well, you know,' I added, the memories coming out thick and fast now that I'd tapped into them.

'No, I don't know, you kept that quiet. That's very creative. And you write, too.'

I laughed at the idea that writing reviews of bands and

various other useless articles was at all creative, but I liked that she said it was, probably just to humour me.

'But you don't dance now, right?' she asked, followed by the questions I dreaded answering: 'Why did you stop? Why don't you ever talk about it?'

I hated talking about it but it's amazing what a few drinks will do.

'I used to dance a lot, but I injured my back so I can't anymore,' I said quickly, the words rushing out. I stopped to take a deep breath and slow down. 'I can't even touch my toes now because everything is so stiff.'

'That's heart-breaking, Little Mouse. When I first met you I thought that you might be a dancer, you hold yourself like one.'

'I do? Is that a thing?' I asked, flattered that she'd thought anything at all about me that first time we'd met.

She laughed. 'Yes, of course it is. And I guess you've already tried things like yoga to help with it?'

'Uh... no... I've never really done any yoga.'

'Really? I'm sure it would help, especially with the stiffness. And I'm sure it would generally strengthen your back too – you could try it... We should go to yoga! Tomorrow!'

'Tomorrow?'

'Yeah, I know a girl running a free class in some exercise clothing shop.'

'Ok, I guess...' I said as I looked at my watch. It was nearly 3 a.m. 'But it's tomorrow now!'

'Perfect. Today, then! What a great idea for the year of Jess and Astrid. Yoga on Sundays!'

I wasn't sure it sounded great exactly, but who was I to say no. Exercise was good and she had only suggested it for my benefit. I had been planning to sleep in a sleeping bag on the sofa that night because a new mattress had been ordered for my bed but hadn't yet arrived. Astrid apparently had other ideas.

'Come on,' she said. 'Let's be each other's alarm clocks; you can crash in my bed tonight!'

So after we'd brushed our teeth, I climbed into her bed and lay there next to her like we had in the hotel bed after seeing Bright Eyes. It was nice not going to bed alone.

***

I think I was still drunk the next day when we were getting ready for yoga. We woke up after not enough sleep and giggled as we struggled to pull on tight patterned leggings. I borrowed a pair from her. She made us a strong coffee. It tasted odd when I took a sip and I peered into it, trying to understand what it was.

'Irish,' she said, with a sly smile, when she saw me scrutinising it. 'With coconut milk, of course.'

It felt slightly mad to be drinking alcohol in the morning, especially before a yoga class. Then I looked at her, and suddenly it made sense. We were rebels.

We walked into town arm in arm, singing again. I felt so light and happy, which was strange considering how recently I had been so upset about you leaving. But that was one of the beauties of Astrid. You couldn't be around her and *not* have fun. Adventures were always just around the corner and the world felt like an ocean of possibilities.

We got to the shop around 11 a.m. I guess over the years, I had purposefully avoided anything that reminded me of my injury, or the things I had lost. I'd found ways to get out of anything dance or gymnastics related at school after the accident, because it felt like too much of a reminder. I'd thrown myself into dance after my sister died and it kept me busy. When that had ended, I'd been left feeling like I had nothing again. I'd never thought about the significance of it before, but suddenly, as we were sitting on the mats between the shelves of clothes, it all came flooding back. My failure at not being able to dance anymore, my parents' disappointment, memories of my sister. I started to cry. As I moved into the 'downward dog' position, tears were falling onto my mat. Then I felt a hand on mine. Astrid had reached over from her mat beside me. She peered out from under her arm and smiled and then I did too.

When the class finished and we'd rolled up the mats and put them in the corner, Astrid gave me a huge hug, one that I didn't want to end. But I was feeling a lot better by then. I felt good, actually. Surprisingly good.

'Well, we could make this Droga a thing, I think!' said Astrid as we left the shop.

'Droga?' I asked.

'You know, drunk yoga! Droga!'

I laughed. Of course. Droga.

'I think I started sobering up halfway through that class,' she said. 'Apparently it's national margarita day. Shall we go to see if we can hunt some down?'

Within the hour, we were sitting in the window of a Mexican restaurant-slash-bar and had made our way through a pitcher of watermelon margaritas. So much had happened over the past couple of weeks. My whole life had changed; things I'd dreaded had actually happened, and yet here I was, feeling so happy. I felt slightly guilty for being happy, and I did wonder how you were feeling – were you missing me? Or were you out having a good time? I thought you would probably have wanted me to be enjoying myself, so I let go and surrendered to the moment.

Chapter 15

Our new flat was everything I expected a house for uni students to be. None of the furniture matched and some of it was so strange that we couldn't work out what it was supposed to be. There was a dark wood cabinet with no back or shelves by the doorway to the living room, a strange heavy ornate table by the wall near the kitchen, and a sofa so low it was almost like sitting on the floor. There was a weird wooden box hanging on the wall outside my bedroom, which Astrid dubbed 'The Church Box' as it had a cross carved into it. We had no idea what it was meant for, but Astrid started filling it with dried roses.

'See, they've had the life sucked out of them by the Church Box!' she said as she arranged the dry, crunchy roses. I'd giggled. To her, it was just a bit of fun but to me, it was an act of rebellion, one that my parents would not approve of.

She quickly made friends with the person who ran the local florist and started rescuing the less perfect flowers at the end of the day that could no longer be sold. If there were ever roses, she would dry them for my church box. As well as flowers, we filled our place with pot plants and fairy lights. Astrid had done some paintings to hang on the walls. She was so humble about them – 'Oh, it's nothing, I was just bored' –

but I thought they were fantastic. She presented me with a picture of a Labrador puppy for my wall and had painted a fox for hers. She joked that the fox was her 'spirit animal'. I knew she didn't really believe in that sort of thing, and neither did I, but I couldn't help but think how fitting the fox was for her. How stunning and independent they both were.

Astrid decreed that the first order of business, after the adornments, was to throw a housewarming party. I agreed, thinking we'd just invite a few people over for drinks. But Astrid had other plans.

'I think we should have a beat poetry night,' she'd said. 'It seems only fitting.'

'A what?'

'Beat poetry. You know? The beat generation – free expression and pushing boundaries. Who doesn't love the literature and poetry that came from that time, not to mention the idea of people getting together to create... Perfection. So, I think it would be only right if our housewarming pays homage to all that.'

I had obviously agreed, even though I hadn't entirely understood what she meant. I clearly had some research to do to catch up.

The paper invitations were hand-made by Astrid on sheets of thick white card and sent out in the post. She handed me a stack of invites and asked who I was planning to invite. I had no idea. I didn't want to invite your lawyer friends, I was sure of that. I'd sort of made a couple of friends in class, people who I'd been put with for group work or sat next to all term... Maybe I could ask them.

The invitations themselves, were perfect. They read:

Join Astrid and Jess in christening their new digs with a

celebration of solitary Bartlebies and intense conviction. Channel your favourite Beat poet – Ginsberg, Kerouac, Burroughs – and come and indulge in a night against social conformity and literary tradition. Bring red wine and poetry. Dress as your best misrepresentation of Beat Culture –stripes, berets and turtlenecks will be very welcome – and get ready to party!

Astrid went out for supplies the morning of the event, before I'd even woken up. By the time I was up and about, she was back with bottles of cheap bubbly, red wine, and various snacks. I found her at the dining table making posters on cardboard. One read *'Poets Read Every Saturday Night at 2 a.m.'*, and another featured a quote from Ginsberg, apparently.

'Oh, wow! You've been busy!' I said as I got down the stairs.

'Party day, party day!' she said excitedly, looking up at me and smiling a huge smile. 'There's nothing quite like it!'

I don't think I'd ever hosted a party before, but I was ready to get swept up in it all.

'I don't know how you do it. I need coffee.'

'Yes please!' she said, and went back to her poster making.

I walked into the kitchen and got out two mugs, made a pot of coffee for us both and took a cup to her in the living room. I sat down on the sofa to drink mine while she kept working at the table.

'Have you already got your poetry ready for tonight?' she said as she stopped for a moment to take a sip of her coffee.

'Poetry?'

'Yes... did you not read the invitation?'

'Well, yes, I did, but I didn't think I needed poetry...'

'You know how there was a part that said, "Bring red wine and poetry"?'

'Yeah but... *I* don't have to do anything do I?'

'Come on, Mouse! We'll be reading poetry all night. You're the writer! You can't not read something!'

'I...'

A feeling of panic started rising in my chest. I hadn't intended on being involved in the night's poetry, I'd planned on just listening and watching.

'What are you worried about?' she asked.

'I can't write poetry! I've only ever done it for assignments back in school. And I certainly wasn't very good at it then. I mean... What if it's terrible?'

'People will be too drunk to know. And besides, it's poetry, it can't be terrible. There's literally no such thing. That's the beauty of it!'

'But I don't know how to write a poem! I wouldn't even know where to start.'

'Everyone knows how to write a poem because there's no correct way to do it. You just write. Honestly, even a shopping list can be a poem. There are no rules. One of these days you're going to have to start living your life, you know, not just keep hiding away from it...'

'I... uh...'

'You can always just perform someone else's poem. Or write one and I'll read it. But I reckon you should just do it: write a poem, read it out. Easy. It's so safe, we'll be amongst friends.'

Amongst *her* friends... I didn't know most of them aside from meeting a few here and there. I was certain they would laugh at me if I read something, especially if I'd written it.

'I'll help you if you like. Or I can read over it when you're done – whatever you need. I'm going to write something after I've finished this if you want to join me. We can have a little writing sesh together.'

She said it so easily, as if it were such a simple thing. Just throw together a poem. Then read it in front of lots of people. Sure. Fine. Just like that.

I went to have a shower and panic. I decided, whilst I showered and dressed, that I couldn't do it. There would be plenty of other people who would step up, I was sure, so I could just stay in the background and not get involved. I didn't like being the centre of attention. That had been Emily's role, it was the way we always worked together. Then I guess it became yours and now it was Astrid's. The fact that you were all assertive people meant that the pressure was off me and I generally didn't have to do anything that scared me. But she was threatening to throw that all upside down. I went downstairs with the plan to tell her that I didn't want to do it – I just wanted to watch. Maybe next time I would get involved.

I couldn't find her in the flat, so I went out the back door to look in the garden. The sun was out, and she had set up a picnic blanket, got some snacks and a pot of tea, and there was soft classical music playing from her portable speakers. Laid out in front of her were two notebooks and lots of coloured pens. It looked idyllic.

'Yay! You're here!' she said with a huge smile, holding her arms out above her head. 'Come. Come join me!'

As soon as I saw her there, with excitement in her eyes and so much warmth in her smile, I knew I couldn't say no to her. I couldn't disappoint her. I walked over and sat down next to her.

'Here!' she said as she passed me one of the notebooks, a green pen – my favourite colour, I wondered if I'd mentioned it somewhere along the way – and a cup of tea. 'Just start writing! Let me know if you need a prompt.'

I nodded and managed a small sounding ‘Thanks’, which I followed with a tentative smile.

I began to write.

Chapter 16

People started turning up for the party from around 6 p.m. Everyone was dressed in striped shirts and scarves. Astrid had got us both striped shirts from a charity shop, and she had a beret on, like she had on the first night I'd met her. She paired her shirt with cute, almost Parisian looking shorts, and I wore jeans. People were milling around chatting and pouring themselves glasses of wine. Red wine bottles were mounting up on our dining room table as people added more to the collection.

I got chatting with someone called Freddie, who looked like Andy Warhol and had a soft air to him that felt comforting. He was telling me about an art exhibition he had coming up at a warehouse on the outskirts of the city. It sounded so cool. I'd found I was much better at remembering people's name when I met them one-on-one and had a conversation with them – it was the bigger groups that overwhelmed me.

'What kind of art?' I'd asked him, then wondered if it was a weird question to ask, requesting he categorise his work in a sentence.

'I blend together different photos I take, to highlight the environmental crisis that's looming over us all.'

'Oh, wow,' I said. I never understood how people came up

with ideas like that. 'It sounds amazing.'

'You should come see it if you want,' he told me. 'It starts next month – let me know if you'd like to, and I'll put your name on the door so you can get in free.'

'That's so kind of you, thank you! Yes, I'd love to! Maybe I can write a review of it if you'd like – I write for the uni paper.'

'That would be great if you could! I'd really appreciate that, you're the best!'

I blushed, enjoying the fact that my ability to write about events could make me appreciated. We even exchanged numbers so that I could let him know when I wanted to go.

After a couple of hours of chatting to people and occasionally dancing to the songs that played, the party had really got going and it seemed like most people were there.

Astrid came and found me while I was captivated by another of her friends talking about his recent trip to Florence for his Art History degree. She gave me a hug and a kiss on the cheek. 'Can you make sure everyone has a Prosecco please?'

I went into the kitchen to get the bottles of Prosecco she'd bought earlier, and once people realised what I was doing, they started lining up to hold glasses out to me. Except that they weren't all glasses; people were drinking out of mugs and cups, and someone even handed me a bowl to fill. Another person had found a shot glass. Our glassware-to-guest ratio was out, but it didn't seem to bother anyone. Astrid had pulled a chair into the middle of the room, which she was standing on. I noticed she had a full glass herself, which someone must have got for her. I poured myself a Prosecco and stood at the back watching her.

The room came to a natural hush and Astrid started talking.

'Thanks everyone for coming. This feels like something

really special here tonight, here with you all. When I was younger, the first thing that really got to me about life was its potential to be unremarkable. Everyone around me seemed so unremarkable. They all went off every day to their jobs, which most of them seemed to hate. I remember asking the adults I knew how they spent their days, and if they loved it. None of them said yes. None of them. Oh, except my first-grade teacher, Mrs Grey. She said 'Of course I do. Aren't we having a whale of a time?' She thought she was making a tremendous joke since we were doing a module called 'Under the sea'. I decided she probably didn't count.'

Everyone laughed. I looked around and they were all smiling. I couldn't help smiling too.

Astrid continued: 'I did quite like Mrs Grey though, because she was always getting us to be creative. We did lots of writing, lots of art. Everyone in my class used to draw pictures of themselves or their parents or their dogs – which I thought was so boring. I drew the places I wanted to go, the people I wanted to meet...' She paused for a moment to indicate the people in the room. '...And I made a promise to myself then, that I wouldn't grow up to be like those adults who seemed to just coast through life, eyes closed, not enjoying themselves. I swore to always look for the beauty, the joy, the wonderful moments, never settling for the mundane.'

There were noises of agreement and a couple of claps from her audience.

'I still think life should be remarkable. And I still think the most important thing is to create. Creating is the essence of what makes us human. So I invite you all to be both remarkable and creative tonight, and this year, and forever.'

People started making louder noises and claps and so Astrid

raised her voice above it.

'This is our new home, Jess and I, our Den of Iniquity. You are all welcome here, any time you like. May it always be filled with remarkable people and creativity! So I'd like you all to raise your glasses to the future of this flat, and all the wonderful things that will happen between its walls. To the Den!'

Everyone echoed the toast in response and raised their glasses. I did too, feeling completely in awe of her. She really did see the world differently, in technicolour.

'I'd like to invite you all to use this space tonight to read poetry and dance and talk and above all, please enjoy! You may stay as long as you like. Our haven is your haven!'

Everyone cheered again and started chattering amongst themselves as she stepped down from the chair to be met by people wanting to talk to and hug her. I made my way over and hugged her too.

'You are amazing, you know? Absolutely amazing,' I said to her.

'So are you, my dear Little Mouse!'

I was swept up in the fanfare of it all. So swept up that I'd forgotten completely about the whole poetry reading thing.

'All right, all right,' she said to the room, raising her voice above the chatter again, then indicating to the chair. 'Who's got some poetry to read us?'

Someone volunteered to go first, and I felt a huge sigh of relief leave my body. I never understood those types of people – those who willingly spoke up in class, who put their hand up to do their presentation first – but I was glad they existed. Astrid had read over my poem, and she'd said it was good, but of course I didn't believe her. She was just humouring me,

I knew it. And as we got into the poetry readings, I became more unsure of myself – I'd written a rhyming poem because that was what I thought poems were, but I realised that a lot of the poems people were reading didn't rhyme at all.

After a few people had gone, Astrid squeezed my arm gently from where she was sitting next to me. When I looked at her, she smiled at me and nodded, before standing up, moving to the front, and addressing everyone again.

'Now everyone, we've got a treat,' Astrid said. 'I was a bit of a monster and I made poor Jess write her first poem to read tonight.'

Her next words were drowned out by a surprisingly huge cheer from everyone in the room and lots of enthusiastic clapping. I was so startled by the support that I forgot for a moment to be scared.

'I know, I know, it's a momentous occasion,' Astrid continued, as the cheering died down. 'It's such an honour that she would grace us with this. She is our resident writer, some of you will have read her articles in the uni paper. And I told her that I knew you would be the most supportive audience around.'

There were murmurs of agreement. As she was speaking, I noted that there was a box of red wine being passed around, filling glasses. I quickly finished the rest of my glass hoping it would give me some courage and held it out for someone to refill before I went up.

'So, without further ado, as they say... Our Jess!'

Everyone clapped and whooped and instead of freezing, my legs seemed to propel me forward towards the chair. Astrid hugged me before I sat down on the chair and then she handed me my notebook, which I'd evidently left somewhere, perhaps hoping it wouldn't be found. Then she left me, moving to the side of the stage area.

Everyone was clapping still, as I sat down in the chair facing them all. I don't know what they were expecting but I suddenly knew I was going to let them all down. I looked around at the sea of faces, many I barely knew, but then I saw Astrid. She was hugging her arms around herself and smiling at me with a look on her face that I could only identify as... love. I could do this, for her. I couldn't bear to let her down.

'Hi everyone,' I said nervously as I looked around at the smiling faces. I could feel the wine in my head. 'I'm fucking terrified!'

Some laughed, others called out encouraging things like 'You'll be fine', or 'Go Jess'.

And then, I looked at the page, focusing my eyes on it and not on all the people and I just started reading. My voice started out shaky but as I realised no one was laughing at me – not out loud, anyway – it seemed to become stronger.

I was raised on stories my parents told
And their parents before
We tell the tales that brought us here
Weave history with folklore

We hold our grief in empty hands
Held tight to keep it safe
We cycle it for years to come
Passed down for all to take

I see it in my father's face
Each time we say goodbye

Shadows drift across his eyes
Reflected in the sky

Each generation takes its turn
Evolving tales to fit
As oceans surge and forests burn
They all weave into it

Collective stories grow our world
We watch it from the fence
Then take our chance to speak our truths
In search of moral sense

There was silence when I finished, and I looked up in a slight panic. Then they all erupted in applause. Astrid bounded over and pulled me up into a big hug.

'See?!' she said. 'You can do *anything*! I'm so proud of you!'

I hugged her back as relief washed over me and I thanked her for pushing me to do it. I glided through the rest of the night. There was more poetry after mine, someone even read a limerick. Astrid read the last one of the night and it was so captivating – it was like a story told through poetry. She spoke of the ocean and the spirits of the sea and sky, and of pilgrims who make their way to be reborn in the water. The room was so silent for the whole poem, completely captivated by it. There was another huge applause for her. When it died down, she spoke again.

'Well, I must thank you all for this wonderful, fitting welcome to our flat. Thank you for joining in with my whims, for being the exact people I want to fill my life and this flat with. I was thinking, though, who of us here could consider ourselves pilgrims? Aren't we all searching for answers, for meaning, for enlightenment?'

The cheers that met her question indicated that it applied to everyone, apparently.

'Well then, follow me.'

She grabbed a bottle of wine, and everyone got up and followed her as she made her way out to the garden, some grabbing bottles on the way. I had no idea what she was planning, but I followed along behind everyone else, pulling closed the back door behind us.

Once we were outside, the cold night air buzzing against my skin, someone handed me a bottle of wine and I realised people were just swigging straight from the bottle, so I did the same. People started cracking glowsticks, and I realised Astrid was handing them out along with sparklers.

'You may or may not have noticed that the moon is in fact full tonight, shining in all her glory,' she said, her voice quiet in the still night. 'The Sturgeon Moon, if you were wondering, and indeed if we were by the water, I would insist we swim. But alas.' She started walking around to the people closest to her, lighting their sparklers and handing out a couple of extra lighters for people to help. Once we were all sparkling, she raised her voice slightly. 'But that doesn't mean we can't be reborn by moonlight, my pilgrims. Let us show her our support by calling her in true nature...'

And before I could wonder what that meant, she howled. Like a dog, or indeed a wolf would, her high-pitched call piercing the silence of the night. When she finished, everyone was silent, her voice echoing out into the darkness, well beyond the bounds of our little flat. Then, after a brief pause, everyone else did the same, and even despite my brain immediately worrying about the noise we were making, before long I was doing it too, joining in with the chorus of howls. It felt oddly liberating and connected me to the group in a way that felt so visceral, so primal. When we'd finished, an electric hum hung in the air. Then an actual dog howled somewhere nearby, and we all broke into laughter.

This was it. No one would ever forget this party. I would never forget this night.

Chapter 17

Not long after we moved in was my birthday. It was late September and starting to get cool and I didn't know how I felt about turning 20; Astrid said birthdays were always worth celebrating, especially when it involved entering your 20s. But for some reason, my impending 20th didn't feel particularly iconic. I think part of me hoped you'd come back for it, though I knew that was ridiculous as you'd only just left. I had this fantasy of you turning up on the doorstep holding flowers, but it was an impossible thing to wish for and I berated myself for even letting the thought enter my mind. I always had such unreasonable expectations.

I'd told Astrid I didn't want to do anything for my birthday. I didn't really have any friends other than you two – not that were truly *my* friends, anyway. And I doubted anyone would want to come to a party for me. So I said it just wasn't my thing and that I didn't like being the centre of attention.

I'd hoped at least to hear from you but as the day dragged on, I still hadn't. Obviously there was a time difference, but I thought maybe you could have messaged overnight so I had something to wake up to, but you hadn't. I was moping around the house when Astrid decided I needed to stop.

'All right, I've had enough of this. Birthday girl, let's go for a drive,' she said.

'Where to?'

'Anywhere.'

'Ok.'

Sometimes we did that – just went for a drive. She called it *cruisin'*. As we got in her car, she handed me a new mix CD to put on that she'd made, and she drove us out to the ocean. I was slightly surprised that all the songs on the cd happened to be ones I loved – Bright Eyes, Franz, Bowie of course, The Arctics... It was such a nice coincidence and even despite myself, I found myself singing along, with Astrid joining in.

It was late afternoon when we arrived at the seaside. There's a specific sort of calm that always washes over me when I look out at the horizon, and seeing the water automatically made me relax. The vast expanse of blue stretching out from the shore gave me a sense of perspective of how small and inconsequential I was, which felt somehow freeing; birthdays meant nothing in the grand scheme of things, and it was silly being upset about how disappointing mine had been. Especially when I'd made it clear I didn't want any fanfare around it – I had no right to be upset when people honoured that request, even if, being honest with myself, I guess I'd secretly hoped they would anyway...

Astrid turned off the engine and we got out. It was hazy; it had been a misty day and the fogginess hung in the air making everything seem darker and colder.

'Come on, let's go for a walk,' she said.

We walked up to the top of the headland, weaving up a path and through some bushes. When we reached the top, there was a group of people up there, all standing together. It took a moment to realise they were all people I recognised; Astrid's friends, people who had come through the house who I had met here and there. I wondered why they were all gathered without Astrid, and in such a strange place.

'Happy birthday!' they said in near unison as they came over to us.

Astrid stood beside me grinning at me.

'Happy Birthday, my Little Mouse!' she said and threw her arms around me, kissing me on the side of my head. I was in shock. Everyone was standing around looking at me.

'Is this for me?'

'Yes, silly, it's your birthday!'

'This is... wow. What... Wow...'

I was speechless. No one had ever done anything like that for me before. I certainly didn't expect anyone to care enough about me to go to so much effort.

'Come on, we've got wine and snacks!' said a male voice, and I looked over to see Freddie, the artist I'd met at our housewarming. Seeing him made me feel that they weren't just Astrid's friends, they were becoming mine too. And it made me feel so warm inside.

Blankets were laid out on the ground and food was spread out like a banquet. Someone started pouring plastic cups of red wine and passing them around. I took one and had a big sip. I couldn't believe she had done this all for me. Surely, I didn't deserve any of it, I wasn't the type of person that people organised parties for. The sun was starting to set, and everything seemed so magical. I couldn't have been happier in that moment. I did take a moment to wish you were there, I really did, but I'm not sure it would have been your thing anyway.

We all just sat around chatting, and I felt like I was really part of the conversations, rather than sitting on the outside like I usually did, not knowing what to say. But they were all such interesting people. We talked about music – there appeared to be many Bowie fans – we discussed art, literature, and they talked about travel, and each of them had interesting projects they were working on which they spoke about with such passion that even I felt inspired.

Astrid pointed out the view from the headland, and it was indeed spectacular. She said it was such a magical place, being up so high above the world, looking out onto the ocean. She mentioned that there might even be whales passing by, but we couldn't see any. By the time we'd finished the wine, it was starting to get properly cold. The mist had lifted, and it was turning into a beautiful evening, but the temperature was dropping. I hadn't prepared for being outside so late. I pulled my legs up into my chest and wrapped my jumper down over them. Astrid noticed – she always noticed things like that. She always seemed to know what everyone was doing and feeling at any moment.

'Shall we head back down?' she asked the group.

Everyone seemed to agree, and we started packing things up. The walk down the track was harder in the fading light, and with our arms full of things.

We went to the cars to put things away and I assumed we were leaving, but Astrid pulled out more wine and various bags and boxes. She noticed I was looking at her confusedly.

'You'll see,' she said, a smile spreading across her face.

I shook my head at her and laughed. I had learned that the best thing to do was to trust Astrid and whatever plans she hatched, so I helped her with the carrying, and we headed down to the beach. Everyone else was doing the same thing.

On the beach, Freddie had started building a fire and every-one else was laying picnic blankets down around it. Someone had brought portable speaker, and music started playing. More wine was opened, and another plastic cup was handed to me. I looked up and realised it was at least close to a full moon. I gazed up at it, feeling amazed by its glowing presence.

Then Astrid came over to me with a fairly large, flat box.

'Harvest Moon this month,' she said, evidently having noticed me gazing up at it. She then sang a portion of the Neil Young song, which made me smile even more than I already had been.

'She's full on Monday,' Astrid said once she'd finished her serenade, and handed me the box she was holding. 'For you.'

I took the box. It was heavy. I knelt on one of the blankets to open it. She stood above me, arms crossed but smiling, expectant.

I undid the ribbon and slowly lifted the lid.

It was a leather jacket.

It was a leather jacket with red sequins on the back.

It was a leather jacket with red sequins on the back that spelled out 'Rebel Rebel'. Just like the boiler suit she was wearing the night I first saw her.

I stared at it. It was the most beautiful thing I'd ever seen. I couldn't find the words to tell her, my voice was caught in my throat. I started to cry. I looked up to see she was looking quite smug.

'Put it on then, or you'll be cold,' she said.

I stood up and put it on. It felt heavy but comforting. It was slightly oversized but just so perfect.

‘Astrid... I don’t know what to say,’ I managed, finally.

‘You could try hugging me...’

And so I did. ‘I love it,’ I said into her hair.

‘I know.’

‘Wherever did you get it?’ I asked as we moved apart.

‘Jacket’s from a charity shop. I did the words.’

Of course she did. She’d hand-made me a birthday present. I was stunned.

‘I’ll never take it off,’ I said, wiping the tears from my face.

‘Good. Now, let’s do some birthday dancing, shall we? Starting, of course, with the song that was number one in the charts on the day you were born. Though I’m sorry to say in the UK it was “A Groovy Kind of Love” by Phil Collins, which we’re just going to go ahead and ignore because no one can dance to that misery-ballad. So, we’re going to borrow from our friends in America...’

She fiddled around on her iPod, mumbling ‘birthday playlist, birthday playlist’ to herself, before I heard the first notes of ‘Sweet Child of Mine’ by Guns N’ Roses ring out. I don’t think I knew the Phil Collins song, but I was happy to join Astrid and everyone else in headbanging and air-guitaring to Guns N’ Roses, feeling very silly but not caring at all.

It didn’t take long to warm up once we started moving. The fire was getting bigger, and the light from it flickered on our faces. Astrid grabbed a branch from the stash of firewood the others had evidently pulled together earlier; one with some leaves on the end. She put it in the fire where it caught alight. Holding it up above her head, she continued to dance. My eyes were glued to her. Then suddenly everyone was scrambling to find their own branches, and soon we were all dancing circles around the fire, flames held aloft. It felt so wild, like I was living up to the words emblazoned on my back. I decided, in that moment, that it would be my new mantra. I was tired of being boring, cautious Jess. I had lived too measuredly; I hadn't taken risks or experienced enough magic. This was my year to truly live – to live before real life started.

Rebel Rebel.

I started to get tired and threw my branch in the fire to burn. I wandered down to the water's edge and stood there, feeling the wind playing with my hair. My bare feet were covered in sand. To my right, a light shone out, illuminated high up on a pole. To the left were the cliffs that led up to the headland. Out in front, past the waves, was darkness. There were red lights forming a line at about the height I would expect the horizon to have been.

The waves crashed upon the shore, some quite gentle and some more forceful, like they were willing the beach to follow them out into the unknown. Maybe they were willing me too, but the wind felt brisk, and I imagined the water would be way too cold. I was at least warm in my new jacket.

As I stood there looking out to sea, it felt like I could feel the whole world converging; every moment of my past, and a future stretching out ahead. And I wondered how I got to this point, to this place. How I had made it through everything, and ended up being the person standing here?

I turned back and saw everyone still dancing around the fire. It was as if we were the only people in the whole world. At the very least, we were the only ones who mattered.

I made my way back and took a spot on one of the blankets, where I was eventually joined by the others. Astrid had brought a ukulele, as had a couple of the others. There was a mandolin, someone had brought a strange small drum and someone else, a harmonica. Astrid started singing some sort of sea shanty. Everyone joined in the chorus singing strange words I didn't know: something about 'Yaller Girls', and 'Doodle Let Me Go.'

The harmonies were swirling around the campfire. After that came some songs I did know: one mum had in a songbook from her uni days, 'Ilkley Moor Bah Tat' and then they launched into 'Tied Up With a Black Velvet Band'. Astrid seemed to know all the words, and others chipped in with songs they knew too, calling out the chords until the other musicians caught on. In a break between songs, I asked Astrid how she knew them all and she said she'd played at an Irish wedding a couple of years back and had learned a whole lot of traditional Irish songs and sea shanties for it.

'Weddings always pay well. And they're a good set of songs to have up your sleeves for campfire singalongs,' she told me, as if campfire singalongs were a normal part of life.

As the sun started to come up, we were all quiet, lying by the fire, which was still glowing enough to keep us warm. Someone had put on Peter Gabriel, which was wafting out of the speakers over the silence of the beach. The waves were gently crashing on the shore, and Astrid's head was on my leg as she lay stretched out before me. I felt like I was in a dream. A fairy-tale.

I hate to say it, but even though it had been such an amazing night, I was still upset that you hadn't even called on my birthday. I had no messages on my phone, no emails, nothing. I tried not to think about it, but the thought hung over me as we drove back home the next day.

But when I got home, there was a bunch of flowers on the

front step of the flat. My favourites; white lilies and purple irises. It had a note attached:

- *Happy birthday, sorry I couldn't be there. Love Robert* -

I felt terrible for ever doubting you. Of course you hadn't forgotten, I told myself, scolding myself for ever thinking you could have. I'd jumped to a conclusion that you didn't care. I resolved to try to be better.

Chapter 18

That autumn was beautiful. Though I can't say if it was particularly more beautiful than other autumns, or just that I was just noticing it more. Astrid made me notice things I wouldn't have otherwise thought about. One day she decided she was going out to draw pictures of the fallen leaves amassing in a park a little way from ours. I went with her, of course, taking a book to read while she sketched.

I remember that day so vividly. I watched her turning the leaves over in her hand, scrutinising and detailing each one in their own unique way. I was trying to read my book, but I was distracted by her. She saw the world through a lens of wonder that I wished I had. Or one that I was perhaps learning to use, by being around her.

'How do plants know when to make leaves and when to make buds? Are there some cues that tell them to do one or the other? Is it due to sun and water amounts? Or general happiness levels? Or do you think they just wing it?'

I looked up from my book. I hadn't ever thought about trees in so much detail.

'I don't know, they just do it, I guess. I suppose nature is intuitive.'

'Plants are really clever, you know? Did you know that

they can partition resources to certain parts of the plant if they're being attacked by something? They prioritise one part and keep it healthy, let the rest die off, and the plant itself survives.'

I propped myself up on my elbows. 'Really? How on earth can they do that? That's wild!'

'I know. Clever little things.'

I always felt so close to nature when I was with Astrid. She helped me to realise its beauty. And she seemed to know so many interesting details, like the names of the different full moons and when they would be coming. She once told me that it was worth knowing a bit about everything. I tried to grasp at bits and pieces that she shared with me.

Clouds had begun rolling in, so we packed up our things and started walking home. We were still about ten minutes away from the flat when it started to rain, hard. I suggested we get a bus instead of walking; we hadn't brought umbrellas or raincoats, as it had been fine when we left.

'No way! We walk!' She said, in response to my suggestion.

'We do?'

'Yes! The world gets so much more beautiful in the rain. What an absolute gift to be out in it!'

'More beautiful? I thought it just gets more wet.'

She shook her head, her hair starting to clump together and drip. She kept walking and I had to run to keep up with her as she continued talking.

'We lived by the water for a while when I was younger. We had a yacht. That was back when we felt like a proper family. We used to go out on it at weekends. You're completely at the mercy of the elements out on the sea. If it rains, it rains. If it's windy, you fly with the wind. If it's not, you wait. You could go down into the cabin when it rains, sure, but you could also sit outside. The rain pattering down on the deck and the surface of the water was the most serene sound you could ever imagine. The world transforms when it rains. There's this sense of calm that takes over. It's like nature is reaching out a hand to you. She's saying, "Hello, will you play with me?" And most people run away. They put up their umbrellas and they scowl and they curse her – "How dare you rain on me?" Like they'll never recover. Like their world is ending. This is what she gets for making sure the plants grow and that we have something to drink. She deserves better. I've always loved rain. It rains so rarely here, at least properly, that I almost forget the sound of it falling around me. But it's there. This is life, right here, in this beautiful moment.'

I stared at her in awe. I was used to her monologues and I always welcomed them, but I had no idea where she got them from, or how she formed such interesting views on things. I could listen to her talk forever. I felt silly for suggesting we get out of the rain. She was so right as always, challenging me to rethink the way I viewed the world.

She put her arms up and started spinning around and around in the street. She looked so beautiful and free. I laughed and joined her. My arms stretched out, my head up to the sky. I felt free, too.

When we got home, Astrid went in but I lingered for a moment in the doorway and kept looking out at the downpour. She was right, it was beautiful. And that smell – slightly like newly cut grass, slightly like sulphur, with a hint of freshly washed sheets. I couldn't believe how calm it made me feel. My shoulders felt relaxed. I realised she was right about the rain – she had awoken a memory in me, one from my childhood. One I hadn't thought about in a very long time. It was a memory from when my sister was alive.

When it rained, Emily and I used to run into the conservatory, which had a flat roof, and the water falling on it sounded like elephants were running above us. We'd lie by the windows, giggling and watching it come down. I was suddenly transported back to a simpler time. A reminder of a home I once had. Nowhere had really felt like home since then – not in quite the same way.

When I went back inside, Astrid had put the kettle on. She was drying her hair with a towel, and she'd put one out for me too. I started rubbing it over my head.

She went into the kitchen to finish making our tea and told me to pick an album to put on. I pulled out a vinyl of the Everly Brothers and stuck it on. Almost as soon as it started playing, Astrid came quickly out of the kitchen, stopping the vinyl before taking it off and putting it back in its sleeve.

'Not that one,' she said. 'Pick something else.'

I felt like an idiot for choosing the wrong album, I wasn't good like she was at picking the right music for the time. I went with something I knew was safe and put on 'Aladdin Sane' by Bowie.

She came in shortly after with the tea pot and our two mugs.

'You don't talk about your parents much,' I said as she poured it out. My own memory of my sister had stoked my curiosity and I figured it was a good time to ask.

'Not much to talk about.'

'So they're not together anymore? They're divorced?'

'Not really. They separated when I was about ten, though they sort of pretend they're still together. They're still married but they only meet up once a year, I think. Mostly, mum's still at the house in Germany, and Dad's in Paris, though he travels a lot.'

'Are you close with either of them?'

'Do I seem to be?'

'I guess not...'

'We were closer when I was younger, I guess, but then Dad's job took off and he had better things to do than hang around us. Mum was always busy modelling and then mentoring younger models when we got older. Sofia stayed with Mum in Germany. I tried to follow Dad for a bit but it was useless. He's impossible to find; his work takes him around the world, and he's not the best at making or keeping plans, even with his daughter. Then they decided I was too difficult and sent me to boarding school.'

'You went to boarding school? Where?' I had never pictured Astrid going to boarding school.

'A place up North.'

'North of where?'

'Here.'

'Wait. You went to school in England?'

'Ya.'

'Oh, wow. I had no idea.' How had I never asked her about her childhood? We'd been friends for the best part of a year and now we lived together, and I didn't even know these details. That would explain why her accent was so faint. I felt like she knew everything about me, she was always asking questions and taking an interest, but I hadn't even asked her about her upbringing.

'I mean... It's not like I chose to go or anything,' she said. 'I was sent there.'

'Was it hard?'

She shrugged. 'Home wasn't exactly a joyous place at that time, so it was nice to be away from it, I guess. My parents didn't really have the time or energy for me, I don't think they liked me very much. Sof got to stay, but I had to go. Whatever, I never needed them anyway. And I don't want anything from them, I'm fine on my own. Better, in fact.'

I nodded, taking the cup of tea she handed me and settled down next to her on the couch. The hands-off parenting she'd had sounded like a dream to me.

Chapter 19

Our house, commonly referred to by its nickname, 'The Den', quickly became a place of shelter for people who were passing through or who wanted somewhere to come and hang out and stay the night. Our sofa was generally available to anyone who wanted to stay over. The Jess of the previous year would probably have been stressed by this, but I guess I'd changed somewhere along the way. The new Jess liked that vibe – open doors and flowing conversation. I felt safe with Astrid's friends, and I loved that there was always creativity around.

I was finding it hard to remember the names of everyone who came through our doors. One day, when Astrid was talking to me about someone I was supposed to have met, I asked her how on earth she was so good at knowing so many people's names, when I could meet them so many times and still not manage to remember.

'Oh, it's easy – you trace their name on your palm when they tell it to you,' she said. 'Just use the finger of your other hand. For bonus points, you can then try to use it back to them in your first conversation.'

'Wait, trace their name? Like... right there in front of them?' I asked, thinking I would probably look silly doing that.

'You can – to be honest, people are usually happy if you admit you find remembering their name important. But you can just do it secretly, they don't need to know.'

I made note to remember to try it out. Though I found that even if I thought I knew someone's name, when it came to using it, I often second guessed myself – even if it was someone I knew. My brain was always playing tricks on me.

But whether I remembered their names, just having so many wonderful people dropping by and using our living room as a hub for their creative activities, made me feel more inspired. I started writing more, and recording things that were happening, as if I were documenting my time with Astrid. I thought that one day I might put the things I'd written, the notes I'd taken, into a book – immortalising Astrid in the pages, and myself as the writer. It was a nice dream.

I mentioned it to you in passing once over the phone. I told you that I'd started writing about my life and all the things we were doing. After a pause, you'd asked what on earth there was about our life to write about – we were only twenty, and living such a regular existence... You pointed out that focusing on my articles for the paper, or my uni work, made more sense. It was a good point: in the grand scheme of things, our lives weren't anything special. We were hardly Auschwitz survivors or people who had overcome some great adversity, or anything gripping and lifechanging. I would go back and forth on whether I thought my writing was worthwhile – usually depending on whether I was surrounded by Astrid and her creative friends or talking to you and being pulled back down to earth.

I couldn't really keep track of most of the people Astrid knew who seemed to cycle through our lives. Some became more familiar, and some I never saw again. Freddie had become someone I enjoyed spending time with when he visited or we caught up at a party. He and Astrid had begun collaborating on a series of big canvasses, which they worked on over wine in the living room. We also went to see his art exhibition, which had captivated me. It was a 'group show', with lots of people exhibiting in different rooms of this huge but strange old building that was apparently going to be knocked down in the near future, which someone had secured for the show. Freddie's part was my favourite – using large panes of glass as a canvas, his artworks showed beautiful parts of the world, including easily recognisable landmarks, on fire, superimposed with people pouring kerosene on them and laughing. It gave me chills, and I did indeed write about it – not for the uni paper, but for *The Relativity Cadenza,* as I thought it was more their vibe.

One night, Freddie was over with a group of other people, and we were all drinking wine. It was nice to see him again – I thanked him for the entry to the exhibition and congratulated him on his award (he'd won 'best in show' on the closing night). He then surprised me by thanking me for the article in *The Relativity Cadenza*, which was obviously nothing, but it was nice of him to say so. Apparently, the guys from the mag had got in touch with Freddie and asked if they could use one of his artworks for the cover of next issue.

'They said they're going to make the focus of the whole issue on the climate crisis, so get your environmental and political words sharpened and ready!' he told me, which worried me, as it wasn't exactly something I knew a lot about.

'Oh, I'm not sure they'll ask me to write anything for it,' I said. I don't know why they kept accepting things I sent to them and then actually printing them, but I figured they were just being kind, or were desperate.

'Are you serious? They told me you were their star writer! They just said they wished they got more articles from you. I'm sure they'll want you to be involved!'

'I... did they?' I was trying to work out why they would have said that, when Freddie was pulled off to say hi to someone else who had arrived. I walked around in a bit of a daze for a few minutes after that, trying to mesh together two stories playing out in my head – the one I knew to be true; that I wasn't any good and my articles were banal and formless, and this seemingly completely different person being spoken about who was considered a 'star writer' and who people wanted to hear more from. I couldn't work it out, so I just tried to push it all out of my mind. I didn't dare connect with the possibility of the second story being true, lest I start believing I was good and got lazy or big-headed. They were the worst kinds of people.

There were quite a few people milling around at our house that night. I'd met most of the people here and there, but there was one guy who I didn't know. As the night had drawn on, he'd pulled out a guitar and started strumming away. Someone asked if he could play a specific song, I forget what it was, and he mentioned something about needing to get out his 'caypo'.

'What on earth is a caypo?' Astrid asked.

'This,' he said as he held a strange clip-like thing.

'That's called a cappo,' she said.

It turned out he was Australian, and they said it differently down there.

'Can you use it though?' she was testing him in classic Astrid style. It made me smile to myself.

He could use it. And of course, so could she. It was past midnight and people were lying around our living room, some on the sofas, others on the floor. Then she started singing along as he played. Any conversations halted to make space for their song. Together, they sang more songs, switching who was playing guitar and performing duets they put together on the spot. It turned out his name was Steve, and that he was one of the other guy's friends. He had been playing in the uni bar that night as part of his tour around the country.

'Come with me,' he'd asked her, sometime in the early morning.

'Sure,' she'd replied with a shrug.

Just 'sure', without even a second thought. She didn't worry about logistics or how she could make it work, or even the fact that she hardly knew this guy, she just agreed. I wondered how she could do that; just skip out on classes without worrying about getting in trouble – term had only just started, and I was certain if I disappeared for two weeks, I'd get in so much trouble for missing my tutorials, which I had to sign in for. But even more than that, I wondered how she could give herself over to strangers, trusting that everything would lead to adventure and not ruin. But she showed me time and time again that she could.

So, the next day they left. The next day. Just like that.

I didn't want her to go. What was I going to do for two weeks, in the flat alone without her? You hadn't been gone that long and now Astrid would be leaving me too. But I said nothing.

'Make sure you water my plants, Mouse,' she called back to me as she ran out the door the next morning, guitar in one hand, tote bag stuffed with clothes hanging over her shoulder.

'Of course... I'll miss you,' I called after her, unsure if she would hear.

A moment later, she'd popped her head back around the door, smiled at me, then put her guitar down and came over and kissed the top of my head.'

'You too, Little Mouse. But I'll see you soon.'

It might have seemed soon to her, perhaps, but for me it felt like a long two weeks. It's easier to leave than to be left behind, so they say. I felt at an absolute loss being on my own. I tried to concentrate on writing articles for the newspaper but I felt unmotivated and uninspired. Without Astrid around me to energise me, I just didn't have the capacity to do anything.

I realised that although the fear of being alone played in my mind almost constantly, I hadn't actually spent much time alone since I'd met you, and then Astrid. And with you both gone, I was suddenly plunged back into the loneliness of high school, and I felt the same sense of having no one. During those two long weeks she was gone, I called you more often. I sensed I was being a nuisance, but even that seemed preferable to the quiet of the empty house. I even called my mum. She was particularly happy to hear from me and went on about how she never hears from me anymore, before demanding updates on how you were going and when you were coming back.

'I don't know why you ever let him go all that way in the first place,' she'd said. But when I asked her how I could have stopped you, she didn't really seem to have a useful answer, other than to say I should have found a way to give you more reason to stay.

I watched lots of box sets and ate lots of ice cream. Then I felt bad for eating lots of ice cream and could hear my mother's voice in my head saying I had no self-restraint and that I was going to get fat, and then no one would want me. So I'd go a whole day of only drinking soda water, then that made me feel ill and gassy, so I got pizza again.

Fear and self-doubt crept in even more and my head kept playing the same things over and over again. I had made myself believe that you had left because you didn't love me anymore, and that you would inevitably leave me forever – maybe you wouldn't even come back from America. Then I worried that Astrid would decide she didn't want to come back from her trip either, and convinced myself that it would all be somehow because of me. That I had ruined everything and was destined to be alone.

But then, she'd messaged me saying she couldn't wait to see me when she got back, and that fear was replaced with hope as the day got closer. I decided to clean the house as a nice surprise for her return. I set about vacuuming, tidying and dusting. I even went into her room to vacuum and straighten some things out. I washed her sheets so that they would be nice and clean when she arrived. As I was making the bed, I accidentally kicked something underneath it, and I bent down to see what it was. It was an old shoe box. I couldn't help myself – I looked inside. It was filled with stacks of newspaper clippings. I pulled the top few out and saw that they were all about Astrid. Astrid playing gigs, Astrid modelling on a page pulled from a glossy magazine, Astrid leading a rally about the treatment of women in the Middle East, Astrid going on tour. I was surprised to see a copy of the first review I had written about her too and I felt so special to be part of the canon of Astrid. Further down the pile, they turned into clippings about someone else – a man named Gerhard Wolf.

I knew immediately who he was just by looking at the pictures. He had the same nose, the same chin... it couldn't be anyone other than Astrid's father. I already knew he was some sort of big shot businessman. From the clippings, it appeared that he had founded a large music company, and there were photos of him with Formula 1 drivers. There were far more clippings about him than about her. I realised that, in my hands I was holding a shrine to the person that Astrid had said she hadn't cared about. I couldn't stop reading, couldn't take my eyes off the pictures. He had the same intriguing, commanding air that Astrid had, I could tell that even just from photos. There was also an address scrawled on a piece of blue paper in handwriting I didn't recognise, with 'Gerhard' written above it – 16eme – I knew from French lessons back in early high school that it must have been the address of the apartment she said he had in Paris.

I suddenly got an overwhelming feeling that I was intruding, so I carefully put everything back in the box and quietly left the room. I couldn't work out why she had a box of cuttings of a man she seemed not to care about, and certainly never wanted to talk much about. I supposed family things were perhaps more often complicated than I'd realised. I guess I had assumed everything in Astrid's life was perfect, but the more I found out about her the more confused I became.

It was later that day that Astrid returned, just as exuberant and full of life as ever. She immediately asked me about my two weeks without her, what I'd got up to, what adventures I'd had. I tried to pretend I'd had a wonderful time whilst she was away. 'Reflective and productive,' I'd said. I showed her an article I had written, which was really an old one that I had just proofread and sent in. I hadn't written anything new since she left. But suddenly, everything felt ok again with her back.

I was sitting on her bed as she was unpacking her bag.

'I thought you'd like this,' she said, and something hard landed in my lap. I turned it over. It was a little book of Bowie quotes. 'I picked it up in York on my way back. Saw it in a tiny little shop and knew I had to get it for you. These, too.'

A packet of Beatles playing cards fell into my lap. I smiled.

'I love them,' I said, flicking through the book.

'I know,' she replied.

'So... How was it?'

I opened the book up to a page that said '*For me, the world that I inhabit in reality is probably a very different world than the one people expect that I would be in.*'

She walked over and looked at it over my shoulder, gently stroking my hair.

'Yeah, pretty fun. We played somewhere different every night. I forgot what it's like to play with other people; I haven't done it in a while. It was good. Harmonies are nice. Personalities are interesting. But ultimately, it's all an experience, isn't it. We made some good money, too, which came at a good time. I got us this to celebrate me coming home.'

She pulled out a bottle of Moët and Chandon Champagne.

'Wow! I don't think I've ever had Moët!' I said, amazed. I said Moët with a French accent – silent T – feeling proud of myself for pronouncing it right.

'It's pronounced Mowett,' she replied. 'You sound the T.'

I was about to laugh and make a joke that she'd spent too much time with an Australian, but noticed she didn't look like she was making a joke.

'Wait... Really?'

'Yeah. It's French champagne, of course, but Mr Moët was Dutch. So, it's MOWETT.' She pronounced it slowly with an overemphasis on the syllables.

I was horrified at the fact I'd got it wrong, and it must have shown, because she laughed.

'Don't worry, we've all had the moment where we've found out we were saying it wrong. It's a rite of passage. *Now* you're allowed to drink it.'

She went downstairs to put the bottle in the freezer while she finished unpacking. A short time later, once she deemed it cold enough, she poured us two glasses. It tasted so good. Just as having her back felt so good.

'I found this new band while I was away,' she said excitedly, running upstairs to grab a CD from her room, then putting it on. 'You've got to hear it. I'm obsessed.'

From the first notes of the first song, I knew I liked it. It sounded so different to anything I'd heard, but somehow also familiar.

'Who is it?' I asked.

'They're called Vampire Weekend.'

'I love it.'

'Right?' She replied, as we sat side by side on the sofa, drinking champagne.

'It reminds me of something...'

'Graceland?' She asked. 'Paul Simon?'

'Oh, yeah. I think you're right.'

And I smiled. I couldn't stop smiling. I knew the old saying that absence made the heart grow fonder, but I hadn't really understood it before. But I was like a ball of energy now that she was back; once again, anything felt possible.

Chapter 20

The weekend that Astrid got back, her friend Tom was DJing a set at a fundraiser on the Sunday afternoon. It was to be held down a side street, in a sort of alleyway, which they were turning into an event space for the day. I'd met him a couple of times when he'd stopped in at The Den, and I liked him, so I was excited to go along and see him DJing. I remember him telling me, a few weeks before, that he generally preferred house music (a moniker which meant nothing to me), but that at events like these, people liked to hear songs they recognised, so he would be playing what he called a 'crowd pleaser set'.

Astrid was always so excited by the creative exploits of her friends, and she insisted we go and support anyone doing anything cool. So even if she was tired after returning from two weeks of being on tour the day before, there was no way she was going to miss it.

It was a pretty relaxed event, and although we had our coats to ward against the inevitable cold autumn evening, it was actually quite a sunny afternoon. There was a café and a bar that both opened out into a sort of loading zone, and a brewery had set up a temporary stand for drinks. The event was raising money for local families living in poverty, and some percentage of the food and drink costs were going towards the charity, as well as various raffles that were held throughout the day. There was also a silent auction, and Astrid didn't mention until we were there that one of her artworks was in it. It was based loosely around the fallen leaves she'd drawn that day in the park.

We arrived just after lunchtime and had a coffee while the first act was on. We found a spot with two deckchairs, where we sat down together, and Astrid told me some more stories about her two weeks on tour.

When Tom's set started, we got ourselves some beers in plastic cups from the stall, and started dancing in the space in front of where he was set up. More people joined us, a few who I recognised and others, who Astrid introduced me to, whose names I inevitably forgot. I then managed to lose Astrid for a bit, when she ran off to hug someone else she knew. I then watched her flitting around between everyone, with her huge smile and animated expression drawing yet more people in. I loved seeing her at events like these, she was just so natural. While the area we were in wasn't big enough to properly lose her – I could still see her, even though she wasn't by my side – I was left dancing on my own, wondering if I should keep going.

I recognised a group of people I'd met at our housewarming party who waved me over. So I took a break from dancing and went to have a chat to them, leaving her to do her thing. They all congratulated me on my poetry reading, which I thought was very kind of them to remember. While we were all talking, I noticed Tom beckoning Astrid over to him. I watched her make her way over and for a few moments, they were deep in conversation, before both looking intently down at his decks, as he pointed out various things on it. Then, to my complete and utter amazement, she seemed to take over as he walked off and made his way over to the bathrooms. The switch was seamless, and she looked so vibrant, standing there dressed all in black, one headphone over her ear, looking down at the equipment. After a few moments of hard concentration – biting her lip and looking down with a scrunched brow – she quite quickly found her place and started grooving along to the music. Someone in the audience cheered, shouting out, 'Go Astrid!' and we all joined in, whooping, and clapping.

I was reminded of the first night I'd met her, when I was told that she'd taken time off from uni to model and DJ in Berlin. I'd forgotten about it since then, but I think part of me had thought the story might have been an exaggeration. I know you certainly thought it was 'too good to be true,' as you'd said to me later. But when I saw her standing there, so easily filling in for Tom at a moment's notice, I knew it was true. Of course it was true. I'd learned since then, never to underestimate Astrid.

There was someone within the group of people I'd got chatting with who had been invited along by a friend and hadn't hung out with us before. After a while of listening to them all talk, I realised, happily, that I was no longer the new person; she was. I got talking to her and for a while, the conversation turned to Astrid, who she'd only just met. She was, of course, impressed by Astrid stepping up to DJ, but also mentioned how brilliant she'd been when they briefly spoke earlier. She said that Astrid had seemed so interested in who she was and what she was all about; not just asking 'how are you', but rather wanting to know about her dreams and passions. I thought about the party where I first met Astrid, and how much of an impact she'd made on me, even before we'd spoken. Back then, it had been your friend who first told me about her, and I thought that it was my turn to play that part.

'Oh, yeah. She's brilliant,' I said. 'She just got back from a tour, gigging around the UK.'

The new girl's eyes widened. 'She's a musician?'

'Yeah, she's super talented. She's got this gift for music, and pretty much all creative things for that matter. Honestly, she can do it all. I could never be that good at anything, let alone so many things!'

Suddenly a voice came from behind us. It was Astrid's. When I turned around, I saw she had her hands on her hips, and she was looking somewhat annoyed. I noticed that Tom was back on the decks and Astrid had clearly been released back into the crowd.

'Talented?' she said. 'What do you mean by that?'

'Oh, I just mean you have such a talent, such a gift for music. You're such a natural!' I replied, not sure what was happening, or why she seemed annoyed.

'What, like it's something I was born with, or God gave me?' she said.

'Um... I guess... I just... you're so good...' I felt an immediate sinking feeling that I'd done something wrong, though I didn't know what.

'I hate that word, "talent". It makes it sound like I was born being able to play music rather than having to work hard at it. And that's ridiculous. It doesn't just appear, no one is born a fully formed concert pianist. Like any musician, any artist, I've worked my ass off. I've put in the hours. Of course you could do it too if you wanted, you'd just have to dedicate the time and effort. Don't create false ideas of me and then use it as an excuse for why you can't do something. I'm not special.'

I didn't know what to say, I just looked at the ground and she walked off.

The back of my eyes and nose started to prickle and I knew I was about to cry. I went straight to the bathroom where I had to queue for far too long before I could get in, lock the door and let the tears fall. I couldn't stop them.

I'd never really thought of her as having to work hard for anything, I just thought she was naturally brilliant. But the more I thought about it and her reaction, the more I realised that the word 'talented' took away from the work she'd put in. Of course she wasn't born a musician; how could I be so stupid as to minimise her effort? I had to go and apologise. I dried my eyes and left the bathroom. I pushed through the crowds to find her. She was standing by a lamp post laughing with some guy. I probably shouldn't have interrupted, they seemed quite close (and in fact, I saw them sharing a quick kiss later), but I had to tell her immediately.

'I'm so sorry!' I blurted out as soon as I got near her.

She looked at me and seemed confused.

'What about?'

'About saying that you were talented.'

'Oh. Yeah well, it's ok, I just hate that word. You're the writer, you should think about the words you use. "Talented" implies some kind of natural aptitude. Sure, maybe my mother played me Beethoven and Bowie in the womb, maybe I picked up music by osmosis to some degree. Maybe. They say I always sang in tune. But if you're talking about me being good now, which I am very flattered and grateful that you would, I would prefer you chose your words a bit more delicately and not make out that it's something I was born able to do. Talent just isn't a thing. It doesn't exist. There aren't *creative people* and *non-creative people*, there are just people who have put in the work and those who haven't. Yet.'

I nodded and sniffed.

'Chill out, Mouse, you're not in trouble, I'm not your mother.' She laughed and held her hand out to me. I wasn't sure what she wanted.

'Come on, let's dance!' Her smile was, as always, infectious and I couldn't help smiling back.

'Speaking of 'Let's Dance'... Tom?'

He looked up at her from his decks. She smiled and mouthed the words 'Let's dance' and did a shimmy. He nodded and once the song he'd been playing finished, the unmistakeable first 'aahs' of Bowie's 'Let's Dance' came blasting out. She raised her eyebrows at me, smiling and put her hand out again for me to take. And, as if my mistake had never even happened, we danced. Everyone joined in, the power of Bowie compelling them.

***

I slept in the next morning because I didn't have class until later in the day. When I woke, Astrid was already up and working on something at the table. I went and flopped down on the couch, not yet quite awake. She was so perky and I was still feeling slightly dusty from the previous evening.

'Good, you're up!' she said. 'I was waiting for you to come down so I could make us tea.'

'Thanks,' I called after her, rubbing my eyes.

She came back a few minutes later just as I happened to be in the middle of a big yawn.

'How do you do it?' I asked when she put down my tea in

front of me.

'Do what?'

'Function. Have energy. Find motivation.'

She laughed. 'There are always things to do. Time is short, and nothing scares me more than the idea of wasting any of it.'

'Am... I wasting time?'

'You're spending it in the way you want to. There's no shame in resting and taking it easy.'

'But what about you?'

She sat down next to me before taking a sip of her tea.

'I get restless when I'm not doing things,' she said. 'I start to get stressed. Or depressed. And I hate the medication. So I'd rather just avoid that if possible. I feel much happier with things if I'm busy.'

I couldn't imagine Astrid ever being depressed; she must have been joking. Or at least trying to make some sort of point. Surely she hadn't ever experienced depression.

'Don't you ever sleep?' I asked, stifling a yawn.

She laughed, that beautiful laugh, which always made me want to laugh too.

'Newton only slept a couple of hours a night, you know. Mozart averaged about five hours, I think. Da Vinci grabbed a bit here and there throughout the day.'

'I've heard of that. It has a name, doesn't it?'

'Yep. Don't know what it is.'

'You don't do that, though.'

'Nope, it's not really practical if you have things you actually have to do. What I'm saying is that you don't need a full nine hours every night.'

I groaned, 'I do.'

'Then you do you, Mouse. Nothing wrong with that. We're all different in this beautiful world, and that's what makes it so exciting.'

Her work ethic did rub off on me a bit though. I started finding time to study again, because she was. I'd come to realise she was always working away at something. If not uni assignments, then she would have her guitar our and be working on a new song, or I would hear her in her room, the sounds of her keyboard drifting through the house. Other times, she'd be at the dining table working on a new poem or creating an artwork. We would often sit down together to study or work through our assignments or create something. I realised, in that first couple of months of living with her, that her private life was very different to the persona she showed at parties. That easy, care-free party girl had hidden behind her a hard worker who wanted to do well, who wanted to create constantly.

She also got me back into reading. She was a voracious reader, and I hadn't read for pleasure since I was in early high school, but she reinspired me. I also kept writing things down - bits and pieces of parties and events we'd been to, conversations we'd had - on scraps of paper. It felt good to be spending my spare time creating, if you could call it that. I still struggled with believing I was a *creative person*, but Astrid assured me that the only difference between someone who was creative and someone who wasn't, is that they did the work and actually created things: no one was more suited to it than anyone else, we just all had our own different outlets.

Once I'd had it pointed out to me during the conversation at the fundraiser, I started to notice this different side of her; how hard she worked, how she didn't value things that came easily, though she made things look effortless. There was never an idle moment with Astrid.

Chapter 21

I had initially resisted Astrid's attempts to take me out to a club. I was certain that it wouldn't be my thing, but she had insisted. I guess it just wasn't something I'd really done before. But if Astrid was going to be there then I knew it would probably be fun. I had nothing to lose. Tom and some of his friends apparently went out most weekends, and he and Astrid shared a love of this 'house music' that he'd told me about. So one Saturday night, she helped me pick something out of my wardrobe to wear and we danced around our living room having pre-drinks and getting ready. She did my makeup and made my eyes look all glittery.

I would have been happy just dancing in our living room all night, but at around 11 p.m., she said it was time to go. That seemed so late to me to be leaving, but I was along for the ride. The music at the club was that strange perpetual music that made it feel like you were trapped in a box. It rarely changed, it just kept going in the same way for hours. And hours. Although I was enjoying myself enough just being with her, I found the music incredibly boring. I wasn't sure why everyone seemed to be enjoying it so much.

We hadn't found Tom, and I needed to go to the bathroom. Astrid said she'd come too. Once we'd found the loos, she threw me off guard by following me into my stall – actually into my toilet cubicle. I tried not to act too surprised, but I'd never been to the toilet with someone there with me, watching. She went first, squeezing past me to get to the toilet, before pulling down her underwear and sitting down. I tried to look anywhere other than at her, but she was talking to me about the DJs that were playing, and I didn't know if I was meant to maintain eye contact or stare somewhere else, like at the toilet paper holder, which I ended up fixing my eyes on. I noticed it was broken, and the toilet paper was just sitting on the floor next to the toilet, which freaked me out. Then she flushed and indicated for me to go. We shuffled past each other, then I awkwardly pulled my underwear down and sat there for what felt like ages. I couldn't stop thinking about the fact that we hadn't wiped the seat down with toilet paper first. She kept talking to me and keeping eye contact while I tried to concentrate on going to the toilet. I heard two voices coming from the cubicle next to us too and suddenly realised this must be a thing people did, though I didn't understand why. I eventually finished, flushed the toilet and we went to wash our hands in the gender-neutral sink area with taps that were switched on using a foot pump. I couldn't work out how to make them work until Astrid showed me.

We went back to the dance floor to see if we could find Tom. After a while of listening to the music and trying to dance to it – I had no idea how, and I felt so awkward – we decided to go out to the smoking area for a break. There was no phone reception in the club, so after Astrid lit two cigarettes and handed me one, she sent off a quick text to Tom asking where he was. We stood for a moment, chatting, before a very tall, good-looking guy came over and asked Astrid for a light. She got it out and without saying a word, just smiling her half-smile that always seemed to draw people towards her, she held it up and lit his cigarette as he moved in close to her. They didn't really move apart very much once it was lit, just looked at each other for a few moments, before he broke their silence with a 'Cool, thanks,' followed by an exhale of smoke.

Before I could work out whether I should say anything and risk breaking the silent connection between them – their chemistry, even in those first silent moments, felt palpable – his three friends also appeared around us, laughing and clapping him on the back and introducing themselves.

They all had names, of course, but I only remember two – Jerome, the guy who Astrid was standing so close to that their bodies were touching, and Grant, his loudest and goofiest friend. He seemed to be making an effort to talk to me and when he'd told me his name, I tried Astrid's trick of secretly tracing his name out on my palm to help remember it. I guess it had worked, because it's still in my mind, even now. He made a big fanfare around kneeling and kissing my hand when I told him my name, which made me giggle.

As we all stood around chatting and laughing, I couldn't help watching Astrid and Jerome out of the corner of my eye – her hand occasionally on his shoulder, his arm, his face, his eyes mostly on her. His friends mainly kept up the conversation, talking about their uni work and debating about whether one of their lecturers was good or bad – they all seemed to have classes together. Astrid and Jerome didn't add much to the conversation, they were more interested in whispering in each other's ears and making each other laugh.

'What do you study, Jess?' Grant had asked me, jolting me out of my thoughts.

'I uh... Economics,' I said, my eternal shame at studying such a boring degree feeling strong. 'How about you?'

'Bed,' he said with a wink, an eyebrow raise, and then... he bit his lip.

I was slightly taken aback at his boldness – it seemed like such a suggestive move, and I wondered if he was hitting on me, which made my stomach flip with something that felt like... excitement. Which confused me. But before I got too carried away, I immediately reminded myself there was no way *he* would be even remotely interested in *me.* Especially not that quickly, I wasn't Astrid. I must have misheard. I realised my shock was showing on my face when he laughed and clarified.

'Bachelor of Education. You know, B-Ed... Bed.'

'Oh! Oh, right!' I said quickly, and the others all laughed. I'm sure I was blushing with embarrassment.

We all went back inside to dance after a while. I liked being part of a group. I couldn't miss seeing the tall pretty one kiss Astrid. They looked perfect together.

Grant started doing the worm in the middle of the dance floor, which made me feel a little embarrassed for him, but everyone seemed to be laughing. Astrid caught my eye and we smiled, sharing a moment between just the two of us amongst all the people in the whole club.

Hi friend, I see you.

Grant kept me company as Astrid was getting more interested in Jerome. I certainly didn't want to get in her way, and it was nice to have someone entertaining me. At one point, he showed me to this part of the club where there was a hidden shelf sitting up above the dancefloor. He said we should get up there and I thought he was mad, but somehow, he managed to boost me up (I had memories flooding back from the magazine launch house party we'd crashed so long ago), and he climbed up after me. From our vantage point above everyone, we looked out onto the crowd. Swathes of people were moving back and forth, sometimes together, sometimes apart. It looked amazing from our spot, and I smiled to think that I was having my own little adventure.

'Do you actually like this music?' I asked him from where we sat, looking out at everyone.

'Yeah, it's fun to dance to,' he said.

'Is it? I guess I don't really get how to dance to it,' I replied.

'It's easy, watch them.'

We sat watching everyone dancing to the never-ending beat which never changed. They just sort of shifted back and forth, bopping in time. Well, some of them were in time. It was at least something I could easily do, but even though I was drunk, I didn't feel drunk enough to do that for hours on end.

After a few minutes of watching everyone, he said excitedly to me: 'I can do a backflip, wanna see?'

It was about the last thing I was expecting to hear from him, and I replied in shock: 'Really? Here? Even after drinking?'

'*Especially* after drinking,' he said to me with a wink, then he jumped down and proceeded to actually do a backflip in the empty space on the stage-like area below our ledge. I applauded, amazed, and he did a deep bow. He then put his hands up for me to take and jump down, and we found our way back to the others, who were dancing. I joined in, enjoying knowing that I was part of the ever-moving whole I had witnessed from the ledge.

Another trip to the smoking area told us that Tom had ended up getting too wasted at home and hadn't made it out. Astrid rolled her eyes as she read out his message, shaking her head.

'He would,' was all she'd said.

When it was time to leave, Astrid said she was going to go home with Jerome, and asked if I would be ok to get home myself. It turned out that Grant lived near ours and would be heading the same way as me so we could split a taxi.

I nodded, wanting to be cool with it and not stop her having fun. I felt comfort in knowing that there would be someone else there who would make sure I got home. He seemed harmless, I felt safe enough with him. Astrid gave me a big hug before she left. I felt strong and like I was in control. I could do this, make my own way home.

The taxi home was unmemorable. Grant was talking about his sister who wanted to do a year abroad in Spain, but I wasn't particularly engaged with what he was saying. He was good enough looking, though his joking personality made him more funny than sexy. But as I sat there next to him, I wondered if I asked him to come in with me, if he would. I tried to think if I could see us together, Jess and Grant. No, of course I couldn't. But part of me wanted to go home with someone too, have a night of debauchery, then never see him again. Astrid and I could debrief and exchange notes from our living room over coffee the next morning. But I'd already told him I had a boyfriend, so he wasn't going to push it, even if he was up for it. When we pulled up to mine, I said goodbye and got out of the taxi. As I left, I heard my name being called out.

'Jess?'

I turned back around, leaning through the door. Perhaps that wink earlier on *had* been suggestive, I thought maybe I was heading for a poetic movie moment where he asked to come in for just one drink? Or say that he thought I was a 'great gal' and he'd like to see me again? Or maybe he just knew that we could be great together if only circumstances were different?

'Do you have £10 for the taxi fare?' he said, his face half in the shadows.

'Oh... yeah...' I felt suddenly stupid. 'Sure, one second.'

I buried my wistful hopes down deep as I rummaged in my tiny purse for a folded-up note.

'Here,' I said as I handed it to him.

'Great, thanks. Bye then.'

'Bye.'

I stepped back and stood beside the car, watching as it drove off. The flat was cold and lonely when I got home.

I couldn't help thinking about what would have happened if he had come in. What if we'd had a whisky, or a wine, and then we'd stayed up chatting for hours. And, as the sun began to rise, we'd shared a beautiful, meaningful kiss and I had taken him to bed... I wouldn't have been alone, for a start. And it would have felt good to think someone liked me, that I was special enough that someone I'd just met would decide they liked me enough to want to go home with me...

But I had you. I wanted to be with you. I hated myself for even having those thoughts. What was wrong with me? Just because you weren't around, that didn't mean you didn't exist... Why was I dreaming of a throwaway encounter that would mean nothing and would clearly not be fulfilling? I pushed the idea down deeper and tried to forget I'd even contemplated it. These were the wicked thoughts that lived deep inside me that I would not – could not – listen to, even for a moment.

I went to bed and slipped between the cold covers. My duvet

didn't feel warm enough. Nothing did.

Astrid came home not that long after I went to bed, which I hadn't been expecting. It had only been a couple of hours since we left the club. I was still lying awake when I heard the door open. I thought, for a moment, that maybe she had brought the tall boy home with her, but I heard just one set of footsteps come up the stairs and make their way towards her room. I wondered what had happened in her parallel night.

The next day, I made my way downstairs to where Astrid was already sitting at the dining table, working on something, and listening to music.

'Good morning,' I said, as she looked up. 'Who's this?' I asked, pointing to the speakers. Some very groovy, very fun, upbeat sounding music was filling the room, and I liked it.

'Accessible Dylan,' she replied.

'That's their name?' I asked, thinking it was an odd choice for band name, but then again, there were plenty more odd ones than that out there.

'Oh no, sorry, they're called The Redwalls. Aren't they good?'

'Yeah, it sounds so cool.'

I sat down on the sofa, curling my legs up under me.

'So how was the rest of your night?' I asked, and she laughed.

'Well... It was pretty funny actually. It turned out he lived miles away, and I was like nah, no way. But his car was nearby so I suggested we go there for a bit of action and then I came home.'

'What? In his car?'

'Yeah.' She shrugged. 'Seemed the easiest option. I don't think it was how he'd envisioned the night, but I don't really care. He's already texted me saying he wants to see me again but like, who can be bothered with that?'

Somehow this act sounded impressive coming from her. And empowering. I was sure that had I been in that situation it would have felt seedy, but it clearly wasn't for her. She knew what she wanted, and she got it. I admired that so much. I tried to picture them in his car – how would their limbs have fitted in around each other? Would they have spread out in the back seat? Leaned the front seat back?

She came and sat down next to me on the couch and asked if I was ok. She asked if I hadn't been feeling too lonely. I wasn't sure if it was a throwaway jokey comment, or if she was seriously talking about my current situation.

'Have you ever been in love, Astrid?' I asked her.

'I once fell in love with a barista.'

'Oh? What was he like?'

'I didn't know him of course, not properly. It was like all the best loves; ones that can't be marred by the passing of time, by disagreements that ruin lazy Sunday mornings, or by the monotony of consecutive days in each other's company.'

'What did he look like?'

'Shorter than I would have liked but in fantasies, I'm not sure practicalities have a place. I will almost always fall in love with a good-looking person who makes me good coffee. But it has to be really good coffee. I found out his name was Emerson and as well as making coffee, he rebuilt vintage motorbikes. There was a space of time when he was away, and I asked the fill-in barista where he had gone. Apparently, he'd fallen off his bike in the rain. I could see it; the downpour, the dark night, his headlights misting as he edged closer towards the shiny road, eventually coming into contact as he and the bike spun off in different directions... I could almost believe I was there. Presumably by the time he came back to work I had left – off finding new adventures, as I tend to do. But I never forgot him. Sometimes I wonder where he is now.'

'You never saw him again?'

She shook her head. 'In fact, I went back a while later when my travels took me near the café again, and I asked after him. I was told he now worked in a different café on the other side of the city. I knew a girl who lived nearby so I called on her for a visit. On a sunny Sunday morning we walked down to the waterfront where the café was. It was filled with dark wood, exposed brick, and Edison bulbs. It had long, high tables, with the café's name etched on the corner of each one, and everyone had to share. But of course, he was nowhere to be seen. Even now, I think about him sometimes. It was the kind of love that will remain pure, bereft of disappointment, completely protected by the absence of time spent in close proximity.'

'Don't you wish you'd been able to find him?'

'No, not really. Life is just a combination of fleeting moments and connections. That's the beauty of it all.'

I smiled. I liked the story, but it didn't seem like Astrid at all. She never chased anyone. If anything, that story would make more sense told the opposite way, from perspective of the person in love with her. I wondered if it was true, or if she was just trying to make a point.

'Are you trying to say that nothing is ever as good in reality as it seems, and that love isn't always perfect?' I asked her, trying to piece it all together.

She smiled, rubbed my arm, then got up and said 'I'm going to go make some breakfast. Scrambled eggs on toast?'

'Oh, yeah, sure. Sounds good,' I said. As she made her way to the kitchen, I called after her: 'Hey, Astrid?'

'Mmm?'

'Was that a true story?'

'What do you think?' she said from the kitchen and didn't offer up anything more.

Chapter 22

If we didn't have people staying over at The Den, Astrid would sometimes come home late and when I'd asked her where she'd been, she said in such a non-committal way, 'with a guy'. I wondered if she had a couple that she was seeing regularly (but I didn't know of any), or if she was just going and sleeping with lots of random guys… Where was she even finding them? But then again, finding new people was like a superpower of hers. I wished I'd had the confidence to just go and talk to people like she did. She once told me she never started conversations, but she happily kept them going. I tried to figure out how that worked. If I didn't start conversations (which of course I never did), then no one would talk to me. Yet everyone wanted to talk to her…

I was at uni one day having just finished a lecture, when someone stopped me.

'Oh, hi! What time for tonight?' he said.

I wasn't sure if he was talking to me at first. I tended to be in my own world when I was at uni. The novelty of actually being there had never quite worn off. Even three years in, I was still overcome with just how amazing it all was, being at university, especially whenever I was walking around campus. I'd spent what felt like so much of my life wanting to grow up and now I had, I still couldn't quite believe it.

'Jess?' he said, and I figured he must have been talking to me, since he seemed to know my name.

'Hi,' I replied.

'What time should we come over tonight?'

He was quite pretty, and tall, with dark hair. I tried to work out if his face was familiar. I wished I could remember people's faces and names better.

'I'm not sure what you're talking about, sorry.'

'I... heard there was a party at your place.'

'Oh, is there? Probably, I'm not sure. Maybe ask Astrid?'

'Ok, yeah, maybe.' He seemed suddenly unsure.

'Cool. Well, might see you later then, I guess.' He walked off and I started to make my way home.

When I got home I asked Astrid if she had planned a party.

'I wouldn't call it a party. I just invited a few people over.'

'And you didn't tell them when to come?'

'No, I did. I think I just said come around from like seven-ish.'

'Ok, cool. It's just that someone came up to me at uni and asked what time to come around.'

'Who was it?'

'I wish I knew.'

'Oh, Mouse, you never cease to make me laugh. Well, I'm sure they'll work it out.'

She was right, it wasn't a party by party standards, but there were still quite a few people. There was a guy who I recognised because I'd seen him in my kitchen one morning. So I guess that meant she'd probably slept with him. They weren't being couple-y or anything though. I'd got the idea Astrid didn't like to do that though, she kept these things relatively private from the outside world, but I knew they had a vibe and I assumed he'd be staying over. He was so her type. Tall, good-looking, and wearing a leather jacket – although this one had blonde hair. Usually she liked guys with dark hair.

I wondered if the one who had found me earlier that day was going to turn up. Eventually he did, accompanied by another friend. He was drunk already, and he came straight up to me and hugged me, then asked where Astrid was. I suddenly worked out who he was; the guy I'd seen Astrid kissing at Tom's fundraising event. This was bound to be interesting.

I indicated where she was, and he made his way over. They hugged and I saw her ask him if he was ok. He nodded and walked off to get a drink.

Later, as Astrid and I were dancing together, wine cups in hand, he appeared again, wanting to talk to her.

'I'm not doing this,' she said, and walked off into the kitchen.

He looked like he was going to follow her, then I said, 'Hey.'

Just like that; *Hey. Look at me, not her.* And he did.

'Come on, let's get some fresh air for a minute,' I said, and he nodded, looking a bit wobbly. We went out the front of the house to sit on the step at the entrance.

'Why doesn't she want me anymore?' he asked, swaying slightly where he sat.

I liked this role. I felt important, like I had the knowledge he wanted.

'Wasn't it quite a while ago you two hooked up?' I asked. It was a guess, I didn't really know if she'd kept seeing him, but considering I'd not heard anything about it, I took a punt that there wasn't anything serious between them.

'Yeah, but I saw her in town a few days ago and she told me

about tonight, so I figured she wanted me here.'

'I'm sure she did. I just don't think that means that like... she's yours or anything.'

He put his head in his hands. 'I just wanted to speak to her,' he said.

'Are you going to be cool about it though? Or are you going to make a scene?'

'I'll be cool, I promise.'

'Ok, you can probably speak to her then...' I was hardly going to stop him.

He got up, a little uneasy on his feet, and went inside. But even without being in there to see what happened, I soon knew that he hadn't been cool about it. Within a few minutes, his mate and another guy were marching him out. I walked inside to find out what had happened. Astrid was standing with her arms crossed, evidently having just watched him being taken away. She shook her head and then walked off in the other direction. I wondered how many times she had seen him and why he had acted like that. It seemed like a pretty intense reaction if they'd only spent one night together, but then again, it was Astrid. I couldn't imagine what it would be like to have someone acting like that over me. I watched her sit down on the sofa with the blonde guy.

'You ok?' I mouthed to her as I went to grab us both another drink.

She rolled her eyes, then smiled and nodded as I handed her a cup of wine.

The blonde did stay over.

I stood in the hallway after I'd brushed my teeth, wondering if I'd be able to hear them together in her room. I crept right up to her door but couldn't hear anything.

I went to bed alone.

It was only a couple of days later, as I was making some breakfast, that Astrid headed out the door, calling: 'I'll be back in a couple of hours, just going to see my psychologist.'

This was new information for me, I had no idea she was seeing a psychologist. I spent the whole time she was out feeling terrible. How had I not noticed there was something wrong? Surely, she wasn't depressed or struggling... She seemed to be so together, so in charge of herself and her life... I wondered if she'd been affected by the way the guy had acted towards her at the party, but surely it couldn't be that? Maybe she was dealing with some trauma I didn't know about? Or had I done something to hurt her? I couldn't think of anything, but in the time she was out, I'd almost convinced myself I might have.

As soon as she got home, I rushed to give her a hug.

'I'm so sorry I didn't realise something was wrong. Are you ok? Do you want to talk about it?'

She returned the hug at first, but then pushed me away at arm's length and looked at me strangely.

'What are you talking about?' she asked.

I felt awkward talking about it but I was her friend, so I could do it for her. I couldn't believe she hadn't felt comfortable telling me what was wrong.

'Well... it's just that... you went to see a psychologist. Did something horrible happen? You don't have to say, of course, I just want to be here for you.'

She laughed, which seemed like a strange reaction.

'No, nothing horrible happened... I mean sure, I started seeing a therapist when my parents first split up, they insisted on it. And I still make sure I go often enough. You shouldn't just go see a therapist if something is *wrong*, it's an important tool to help you get through life. Mental health is important, you know.'

'I thought they just treated depression and stuff like that.'

'Well, yes, they obviously do that too. Can we get out of the hallway? I want tea.'

'Oh, gosh. Yes, sorry, of course.'

I followed her to the kitchen as she set about making us tea. 'So... there's nothing wrong?' I asked, still not entirely sure if she was ok or not.

'Well... Life is wrong. We've created such a strange society where there are lots of stresses and things that come and go. It's much easier to navigate when you have someone to talk things over with. Surely you understand that. I imagine you saw someone when you were younger to deal with losing your sister?'

'Well... no.'

'Really? Not even for a bit?'

'No, it wasn't really an option.'

'What about your parents? No family bereavement counselling?'

I shook my head.

'Well, what support *did* you all get to process it all?'

'None really, I guess. They got pretty into church after she died but I don't know if that counts.'

'Geez. See, *this* is what's wrong with the world. Everyone should have a therapist when something difficult like that happens and yes, I'm well aware that calling it "something difficult" is a massive understatement. I'm also aware that having a psychologist is a privilege not immediately available to everyone – it's terrible that a lot of people can't afford it or get access to it. I love our healthcare system, but this is where it fails. We prioritise physical health and completely ignore mental health. But I try to prioritise getting mental health support over many things. And losing a sister and daughter is definitely something you would need help to work through and survive without losing your minds. I can't believe you never had any for it. Anyone who can have therapy, should. It's the best thing.'

I was surprised by the way she was speaking. Getting therapy would be a sign of failure in my family, they were more the stoic find-a-way-to-deal-with-the-situation and never-ask-for-help type people. But it made sense when she said it.

'You and Robert should definitely have some therapy.'

'Me and Robert? Why? We're not that bad...'

'Whether or not you're "bad" isn't relevant. Therapy would absolutely be helpful. It might have helped him to actually discuss his leaving plans with you, as opposed to just saying it was the way it had to be...'

I suddenly didn't want to talk about it anymore. I didn't like seeing myself through those eyes. They didn't seem like eyes that understood me or my relationship. I went to pour the water into the teapot while Astrid got the milk from the fridge. We went and sat in the living room.

'Don't you want to be in love, Astrid? Don't you get tired of not having someone who will always be there for you?'

'Not if I can avoid it. It just gets in the way.'

'Really? How?'

'It forces compromise. Makes me less who I am. Being in a relationship is way too much risk of losing yourself, it's better to just steer clear entirely.'

'I don't know. I think I'm worse on my own.'

'Yeah, I know you think that. But that's just because you don't like yourself. I wish you'd work on that. It's hard seeing you always being so down on yourself.

I felt uncomfortable hearing her say that. There really wasn't much to like.

'Anyway,' she continued. 'I like to think I can get that kind of love and support and connection through my friends. And there's nothing greater than walking the streets at night, alone, with the right music in your ears, no pressure to be anyone or anything, nowhere to be, no one you have to go home to, just able to be purely yourself. I'd hate to think I was ever expected to be somewhere, just to make some man happy.'

'How do you know if it's the right music?' I asked, leaving the rest.

'One sec,' she said, before running upstairs and coming back with a USB and my laptop. She got up my iTunes and dragged a whole heap of files into it from the USB, putting it in a playlist named 'Out Into The Night'.

Chapter 23

One night when we were out at a club, I lost her. We'd gone out together, starting with drinks at our place, where Astrid had invited a couple of friends over. They were dance music types and seemed nice enough.

I'd asked Astrid where her love for club music had come from – I obviously hadn't really seen this side of her life until we'd moved in together, though she had mentioned a few times that she liked 'every type of music, except maybe opera'. She said she was saving opera to discover when she's older, because she wanted to know there were still new things out there which she didn't yet like. She told me that liking electronic, particularly 'house' music was in her veins, and part of being German. And that if you wanted a night out of getting dressed up, dancing and meeting people, it was the way to go. She also said she was currently in *that mood*, which is why we were going out to clubs more. I went along, now quite enjoying being out late at night, and the possibilities that the dark nights and bright lights might hold, but I still wasn't convinced by the music.

One of the people who had come over to ours before heading out, Chris, had such beautiful eyes and I couldn't stop looking at him when he spoke to me. We ended up sitting on the sofa together, talking about anything and everything. He told me about his big Italian family who lived not far away, all still in and around the town where he'd grown up. He said he was the black sheep of the family, having moved to the big city, but he went back to visit them often. He told me about his mum's cooking and his three brothers, and I was captivated by the stories he told. He was so open and so interesting and seemed genuinely interested in me and what I thought about things. The conversation felt easy, and I hadn't really felt that with anyone new, other than Astrid. I felt immediately safe in his company. Astrid and I were both in the kitchen at one point and she noted with a smile that Chris and I were getting along well.

'I'm glad you two met,' she said with a twinkle in her eye. 'He's nice. Really nice. He'll take care of you, that one.'

I brushed it off, feeling embarrassed that she'd noticed we were talking so much. But it didn't stop me going back and sitting next to him again.

That night, we went to a club I hadn't been to before. It had the most confusing layout and walking around was difficult – one minute I was sticking to the floor, the next I was almost slipping over. I was wearing silly high heels that made the balls of my feet go numb and tingly. I couldn't work out where we were going at any point and it was so busy. We all danced together for a while, Chris and I next to each other, occasionally getting close, which made my stomach flutter.

We moved between the different stages at the club and though I tried to stay close to Astrid, inevitably, I lost her.

I tried to send her a message, but my phone had died. The reception inside had been patchy anyway. Surrounded by strangers, and with no idea how to even get out of the place, I started to panic. The repetitive beat of the music was drilling into my mind as I passed bathrooms, a dance floor, another bathroom, a different dance floor, and eventually I wound my way up to the smoking area, the cold air hitting my face as I burst out the door. Where was she? What if something had happened to her? Was she looking for me? I suddenly couldn't breathe. I felt abandoned. Had she left? Why hadn't she told me if she had left? She'd never left before without at least telling me and checking I was ok with it... Maybe I had annoyed her. Did she hate me?

My hands were clammy even though I was cold, being outside without my coat, which I'd checked into the cloakroom. The music was still ringing in my ears and my heart felt like it might break out of my chest. I found a dark corner in the smoking area where I thought no one would see me, sat down and closed my eyes as tightly as possible. As I sat there with my heart thumping in my chest so loudly I could hear it in my ears, I couldn't tell how much time passed.

Suddenly there were hands on mine. They were pulling me, grasping me, tearing at me. I gasped for breath. I heard my name, and I looked up and saw a face. I felt hands resting gently on mine – they were not in fact pulling at me at all, they were just resting.

'Jess?' He knew my name. He had kind eyes. Kind blue eyes. Deep, shining blue. Like two oceans that I wanted to jump into and disappear.

'Jess? Are you there?'

After a moment, I recognised him. It was Chris.

I tried to speak but couldn't get the words out. Eventually I managed to say her name.

He put his hands gently on either side of my face, forcing

me to look into his eyes. Those blue eyes.

'Breathe with me,' he said, calmly. He breathed in deeply, then out. In, then out. I tried to match my breathing to his. My breath rattled through me.

'Astrid's gone...' I finally managed to say.

'Everyone's almost gone, the club is just about closing.'

'But... but... Where is she? What do I do?'

'Do you want to go home?' he asked as he removed his hands from my face.

I started to panic again. I couldn't even think how to get home. Astrid always got us home. What if she wasn't there? Where was she? I didn't want to go home alone... I realised I was shaking my head in answer to his question.

'Look, I live just around the corner. Do you want to come back to mine, and I'll drive you home in the morning?'

That sounded like a better option. I nodded. I really didn't want to be alone.

He helped me up from the ground. With his arm around me, he guided me towards the cloak room. I got my coat and we left. The world was still spinning. We walked arm in arm through the streets as I tried to concentrate on my breathing.

I don't remember the house. I just remember him making me stand at the sink and drink lots of water. I finished one glass, and he poured me another.

Then I guess we went to bed. I remember him putting his arms around me. He held me and it suddenly felt like all the chaos of the night was quietening down. I felt safe.

***

My first thought when I woke up was that I was back in the upside-down room of my first night at uni. Then I remembered I'd moved. But I wasn't in the flat either. I looked around, searching for some sort of sign to tell me where I was. Then I looked over and saw Chris lying next to me. He started to stir.

'Where am I?' I said, mostly to myself.

'Good morning,' he mumbled as he slowly sat up. 'You're at my place.'

I tried to piece together the previous night. It was all pretty hazy.

'What happened last night?'

'You were a bit stressed, so we came back here.'

I tried to think back, then thought about the fact we were sharing a bed, and suddenly panicked that something more had happened. I made a quick check that we were both fully clothed, which was a relief. But I still wasn't sure.

'Did we...?' I croaked, not able to hide the worry in my voice.

'No.'

I breathed a sigh of relief.

'I did say I wanted to kiss you though...' he continued. 'But I obviously didn't,' he added quickly.

'Oh... what happened?' I couldn't remember that at all.

'Well, I was going to leave you here and go sleep on the sofa, but you insisted I stay. You wanted cuddles and you had your head so close to mine. I probably shouldn't have, but yeah, I wanted to kiss you. You said that drunk Jess wanted to, but sober Jess wouldn't. You said Jess had...' he paused for a moment, scrunching up his face as he was thinking. '... That Jess had become accustomed to doing what she feels she should do as opposed to what she wants to do and although she wanted to kiss me too, she shouldn't.'

'Well... that's embarrassing. And I spoke about myself in third person?'

'Yep. For what it's worth, I thought it was cute.'

'I have a boyfriend,' I said.

'I know. You said. And you feel like you owe him loyalty even though you don't want to.'

'I said that?'

'You didn't need to.'

'I'm sure I was just drunk. I wouldn't read too much into it.'

I was starting to remember snippets of the night before. I had made such a scene and acted so insane, yet he had been so sweet to me. And to give me somewhere to stay when I'd been so weird about not wanting to go home... I didn't understand why he'd put up with me being like that. I didn't even know why I'd acted like that. At the time it had seemed so all encompassing, but in hindsight, there had been absolutely nothing to panic about. I felt ridiculous. I suddenly felt like I needed to get home. He offered to drive me, so I said yes.

We made small talk all the way. When we arrived, I thanked him again and he assured me it had been nothing. I got out and waved him off. Out on the street, in the morning light, I was aware of the state of myself: my dress that was clearly from the previous night, my silly heels in my hand, walking barefoot to my front door. I was one of those people. Not where I was supposed to be, outside of time and space.

I found my way to the front door, managed to put the key in the lock though my hands were shaky, and opened the door.

Silence. I closed the door and walked in.

Then suddenly she was there.

'Mouse! My little Mouse!

She swept me up in her arms. She pulled me in, in her arms, and we collapsed on the sofa.

'Where did you go?' she asked.

'I thought you'd left.'

'I did. I thought you had too. Then I called you and you'd turned your phone off. I sent messages too.'

'Yeah, it died. I guess I hadn't properly charged it.'

'No one knew where you'd gone. I called Chris, in case you were with him, but I guess his phone was dead too. I stayed up waiting for you to come home.'

'You didn't bring anyone home?'

'No, no, I was worried. Where did you go all night, Mouse?' she asked me.

'I stayed at Chris's place.'

'Oh my god!' She sat up and stared at me. 'Did you...?'

'No!' I answered quickly. Too quickly?

It sounded like she was unhappy with me at the mere thought of it, as she should be – I'd spent the night with someone who wasn't my boyfriend. Although nothing happened, I decided not to tell her that he'd wanted to kiss me. There was no need to mention it. It had been nice knowing that someone had liked me enough to want to kiss me, but I tried to push it out of my mind and bring myself back into my real life, away from this life of fantasy, of fleeting connections and meaningful passing moments... I didn't need to play any games. I only needed you.

Chapter 24

'What are we doing for Halloween?' she'd asked me one Sunday morning, back in October, soon after she'd returned from her tour.

'We're doing something?' I asked, thinking Halloween was just a kid thing.

'Of course we're doing something. An excuse to dress up and celebrate? There's no way we're missing that.'

I liked how serious she was about events and having fun.

'Ok, well, sure. I've never really done anything for Halloween before,' I replied.

'A travesty if ever I heard one. Leave it with me.'

A few days later she came back to me with a plan.

'So I've been thinking about it, and I've decided that holding a Halloween party is boring and obvious,' she said as she sat at our dining table, a pen in her hand and a list written in front of her. 'What would we do, haunted house and peeled grapes pretending to be eyeballs? We're not children. Let's go to a rave. I've found a Halloween themed one held in this cool old building that is currently empty and waiting to be fixed up, though it's a couple of weeks after actual Halloween. There should be people we know there, or at least we will after a few minutes. Keen?'

'Keen.'

And so a rave it was.

On actual Halloween night, we'd dressed up in matching skeleton onesies Astrid had got us, and eaten sweets and popcorn while watching a strange erotic-horror-vampire movie with Bowie in it, called 'The Hunger'. It had some lesbian love scenes which made me slightly uncomfortable to watch in a room with my friend, but overall, I quite enjoyed the weird movie. Bowie played an aging vampire who starved himself to death, via a very impressively done and swift aging process. Once his character had 'died', we kept waiting for him to return, but he never did.

Two weeks later was the rave. We'd started at ours with a few drinks, as was becoming tradition for our nights out. Astrid and I watched live clips of our favourite bands while we got ready. We were in and out of our bedrooms to get changed, the bathroom for makeup, and the living room to dance as the songs we loved came on.

I dressed as a cat. It seemed easy enough, I just wore all black and little wire ears on a headband. Astrid drew my nose and whiskers on for me in eye liner pencil. I thought I looked pretty convincing.

Astrid went as Bowie. She was stunning. She'd coloured her hair temporarily red and drew the Aladdin Sane lightning bolt on her face. She had bright red sparkly tights and a red sequin jacket, which she put over a shiny black shirt. As we were ready to leave, she pulled on knee-high sparkly silver heeled boots. Her cheek bones looked so angular, and she looked so tall and thin, like a model. I remembered that first story I had heard of her, modelling in Berlin.

I couldn't take my eyes off her, to the point where she asked me what was wrong.

'Nothing,' I eventually managed to say. 'It's perfect. You're perfect.'

She wasn't wrong about the venue being cool – it was set back off the street, on the edge of a little plaza type thing – an area that was otherwise closed, as it was going to be done up and turned into some sort of local hub. The building that the rave was in was a huge old building that had been completely cleared out, and had lots of different floors, each of which had a different DJ playing.

Inside it was dark, but the lights were bright and beautiful. There were lots of people there, but nobody stood out as much as Astrid, the lights glinting as she moved, her jacket shimmering like a slinky, sparkly, second skin.

She'd told me the music was going to be 'Deep House', specifically, whatever that meant. I quickly learned it wasn't really my thing, but I hadn't expected it would be, and at least Astrid seemed to enjoy it.

As usual, Astrid kept running into people she knew. We were dancing when a girl we had said hi to earlier came up to Astrid and whispered in her ear. She grabbed me by the wrist, and we all went into the bathroom, the three of us going into the same stall. I'd been to the toilet with Astrid before, but I wasn't sure how I felt about there being a third person watching…

'Ok so I've got enough for three,' her friend said. I'm sure Astrid had mentioned her name, but I didn't catch it, or couldn't remember. '10 each.'

'You got ten pounds, Mouse?'

'Umm yeah…' I pulled out my wallet and extracted a folded note, handing it to Astrid.

'There, that's us.' She passed it on to the friend, along with another ten pounds she pulled out of her bra.

'Cool, we'll use the back of my wallet.' She seemed to be inspecting the notes we gave her, before shaking her head. 'These won't do, hang on.' She put them in her wallet, a big flat thing, and pulled out another note that was flat. 'Ok here, hold this.'

She gave Astrid the wallet and pulled out a little bag of white powder. Only then did it dawn on me that we weren't going to the toilet, and I suddenly realised what was going on.

"Uh... I don't think... I...'

'It's ok, Mouse, you've got me.' she squeezed my hand and smiled.

The white powder was emptied onto the back of her wallet and the friend pulled out her ID and started to move it into three lines. Astrid went first. I tried not to look too shocked when she breathed the powder up her nose through a rolled note. I didn't want to be the boring, square person who refused to be involved, but this wasn't part of my plan. I was always told drugs were dangerous. But I realised, watching Astrid, it didn't feel dangerous. It felt... strangely exhilarating. Her friend went next. Then it was my turn. A rolled-up ten pound note in hand, I somehow just stopped thinking and went for it. I was expecting it to burn, or at least that I would feel the need to sneeze or something, but I felt nothing.

'You missed it. Try again,' the friend said.

I felt like an idiot, but Astrid reached out and rubbed me on the shoulder. And so I tried again, finally succeeding. It was an odd sensation but not too unpleasant.

Astrid hugged me.

'Come on, let's go,' she said as she unlocked the cubicle door and led me out by the hand. Her friend lingered in the stall, licking her wallet.

We went back to dancing and I don't know how much time had passed, but after a while the music started to sound sweeter, and breathing suddenly felt like a brand new sensation. I was distracted by breathing in deeply through my nose, the air rushing in, tinged with the smell of smoke machines. I suddenly appreciated the beauty of our relationship with trees that allowed this fantastic mechanism of breathing to take place. And I began to see the interconnectedness of humans. On the dancefloor, I got this rushing feeling creeping up on me, from somewhere behind my shoulders. The hair on my neck prickled and I shivered. I looked around for Astrid. She was leaning back against a wall beside me, arms crossed, smiling at me.

I grinned back.

She nodded slowly and handed me a glass of water and two pieces of gum. I didn't even notice her going to get them.

'You're cool, Little Mouse, you're cool,' she whispered in my ear.

And I *was* cool. I'd never felt cool before, but in that moment, I was. I was cool with what was going on and I felt cool – in the way that Astrid was cool.

Any drunken haze that had been hanging over me lifted and I felt lucid and aware.

And happy.

Pure happiness.

And we danced.

My feet just wanted to be moving. To the right. To the left. Shifting. Shifting. This way, then that. The lasers layered in the smoke and the people all moved as one. The beat of the music was in our legs, our chests, our hearts, our souls. The whole club stretched out in front of me. Everyone was smiling. It felt like we were all part of something big. Something bigger than us all. As people moved past me, complete strangers, I felt compelled to tell them how beautiful they were. And I did, without fear, without holding myself back. And they smiled and told me I was, too.

I don't know how long we danced, it could have been minutes or hours. I was even enjoying the music, feeling the beat mixing with my own heartbeat. Then she beckoned me to go outside with her. I didn't want to leave the dancefloor, but I didn't want to leave her either, so I followed, and we went and found the smoking area. We could still hear the music from inside spilling out and my body was moving to it. She lit two menthols and passed me one.

'Thank you,' I said as I took it. 'For everything. For this. For tonight. For every night. For every day. For saving me from myself. And everyone else. I don't know where I'd be without you. Thank you, thank you! I love you. I love you so much.'

I didn't care that I was gushing at her, I didn't want to hold back. I needed her to know how important she was, how much she meant to me and how much she had saved me. She smiled and cupped my cheek with her hand.

'It's a good night, Little Mouse. I'm glad we're here. Happy Halloween.'

'Astrid?'

'Yes?'

'Why do you call me Little Mouse?' I liked that I had a nickname, and it made me feel close to her, and special. But I had never asked about why she called me that.

'Oh, I didn't even think you might not know what it is – it's German. It's from the word 'Mauschen'. We use it for the ones we love and care about.'

I had always thought she'd called me that because I was mousy. Plain. But it was affectionate. I felt surrounded by love and full of hope and possibilities. All my worries had melted away. I was light, I was free.

We went back inside and danced some more. We danced by ourselves. We danced together. We danced with everybody else.

We walked home that night. We held hands all the way and she said she loved me too. When we got home, she poured us whisky. I asked her what the powder had been, and she said 'MDMA'. I didn't really know what that was, but I'd decided I liked it. I asked her if we could have it again, and she said yes, she would get us some more. We stayed up for hours listening to music, still in our costumes. She kept putting on songs that felt so perfect for the moment. From the groovy, moody 'Station to Station' – we always made sure to start and end with some Bowie – to singing along together to 'Psycho Killer' by Talking Heads, and I also think that was the night she introduced me to a Canadian band called The New Pornographers, who I grew to love. Each song she chose had some sort of significance.

We watched the sun rise from our living room window, the light creeping across the floor as we were still drinking at 7:30 a.m. We toasted the sun as it made its way up into the sky. That night, that morning, felt so removed from everyday life. I couldn't believe how carefree I felt. Or, in fact, *happy*. It wasn't a word I'd connected with very often, but I really felt it that night. When we finally went to bed, she crawled in with me and we slept until after midday. Then we woke up and dragged my duvet into the living room and spent the rest of the day watching movies on the sofa. We ended up ordering pizza and ate it while we watched ‘Labyrinth’, both quoting lines along with it. It was a perfect day to follow a perfect night. I felt tired but alive, and I carried that feeling through to the next weekend, and the next club.

Chapter 25

Amongst everything else that was happening, Astrid was still playing gigs regularly and I went along to them all. She had a regular mid-week spot at a café/bar not far from our house, playing from 7-10pm, just her and her acoustic guitar. I felt so special being part of her support crew. She would come and sit with me in her breaks, and when people came to talk to her after she played, congratulating her, and saying how amazing she had been, I was right there next to her. Sometimes I reviewed her gigs, otherwise I would just enjoy the evening without having to put words to the experience. I'd written a profile on her, which I'd sent to *The Relativity Cadenza*, incorporating gig review information with photos and just some general words about her. As always, I'd panicked that it wasn't what they'd want to print but was shocked and relieved when they'd happily published it. She'd been so excited about it and so grateful, showering me with praise I was sure I didn't deserve.

One evening while she was sitting working on something with her guitar, she came out with a bombshell.

'You know the gig next week?' she asked, making me look up from where I was sitting at the table doing some work.

'Yes, of course. I'll be there.'

'You're coming up to sing with me.'

I laughed at what was clearly a joke. But she wasn't laughing. Why wasn't she laughing?

'Wait, you're not... serious...?'

'Of course I am.'

'I'm not getting up there! Are you mad? I can't perform on stage. There's no way! I can't sing! And certainly not in front of people!'

'That's just fear talking. It's not real. Fear lies to you. Look, our whole lives are just one great performance,' she said, throwing her arms in the air. 'Every single day. A performance we never get to rehearse for but we each attempt to orchestrate. We're all our own Shakespeares. That's just life. But, my friend, will *your* performance be a comedy or tragedy?'

She paused and looked at me, and I wondered if I was supposed to answer. She was trying to distract me, I could tell.

'Oh, um...My life, you mean? Well, a comedy I suppose. I certainly don't want it to be a tragedy...' I didn't really know what she was asking.

'No, Little Mouse,' she said, and perhaps I should spell it *Maus* now since I know the reason for my nickname – I looked it up a few days later and it was there plainly: Maus [Mouse] or Mauschen [Little Mouse], are used in German as terms of endearment.

'It is both!' she continued. 'And everything in between! We wake up every day and we put on our costumes and we go out to see where the current scene is heading. Some people don't know how to act at all. They wear the same boring clothes every day and they say the same old boring lines. And they don't *want* to be the heroes of their own stories. But we do.

And, as our narratives interact, that's when it gets exciting. And it doesn't always go right, and it doesn't always go wrong. But here we are, trying to get in all our lines before the final curtain call.'

'Right, ok... So... That's great, but what does any of that mean...?'

'This is life, and it's your only one. Just get up and do it. One song. Three minutes. We'll do 'Zombie', just like we did that night walking home.'

My head was spinning. I tried to think of reasons why I couldn't do it. I knew that saying 'I'm scared' was not something that would convince Astrid to let me off the hook.

'What if I'm not any good?'

'Wouldn't matter, but I know you can sing so that's irrelevant.'

'Well, what if I freeze and can't sing?'

'Then you don't sing. But you'll forever regret it.'

'What if—'

'Your excuses bore me. We'll practise it lots so that you're prepared. You're doing it, and that's all there is to it. Just come up and sing with me. When have you ever felt unsafe with me, my Little Mouse?'

'Well... never. But—'

'No, we don't do buts. We just do. The risk is low, you're doing it.'

It didn't sound like I had much of an option. I was terrified, but I couldn't deny that there was a tiny part of me that wanted to be that person on stage – that wanted to be there next to Astrid, *my* Astrid, singing by her side. The thought gave me chills and sweats in equal measure. Could I allow myself to do it? Would Astrid allow me not to?

That week, I came up with so many reasons why I shouldn't do it, but when I spoke them out loud, they all seemed silly. She was so good with me. She was so loving and supportive and patient, and just like she promised, we practiced a lot. I had this complete feeling of dread about the whole thing, and I felt slightly ill every morning when I woke up, knowing what was ahead of me. It would be so much easier just not to do it. Then no one would hear me and decide I was bad. No one would wonder why the hell I was up there. No one would scoff at the fact I dared to think myself worthy of being onstage. No one would decide they never wanted to see me again after hearing me ruin the show. And most importantly, then Astrid wouldn't realise how bad I really am, and that she'd made a horrible mistake.

I flipped between moments of being excited and maybe even a little bit confident – when she and I practiced, it sounded quite good – and moments when I played over and over in my head the images of my inevitable failure.

I even called you to talk it through. I had no idea what I wanted you to say. I think I was hoping you'd tell me not to do it, give me some sort of way out. You were certainly surprised; I'd never talked about singing before and I don't think you really understood why I would be joining Astrid onstage. But you said it probably wasn't a big deal and that if Astrid wanted me to sing, then I must be ok. When I suggested that maybe she was just doing it to be nice, you'd replied that you didn't think Astrid ever did anything 'just to be nice'. I hated when you spoke about her like that, you often said things that didn't feel true – that she was using me, that she wasn't genuine, that she only cared about herself, and the one that scared me the most: that she would cast me aside as soon as I was no longer of use to her. But you didn't know her like I did and somehow, that chat with you gave me more resolve to actually do it.

The morning of the gig, I was a bundle of nerves. I woke up early and eventually decided I wanted a coffee. She was already downstairs, tinkling on her guitar.

'Just black for me please,' she called out. 'No dairy on the morning of a gig, it ruins my voice.'

I thought I'd better do that too, but it turned out I hate black coffee so I put a generous dash of milk in my cup. She watched me dithering about probably looking stressed, and she laughed.

'My darling, come here.' She held her arms out to me and I put down my coffee cup and went over to her. She bundled me up tightly in a hug. 'You're cute when you're nervous.'

I gave her a half smile.

'These are such low stakes. You can do this. It's going to be so nice for us to sing together! This is going to be such a beautiful moment. I can't even begin to tell you how excited I am! I'm so used to playing the same old songs, but it's going to be so amazing to have you up there with me for our special song. You just need to get out of your own way. All your fears are in your head. I want you there more than anything, and the audience will love it. I'm sure you'll enjoy it once you're there, and that's all there is.'

My shoulders dropped just a little and my breathing slowed. I was so caught up in my own nerves, I hadn't stopped to think about how nice the moment could be, and how it was about more than just me.

'Right. Now, remember that moment when you felt you should never sing again? When the teacher told you to sit down and not sing the harmony?'

'Yeah...'

'Did you like that teacher?'

'No, not at all.'

'Then fuck her, this is your chance to prove her wrong! And...' she continued, more gently. 'I'm guessing you haven't been onstage since you last danced, have you?'

Oh. No, I hadn't. Of course I hadn't. I shook my head.

'I think it's time we made a better memory to override those two, don't you? The shame caused by the teacher and the sadness caused by your injury... They shouldn't be your last memories of performing. We can do so much better.'

I hadn't linked it all together, but she was so right. I realised there was part of me that was scared that if I performed, something bad would happen. Not just that I'd be laughed offstage for not being able to sing, though that was certainly there and felt very real, but something deeper. That by opening that side of me, I would hurt myself, somehow. *Damage* myself. Even though I knew that was ridiculous in theory, my body was holding on to something so much more than shame, it was a deep fear that everything would go wrong, that my life as I knew it would end. It felt huge to realise that, and somehow also a relief.

'Thank you,' I said as I held onto her and hugged her tightly, feeling tears welling up in my eyes. 'Thank you.'

'You've totally got this. And you won't be alone. It's going to be so much fun!'

I managed a smile. I could do this. I was going to do it. *Come on, Jess.*

The venue was a small bar in town. I'd been there so many times before to see her play, so I knew the layout, which helped with my nerves. We got there early, but the place was already filled with about 50 people. I actually felt excited. I reminded myself that this was the year of Astrid and Jess. I could be bigger, better – fantastic, even – with Astrid by my side.

Her set was amazing – she played some new songs I hadn't even heard before. She'd said that regular Wednesday night slot was a great playground for testing out new ideas. I didn't know how she did it, but every time she played, she pulled out something new – something more amazing than the last time. She spent her breaks between sets reassuring me that everything was ok. It was getting near the end of her final set when she asked me to join her onstage. I'd been so transfixed by her performance that I'd somehow complete forgotten that I should be stressed and anxious. When she called my name, I just went up towards her. She was smiling at me, and she put a hand out to squeeze my shoulder when I reached her. Then she announced into the microphone, 'This is my girl, Jess. You all know her, you all love her, so give it up for her vocal debut!'

I'll always remember that.

We shared a mic. We stood so close on either side of it, her guitar taking up one side, with me fitting in around it. Standing across from each other, I could feel her breath on my face.

She started playing the chords, then started singing and I joined in. I started tentatively at first, trying to hear my voice coming back to me through the speakers, which was a strange feeling. I listened carefully, trying to make sure I was singing in tune. We sang together, then when it got to the next part, she went to a harmony, like we'd practiced, and I stayed singing the tune. I was singing. I was actually singing.

And in front of people, no less. I didn't stop to take it in, I just kept my eyes on her and kept going. In hindsight, I wished I'd been able to enjoy it more as the moments seemed to slip away while I held on tight to my resolve. When we came to the end, I almost didn't want it to finish. People were clapping and cheering as Astrid played the last chord. She smiled at me with so much warmth that I felt like I was floating. Then she hugged me over her guitar.

I returned to my seat in a daze. As she finished her last couple of songs, I sat in the audience grinning and wondering how on earth I'd done it. But I knew that Astrid was how I'd done it. She was the whole reason I could. So many people congratulated me after. They were amazed it was my first time getting up there singing.

'You're so brave,' some of them told me, 'I couldn't do it.'

And I thought they probably could, if they'd practiced like we had, and had Astrid as a guide. I wasn't special, if *I* could do it, anyone could. And for a moment, I understood Astrid's annoyance at people saying she was 'talented'. It was work that got me there; practicing the notes over and over with my patient friend, but also a constant struggle with my terrified brain that didn't want to let me do it. I didn't want to be used as an excuse for why others couldn't do something similar, like I was *the type of person* who could, and they weren't. It amazed me to think I'd crossed over to Astrid's side of the fence in some small way. She'd made me special.

As we left, Astrid went to the bartender and came back with an envelope. I'd seen her picking them up before but hadn't really thought about why. She opened it and handed me a £20 note.

'Your cut,' she said with a smile.

‘Oh, wow, thank you!’ I hadn’t realised she got paid for her gigs, how cool to get given money for something she loved doing.

I was on such a high for days after. I wish you’d been there to see it because when I talked to you later, I don’t think you realised how amazing it had been. But I knew.

Chapter 26

As the temperature was dropping and November moved towards its end, autumn still seemed to be hanging onto a semblance of warmth long past when I thought it would. I was getting my usual winter conversations ready – about how cold it had become, about pulling out my winter coat from the back of the cupboard, but Astrid pointed out, that the chill hadn't set in yet.

'Oh,' I'd said when she mentioned it, realising that she was right. 'Yeah actually, that's true. Wow, that's abnormal for this time of year!'

'Not really,' she'd replied. 'The run down to Christmas often isn't that cold here. It's the Jan-Feb you've got to watch out for. Very dark, very grey. But alas, we're not there yet!'

And to signify that, we'd all gone to the park on the Friday after the gig, as it happened to be a particularly sunny afternoon. We all had jumpers and coats and blankets, but the sun made it still just warm enough to sit outside, though we did our best to stay in the sun. We'd spread blankets and towels out on the ground to sit on and everyone brought stuff for a picnic. I think we were celebrating something. There seemed to be celebrations wherever I looked those days. Astrid once told me that life itself was a cause for celebration and I'd laughed, but it certainly felt like it at that time.

It was that afternoon that I saw Chris again, when he turned up with a few friends. I didn't realise he was coming. I hadn't seen him for a few weeks – not since that night. We'd already accumulated a few empty bottles of wine by the time he arrived, and I was feeling bold. He waved at Astrid but came and sat down next to me.

'Hey, you,' he said as he opened his beer using a contraption on his keyring. Voices swirled around us as the others continued to talk.

'Well, hello,' I replied with a smile.

'So, what's been up, party girl?'

'Am I?' I asked, feeling like I was blushing.

'Only if you wanna be...' he said with a sly smile.

To be fair, I couldn't really fault that assessment, as I went on to tell him about the Halloween party we'd been to, though I left out the bit about taking drugs, I wasn't sure that was something I should talk openly about.

'What did you go as?' he asked.

'Just as a cat.' I replied.

'Bet you looked cute.'

'Oh, not really,' I said, feeling uncomfortable with the compliment. 'Astrid looked amazing though, you should have seen her – she dressed as Bowie.'

Then I went on to tell him about the gig, about how I'd got up and sung with Astrid. I talked about how mad the whole thing had been but how I'd found myself enjoying it in the end.

'Hey, where was my invite?' he said, putting his hands on his hips in mock anger. I laughed, but he continued. 'No, seriously, I would've loved to have been there.'

'Oh, don't worry, it wasn't much, we just did one song. I mean, Astrid was amazing though, she did three sets. She did this new song she'd written, and it was so—

'No, I want to hear about your bit. What did you sing?'

'Oh, ok... we did 'Zombie' by the Cranberries.'

'Nice! I love that song. It's one of my mum's favourites.'

'Mine too,' I said, for some reason, though I don't think it was necessarily true.

I have a memory of people playing games around us, throwing a frisbee maybe. But the more we talked, and the more I drank, the less I noticed anyone else.

'What about you?' I asked. 'What have you been up to?'

'Not much, nothing like you, superstar. Just working, mainly. I went to visit my parents for a bit, got some of mum's cooking to keep me going.'

'You said she was Italian?'

'Yeah, very much. She and Dad came here when they were in their 20s. They still mostly speak Italian together.'

'Wow! And do you speak it too?'

'Bits and pieces. I can understand more than I can speak.'

'Have you ever been to Italy?' I asked.

'Yeah, a few times. My grandparents are still there. They speak practically no English, so that's always a fun game of charades. But they're great.'

'Wow, I would really love to go to Italy.'

'You've never been?' he asked, taking a swig of his beer.

"No... no, I haven't travelled as much as I might like...'

The sun went down and eventually people started leaving. Somehow, it ended up being just the two of us left there. I was quite drunk by that stage. Astrid had gone off with a few of the others in search of a party but for some reason we stayed.

'Don't stay out too late...' she'd said, with a wiggle of her finger, as she went off.

I wondered whether that was meant to be a warning, a reminder to behave. I knew how important respect was to her, and even though she didn't seem to like you all that much, it would obviously be incredibly disrespectful for me to go and get involved with someone else. I had no intention of anything happening anyway. We were just enjoying chatting. That was harmless.

But as it got colder, we seemed to be sitting closer, until our legs were touching. I felt the warmth of his leg against mine so acutely, like it was the only thing that existed in the whole world. Then his arm was against mine too, and it seemed like we were pressed up against each other. Then as we were talking, his head got so close to mine and I could only focus on his face, his lips. It was as if I was being pulled in by some invisible force – his body was calling mine towards it.

We kissed.

We did.

It happened.

All the tension seemed to melt away. The world was swirling around us with just the two of us in the centre. I forgot everything I was supposed to be, and I was just there in that moment. I'd read about moments like this in books: storms could have raged around us, with rain falling and lightning strikes filling the sky, but I wouldn't have noticed.

I'd never kissed anyone other than you before that moment, but this felt electric. It felt as if every part of me was tingling, and my lips ached for his.

Chris walked me home, nearly all the way to The Den. I had objected, of course, not wanting to take him out of his way, but he'd insisted. We walked, linking arms, until the point where we parted ways as he hurried off to get on a night bus to avoid having to wait another hour. He checked that I was ok to walk the last couple of blocks on my own, and I nodded, certain that I could do anything in that moment.

Then, as I went to walk away, he reached out and grabbed my hand, pulling me back to him before kissing me again, his hands buried in my hair. He then ran for the bus stop, turning around to wave at me one last time.

It had got so cold by that stage but as I walked home, I'd hardly realised. I was on such a high from the perfect evening we'd shared, I felt like a different person, all light and carefree. When I got home from the park, Astrid was still out, and it started to dawn on me what I had done. I paced around the house, trying to make sense of everything. Back and forth and back and forth. Eventually I went to bed. I was still buzzing but below the surface was this growing feeling of dread.

The next day, the guilt hit me properly. I couldn't believe what I had done. It felt like such a terrible, drunken decision. I was pathetic, I had no self-control. A few drinks and suddenly all my values had disappeared. I'd given in to the first person who showed me any attention. What was wrong with me? I had everything sorted. I had my relationship, my life was on track. It was meant to be you and me forever, why was I jeopardising that? I felt remorse, I promise. So much of it. I knew then that it would have to stay a secret and never EVER happen again. I wouldn't even tell Astrid; I couldn't handle her disappointment.

I'd tossed and turned through the night. Astrid didn't come home until early; 9:23 a.m. I heard her come through the front door but I wasn't sure I could face any questions about my night, so I stayed in my room a while longer, pretending to sleep. I eventually decided to push it all to the back of my mind and pretend nothing had happened. Fine, I could do that. I just had one thing niggling at me – I worried Chris might say something, and I went around in circles wondering if I should text him. In the end I did. I typed and re-typed the message so many times, nothing seemed right. But I sent it anyway.

Hi, hope you're feeling ok this morning. Do you mind if we don't tell anyone about last night? I just think it would be best, if that's ok xx

I put two xx's at the end, thinking it would soften the blow. Then after I sent it, I wondered why the hell I'd added them.

The response came almost immediately:

On it, 99. X

It took me a moment to decipher that, until I remembered that old show I'd watched a few times when I'd got home from school – Get Smart. It made me giggle, which helped to diffuse some of my stress around the whole thing. And indeed, I have to admit that part of me did feel like a spy, hiding the truth from the world and pretending to blend in like nothing had happened. But most of me felt terrible. I was such a failure. It was a silly mistake, it meant nothing, it would not happen again. In fact, nothing had happened in the first place.

Chapter 27

The night I discovered trance music, it felt like everything changed.

It was a 'gig' night as opposed to a club night, which meant an act was DJing rather than one of the club's resident DJs. I didn't really understand this whole new electronic music world, but Astrid said they were decent. Apparently Chris had told her we should go. I'd been trying to avoid him, but I couldn't really say I didn't want to go or she'd know something was up. And surely it would be fine. The kiss had happened, it was done, and it was all over. I knew not to let it happen again.

I'd felt slightly distant from her, knowing that I was keeping such a big secret. I didn't like it, but I wasn't sure how to pretend everything was ok if I said it out loud. Sometimes I thought it might burst out of me as we sat in the living room together, her working on a new song, me reading or finishing an assignment. I kept trying to take myself out of the room in those moments, but I was sure she sensed something was off.

Astrid handed me a capsule of MD before we went into the club. It was one that she'd made herself after grinding up crystals of the stuff into powder with the bottom of a glass at our dining table. I'd watched her acquire it earlier that day, going out and getting into a random car, before coming back with a small package. I don't know how she did things like that, just launching herself into the unknown...

She'd put the remaining caps in her shoe to get through the security at the door. She smiled so sweetly at the security guards, but they weren't going to stop her anyway.

I *felt* the music as soon as we entered, it grabbed my attention in a way it hadn't on any of the other nights we'd gone to a club.

'Who's this?' I asked her in a rush.

'Oh, it's just the support. The main isn't on for a bit. Let's go have a smoke and get a water.'

I wanted to stay and listen, but I followed her out. Chris was already there in the smoking area with a couple of people. He was standing next to a beautiful girl, and they were laughing together. I felt something when I saw him, but I pushed it down.

We all greeted each other with hugs and kisses. I felt like Chris hugged me for longer than he did the others but then I decided I was probably reading too much into it. He told me that the headline act was his favourite – they were called 'Above and Beyond'. I'd never heard of them, but I told him I'd liked the music that was playing when we came in.

'Oh yeah, he's great too. He's on one of Above and Beyond's labels. They have two – the Trance one is their main, but they also have more of a Deep House one too.'

I nodded, pretending I was following. But mostly I was just coming up as the drugs kicked in and I was distracted by the deep pools of his blue eyes in front of me and the way his cheeks moved when he talked. I also wanted to dance. Everyone looked so pretty, like they were sparkling.

Eventually we went back inside – though not quickly enough – and got to the dance floor. Astrid gave me my two pieces of gum and another water, and we started to dance. Left-right-left-right, shifting, shifting, side to side. I closed my eyes. It was perfect.

I could tell when the main act came on, the whole vibe shifted. Above and Beyond's music was melodic, it was beat driven, it ebbed and flowed. The music built up and built up and built up until I felt like I might explode, and then the whole thing sort of dropped, coming at me in a rush and completely taking me over. My body moved without me telling it to. It felt like I was being lifted up and up and up.

So this was 'trance' music. *Trance.* I didn't think the name sounded fitting. I thought 'trance' would be more like the music we usually heard, which Astrid told me was 'house' – the repetitive stuff that never changed, all on one level, less ups and downs. I could picture that putting you into a trance. But this was something else. I thought I was going to take off from the ground and fly, I felt so free, so light. What were any of these names anyway? House? Trance? They meant nothing. Did they mean something to other people? Had I just thought them so many times in a row that they had lost all meaning? But then again what did any of it mean? Rock music? Pop music? No, they made sense, they were shortened from longer terms. I was buzzing. Astrid brought me more water and we danced, and we danced, and we danced.

I couldn't help myself – I looked over at Chris. He was looking at me. He moved closer, weaving around a couple of people to get next to me. Everything felt so big, so real. He took my hand and mouthed the lyrics to me, along with the song.

Then the music took off and soared above us. And we kissed. Again. Right there, in the middle of the dance floor. And in that moment, I didn't care who saw. I didn't think of consequences, the two of us melting together was all that mattered.

I didn't want the night to end. I was so high on the music, the love (and the drugs). The audience exploded at their final song – jumping and singing and surging – and I wasn't ready for it to be over.

Chris was next to me when the lights came up, but I couldn't see Astrid anywhere. I thought she would have told me if she was leaving. Maybe she'd met someone and gone home with them. I didn't care. I was still moving, still grinning, still flying high. It felt like such a different experience from the last time I'd lost her. How could I panic when I was feeling so good?

Chris followed me around the club as I tried to find Astrid, everything looking so different under the house lights, but it soon became apparent we wouldn't find her.

'You can come back to mine if you like, I've got drinks and we can listen to more music,' he said.

'Trance music?'

'Yes. This is my music, you know.'

'Yes. Take me. I need more!'

We ran into one of his friends as we were leaving and we all decided to split a taxi, since they lived near each other. I was usually terrified of taxis – trying to flag one, telling them where to take me, trusting a strange man in a car to get me home and not rape me, not knowing whether to make small talk or be silent, to sit in the front or the back... But that night I wasn't. I was cool.

Chris sat in the middle, with me on his right. He was sitting so close I could feel the warmth of his body next to mine. His jacket was open and the zipper was resting on my leg. The lines where he ended and I began were blurred with the weight of that zipper. My heart thumped so loudly that I wondered if the others could hear it. I could even faintly smell him. It was a scent I hadn't realised was familiar. It felt like lifetimes ago that we'd met, and I'd first told him nothing would happen between us. But as my eyes traced the slender curve of his wrist poking out from the bottom of his shirt cuff, I doubted every word I'd ever said. I tried to think of you but, in that moment, I couldn't even picture your face. You were slipping away from me.

The taxi dropped us off at his friend's place because it was closest and therefore cheapest. He linked his arm with mine as we got out of the taxi, waving goodbye to his friend. As we walked to his house, I found it hard to think about much more than his arm being wrapped around mine, holding it against his body. By the time we'd arrived my arm felt like it belonged in his.

He unlocked the door as I waited behind him, feeling the cold and the momentary distance between us that I wanted so badly to close. We went to his room, and he said to lie on his bed. I must have hesitated a moment, unsure what lying on his bed might mean, but he explained he'd lined up speakers underneath the bed and to get the full experience, it's where I needed to be. Satisfied with the answer, I sat down on the side of the bed, took my shoes off, then swung my feet up and made myself as comfortable as I could in a situation that felt very nearly out of control.

'I have just the song for you,' he said. He was looking

through his phone to find it, which was hooked up to his sound system.

'Is that so.'

'Yep, it will actually blow your mind.'

I wasn't sure my mind could be any more blown, but I felt alive with the knowledge that he was playing a song he'd thought of just for me.

'It's a bootleg of a song you might know.'

'What's a bootleg?' I asked, the situation, the drugs, the music making me bolder than I usually would be, and apparently happy to admit that I didn't know what was going on.

'Oh, it's like an unofficial recording I guess, though I'm not sure how far that term stretches. But for the purposes of our listening, it's just a remix.'

The song started and he came to join me, lying next to me on the bed. I got that unmistakeable familiar feeling of nothing else in the world existing. But also vying for my attention was the music. The speakers under his bed meant that when the music played, it surrounded and engulfed us. I felt it in my chest again, like I had at the club, and I couldn't tell the beat of the music apart from my own heart beating.

I didn't think I recognised the song; its intro was long and repetitive and I found myself getting bored with it. But then the singing started, and I realised it was a remix of a Massive Attack song. No, a bootleg. It sounded nice enough, but nothing like what we'd been listening to earlier.

'Close your eyes,' he said.

And I did. I lay there, side by side with him on his bed, my eyes closed. I tried to concentrate on the music and not the fact that his arm was touching mine. Until suddenly, I no longer had to try. After the verse, it all changed. The timing, the music, the feeling – it had that same building quality that I'd heard earlier in the night. The music was all around me. It was holding me, moving me, lifting me – I had goosebumps all over my body. I hadn't been sure I'd feel that again – the way I had felt on the dancefloor that night. But here, in his room, only the music and I existed, and I didn't even mind. Even Chris had dropped out of my consciousness.

It felt like the world was ending. Or maybe just that it would be ok if it did. I was being lifted out of my body and I was flying. It was the feeling of coming up again on MD, but I wasn't. The effects of my earlier caps had mellowed into a happy buzz. But this music was taking me somewhere else. I felt like I could suddenly understand the world. I felt so big and expansive, and so connected to everything. How had I lived grounded for so long?

When the song ended, I opened my eyes and saw he was propped up on his elbow, looking at me and smiling.

'You see?' he said.

I couldn't find the words to encapsulate any of the feelings I had just experienced, so I only nodded.

'More?' he asked.

'Yes, please,' my voice sounded breathless.

He put a song on that we'd heard earlier in the night. 'Stealing Time,' he said it was called.

It had started raining outside. I could see drops falling against the window. We just lay there in silence, listening to the music and each other's breath.

At some point, my fingers absentmindedly found their way to a necklace he was wearing that I hadn't noticed before. I twirled it in my fingers.

'What's this?' I asked him.

'It's a necklace.'

'I know, but what is it? Where did it come from?'

'A girl gave it to me.'

'What girl?'

'Just a girl who I loved.'

'Oh? Where is she?'

'She's in London.'

'Why aren't you together?'

'Our lives went in different ways. She didn't want to stay.'

'But you were together?'

'Yeah, for a couple of years. I loved her and I think she loved me but... some things just weren't meant to be.'

'What was her name?'

'Cassie.'

'Nice name.'

'Yeah...' He reached over with his hand and started playing with my hair. 'I've moved on... I've been with other girls, had other girlfriends since then. I think part of me will always love her though.'

I didn't know why he was justifying himself to me, but it was cute.

'Why do you still wear it?

'I suppose it's a reminder to not let myself get hurt again.'

He moved to sit up against the headboard of his bed and I shifted so that I had my head on his chest. I don't know if it was the remaining drugs in my system, or the music, or something else, but I just wanted to be close to him. I needed to feel a connection – our bodies touching.

'Your heart is racing,' I said, feeling it through his chest.

'I've got a hot girl lying on me. What did you expect?'

'Is mine?' I asked.

He put his hand on my chest. It felt heavy pressing against me, and strangely intimate.

'Yes,' he whispered.

And just as we had before, again we kissed. I couldn't stop it, I couldn't deny how desperately I wanted it, needed it. No, we didn't have sex. But I think perhaps I wanted to. I felt everything so strongly that night. It was overwhelming. I'd become so good at pushing my feelings down that when I let go, it all hit me with a rush. I kept feeling like I was coming up all over again, but I wasn't. I guess this was a sort of happiness.

The next morning, he cooked me breakfast. I didn't feel like eating it, but I did anyway. I didn't want to be rude.

'I wonder what everyone would have thought?' he asked me as he took a bite of his bacon.

'What everyone thought of what?'

'Of the kiss.'

'What kiss?'

'The one we had on the dance floor.'

I couldn't quite put it together.

'What do you mean... wait... Oh my God, we did, didn't we. Do you think everyone saw? Do you think Astrid saw?'

'Um... I guess so. I don't know, they were probably more interested in whatever they had going on, but I would've thought someone might see. We were hardly discreet.'

My heart started to race and I struggled to hold my breath steady. I didn't know she'd seen. Of course she'd left. She must have been so disappointed in me. The reality of the situation dragged my elation back to earth. What had I been thinking? Kissing someone else on the dance floor. Right out there in the open like I didn't care for anyone. Now Astrid knew. Who else knew? I tried to work out if anyone you knew might have been out that night. It seemed unlikely but my brain quickly made some tenuous links that were enough to convince me I had to do something.

'Take me home. Please.' I said to him, an urgency in my voice.

'What, now?'

I hadn't even finished half of my breakfast.

'Yes.'

'Ok...'

I had no idea if he was safe to drive but I needed to get home. I needed to do some damage control as quickly as possible.

Astrid wasn't home. She didn't get home until much later that evening. I'd had to go to bed because I was so exhausted. I would face her when I was rested and feeling stronger.

Chapter 28

I made the inevitable trip home for Christmas. I wanted you to come back, obviously. I desperately wanted to see you – I wanted a reminder of you, of us, of what we were together. But you'd decided to stay in America and spend Christmas with your uncle, leaving me to brave my family. It was fine, but I felt guilty for not enjoying it more. For not making the most of the time with my parents, for regressing back into a fifteen-year-old as soon as I stepped foot back in that bedroom, for not trying harder to make it easier for my parents.

But I have to admit, no matter how much I wish it wasn't the case, mostly, I was thinking about Chris. We texted constantly. He, at his family home with his huge Italian family, and me alone, rattling around my parent's house.

And I missed Astrid. We weren't really text-friends, so we didn't message much when we were apart. I felt the absence of her in my life so heavily while I was surrounded by my parent's floral-patterned sofa, lace curtains and Emily's ballet shoes. I felt so far from the life I'd carved out for myself, and my mind played tricks on me, assuring me I had made it all up and none of it existed.

Astrid and I had set up a tree in the flat in the weeks before we'd both left for our respective family Christmas, decorating it together while drinking mulled wine, and singing along to songs like 'Do They Know It's Christmas' by Band Aid, and Paul McCartney's 'Wonderful Christmastime'. We'd had our own little Christmas celebration too, exchanging presents. There were also two extra presents that had appeared under the Christmas tree too, with a tag saying they were from *Santa Claus*, though with the German name for him which I loved, though I can't for the life of me remember what it was. Inside them were two mugs: mine had a gold J on the front, hers an A.

You and I had kept talking, of course, occasionally with phone calls and more often with emails, but life kept getting in the way – for both of us, I think. Speaking to you for the first time after I'd kissed Chris made me feel terrible. I wondered if you could guess what had happened in the words I didn't say, if you could sense it through the phone. But over time it became apparent that I'd got away with it, and it started to bother me less. In a way, it made me feel stronger, more powerful. I had a newfound confidence in myself. I hadn't really done anything too wrong, and we were apart anyway. Who knew what you were doing that I didn't know about. I needed to think about myself for a while – you were the one who left after all.

Astrid had gone back to Germany for Christmas, though she hadn't wanted to. She said Christmases were always tense, her parents requiring them all to pretend they were a big happy family while the grandparents visited, but she said the inauthenticity didn't sit well with her. We were both happy to be back in our flat together once the new year had turned.

I wrote on my list of new year's resolutions to stop seeing

Chris, but I broke it almost as soon as I'd written it. He and I existed together mostly after midnight, in the lights and smoky haze of a club, or back at his after being out. Part of me would like to say that nothing more happened between us. But only part of me.

I'd been wanting it for some time. I'm sorry, but I just couldn't help myself. He was everything I couldn't have, and it made me want him more. I saw him soon after the Christmas holidays ended and was standing in his room after we'd been at a club. Astrid had gone off earlier with someone called 'Joe', though when she said his name, it sounded more like 'jaw', an affectation of her remaining German accent. Reminders of English being her second language came out in the sweetest of places, like how she said she 'can't be asked' to do something rather than the much more boring 'can't be arsed'. As she was leaving, she'd asked if I'd be ok, and I was able to smile at her, nod, and say that Chris would look after me. We made our pilgrimage back to his flat.

He'd put some trance music on, and I was standing looking out the window while he went to get us a drink of some sort. He came in and put the drinks down on the bedside table and I noticed after a while that he was looking at me. He had an odd look on his face, sort of sad.

'What is it?' I asked him.

'You don't like me, do you?' he said.

'That's not true.'

'Ok, well, you don't like me *like that.*' He closed the distance between us and put his hands on my arms, the feeling of his skin on mine making me. 'Not like I like you.'

'No, I—'

'It's fine. I get it. I know I'm not good enough for you.'

Not good enough for... me? It felt like I was in some parallel universe. I wasn't too good for anyone.

'I—'

'Don't. I don't want to hear it. I'll get over it.'

I don't think I'd really thought about him liking me, not seriously. I thought I was just a bit of fun to him, just someone to pass some time with. I put my hands up on his chest, the fabric of his shirt pooling under my fingers.

'I do like you!'

He wouldn't look at me, his eyes were moving left and right.

'I think... if anything... I like you too much!' I blurted out. 'More than I should.'

He looked at me and we just stood there staring into each other's eyes, our breath hanging between us. Shivers ran down my back and over my arms. In that moment, anything felt possible.

Then his hands were on my face, in my hair, he pushed me backwards and as my back hit the wall, his lips found mine. Everything else faded away, just like it had in the park, that first time. I needed this; I needed him. No matter how much my mind was used to reminding me he wasn't what I wanted, my body felt empty without him. He kissed down my neck, and it was as if my skin was on fire where he touched me. I moaned. He bit my neck.

He pulled his head away and pushed on my shoulders, so I was held harder against the wall, passion raging in his eyes, an immediacy to his actions that encompassed me. It felt like we had to be together, needed to, as if the universe required it. He looked at me as if trying to work out what he would do with me.

Not being able to stand the tension anymore, I surprised

myself by uttering: 'I want you.' Then, as if coming out of nowhere, 'Do what you want with me. I'm yours.' And from somewhere inside me, a feeling arose until I gave into it – I bit him. Hard, on the shoulder. It felt like my own Astrid moment – seeing how he would react, tempting him, wondering what he would do. I felt so in control, even though what I really wanted was for him to control me and have his way with me; to use me, to hurt me, to dominate me. I knew I could trust him; I knew I was safe, but I wanted to really feel something.

He looked at me, a stunned look on his face, then said 'ouch,' followed by 'you cheeky thing,' which reassured me I hadn't gone too far. He kissed me even more passionately, before pushing me sideways, where I crashed down onto his bed. I didn't have more than a moment before he was on top of me, his weight holding me down. He ran his hands up my stomach and I flinched from the feeling of hands on my skin. Before I realised it, he'd swept my top up and used it to pin my arms above my head. I was suddenly very aware that I hadn't worn a bra, which was very unlike me, and my chest was suddenly exposed to him. I couldn't touch him, but I wanted to, and it drove my need for him into a frenzy. I squirmed to get my hands free so I could pull him into me.

He was looking down at me, a wild look on his face. I'd never been more attracted to him than I was in that moment. He leant down to kiss my right nipple, tracing around it with his tongue, before biting it gently. I'd never felt something so sensitive, it coursed right through my body, making me tingle between my legs, and I let out a soft, breathless moan. The feeling caught me off-guard.

He let go of the shirt holding me down, but put his weight on my upper arms so I still couldn't move. His knee was between my legs, and I squirmed to get closer to him, to get some sort of contact. I needed him. He kissed me, hard, fast, desperately. My heart was racing. His hands closed gently around my neck, and I felt the power he had over me, completely at his mercy. I heard myself mumble 'more,' before pulling my arms free – which I realised I could do easily, if I really tried. I dug my fingernails into his back, trying to leave proof that I had been there. My body ached for him until finally, it got what it wanted.

Chapter 29

I made the inevitable trip home for Christmas. I wanted you to come back, obviously. I desperately wanted to see you – I wanted a reminder of you, of us, of what we were together. But you'd decided to stay in America and spend Christmas with your uncle, leaving me to brave my family. It was fine, but I felt guilty for not enjoying it more. For not making the most of the time with my parents, for regressing back into a fifteen-year-old as soon as I stepped foot back in that bedroom, for not trying harder to make it easier for my parents.

But I have to admit, no matter how much I wish it wasn't the case, mostly, I was thinking about Chris. We texted constantly. He, at his family home with his huge Italian family, and me alone, rattling around my parent's house.

And I missed Astrid. We weren't really text-friends, so we didn't message much when we were apart. I felt the absence of her in my life so heavily while I was surrounded by my parent's floral-patterned sofa, lace curtains and Emily's ballet shoes. I felt so far from the life I'd carved out for myself, and my mind played tricks on me, assuring me I had made it all up and none of it existed.

Astrid and I had set up a tree in the flat in the weeks before we'd both left for our respective family Christmas, decorating it together while drinking mulled wine, and singing along to songs like 'Do They Know It's Christmas' by Band Aid, and Paul McCartney's 'Wonderful Christmastime'. We'd had our own little Christmas celebration too, exchanging presents. There were also two extra presents that had appeared under the Christmas tree too, with a tag saying they were from *Santa Claus*, though with the German name for him which I loved, though I can't for the life of me remember what it was. Inside them were two mugs: mine had a gold J on the front, hers an A.

You and I had kept talking, of course, occasionally with phone calls and more often with emails, but life kept getting in the way – for both of us, I think. Speaking to you for the first time after I'd kissed Chris made me feel terrible. I wondered if you could guess what had happened in the words I didn't say, if you could sense it through the phone. But over time it became apparent that I'd got away with it, and it started to bother me less. In a way, it made me feel stronger, more powerful. I had a newfound confidence in myself. I hadn't really done anything too wrong, and we were apart anyway. Who knew what you were doing that I didn't know about. I needed to think about myself for a while – you were the one who left after all.

Astrid had gone back to Germany for Christmas, though she hadn't wanted to. She said Christmases were always tense, her parents requiring them all to pretend they were a big happy family while the grandparents visited, but she said the inauthenticity didn't sit well with her. We were both happy to be back in our flat together once the new year had turned.

I wrote on my list of new year's resolutions to stop seeing

Chris, but I broke it almost as soon as I'd written it. He and I existed together mostly after midnight, in the lights and smoky haze of a club, or back at his after being out. Part of me would like to say that nothing more happened between us. But only part of me.

I'd been wanting it for some time. I'm sorry, but I just couldn't help myself. He was everything I couldn't have, and it made me want him more. I saw him soon after the Christmas holidays ended and was standing in his room after we'd been at a club. Astrid had gone off earlier with someone called 'Joe', though when she said his name, it sounded more like 'jaw', an affectation of her remaining German accent. Reminders of English being her second language came out in the sweetest of places, like how she said she 'can't be asked' to do something rather than the much more boring 'can't be arsed'. As she was leaving, she'd asked if I'd be ok, and I was able to smile at her, nod, and say that Chris would look after me. We made our pilgrimage back to his flat.

He'd put some trance music on, and I was standing looking out the window while he went to get us a drink of some sort. He came in and put the drinks down on the bedside table and I noticed after a while that he was looking at me. He had an odd look on his face, sort of sad.

'What is it?' I asked him.

'You don't like me, do you?' he said.

'That's not true.'

'Ok, well, you don't like me *like that*.' He closed the distance between us and put his hands on my arms, the feeling of his skin on mine making me. 'Not like I like you.'

'No, I—'

'It's fine. I get it. I know I'm not good enough for you.'

Not good enough for... me? It felt like I was in some parallel universe. I wasn't too good for anyone.

'I—'

'Don't. I don't want to hear it. I'll get over it.'

I don't think I'd really thought about him liking me, not seriously. I thought I was just a bit of fun to him, just someone to pass some time with. I put my hands up on his chest, the fabric of his shirt pooling under my fingers.

'I do like you!'

He wouldn't look at me, his eyes were moving left and right.

'I think... if anything... I like you too much!' I blurted out. 'More than I should.'

He looked at me and we just stood there staring into each other's eyes, our breath hanging between us. Shivers ran down my back and over my arms. In that moment, anything felt possible.

Then his hands were on my face, in my hair, he pushed me backwards and as my back hit the wall, his lips found mine. Everything else faded away, just like it had in the park, that first time. I needed this; I needed him. No matter how much my mind was used to reminding me he wasn't what I wanted, my body felt empty without him. He kissed down my neck, and it was as if my skin was on fire where he touched me. I moaned. He bit my neck.

He pulled his head away and pushed on my shoulders, so I was held harder against the wall, passion raging in his eyes, an immediacy to his actions that encompassed me. It felt like we had to be together, needed to, as if the universe required it. He looked at me as if trying to work out what he would do with me.

Not being able to stand the tension anymore, I surprised

myself by uttering: 'I want you.' Then, as if coming out of nowhere, 'Do what you want with me. I'm yours.' And from somewhere inside me, a feeling arose until I gave into it – I bit him. Hard, on the shoulder. It felt like my own Astrid moment – seeing how he would react, tempting him, wondering what he would do. I felt so in control, even though what I really wanted was for him to control me and have his way with me; to use me, to hurt me, to dominate me. I knew I could trust him; I knew I was safe, but I wanted to really feel something.

He looked at me, a stunned look on his face, then said 'ouch,' followed by 'you cheeky thing,' which reassured me I hadn't gone too far. He kissed me even more passionately, before pushing me sideways, where I crashed down onto his bed. I didn't have more than a moment before he was on top of me, his weight holding me down. He ran his hands up my stomach and I flinched from the feeling of hands on my skin. Before I realised it, he'd swept my top up and used it to pin my arms above my head. I was suddenly very aware that I hadn't worn a bra, which was very unlike me, and my chest was suddenly exposed to him. I couldn't touch him, but I wanted to, and it drove my need for him into a frenzy. I squirmed to get my hands free so I could pull him into me.

He was looking down at me, a wild look on his face. I'd never been more attracted to him than I was in that moment. He leant down to kiss my right nipple, tracing around it with his tongue, before biting it gently. I'd never felt something so sensitive, it coursed right through my body, making me tingle between my legs, and I let out a soft, breathless moan. The feeling caught me off-guard.

He let go of the shirt holding me down, but put his weight on my upper arms so I still couldn't move. His knee was between my legs, and I squirmed to get closer to him, to get some sort of contact. I needed him. He kissed me, hard, fast, desperately. My heart was racing. His hands closed gently around my neck, and I felt the power he had over me, completely at his mercy. I heard myself mumble 'more,' before pulling my arms free – which I realised I could do easily, if I really tried. I dug my fingernails into his back, trying to leave proof that I had been there. My body ached for him until finally, it got what it wanted.

Chapter 30

I already thought about Chris a lot, but after that night, I thought about him almost every second. I'd never experienced anything like that before. The sex itself was great but more than that, the power play, the dynamics of our interactions left me wanting more. The memories of it filled my mind.

It was nothing like what you and I had. With you it was nice, but I never felt like I was completely there. I was so preoccupied with making sure you were satisfied, and that I was doing it right, that it was hard to let go and enjoy it properly. Having sex with you seemed to highlight how broken I was – unable to orgasm no matter what, although it did sometimes feel nice. But with him I no longer felt broken. No, I didn't orgasm then either, but I felt like maybe one day I could... Or at least, I felt closer to it than I ever had. And somehow it didn't matter that I didn't, because it was all about the game, the roles we were playing, rather than having an end goal.

He crept into my thoughts as I was sitting in class or as I tried to concentrate on the assignments I kept accidentally leaving to the last minute. I would find myself randomly smiling and then realise it was because I was thinking of him. Any time he wasn't around, I wished he was.

Astrid noticed that I was happy and relatively distracted too. One day she commented on it as we were out walking in town. It was a Sunday and we'd been at yoga (though not droga, as she had played another wonderful gig the night before and we hadn't stayed out much past midnight). We were going to the record store and then picking up something for dinner on the walk home. I enjoyed our domestic Sundays together on the days when we weren't too hungover to function – they made me feel like such an adult.

'I think someone might be a little bit in love...' she said in a light, teasing voice as we were walking around. I inadvertently looked around to make sure there was no one you knew in earshot.

'Me?' I answered quickly. 'No I'm not!'

'All right! Chill! You just have that typical dazed lovesick look on you.'

'No I don't... Do I?'

She shrugged. 'I think it's nice, though a little distracting.'

'Sorry, I guess I've been a little bit out of it. I just... I dunno, it's just a silly crush thing.'

'Sure, it's nice to get attention.'

'Yeah.'

'And good sex?'

I'm sure I blushed while trying to work out what to say. I didn't feel comfortable talking about sex, it just wasn't what was done. Especially not as we were out walking in public. It also felt strange to be talking about Chris in the light of day, like he was a regular person, not just a late-night secret.

'You have had sex, right?' she asked. 'I feel like something's changed.'

As always, she was so observant. I looked at her and bit my lip before saying 'Yeah...'

'And?'

'It was... so good,' I said quietly.

'Brilliant. Fun?'

'Yeah. And like... it feels...' I felt odd saying it, 'kinda dangerous? I mean... I'm not actually in danger. God, is it weird that that feels like a good thing?'

'Not at all. That's what we want – the thrill, the game, the power struggle. Sounds like exactly what you need. Completely different from what you're used to, I suppose?'

'Um... yeah. Very.'

She nodded. 'Perfect.'

I always loved going on trips to the record store with Astrid. The CD section was categorised by name of artist, in alphabetical order, with sections of specific bands for each letter of the alphabet. But at the end of each letter's section, they put all the lesser-known bands and artists for that letter, randomly lumped in together. Astrid said that's where the magic lay, and she would go through every single one, looking for small bands she'd never heard of, then get a stack of EPs and singles that were only a pound or so each. They were often local bands, or smaller British bands. This was one of the main ways we found out new music. Or by making sure we got to gigs early enough to catch the support bands. Or just randomly going to gigs at Phoenix Bar, or any of the other small live music venues. The nights Astrid played usually had some interesting musicians too.

That day we picked up 4 EPs of bands we'd never heard of to go home and listen to. We then went and got the supplies for the mushroom pasta Astrid was craving.

Along the walk home she stopped outside someone's house, and I realised she was no longer next to me.

'What are you...'

'Look at these!' She held up two white bowls. I hadn't even noticed them as we walked past. 'They look cute. Someone clearly doesn't want them anymore. Shall we have them?'

'Yeah, I guess so. Why not?'

'Hey, this looks good too! I have an idea for something we can do with it!'

I looked to see what she was referring to and realised the bowls were sitting on top of a little copper and glass trolley on wheels.

'Sure, but how are you going to get it home?'

'Here take these...' She handed me the bowls and her shopping bag, lifted it up and held it behind her against her back. 'Cool, let's go!'

We were only a few blocks from home, but she carried it like that the whole way. I would never have thought to pick something up on the side of the road, I hadn't even noticed they were there. I wondered what she'd intended on doing with it.

We ate our pasta out of those bowls that night. They were the perfect shape and size for our meal, the flattish base made them different from our bowls.

The trolley found its home in the living room as our new drinks cabinet.

Chapter 31

As I realised that the repercussions I'd been worrying about – you finding out – still never came, I got more confident. We were still discreet; we (almost) never kissed in public, and I made sure Chris wasn't at any parties we threw, just in case. In the lead up I always wanted to go back on my resolve and invite him, but I was always glad I didn't. Although we'd orbited away from any real cross over with people you were friends with, occasionally someone you knew would turn up at a party and it reminded me of what a difficult thing I was balancing. I probably shouldn't admit that part of me enjoyed that fact, though. It made me feel stronger, more in control knowing I was orchestrating it all quite well.

Despite my insistence to Astrid that it was merely a crush, it didn't take long for Chris to tell me he loved me.

We'd just got back to his after another night out and as soon as we got in, he grabbed me by the wrist and took me to his room. There was an urgency in his eyes and I wondered if something was wrong.

'I've not felt this way in a long time,' he'd said.

I'd never been spoken to in such a big, important way. And in response to that feeling, I rushed to tell him I loved him too.

Maybe I did, it was all very confusing. I was overcome with so many emotions, I felt like they might explode if I didn't say them.

'I don't think I have either,' I said. 'But... We can't. We can't keep doing this forever...'

He shook his head then rested his forehead on mine, I could feel his breath on my face.

'You have Robert.'

'And your heart belongs to Cassie.'

Then he kissed me with so much force, like he needed it to survive. As he was kissing me, I wrapped his necklace around my finger. I had become slightly obsessed with it, with his past, with the girl he loved; the part of him I could never touch. I must have pulled too hard because it broke and came off in my hands.

He jumped back, both of our eyes drawn to the chain hanging in my fingers. For a second, I was shocked. I almost started apologising, but I realised that I didn't want to. Instead of feeling bad, I felt some sense of victory – like I had erased part of his past, and I was now the only one in his life. After what felt like an age of silence, with both of us paused in that moment, he drove me back against the wall, pushing me hard up against it. I could feel his breath on my neck as he held me there. Every moment seemed to pass by so slowly. I was unsure of what he was going to do. I needed him to do something. I needed to feel something. I needed to know it was real.

'Hurt me,' I heard myself say. My voice came out breathy, almost as if it wasn't coming from me at all.

He moved back slightly to look at me. I almost panicked that I had said the wrong thing, that he would be disgusted and hate me for it. But moments passed, and I didn't take it back or say that I hadn't meant it.

And then, he slapped me. Right across the face. Not hard enough to do damage, just enough to shock me. My face tingled, then burned. I could feel all the places he had touched me. He grabbed my face and made our eyes meet before kissing me again.

Then we were clawing at each other, tearing at each other's clothes, desperate to get them off. He bit my shoulder, sinking his teeth in, holding me against the wall for a bit longer before throwing me on the bed. We had rough, wild sex for hours and I'd never felt so alive. I was no longer the supporting role, in these moments I felt like the main character. People would write stories and songs about this kind of Jess.

For days after, I ran my fingers over the bruises I didn't realise I had. I counted three. I took my shirt off and found the one forming on my shoulder where he'd bitten me. I touched it, pressing down slightly so that I could feel it ache. It made me smile. Tangible proof of the night Chris had left his mark on me.

Being with him felt increasingly more and more different to being with you. With you it felt like how it should be in a relationship; reliable, dependable, nice. When we were making love, it made sense. But with him it felt chaotic, exciting, dangerous. At times it felt like he worshipped me, like I was the most important person in the world. But I knew that no matter how real it felt in those moments, it wasn't real life, it was just an escape. It was me giving in to animalistic urges, and I knew I was ultimately better than that.

Sometimes – and I couldn't pinpoint what caused it – I felt destructive. It was such an overwhelming and exhilarating feeling, and it made me feel for a moment that I was in control of something. I no longer cared what other people think of me, what they might say about me or whether I offended them. I didn't care what happened to me, as long as I felt something. I felt almost invincible but at the same time very fragile, like I was walking on a high edge, and I knew that at any moment, I could fall.

I wondered if Astrid ever felt like that, like she could tear the whole world apart, given half a chance. But I didn't think she would – she was so measured, so composed. She always looked for adventure and fun and thought of wild things for us to do, but I had never seen a destructive side to her. Surely that was just me.

Chapter 32

I knew you were going to come back. It was always in the back of my mind. And I was looking forward to it – really, I was. Your return would force an end to my season of debauchery. I would be transformed back into the person I was meant to be. I needed you to come back, I needed to be fixed.

I mentioned something in passing to Astrid about your return, and I was surprised at her response, considering I thought she knew my future was with you, in London.

'Haven't we got past this?' Her hands were on her hips. 'I thought you'd got some confidence. I thought you'd finally realised that you don't owe him anything. Wake up! Why are you even with him? He does nothing for you! He just runs off to America without even discussing it! You're nothing alike. You have basically nothing in common. He's just another mediocre man, and you're destined for so much more. But you've got to chase it, not just settle for things. Come on, haven't you realised yet that you're so much better than that?'

I loved her and valued her opinion, but she didn't get what it was like to be me. I wasn't her and I'd never be her. I wasn't the sort of person who compelled people to drop everything and follow me. I'd found someone who would put up with my flaws and love me, someone who saw a future with me – I wasn't about to go throwing it away. I wasn't the type of person who just runs off with the first person they find when things get hard. Real, adult love took work. She just couldn't understand.

'Robert's good to me. And it's not like there's anyone else lining up.'

'What are you talking about? There's Chris for a start.'

Hearing his name come from her mouth in that moment felt abrasive; he didn't belong in that conversation. We would never work. We couldn't. That was a parallel life, not the one I'd been working towards for so long. Any time my mind tried to go there, picturing a different future with him in it, I panicked and pushed it back down.

'He just wanted a bit of fun,' I said. 'We both knew nothing more could ever happen.'

Sure, he made me feel like I was the only person in the world. Time seemed to stop when we were together, but that wasn't sustainable.

'Aah, playing the star-crossed lovers game, eh? Love each other but can never be together? Very Romeo and Juliet, very emotionally safe. You can throw all the love at it but never have to deal with any realities.'

'I'm not sure we're playing a game...'

'Ok, ok, whatever you say. Anyway, he's not living here.'

'What, Chris?'

'No, Robert!'

I didn't say anything.

'You weren't going to say he's moving in here, were you? This is our place! Not ours and your boyfriend.'

'I suppose not.'

'And you're not leaving me, are you?'

I was quiet again. All these thoughts had entered my mind, but I hadn't wanted to address them.

'Come on, tell me you're not moving in with him. You can't just suddenly throw that at me.'

I guess I had assumed that since we'd be back together in the same place that we would live together again. My plan was always to stay an extra year while you finished your degree, but Astrid and I had also been discussing signing another year's lease on the flat...

She and I talked about it for a while that day and in the end, I decided it would make sense to stay with her for another year rather than try and find somewhere new. But I wasn't sure how you'd take it. We hadn't really discussed plans for when you got back so I endeavoured to bring it up the next time we spoke. So after catching up on what we'd been up to, I dived straight in.

'I was thinking maybe I'd stay in the flat with Astrid another year.'

'Yeah, I figured you would.'

'Oh, right,' I replied, unsure how you'd come to that conclusion even before I had. 'Ok well... it's only the two of us on the lease.'

'Yes, I know. I am aware of where you've been living for the past year...'

'Oh yeah, right. I just... I guess I thought... maybe you and I would live together when you get back.'

'Ethan has a spare room going in his flat, so I thought I'd just move in with him. You're already set up there and you'll have finished uni next year anyway – I'll just be studying a lot so it wouldn't be much fun for you.'

I was starting to wonder if I had unrealistic views of how relationships were supposed to work... Things people were saying kept catching me off-guard. I wondered why you didn't even consider wanting to live with me. I didn't say anything for a moment.

'Babe, we've got the rest of our lives to live together,' you continued. 'Let's just enjoy our last year and we'll get our own place when we get to London.'

I thought that maybe you and Astrid should be together – you were sounding like the same person. I seemed to be the only one who thought it made sense for me to live with you – no one else had even considered it. I thought we'd take a step forward from the big house we'd shared with the others before you left and maybe get somewhere just the two of us. But if you both thought it was reasonable for us to be living apart, then I suppose I was the one with the unreasonable expectations.

'Babe? You still there?'

You'd never called me 'babe' before, it must have been something you'd picked up in America. I tried to work out whether I liked it or not. Then I realised I still hadn't said anything in response.

'Oh yeah, sorry. I'm here.'

'It's not like we won't be seeing each other loads anyway.'

'Yeah, of course.'

I was grateful to get another year with Astrid, but it just shocked me that you'd never considered us living together.

'I've organised a surprise for you when I get back. I can't wait to see you. I've missed you,' you said.

That made me smile. You could be so sweet. Of course you'd organised a surprise. There I was, stressing out that you didn't love me anymore because you didn't want to live with me, but you clearly did. I felt a pang of guilt for everything I'd done while you'd been away. For all my indiscretions, all the late nights with Chris, all the times when it was he who'd filled my mind rather than you. But I pushed the thoughts away.

'That sounds lovely. I can't wait to see you.'

Astrid and I finalised signing the lease for another year that week.

'Another year of The Den!' she cheered.

'He will be coming over though...'

'Of course. He's not like... banished. Mouse, it's not that I don't like him. I'm only thinking about you. I only want what's best for you.'

I was so glad I had her.

Chapter 33

My third year was slipping by, and it was only four months until you would be back. I marvelled at thinking back on how slowly my school days had crept by; the weeks taking months, the months taking years... I honestly felt like they would never end. Yet here I was, hurtling towards the end of my degree, getting ready to sit my final exams. The year of living with Astrid had absolutely flown by. I think I'd tried to put the whole thing out of my mind, but the truth was that my degree was ending, provided I could pass those damn exams...

Despite all the partying, I'd actually been doing better in class. Once you returned, you would still have another year of your degree left and since Astrid had deferred her first year, she also had another year to go. So I was hanging around for one more year too, as had always been the plan. I knew I'd have to find some sort of work to do for the year before we moved to London, but I wasn't sure where to start. My heart ached slightly at the thought of leaving our lives for the unknown, but I was also looking forward to things being back on track.

There was a book I needed to pick up a copy of – I was supposed to have read it before my exams but hadn't even got a copy yet, so Astrid drove us over to our favourite independent bookshop. I was in the economics section trying to sing the alphabet song to find where to go, when Astrid came rushing up and thrust a piece of paper at me. I took it, smoothing it out on the shelf, where it had been crumpled in her fist.

The bookshop was hiring. I looked at Astrid and she was grinning back at me, nodding. It certainly seemed like a good idea to enquire, so with Astrid's support, I went to chat with the owner, who introduced herself as Freya. She told me that she needed someone to help out here and there at first, and that they were flexible about hours, but that it could become more involved over time.

'She'd be great for the job,' Astrid said, leaning over from where she was pretending to be looking at a book nearby.

I laughed. 'Yeah, it sounds good.'

Freya asked me to drop my CV by during the week sometime. I'd never made a CV and the one I pulled together felt so pathetic. I had no experience at all and typing out my A-Level and GCSE results seemed so irrelevant. I felt stupid for thinking they would ever consider hiring me. But when Freya skimmed her eyes over it, she said, 'Ooh, you've been writing for the uni paper. That's perfect! Exactly the type of person we want.'

I smiled to myself. *Perfect.* I'd never been considered perfect for anything before.

And so, to my complete surprise, she said she'd be delighted to give me the role.

I started, picking up the occasional shift here and there as I finished my final year. It didn't take me long to get the hang of the cash register and the stock database.

I quite liked working in the bookshop. I got to put the books in alphabetical order, which appealed to me. I also got to create the displays. Whenever Astrid came in while I was working, she would pick up a book off the shelf and bring it to me to put on display, so I would add it in. It made me smile to see her rifling through all the books and picking ones that she thought people needed to read. People seemed to be drawn to her selections, and would often come back and comment on loving the books she'd picked, asking for another recommendation. I would then direct them to her latest selection and send them off a happy customer. Freya mentioned a couple of times that I was really good at picking out books for the displays and I must admit, I took credit for it, though it was all Astrid.

In return, I shared my staff discount with her. She usually rifled around in charity shops to stock up her ever-growing bookshelves but she started getting a few from my shop once I started working there. She didn't seem to use it as often as I thought she would, though.

It was good to have some money, too. Astrid didn't seem to need to get a job to have money, her parents must have just paid for everything. Mine helped, but it was nothing like hers seemed to.

I was glad for being able to start working only occasional shifts because, while studying was ramping up, so was the partying. I think Astrid was trying to fit as much in as possible before you came back. I kept trying to tell her that nothing was going to change between her and I when you returned, but she didn't believe me in the slightest.

I was still trying to juggle it all – work out how to get to the end of the year and into the next.

Astrid and I had stayed in the flat over the Easter holidays. With my parents being religious, Easter was a big thing and I think they would have liked me to go back and spend it with them, going to Church and all the other things they usually did. But between my new job and the fact that exams were starting just after the holidays, I managed to convince them it was better if I stayed.

On Easter Friday, we ate hot cross buns topped with so much butter – she'd insisted on getting French salted butter which came in a block, and I didn't think I'd ever eaten anything so delicious. We agreed that the buns were mostly just a socially acceptable way to consume large amounts of butter. As we sat eating them, we listened to the bells from the church down the road from our house, which seemed to almost always be tolling over that weekend. It felt so rebellious to not enter a Church at all over Easter – I knew my parents would be attending a couple of services, and I pretended that I was too, when they'd asked.

On the Sunday, I woke up to the sound of her writing music on her guitar. As I left my room, I noticed three little eggs balanced on top of the banister of the staircase: The Easter Bunny had come. Astrid had hidden small Easter eggs around the house, and once I was up, we ran around, excitedly collecting them all, then proceeding to eat them for breakfast.

These were moments of pure joy. But it also scared me when I was happy, as I knew it could only change. All things must end.

Chapter 34

Chris had been trying to get me to go around to his place so he could cook me pasta. He said he wanted to cook me his Nonna's famous pasta dish. I'd had a huge week; between work and trying to study for our upcoming exams, I was stressed. I just wanted to get through to the weekend and go out with Astrid, but he insisted. I supposed it was a nice thing he was trying to do, so eventually I agreed to go. I felt like I owed it to him, anyway. He'd had me over so many times after being at the club and so often drove me home the next day... The least I could do was go for one dinner.

He texted me the morning of, asking me to bring some beer. I didn't really drink beer so I'd asked Astrid what I should get.

'Mouse...' She said, staring at me for a moment before continuing. 'I don't want to alarm you, but... you realise you're going to his house for a date, right? This is sounding a tad more serious than late night adventures.'

'No, it's not,' I said, shaking my head in defiance. 'It's not... is it?'

'I know how this goes, I've been there before... Next thing you'll be telling me he tells you he loves you...'

I didn't respond. I didn't need to. She read it all over my face.

'Oh, ok. Well... things have changed a bit, haven't they.'

'Yeah, I guess so,' I said, feeling suddenly heavy with the weight of it all. I'd been going along just enjoying how things played out, but somewhere along the line I'd got in deeper than I'd intended. I hadn't thought about the simple invite to dinner as something so big, but once Astrid pointed it out, it did sound suspiciously like a date. Before then, it had just been sex, drugs and trance music. Unplanned. Spontaneous felt fine, it felt somehow safe; I was in control while we were confined to late nights and early mornings. But this was premeditated. I was getting so lost in my thoughts, a feeling of distress growing within me, that I didn't notice Astrid put a six-pack of beer next to me.

'Take them. They were left here by someone.'

She patted me on the shoulder in a way that seemed affectionate.

'Be brave, Little Mouse.'

I nodded, slowly.

'Maybe it will all just... fizzle out?' I asked hopefully, desperate to avoid any difficult conversations, not knowing how I'd say 'no' when the time came. Saying no was possibly the most difficult thing in the world.

'I don't think there's any chance of that. You give him the attention he wants. Why would he want to give that up? And he knows you won't leave Robert, so it's easy for him. Low risk. He can do and say all these big things without consequence. He'll never be expected to follow through.'

'Well, I'll stop giving him attention. Easy. I'll fizzle him.'

'Nah, that won't work, he'll just get clingy and start trying harder. They always tend to get clingy.'

That seemed unlikely. No one was going to get clingy with

me, that just wasn't how it worked. That was Astrid's world, not mine.

'Just you wait and see,' she continued. 'When they feel like their status is being threatened, they cling.'

I felt slightly annoyed at the fact she thought I could be anything like her, that my situation could somehow parallel her own experiences. She would never get what it was like to be me. No one would ever feel that way about me.

Somehow the dinner had turned into something bigger than I'd realised. I readied myself for it – I knew I could just smile, say the right things, and then it would end. And that would be fine. But I didn't know how long I'd be able to lie to myself that I was keeping it together, because I was starting to feel like everything could all unravel at any moment. It was all suddenly feeling a lot more real.

I couldn't help having all these thoughts hanging over me when I walked up the three steps to his flat. I'd been there in the night, when I was drunk and feeling alive. But now I just felt worried. I didn't want to go. Why was I even going? Because he wanted me to. Because I had done this; I had made him think he should cook me dinner. I'd led him on. I should have said no at that first kiss, that first night we slept together... But now it seemed I'd led him to believe that maybe we could have *that* type of relationship; one with dates. I had said all the words, so certain that they were safe to say because we knew what it was and what it couldn't be. It was my fault I was in this situation, and I had to face the music. Astrid told me that I would have to have a conversation and end things, if that was really what I wanted (of course it was) but I was still hoping I wouldn't have to. I couldn't handle even the thought of a confrontation.

I'd got to his house early because I was always early. I walked around the block a few times, going over in my head what I actually wanted. The problem was that I didn't know.

When I finally rang the doorbell, he came to the door wearing an apron, and he looked so sweet that I laughed when I saw him. He kissed me, in the broad daylight, and invited me in.

I handed him the beers, which he put in the freezer to cool quickly.

'Take a seat,' he told me and indicated the stools by the bench on the outside of the kitchen area. I sat on the one closest to the edge and watched as he pottered around.

'I've got a bottle of wine airing, but I still have some cooking to go so I thought we'd have some beers first.'

'Sounds great,' I said.

After about ten minutes he got two of the beers out of the freezer, took the caps off them and handed me one, holding his out to cheers. I felt very much like I'd stepped into a male's world.

Dinner was a fairly standard tomato sauce over pasta, but it was sweet he'd made the effort. My mind was still thinking about all the things I didn't yet know for my upcoming exams, and the fact that the year was ending. I refused to let it think too much about what was currently happening, and the conversation I'd had with Astrid. As a result, the conversation seemed to turn to talking about what we wanted to do with our futures. I spoke about wanting to live in London after I finished my degree and my dreams of getting a job in the city. Then I told him that I also wanted to travel, like Astrid had told me so many times I must, making sure I went to all the wonderful places she'd told me about.

I knew he had already finished uni, having studied exercise physiology so he could be a personal trainer. He'd met Astrid when they'd had a cross-over elective together. But I don't think I'd realised that he wasn't currently actually doing anything with his degree; he had been working at his uncle's dry-cleaning business.

'You don't want to travel?'

'I went to visit my cousin in Canada for a month before uni started. That was enough travel for me.'

'What about moving somewhere else for a while?'

'Nah, I could never move away. My parents wouldn't approve. They want us all to stay living nearby. We would be betraying the family if we left. I've gone about as far as is considered acceptable.'

'So you're just going to stay here... forever? You have no wish to go anywhere else?'

'No, not really. It's not like I still live in their town or anything, I'm pretty happy here. And it means I'm close enough to visit them whenever I want. The others all stayed though, I'm the black sheep of the family, I think,' he said with a chuckle.

'And you're just going to stay working at the dry cleaner's forever?'

'Is there something wrong with that?'

'Oh, no. Sorry, of course there isn't. I'm just curious. Don't you have any other, you know, dreams? Isn't there something you love doing? Something creative maybe?'

I'd been pulled headfirst into a world where I had been made to sing and write poetry and it was so exhilarating. I figured that if Astrid had shown me that I could do it, maybe I could unlock something in Chris too.

'I... no. Not really.'

'Not really?'

'Well... It's stupid. It's nothing. You'll think it's stupid!'

I felt a flutter in my stomach – it was my turn to pass the baton, to coax a creative dream out of someone.

'I won't, I assure you.'

'Well, I used to write match reports, like of football games. Just for myself to read. And I guess I kinda thought one day I could do that for real. But that's just silly. I'd probably have to go back to uni and start again.'

'A sports journalist! Cool! You wouldn't need to study. Look at me, I just started writing for the uni paper. If you love something, you'll find a way.'

'No, I'm really not a great writer. I don't think I've got a creative bone in my body.'

'I thought the same but now I've sung onstage and read out poetry and written loads of articles and I think... If I can do it, so can you! Anyway, you learn as you go.'

He sighed, scrunching up his face before reaching out to squeeze my arm. I think maybe I'd said the wrong thing.

'Nah, it's not for me. It's sweet that you're trying, but I think your energy is probably better spent elsewhere.'

I could tell the conversation was over. I'd failed. I wasn't compelling like Astrid; I couldn't work out how to convince him that if I had done it then he could too. Maybe he just didn't want it enough.

I suppose part of me had been secretly wondering if there could be any chance of a future for Chris and me, but every time I thought of it I got panicky and stopped myself. Suddenly, what Astrid had said about finding out what I wanted made sense. I realised I needed to be with someone who wanted to move to London, and who wanted a career there. And I wanted to be able to travel. That was not Chris.

Chapter 35

To celebrate 'all the things', which encompassed my new job, exams finishing, the end of the year and in fact my degree, as well as us heading into another year of living together, Astrid announced that we were going to have a festival at our flat.

'A... festival?' I asked, feeling unsure. I thought of festivals as muddy groups of thousands of people tramping around the countryside, listening to live bands. It sounded exhausting.

'Yep, a festival. Of... Hmm... I was thinking of Apollo... and Aphrodite? A weekend of creativity and debauchery!'

I had been studying a Greek history module as a random elective to fill up my quota, so I think that might have been where she'd got the idea from.

'I see... And what will this festival entail?'

'Well, you tell me. What are they Gods of?'

I had to think. A naming-the-gods pop quiz wasn't really the kind of stuff I had been learning.

'Apollo gives us the arts, I think. Music, poetry, all that stuff.' I started to understand where she was going.

She smiled. 'And Aphrodite?'

'That would be beauty, love and... desire, I guess.'

'You see?'

'I think I do.'

'So it will take place over the whole weekend, people will come and go as they please. We will get lots of wine—'

'That's starting to sound more like Dionysus than Aphrodite.'

'What was he all about?'

'Wine, parties, festivity...'

'He sounds like my kind of guy. How did I miss him?'

I shrugged. 'But if we do Apollo and Dionysus then it'll all be men...'

'Gross. Not exactly our USP.' She twirled her hair in her fingers, as she often did when she was thinking.

'USP?'

'Unique Selling Point.'

I laughed.

'I've got an idea,' she said suddenly. 'Pass me that pen and paper.'

I did as she asked.

'What does Apollo look like?'

'Um... He's the one with the lyre – one of those weird old instruments. And maybe a bow and arrow.'

She started sketching a picture of a woman with long floating hair, holding a bow and arrow, a lyre sitting beside her. It was rough, but I got the idea. When she finished, she wrote 'Apollo' in cursive writing underneath then looked up at me and smiled.

'And Dionysus?'

'He's got a crown of ivy and a cup of wine.'

'What a lad.'

She got to work at creating a female version of Dionysus, hair half up, cascading down around an ivy crown, standing under a grapevine and with a cup of wine in one hand. She finished it with the name written in matching letters.

'What do you think?'

'It's perfect.'

It really was. By the end of the day she had done detailed coloured sketches of them, both draped in gold but partially naked, and had turned them into invitations. The only rule for the party, written on the back, was 'Live freely, love, and create beauty.' I couldn't work out if it sounded pretentious or inspired. But either way, I was onboard.

We spent the Friday before the party decorating the flat. Astrid had come home with a few rolls of velvet, which we draped around to look like curtains. We put cushions and blankets on the living room floor for people to lie on. We placed bowls of grapes around the place and covered the dining table in bottles of wine. Our Den of Iniquity was in its full glory. Guests were asked to bring musical instruments, art supplies and wine.

Even after all this time, I still marvelled at the people who were around me. I didn't quite understand how I had managed to get myself in this circle. I never stopped feeling like an imposter. It wasn't that anyone made me feel like I didn't belong, quite the opposite. But deep down I knew I wasn't quite the same as these people.

I couldn't believe it had been almost a year since Astrid had made me get up and read my poetry at that first party in front of a room of people. I had been so scared and yet had ended up feeling so safe and supported.

People started arriving in the evening, dressed in white and gold, or various other Greek-style costumes. Astrid wore a stunning black and gold bodysuit with a long black mesh skirt attached to it that started at her sides, leaving the front open, and hung down at the back. It floated along behind her when she walked. She had wound a sort of flat material imitation vine around her legs and arms and looked amazing, as usual. I just wore a mid-length white dress with a gold belt and gold earrings. Astrid had put my hair half up and pinned it with a gold hairpin, curling the hair that hung down into soft waves. I don't quite know how she did it, but I thought I looked pretty good too.

It wasn't long before our house filled up with the rabble of party guests, all holding cups of red wine and chatting excitedly. There was always such a happy hum of ambient enjoyment that filled our flat whenever we had groups of people over (and especially at parties), and it made me smile. I enjoyed having so many wonderful people around. I sometimes just took a moment out to sit down somewhere by myself and take it all in.

A few times when I went to find Astrid during the party weekend, she'd be strumming a guitar, with people sitting around her. Others also took over music duties and there would always be something on the record player in the living room. I distinctly remember at some point over the weekend, lying on the floor with Astrid, both of us staring at the ceiling and holding hands while Pink Floyd's *Dark Side of the Moon* was playing. I just lay there not quite sure how to process it all. The intensity of the moment made it seem almost unbelievable.

Other parts of the weekend were hazier. The last night was the biggest. I suspected there might have been something like mushrooms or acid going around, which made the event seem weirder than other parties we'd had before. I had obviously become familiar with MDMA, but those other drugs sounded serious and scary. Though I have to say, the conversations that were taking place were also more wonderful – it felt like all the world's problems were being solved. And the music that was being made was better than anything I'd heard before. And the art too.

At some point I realised that someone had lined the hallway with small tea-light candles. I followed them down and out into the garden, where about eight people were standing in the dark, holding candles. Someone was chanting in a different language. A weird hush hung around it in the air. It felt like some type of ritual. I stayed for a little while before heading back inside to see where Astrid was.

Around midnight of the final night, Astrid pulled the sheet off her bed and hung it on the wall of the living room. She found another one from somewhere and put it on the floor underneath, presumably to protect the floorboards. It could have been mine, for all I cared at the time, although mine was still on my bed the next day.

She put her hand in blue paint and stamped it on the sheet. Someone poured green paint on her hair, and I went to run in and help, but she just laughed. She went and stood up against the wall sheet and imprinted it. Suddenly everyone had body parts covered in paint and were taking it in turns to put their mark on the sheets. Most people had stripped down into their underwear or were suddenly naked. We were lit only by candlelight, and folk music was wafting from where someone was playing guitar. The sheet became covered with a plethora of different colours, and everyone was laughing. I even joined in after Astrid came and hugged me, green, blue and purple paint transferring from her skin to mine.

We all took it in turns to have quick showers when we were done to get the paint off, and we danced into the early hours of the morning as our bodies dried. The last bits of paint still clung to our skin, remnants of the greatest party I'd ever been part of.

I woke up the next morning, draped on and under people on the sofa. Clammy bodies were pushed against each other, making me feel slightly sticky in places. They were all still asleep, or at least happy staying in their positions, as no one was moving. I felt restless, so I thought I'd get up and start pottering around and tidying up. Astrid was on the couch, her head resting on the bare chest of a brunette girl. Her usually perfect blonde hair was sitting all wrong, but she looked so beautiful.

I realised I was only in my underwear, so I went and put a t-shirt on. I had bits of paint in my hair, and a partial line of blue across my stomach. It made me smile. I wasn't ready to let go of it all yet.

I made my way around the kitchen, picking up wine bottles and putting them in the corner to take out to the bin.

Then I heard a voice behind me, deep and quiet. I recognised it immediately.

'What the hell is going on in here?'

I turned around slowly and saw you standing in the doorway with your hands on your hips.

'Hi,' I said slowly. 'What...' my voice trailed off. You were the last person I'd expected to see standing in my kitchen. I thought you were thousands of miles away.

'Surprise...' you said, your voice sounding thick with contempt. I could tell you weren't at all happy.

'How... how did you get in?' I stammered.

'The front door was unlocked...'

'Oh...'

I knew I had to do something. I went and put my arms around you and kissed you. You let me, before breaking apart. I wasn't sure how to put all the details together. I hadn't seen you in months, and suddenly you were there. Maybe I had taken psychedelics without realising it and was making the whole thing up... But no, you really were standing in my kitchen. I went into autopilot.

'I missed you so much. Why on earth are you here?'

'Are you not happy to see me?'

'Of course I am, I just wasn't expecting you to be here now.'

We were talking in quiet voices, so as not to disturb the people sleeping in the living room, but I worried that someone might hear us.

'I did a nice thing and surprised you and you're not even happy?' You had your arms crossed, and a frown on your face. I tried to keep my voice light and a smile on my face, hoping to drag you out of your anger.

'Of course I am. What a lovely surprise!'

'Why don't you have any trousers on? And why are there naked people in the living room? Did you have an orgy?'

I laughed. It sounded nervous.

'No, of course not,' I replied. 'We just painted and danced and sort of... celebrated life and creativity and things...'

'Is that why you have paint on your face? And why it's all over the living room?'

'Is it?'

'Mostly just on some sheets.'

'Oh, that's probably ok then.'

You breathed out slowly and ran your hands through your hair. You always did that when you were annoyed, and it gave me hope that what had started as anger was fizzling into annoyance. That was easier to deal with.

'Well...' you said eventually, breaking the silence that was starting to consume me. 'It's nice to see you. Let's get out of here.'

'Out? Out to where?'

'Anywhere. Why are you cleaning up after them anyway?'

Something inside me wanted to shout at you, say that it was as much me as it was them, and that you shouldn't judge all these wonderful creative people. But I didn't want to ruin your return and make you angrier than you already were. I must have taken a while to think about my reply because you spoke again before I could.

'Come on.' Your voice had softened, and you put your arms around me, pulling me in tight. I melted into your arms, where it felt warm and safe. 'How about I get us a hotel for a couple of days so we can spend some proper time together, just the two of us.'

'Oh, that's so kind of you. Are you sure?'

'Of course. Go pack a bag, I'll wait in the car.'

'Ok.'

We seemed to have not disturbed the sleeping masses, and still nobody had moved as I made my way up to my room to gather up my things, so I assumed they were all still conked out or at least pretending to be. So much had happened over the days of the festival. Astrid had pulled it all together and it was just this intensely perfect weekend that was already starting to feel like a dream. I made my way slowly up to my room to put some things in a bag, absent-mindedly pulling a random array of clothing together. My mind wasn't with me; it was still in the living room with everyone else.

I wrote a note on a piece of paper for Astrid, folded it and put it on the table by the door as I left.

Sorry, my love. Robert turned up early as a surprise and he wanted us to stay in a hotel for a couple of days. Be back soon xxx

Chapter 36

It turned out your exams had finished early, so you decided to come back and surprise me for a few days before heading back to your parents' place for the summer holidays. It was such a sweet gesture, and it did make me feel special, it was just awkward timing. I tried to ignore a weird feeling of resentment sitting somewhere inside me and wished I was better at appreciating surprises. I just couldn't help thinking I would have preferred to have known.

We holed up in the hotel room for a few days, spending our time eating, going for occasional walks and watching movies. We even got room service one day when we didn't feel like going outside. It was nice to spend a quiet couple of days, especially after the big weekend I'd had. It felt good slotting back into being actively in a relationship. I realised how much I'd missed it, how much I'd missed you.

I hadn't heard from Astrid, but I figured she was just busy, so I didn't bother her. I'd be seeing her soon anyway.

'Why are you so obsessed with her?' you asked me over dinner after I'd told you about a gig she had coming up that was at a new venue that we were really excited about. 'I don't think she's that good for you. Look at the state she left your flat in.'

'I'm not obsessed with her... She's my friend. We have fun.'

'Fine, whatever. I won't tell you who you can and can't hang out with but I'm not sure I like what she's turning you into. She doesn't care about you, you know? She just keeps you around because you're useful to her in some way. She's a narcissist. Everything is all about her.'

'She's not a narcissist. She's always doing things for me.'

You laughed, and it sounded like you were mocking either me or her. I didn't like it.

'She probably only does things for you if it suits her in some way. It's just what she's like. She doesn't care about anyone but herself.'

I felt my chest tightening, wanting to jump to her defence. But I didn't want to cause an issue or make you mad, so I decided it was best to just leave it.

'I don't want to argue with you,' I said. 'Let's just have a nice time.'

And we did. I didn't bring her up again. I made sure not to say anything that would anger you, I didn't want to be the one to ruin things.

You didn't come in when you dropped me home. You said you had to leave, as your parents were expecting you. I got out of the car and watched you drive away. The time we had together was so nice, but I felt weird watching you drive away – like you were the part that didn't belong. But I knew that must be because you'd been away for so long. I was sure it would all be back to normal once you were back for good. It would just take some adjustment.

I went inside, relieved to be home.

I called out to Astrid. No reply. I knew she was probably in, as her car was out front. I tried again. Still nothing. I went up the stairs to find her in her room.

'Hi, I'm back!' I said, cheerily.

'Oh look, it's you. You're alive.' She wasn't smiling. She wasn't even looking at me.

'What's wrong?'

She sighed audibly then looked up at me. Her face looked angry.

'Where the fuck were you? Someone said they saw you leave with some guy who turned up, who you apparently knew...'

'Oh, yeah, Robert came back early without telling me and wanted to go to a hotel. I left you a note.'

'What note?'

'A note. On a piece of paper. I put it on the table by the front door.'

'You mean the table covered in empty wine bottles? I was supposed to somehow know that there was a piece of paper on it I needed to read?'

In hindsight it did sound a bit ridiculous.

'I'm sorry, I guess I wasn't thinking.'

'Standard. Why didn't you message me?'

Standard? I didn't know how to take that, so I ignored it.

'Oh, I guess I just didn't want to bother you. Sorry. You could have messaged me if you were worried.'

'Why is it up to me to chase you? You shouldn't have to be told to extend common courtesies. What am I, your mother?'

'I'm sorry, Astrid.' I felt terrible. I didn't want to upset her and I really didn't want to fight. Why was I always such an idiot?

'And you left me with all the cleaning. Thankfully some people stayed and helped. I organise us a party and you're all for it, then you just bail. You could have told him you would meet him later. He turns up unannounced and suddenly you have to drop everything to go see him? You drop me without a second thought! He expects you to flake on your friends whenever he tells you to? It's pathetic, Jess. You're pathetic.'

I started to cry. I didn't want her to think I was pathetic. I wanted to say something to make it ok, to make her happy. But I didn't know what to do.

Astrid stared at me for a little while, arms crossed. She seemed so angry. All I could do was stand in the doorway of her room and cry. Eventually she spoke, her voice was softer.

'Always with the crying. Mouse...'

She came over and put her arms around me. 'It's all right, Little Mouse, I'm sorry. I shouldn't have got angry at you. I just feel like you do these things without thinking about anyone else, sometimes. Without thinking about me.'

I tried to get in control of my tears. The note was a stupid idea, I should have just sent her a message. It was difficult having to think about other people. I guess it still didn't come naturally to me.

She forgave me, though. I'm not sure if I would have in her position. We spent the rest of the day together in the garden. Then, when it got cold, we went inside and had dinner, which consisted of cheese and snacks that were still left over from the party. Then we watched The Beatles' Movie *Help*, from which the title of *The Relativity Cadenza* came from. She was right, it was ridiculous, but I loved it.

Chapter 37

You'd gone back to Hampshire, but Astrid and I stayed in the flat over the summer. It made sense, since we were paying rent and I had my shifts at the book shop to cover. I had expected her to run off to Europe, but she didn't that summer. I liked to think that I gave her a reason to stay.

Though she had quite a few 'jobs', as she called them, that she travelled to different parts of the UK for – she was doing some modelling, so she had a few trips for shoots. It sounded a lot more fun than what I was doing, and I envied her being tall and skinny and beautiful enough to get to do modelling. It must have been so much fun.

I was doing so much better in the times she went away and left me in the house on my own. I felt like such a different person from who I was that first time she went on tour. I no longer panicked that she might never return, and I just made sure I busied myself at the bookshop so that I wouldn't be lonely.

I couldn't believe I'd finished university. Though first year felt like it was an age ago, it also felt like the time had flown. I hardly recognised who I'd been at the start, so much had happened since then. I was still waiting for my results, but I was so sure I had failed and would have to do another year.

Or that perhaps I somehow hadn't got enough credits to graduate, or maybe I'd taken the wrong classes. I kept having dreams where I didn't attend my exams and woke up having to reassure myself that I did, though part of me never quite believed it. I had stepped up my days working at the bookshop. I tried seeing Chris less, but it seemed impossible to get him out of my life without something to force us apart.

Astrid had met a local poet who had recently released something called a chapbook, and she wanted me to organise an event at the bookshop. I was immediately nervous about the idea and told her that it wasn't really my call – I wasn't important enough to make decisions like that.

'Have I taught you nothing?' she told me sternly, 'You *are* important. You are whatever you want to be. If you keep talking about yourself like that, how can you expect anyone else to think any differently? It would be a lot of fun and bookshops are always looking for things they can organise events around.'

She was always pushing me to be more, to be bigger and greater than I actually was. She never let me sit on the sidelines. She never stopped giving me the confidence to believe in myself, even when I found it so hard to. Her enthusiasm, as always, was infectious. She had a way of making anything sound like it had the potential for a unique opportunity.

After her pep talk, I decided to get up the courage to ask the bookshop owner Freya about it. I rehearsed the conversation over and over in my head and put it off for days. But Astrid was counting on me, and I didn't want to let her down. So eventually, I approached Freya to tell her my idea – well, Astrid's idea. I told her about the poet, the sort of work she did, and explained that I thought maybe we could organise a reading at the book shop. I suggested we supply wine and put some chairs around to make it into an event.

'Sounds great!' she said, straight away.

'Really?'

'Yeah, let's do it. I love your initiative, Jess. Maybe we could even get some live music in. I wonder who we could ask... Do you know any musicians? Something quiet and folky maybe.'

I smiled. 'Yes, I think I know someone who would be perfect.'

I busied myself in the project. I was amazed to see how far I'd come. I had gained so much confidence from Astrid's belief in me. Though I suppose I should attribute some of it to Chris too – he made me feel noticed, and that it was ok to be seen sometimes. You had done so much to back me in things too, which helped with my confidence, but I have to admit it felt nice to know that somehow, I might be desirable in some small way, not only to you. Old Jess would never have even put herself out there let alone felt confident enough to pull something like this together.

Astrid helped with the planning. We went and picked up bottles of red and white wine and little plastic cups, as well as lots of fairy lights and to put around the shop. We moved a couple of things around to make a sort of 'stage' area, and in one corner we put a whole lot of cushions for people to sit on and chat, or listen to the poetry reading and the music. Astrid had agreed to play. As people arrived, she was sitting playing acoustic guitar and singing. I looked at her and couldn't help smiling at all we had achieved together. There was a buzz in the air as people milled around and looked at books.

The poet, Leela, wrote politically charged poetry, covering

issues like feminism and the environment. She read her poetry in such an engaging and impassioned way, that at first, I wondered if it jarred with the quiet calm of Astrid's music that had preceded it, and the general vibe of the book shop. But then I realised the ambience we had created only set the scene for her poetry to really soar to greater heights. It reminded me of the feeling I'd got when we'd all sung 'The Guns of Brixton' along with Arcade Fire at the end of their gig, all that time ago.

Running even further with my (Astrid's) idea for the event, Freya had turned it into a sort of panel event and encouraged audience questions after the reading. I could never think of things to ask in that situation (I most certainly never spoke out in a lecture) but people asked really thoughtful questions about Leela's inspiration and motivation, her background, and how she'd developed her style. We sold dozens of copies of her poetry book, which we'd made sure to stock plenty of, and Leela had happily agreed to sign. We also sold a handful of novels people had found whilst they were browsing. The event was a huge success.

Astrid hung around after to help me clean up and as soon as the last person had left, I ran up to her and hugged her.

'What's that for?'

'For being you!'

She laughed and kissed the side of my head. 'You too, Mouse. Now come on, let's finish cleaning up so we can go celebrate your successful night!'

'I couldn't have done it without you.'

'Ah well, we make a great team.'

'We really do.'

We really did.

For some reason, Emily wasn't far from my thoughts that night. She and I had made a good team too, in the few years we'd had together. She'd helped to bring me out of my shell even back then, and now it was Astrid encouraging me to be more confident and get out and do things. I remember thinking that, if Emily were alive, she would have been proud to see me that night. It was a thought I'd never had before, and it gave me an unexpected feeling of warmth.

Chapter 38

When my results came out, I was stunned to find out that not only had I passed, I'd actually done relatively well. My overall grades for my degree could have been better, but for the fact that I'd only just pulled myself through first year, I was pretty happy with the 2:1 I'd managed to scrape. I already had a job to go to after I finished up at the book shop, and our life in London was only a year away. Every day, we inched closer to it.

I'd told Astrid my results in amazement after I read them, and she hugged me, saying she knew I'd be fine. She'd been telling me that my previous good marks and the amount of work I'd been doing would be enough, but I just hadn't believed it. I was so sure something would somehow go wrong. But I figured it was good to expect the worst so that I'd be prepared if it happened, though I was very happy to accept the opposite. It was a nice surprise.

We'd cracked out the bubbly that night, later deciding to also indulge in a couple of celebratory caps of MD ('I have a wicked idea,' she'd said), and we stayed up talking excitedly about all the places we wanted to travel to in our futures, then watched the sunrise from our living room.

The days before you returned to finish your final year of

university were getting fewer. I was looking forward to it but part of me felt nervous, and I had no idea why.

'We're having one last hurrah before he returns,' Astrid had said one day, after she'd got back from one of her trips, playing a couple of gigs up in Newcastle.

I laughed. 'Nothing's going to change,' I told her for what felt like the hundredth time. 'I'll just be spending a bit more time over at his. That's all.' She usually just rolled her eyes and brushed it off but this time she said something.

'Perhaps, but what will he think when you're out all night every weekend?'

I guess I hadn't really thought about it in detail. Maybe I was being naive. I didn't want to admit it, but she might actually be right. We wouldn't be living together, but I couldn't avoid the fact that you would be more involved in my life on a day-to-day basis when we were both in the same city... And I couldn't imagine, after your reaction when you saw the aftermath of our festival, that you'd be too happy with what it had looked like for the past year. And I was adamant that you would not find out exactly what had been going on whilst you'd been gone. There was no need for you to know. It was better for everyone that way. It would be over with Chris, and knowing the details would surely only upset and anger you. And that was the last thing I wanted to do.

'We'll still be able to go out, like we used to before he left. Just maybe not as often, or as extreme as we have been lately.'

'And with less Chris.'

The mention of his name made me feel uncomfortable.

'Yes, with zero Chris.'

'He'll still be around, you know. You can't disappear him entirely.'

'I know.' I wanted to change the topic because it was too painful to think about. 'You can still go out like normal though.'

She scoffed. 'Of course I can. And good Little Mouse will go home when the clock strikes twelve, before she turns into a pumpkin and then I'll be left having all the fun with all the lovely boys and girls and people life has to offer!'

'I'm definitely not going to go all Cinderella on you. I can still stay out, I might just be a little less... debaucherous. But it's not like he'll be telling me what to do.'

'We'll see. I think you might find his grip tightening when he's got you back in his sights.'

I highly doubted it. You weren't like that, which I was grateful for. Though sometimes I think I wished you were – maybe even slightly jealous, so I could be sure you still loved me. But I hadn't given you reason to be jealous. Well, not that you knew of, anyway. I enjoyed the idea of us living fairly separate lives. No one wanted a relationship that involved living in each other's pockets and I certainly didn't want to seem needy. It was nice to have some freedom to be myself.

For what Astrid deemed our 'last hurrah', she'd gathered a whole gang of us together. We started with drinks at ours. I was feeling destructive, like nothing mattered.

'Let's get drunk!' she announced. 'Let's cause some havoc. Let's burn this city to the ground!'

As I replied 'hell yeah' and drank my rum and coke she'd poured me, I thought that maybe she *did* have moments of feeling destructive too. Maybe it wasn't just a dark, shameful part of me. But I let go of that thought almost as soon as it appeared. When I watched her, she was pure lightness, pure perfection, not twisted like I was. We'd toasted – 'to the night, to the light and to everything that's bright' – all of us with a shot in each hand. One, two. The liquid burned as it went down. My throat was on fire. But it didn't even matter. Not tonight.

Three, four.

More people arrived. I said hi, but they could have been anyone.

Five, six.

It was a full moon, Astrid pointed out, a 'Harvest Moon', and therefore we were listening to Neil Young. Though it wasn't quite the right vibe for the night, so she switched it for some Kraftwerk.

Then Chris arrived. He took a moment to check if I was ok before saying hello to everyone else. It was sweet.

'I'm better than ok,' I said, before thrusting my fist into the air. 'Let's burn this city!'

He laughed. 'Ok then. Burn it, we shall.' And he went to get more shots.

Seven, Eight.

What must have been a short time later, we were outside the club, and things were looking good. A quick cap of MD was handed to me by Astrid as we waited in the queue, and I somehow managed to swallow it without liquid, which made me smile to myself. Nothing was going to stop me. Getting nearer the front of the line; standing up straight, small smiles, eyes focused. Sober. *Absolutely fine, sir.* Smile at the bouncer, but not too much or you'll look manic. And no one suits manic.

The music that night was everything. It was trance and I was buzzing. Astrid brought me a water and we danced and we danced and we danced.

Everything felt so clear. Life was something so utterly,

eternally, important. *A combination of fleeting moments and connections.* I remembered Astrid had said that to me at some point over the year and I think I'd written it down, determined to make something of it at a later point. Here I was, experiencing life-changing moments with a room full of people who were all utterly joyous. And Astrid was by my side. She kissed me. On the lips. Not a romantic kiss, but I knew she felt it too: the importance of this moment. In that carefree moment, I realised that she was right: everything was going to change. It had to. But I felt so connected to people that night, and so connected to myself.

Chris pulled me away to go to the smoking area for some time out in the cool air, grabbing a water on the way.

'Tonight is everything!' I said as I threw my arms around him.

'Indeed it is.'

'Isn't it all just so fantastic? It's so extraordinary! Astrid's extraordinary, isn't she? You're extraordinary! I wish I was extraordinary.'

'You could be extraordinary,' he said and tapped me gently on the nose. 'You just need to believe it.'

No one had ever used the word extraordinary in relation to me before.

So I kissed him.

I heard someone scream 'Kittens!' And I looked around, startled by the noise, though I knew immediately it was Astrid. She put her arms around us both. 'Now, now, you two delinquents, I hear this all must end tonight. This...' she pointed at me, 'and this,' she pointed at Chris, 'and perhaps this...' she threw her hands out, indicating (I presume) the night and the three of us.

Chris had understood – he'd known from the beginning that I had my place with you and that he and I could never be together, not properly. He knew it was coming as much as I did. He never tried to say I should leave you or that I should be with him. Neither did I. I knew I couldn't. I knew that wasn't an option. It wasn't a sustainable life I'd been living; it wasn't where I was meant to be. There was no way I was about to throw everything away for what had been some late nights and a stupid crush, of that I was certain. I could never be that type of person, I was better than that. Or at least I *would be* better than that very soon. So it was fine. It was all fine.

That night we'd sparkled so bright. The lasers layered through the smoke and we'd stood above the crowd, the three of us with our arms around each other, watching it all morph together.

Chapter 39

You and Ethan moved into your new place when the summer was over. It was a typical house for two males, so different from the vibe of our flat. While ours was filled with art, flowers, musical instruments, and fairy lights, yours had a wide-screen TV, gaming consoles and nothing on the walls. I never quite felt at home there.

Our first night together after you came back began so well. You'd picked me up and taken me out to dinner. We sat and ate pasta and chatted about what we'd been up to since we'd last been together. Then we went back to yours, where we ended up sitting on the couch together, watching something.

It was me who initiated, leaning over to kiss you on the neck. I wanted to feel something. I wanted to be closer to you. You put your arm around me but kept watching the TV. So I whispered in your ear: 'I want you.'

I know, I'd never been so forward before, I rarely started things between us. But I was different – I'd changed since you'd been away, and I felt like maybe I could ask for something if I wanted it. I wondered if you'd notice it was rather out of character, but somehow, I didn't care. I felt empty and it made me slightly panicky. It wasn't enough. I needed something to happen. You looked at me with your mouth slightly open.

'Oh, ok,' you said, sounding surprised. You switched off the TV and we went to your room. The lights were on, which felt all wrong. We lay down next to each other on the bed and you started to take your jeans off. Then you rolled over and got on top of me and started kissing me. You were a good kisser and I remembered how much I liked kissing you. But it didn't last for long. We started having sex and while it was nice to be close to you, to feel you inside me as if filling some kind of void, it just felt like going through the motions. There was no passion at all. I needed more.

Before I could think rationally, I forgot myself and my voice came out sounding pleading and urgent.

'Hurt me.'

'What?' you said quickly, pushing yourself up to look at me. This time I knew I'd said the wrong thing. 'I'm not going to hurt you, why would you say that?'

'Sorry, never mind,' I said, and for a few moments, you kept going as I lay there, unsure of how to react. I felt tense and the painful feeling as you thrust into me wasn't going away. That wasn't where I wanted to feel pain – I wanted it to feel good, but I also wanted to feel your power over me.

Then you stopped and said, 'I'm not feeling it anymore.'

Neither was I.

I was immediately embarrassed by the whole thing. I hoped you would forget about it and never mention it again or ask where I'd got the idea from.

And you didn't mention it again, thankfully. You fell asleep so quickly. I heard your breathing deepen and you were gone. I lay awake for hours playing the scene over and over in my head. I was so stupid. I didn't know how I was going to get used to regular sex again when I'd had so much more, something that consumed my body and mind and made me ache for it... What was wrong with me? Why did I want this? I knew I needed to try harder to let go of those dark parts of me that Chris had awakened during those late nights.

I resented you for being such an easy and sound sleeper. I'd always struggled with sleep. At night my fears would play across my eyelids. I would dredge up moments from my past: either recent ones, or some from so long ago that I couldn't even remember them properly. I would remind myself of all the stupid and terrible things I had said and done. Then I'd think of all the ways they could ruin my future. I'd think of all the ways that you would find out my wicked thoughts and actions and hate me for them. I didn't want to be hated, I wanted to be better. But I didn't know how.

I always had my darkest thoughts at night time. There were times during those dark hours that I wanted to tell you about Chris – come clean about all of it. I wanted to see your reaction, to know how you'd react. But in the light of morning, I'd realise that it was a stupid idea. I would only be doing it to clear my guilty conscience. It wasn't something that would benefit you.

I was starting to feel so nervous and anxious all the time that I found it difficult to properly enjoy things. I'd noticed that things were starting to feel slightly tense between you and Astrid. Nothing obvious, but just certain comments, and the way you both acted around each other and with me. I was constantly worried I had said or done something wrong to make one of you hate me.

I started to get weird flashing lights in my vision too. Astrid told me it was a migraine. Not a full migraine, but a type of migraine. My mother got migraines where she had to stay in bed for days. I didn't get it that bad, but I smiled at the thought that maybe one day I would, and Astrid, or you, would have to look after me. You would look at each other with serious faces and say things like, 'Oh, poor Jess. It must be terrible for you' and 'Can I get you a cup of tea?' And maybe you would take it in turns to read to me because I wouldn't be able to look at the page. But I never got migraines that badly. It turned out I couldn't even do migraines properly.

The flashing lights had startled me at first, zig-zagging in an ever moving circle across my vision, but then became familiar and I felt lonely when they went away.

I would often wake up at night covered in sweat, desperately trying to pull myself out of my dreams. Some nights it was dogs fighting over my limbs. Other nights I was on some sort of quest to find something, but I was being chased. It always ended the same – me on the edge of a cliff, my pursuer behind me and water and angry rocks baring their teeth out of the waves below. It didn't matter where I was running – at uni, in Paris, in the middle of London, through a field... I always ended up at the cliff and I always had to jump.

I'd wake up with the same choked scream every time. If you were there, you would roll over, put your hand on me and say, 'Shhh'. It gave me some comfort, but I would still lie there keeping myself awake for a while, for fear that I would fall back asleep and suddenly be back on the cliff again.

Sometimes it happened when she and I were together, if we were crashing in her bed or mine, for whatever reason – after a late night, or maybe after falling asleep while watching a movie. She would wrap me in her arms, stroke my hair, or slip her hand into mine. In the morning I would wake up to our fingers still entwined. I felt so close to her in those moments. I never wanted them to end.

Chapter 40

Astrid and I were cooking in the kitchen one night after I'd finished a shift at the bookshop. She was back at uni, but she'd still often come to meet me after work to pick me up, which always gave me something to look forward to.

We were having a night in together and making lasagne. I think we were celebrating the fact that I'd started writing a sort of newsletter for the bookshop, which was a lot of fun, and gave me something a bit more creative to spend some of my work shifts focusing on.

'So, how's Robert life going?' she asked as she was putting out a layer of pasta sheets.

'Fine,' I said absentmindedly as I grated the cheese to put on top of the lasagne.

'Fine?' she said, looking up.

'Oh, yeah, I mean... It's good.'

'Mhm?'

'Yeah... well, I dunno, I guess... I'm kind of struggling to work out where we exist together now. It seems even harder than before. I thought it would be easier. I'm sure it used to be easier. I guess it'll just take some time to adjust.'

'What did you expect?' she said, moving to slicing up an

aubergine. We were listening to Dire Straits' *Communique*, an album I'd never heard before Astrid introduced me to it. 'He's still just same old Robert. Just because he's been away doesn't mean anything is going to change. I honestly don't know why you still put up with him.'

'Yeah, I know you don't. It's just...' There was part of me that could see where she was coming from, but there were also many reasons I was with you. You could be so loving and thoughtful and charming. You often thought of me and bought me little gifts. You helped me out with things when I needed it. You pushed me to do things out of my comfort zone and you helped me deal with my parents. You were my future, and you felt like home. With you around, I would never be alone. I didn't want to throw all of that away. Relationships weren't meant to be easy and working at them meant you were growing up and taking things seriously. I didn't want to be the girl with unrelenting standards who ended up alone; a spinster, with no one to love her. The thought of that possibility sat in the back of my mind, ready to terrify me at any moment. Having to make compromises didn't mean the whole thing should be abandoned.

'Maybe you need to make him jealous somehow... I think I know someone who could help...'

I think she was joking, but I answered quickly anyway.

'No way. I don't want to risk him finding out, I don't want to hurt him, and I can't bear to lose him.'

She shrugged. 'Whatever. Just don't come whining to me when Robert is being Robert. You've always known what he's like.'

'Hey, Astrid,' I said. I'd been wondering whether to ask her something that had been playing on my mind. But I figured if

I couldn't talk to her about it then I'd never be able to talk to anyone, and it felt like it was burning a hole inside me.

'Yeah?'

'Do you... you know... enjoy sex?' I felt embarrassed asking her. I felt embarrassed talking about it at all.

'Sometimes. Depends. Why do you ask? Do you?'

'Yeah, sort of. I mean... what do you mean by *depends*?'

'Well, it doesn't take much for me to get bored. Especially with men. I've had a lot of sex, you know. And it all tends to be the same: some guy grunting away on top of you, trying to get himself off. Unless it's not – unless you push some boundaries, play some games, experiment together... That's where the magic happens. Especially for women. Sex starts in our minds rather than our bodies.'

'It can't always be like that though, can it? I mean... if you're in a relationship...'

'Aha, I understand now – things not feeling as exciting now that you're back to the same old?'

'No, it's just...' I trailed off. I didn't want to say it. I didn't want to voice any of it. I immediately regretted bringing it up. My neck felt hot.

'Doing something you shouldn't is addictive?' she asked, looking at me with a smile.

'It can't stay like that forever though, can it?'

'Probably not in the same way, no. But you know what I think of your view on relationships.'

'I do?'

She put down the knife and turned to face me. 'You have some strange ideas of what a relationship is and, frankly, I think you take the fun out of it entirely. But maybe that's Robert's doing.'

'But surely you can't have comfort and security if you're always searching for things you shouldn't be doing.'

'Why not? Sounds boring to me, otherwise.'

I shook my head and smiled. 'Why does that not surprise me? I wonder if you'll ever change.' I said, teasing her.

'Don't count on it. I'll never settle.'

'Maybe in ten years you'll find you want the fairy-tale ending.'

'I was never brought up on Disney or religion, all that crap means nothing to me. You and I have very different ideas of what the *ultimate goal* in life is. And I am enough on my own. I certainly don't need a man to complete me.'

Maybe that was it. Or maybe it was just that she was spectacular, with a seemingly never-ending line of people desperate for her attention. She could take her pick, when and how she wanted it. It was different for me, I needed to keep hold of what I had if I wanted to survive.

We sat and ate our lasagne over a bottle of red wine. Astrid told me about a party coming up the following week that someone she knew was throwing. I was surprised when she said that I should invite you.

'Really?' I asked.

She shrugged. 'Why not? You want to see where you exist together? Invite him into our world. See how he fits.'

'Yeah, ok, maybe I will. You don't mind him coming?'

'Nah, I quite fancy the guy who's throwing the party anyway, so I'm sure I'll find a way to entertain myself.'

'Yeah, ok, sure. That sounds like a good idea. I'll let him know. See what he thinks.'

I figured it could go either way. You'd either just have no interest in going, or you'd be up for it. I could never quite tell which it would be, it was hard to predict how you'd feel about something.

In the end you'd said yes. I was excited you'd decided to come, but also slightly worried you'd hate it. But I didn't realise that was going to be the least of my worries.

Chapter 41

'Who is that?' you asked.

We had been at the party for a short while when Chris sailed past us, shooting me a wide, yet oddly intimate smile. I immediately felt my cheeks redden. I don't know why it hadn't crossed my mind that he'd be there. Astrid had been fairly vague about the party, and it just hadn't crossed my mind to ask if she thought he might come. As he made his way over to a group of people, he shot back another look at me, and I knew you had noticed even before you said anything.

'Oh, that's just Chris,' I said hoping my voice didn't waver. 'He's in Astrid's club crew.'

'Chris. He looks like he likes you.'

'Oh, no, not particularly,' I scrambled. 'He's just quite a friendly person...' He'd started talking to another girl at that moment, in his beautiful, vivacious way, which made my stomach feel hollow, but I was grateful for the timing. 'See?'

You watched him, nodding slightly.

Just play it cool, Jess. This will pass.

There was no reason you would think there was anything between Chris and me. And anyway, there wasn't. It was over.

After that, you stayed close to me. Part of me wondered if

Astrid had been right, and that a little jealousy might do our relationship some good. You'd never shown signs of jealousy before, but the idea of you feeling that way made me feel important. Like I belonged to you. I hadn't felt that wanted for a while. Not since our early days or, though I didn't want to admit it, the nights with Chris.

It was a particularly loud party, a birthday celebration for that guy Astrid had mentioned. I saw why she fancied him – he was typical Astrid type; tall, skinny black jeans, leather jacket. He had striking cheekbones and collarbones jutting out from under his shirt, which was unbuttoned to the middle of his stomach. I had no idea how she knew him or when they'd met, I guess he was just one of the many people who moved in and out of her life. I noticed that Chris seemed to know him quite well – perhaps he was the connection. Though I pushed that thought aside and tried not to wonder if Astrid had orchestrated a situation where I would have to be in the same room as both of you. I was sure she wouldn't do that to me, not without warning.

As the night went on, I continued to see Chris in the periphery of my vision. He always seemed to be just a few feet away. I could also feel the grip of your arm around my shoulder tighten every time he appeared. I was starting to feel a bit overwhelmed by everything. I went to the bathroom to get away from it all for a moment, lingering as long as I could before someone knocked on the door. On the way back to find you, I noticed there was a cupboard underneath the stairs, and I quietly opened it and slipped inside. I knew it was a ridiculous thing to be doing, and that if anyone saw me, they wouldn't understand. But it was cool and dark and quiet, and I just needed some time out. I could hear feet shuffling past outside, and laughter and shouts muffled by the door, but I felt safe in my hiding spot. I stood beside the vacuum clearer, my plastic tumbler of wine in my hand.

The wall felt cold on my back, and I shuffled my feet to fit better around a bucket that was on the floor below me. I concentrated on slowing my breathing like Chris had showed me that first night we'd met, hoping it would help me to regain some control. After what must have been only five minutes, light and noise suddenly rushed at me as the door was pulled open and two faces appeared in the opening.

'This isn't the bathroom,' one of them exclaimed.

I smiled awkwardly and tried to stammer some apologies. It must have looked so strange to open a cupboard under the stairs and see a person in there, leaning up against the wall.

They left the door ajar slightly after they disappeared, the sounds of the party seeping in and the light from outside glowing around the edges.

In the light, I could see I had managed to spill my wine on my dress. I should have known better. Whenever I wore white, it seemed to coax any nearby liquid to add pattern and colour to its blank slate. Sometimes I felt like that too; like I was a white dress, a blank slate that borrowed pattern and colour from people I met. That was the beauty of life, right? Those fleeting moments of connection.

I knew I would have to go back out. *But just a few more moments of peace...*

Eventually I heard my name being called. The door was flung open again and Astrid appeared. It was almost like she'd known I'd be there. She took my hand.

'You ok, Little Mouse?' she said, a worried look on her face. I knew then that she hadn't realised Chris would be there.

'Yeah, just chilling out for a minute.'

Then you appeared and your face seemed to be leaning more towards anger than concern. I felt immediately bad for disappearing without telling you.

'I've been looking for you everywhere! Where have you been?' you said, hands on your hips.

'Sorry, I just needed some time out. I was feeling a bit overwhelmed.'

'Come on, let's get you out of here,' you said.

You'd driven us to the party and so you weren't drinking. I was happy to get out of there, so I said bye to Astrid.

'Are you sure you're ok?' she said, still looking concerned, glancing at you standing there with your arm around me. 'We can go home if you like...'

'No, no, I'm fine. You enjoy yourself. He's super fit, I can see why you like him. You should go for it,' I said, and hugged her.

'Ok, if you're sure,' she replied, and then giggled. 'And yeah, he is, isn't he?'

We slid into the seats in your car and for some reason, as you began to drive, I started to panic. I knew I should be calming down now that I was with you, but everything just felt too much. I had this strange feeling like the world was ending. I hadn't properly felt that way since the night that Chris had found me in the smoking area and taken me home the first time. I didn't know where we were going but it felt like the journey would go on forever, that it would never end. You seemed to be driving so fast and the world was rushing past on either side of me, like my life was rushing before my eyes. I couldn't slow it down; I couldn't get out. I felt trapped, the panic rising in my chest, to my shoulders and up my neck.

'Can you pull over for a minute?' I managed to squeak.

You glanced over to me, a confused look on your face, then after a moment you pulled into the curb.

I wanted to scream, I wanted to break something, I wanted to climb out the window and run away, out into the darkness of the night.

You flicked on the stereo, putting a song on that I loved – you knew I loved it; it was Bowie. It was on a CD I'd made for you but didn't know you'd ever listened to it. I didn't even realise it was still in your car. The first track was 'Life On Mars', and as it played, you reached over and held me so tight that I couldn't move.

That song that saw into my soul. It got under my skin and gave me goosebumps. Its soaring chorus always felt hopeful to me – like an escape. But that night – that moment – wasn't the right time to hear it. I didn't want to bring Bowie into a time when I felt such panic. Bowie was sacred.

I struggled against your arms, trying to move so that I could change the song. It was too much. But you just held me tighter. You didn't let go. Eventually I gave up and stopped struggling.

I remembered what Astrid had said, when we danced that night after her first gig: *'Don't you think that listening to songs you love feels like being stabbed in the heart?'*

I felt like I had been stabbed in the heart.

'There,' you said, once the song ended. 'Feeling better now?'

I hated you in that moment. I resented you for thinking you knew what I needed, for assuming you knew *anything* about me. There was a whole year of my life you hadn't even been part of. You thought you had calmed me, but I felt broken.

***

It took a few days for me to recover from that night, but eventually, I felt stronger for it. It had helped me realise that there were parts of me you didn't know and wouldn't understand. Parts that you could never touch. And they were all mine.

You took me out for dinner a couple of nights later, to a nice restaurant where they put our napkins on our laps for us. You gave me a necklace. It had two letters on it. R and J.

'So that everyone knows,' you said, 'You're mine'.

I was 'yours'. You'd never spoken like that before. I wondered again if Astrid's suggestion had worked, that Chris had made you feel jealous. I'd not intended it to happen like that, but it did feel like something had changed. You kept holding my hand over dinner and kissing me. That night when we'd had sex, there was a reminder of the fire, the desire I knew we'd felt in the early days back in our first year of uni; pulling each other's clothes off in the darkness to get at what was underneath. It was what I'd wanted for so long, to find that again. All it had taken was a year apart and for me to get a bit of attention from elsewhere. Now things were going to be better than ever, I just knew it.

Chapter 42

After the dinner when you gave me the necklace, I stayed at yours for a couple of days. When I went home to grab some things and change before my next shift at the book shop, Astrid was sitting at the kitchen table writing in a notebook.

'Here she is,' she said, when I walked in. 'I've not seen you for days. I thought we were meant to be hanging out this week.'

'Oh, sorry. I was staying with Robert.'

'I figured. You're coming out this weekend at least?'

'I'm not sure I can. Robert has a thing he needs me to go to.' You had invited me to your law society ball and while it wasn't my first choice of something to do on a Saturday night, I knew it was important to you.

'On a Saturday night? But Saturday is our night.'

I shrugged. I wasn't sure what she wanted me to do. I had to spend time with you, you were my boyfriend and of course I needed to support you.

'Whatever,' she said, closing her notebook. 'Let me know if you ever feel like gracing me with your presence again and maybe we can do something.'

She got up and walked off before I could say anything. Of

course I wanted to see her – I never stopped wanting to fill every moment of my life with her – but things were going so well with you and I didn't want to jeopardise it. I was sure I could find a balance. I just had to try harder.

I didn't see her that Saturday, of course, I went to your law ball. I wore the necklace you gave me, and you seemed so happy to see it. You said it looked so beautiful on me, which made me smile so much. I did my best all night to keep up with all the conversations about lots of things I didn't care about or quite understand. I tried to fit in with your friends again, but I was reminded of how different I was from them. It seemed even more pronounced now. But I should have expected it. That's just how things were.

They had one of those photo booths and we got photos of us together, then some with your other friends, using tacky oversized props. It was nice to dress up and eat fancy food, but I felt like I was only half there. They were all nice people, but I didn't exactly fit in with them. It was fun to try and pretend I did though. I started to view it as a game, see how well I could make myself blend in.

You'd dropped me back home the next morning before you went off to play football, with that 'five-a-side' team you joined, all made up of law students. I wondered how anyone was ready to play the day after the ball – they'd all got so drunk. I'd tried to too, but no matter how much I drank, everyone seemed to be on a different level to me, and they all just got sillier as the night progressed.

I walked into the kitchen back at The Den and was surprised to see a girl I'd never seen before pouring a glass of water. She was beautiful with dark skin and tight black curls. She was wearing those boy-leg undies, a vest, and knee-high socks.

'Oh, hi,' I said. She turned around looking startled. I felt a weird sense of satisfaction having been able to startle her when it was her who was the intruder in my house. Astrid hadn't mentioned having a friend over, not that she needed to get my permission or anything.

'God, love. Creep up on a woman, won't you?' She had a strong accent that came from somewhere up North.

'Morning, Mouse,' Astrid said from behind me, evidently having just come out of the bathroom. She gave me a half hug around my shoulders. She was in just her bra and pyjama shorts.

'Hi,' I replied.

Had I been replaced so quickly?

'Jess, this is Jordan. Jordan, Jess.'

We both smiled at each other, but I didn't know what to do. I'd wanted to make a cup of tea, but I suddenly felt odd being in the kitchen. Astrid saved me by flicking on the kettle.

'What do we all want? Tea or coffee?' she asked us both as she leaned back on the counter.

'Coffee, thanks babe,' said Jordan.

'Coffee please,' I said quickly. It felt imperative that I match her.

'Coffee it is then,' Astrid busied herself making it.

I stood awkwardly near the doorway. I felt like I'd walked in on something strangely intimate with Astrid and this unknown girl in our kitchen in her underwear. I felt overdressed.

'How was *law ball*?' Astrid asked me, stretching out the vowels in the words.

'Yeah, it was fine. Nice. It was really nice. How was your night?'

'Yeah. Pretty fun.'

'Only *pretty*?' asked Jordan, and a look passed between them that I couldn't translate. Did Astrid and I have moments like that? Then, as Astrid was getting the cups down from the shelf, Jordan turned around and put her hands on either side of Astrid's waist, just below where her body started to curve out and then – to my shock – she kissed Astrid on her shoulder. Astrid turned around with three mugs in hand – and this part I always think played out in slow motion – they kissed. On the lips.

I couldn't help staring. It looked so soft, so tender. There was none of the urgency that I'd come to expect from men. Jordan twirled Astrid's hair in her fingers, which seemed so intimate, considering it was an action I often saw Astrid doing herself when she was thinking. When they broke apart, I looked away.

'Stop showing off,' said Astrid to her softly. I glanced up to see that she was smiling at Jordan.

I'd always assumed that Astrid was straight. I'd only ever seen her with boys. She'd never mentioned she also liked girls. Had I ever asked? Was it rude to ask someone about their sexuality? Was it rude to have assumed she was straight? She was acting as if it was the most normal thing. Had she been with women before? Was Jordan the first? What was so special about Jordan?

'We were going to go out to grab some breakfast after coffee. Did you want to come?' Astrid asked, looking over at me.

'Oh, no, you go. I've got to do a few things before work.'

An enquiring look passed over her face when I said it, which I only picked up because I knew her so well.

'You ok?' she asked.

'Yeah, just tired. Big night,' I said, smiling at her.

She shrugged and handed me a cup of coffee, before rubbing me on the arm as she went through to sit in the living room. Jordan followed, so I did too. We made small talk while we drank our coffees. Astrid was sitting on the sofa, and Jordan arranged herself around her, so close that they were touching. I secretly considered the idea that she felt the need to stake her claim on Astrid with me there. And that made me feel suddenly powerful. I realised Astrid wasn't replacing me – their relationship was physical, like the boys that came and went from Astrid's life. They could never have what we had; theirs wasn't true friendship. I felt relieved.

After they'd left to get their breakfast, I had a bath. As I shaved my legs, my armpits and washed my hair, I began to think about what had happened. I had no issue with Astrid being with girls – of course I didn't. It was totally fine with me. Obviously I'd met her sister Sofia, who I guess was a lesbian, but I'd never really met anyone who was bi, at least not anyone I knew well. Did something like that run in the family? But either way, it didn't bother me or anything, it was more just that I thought I knew her well... But it was ok – she didn't like Jordan more than me, just in a different way. Astrid and I obviously weren't like that. I didn't fancy girls. Imagine what my parents would have said if I did! No, I had a boyfriend and things with you and I were getting really good. Astrid and I had a different kind of relationship. And she wouldn't want me anyway, not like that. She couldn't, she'd never tried, so she couldn't have found me attractive... not like that. Of course she couldn't.

Chapter 43

Even though I'd satisfied myself that Astrid wasn't replacing me with the girl in the kitchen, I still felt like there was a distance between us since you'd returned. I knew I had to show her I still loved her, that I was still around – that we were still Astrid and Jess. So later that day, I sent her a message while I was sitting in the square eating a sandwich on my break from work.

Us night on Saturday? Just like old times. Jxxx

After I'd pressed send, I started worrying about what she might say, if she'd be mad. Maybe she wouldn't even want to spend time with me anymore, what if I'd pushed her too far? I kept re-reading the message and wondering if I'd said the right thing. Had I been too flippant? She replied a little while later, putting me out of my misery.

About time X

***

When Saturday came, we decided to have some drinks at home and then go out to a pub, as there apparently weren't any decent club nights or gigs on. We started early – mimosas and a cheese platter at lunchtime around our dining table, then we went out to the same pub we'd been to so many times before, the same one Astrid had taken me to early in our friendship.

I'd started to feel like a local there, with Ada the publican knowing my name and greeting me whenever we went. We settled out in the sun – autumn was still giving us quite warm days, and Ada had pulled a whole lot of tables outside, as she did over the warmer months. Astrid ordered us both an Aperol Spritz, and although I thought it tasted quite horrible, I felt fancy drinking it.

'It's nice to finally see you – now you've got your new life and you're too important to hang out with me,' she said, once she'd brought us our drinks. She said it in a light-hearted way, like it was a joke, but I knew there was some truth in her words.

'I'm sorry I've not been around much, it's just hard navigating it all. Anyway, I thought you'd be happy for me that things are going well with Robert.'

She rolled her eyes dramatically.

'Soooooo happy for you. After all your assurance that it wasn't going to happen like this. You kept saying nothing would change.'

'I didn't think it would.'

'Of course you didn't. Sometimes you really have no concept of reality.'

'I… I'm sorry.'

'I just think it's a bit rude to say you'd be around when you clearly wouldn't. Like, manage expectations, babe. We say we're going to do something and you're just not there… It's kinda exhausting trying to keep up with you these days.'

'It's never stuff we've actually planned that I miss, just when we loosely say we might hang out.'

'And those times are no longer important to you?'

'Of course they are.'

'Doesn't really seem it, to be honest...'

'I'm sorry!' I felt attacked, but I also knew I had let her down. I started to cry. We hardly ever fought like this, and I didn't like it.

'Oh, Mouse.' She got up, came around to my side of the table and put her arms around me. 'It's ok. I'm just upset that I'm not so important to you anymore. It makes me sad that you no longer want to hang out.'

'I do. I swear I do.'

She wiped her eye, and I wondered if she was crying too. Surely not. Astrid didn't cry. Not like me. I cried at literally anything.

'Come on,' she said finally. 'This is silly. Let's have a nice night.'

'I love you, Astrid. I always will. It'll always be us. I'll try harder.'

'I love you too.'

After holding me for a moment longer, she went back to her chair and we both finished our drinks, sitting in silence for a moment.

'I've got an idea,' she said after a while, with a familiar smile I hadn't seen for a while. 'Let's get a tattoo!'

'What?'

'Tattoos! Matching Bowie tattoos. How about lightning bolts? Just small ones. That way we'll always know it's the two of us, even if we have to be apart. And when I look at it, I'll know you're with me even if you're off with Robert.'

It had been so long since I'd felt the thrill of her testing me, seeing if I would rise to the challenge. I wanted to show how her how much I still loved her – that I would follow her to the ends of the earth. I knew my mum would freak out if I actually did it, and that you probably would too. But in that moment, I didn't seem to care. It was my life, wasn't it? And I was feeling so overwhelmed by my love for Astrid. She had only been angry because she loved me so much too. And if we did this, we would always be linked.

'Ok,' I said slowly, then with more conviction. 'Let's do it.'

'Now!'

'Wait, now? What do you mean now? How can we do it now?' I was thinking I'd have time to build up to it, to prepare.

'I'll text Fab – I'm sure he'll be working and he'll fit us in.'

'Who's Fab?'

'You know Fabien... We met him together.'

I looked at her while I scanned my brain for any memory. I slowly started to shake my head. I couldn't think of anyone called Fabien.

'Come on, remember that rave we went to in that warehouse place just out of the city?'

I remembered the night, it had been the previous year, one of the many random clubs we'd gone to. I remember it being hard to get home because we couldn't get a taxi. I remember getting quite wasted. And I remember there being lots of seedy men trying to openly sell drugs on the dance floor.

'You know the group of French guys?'

'Oh yeah, we sat with them for a while in that weird booth area.' I remembered Astrid talking to them, I'd been sitting next to her, distracted by the loud music.

'Then you remember Fabien?'

'I guess...'

'We all followed each other on Instagram.'

I half shrugged, half nodded. She laughed and shook her head at me. I wondered if she'd slept with Fabien and that's why she still had contact with him.

'Why don't you see if Ada can make us a couple of Whisky Sours, and I'll text him,' she said, getting out her phone.

'Ok, yeah, sure.'

I went inside and waited until Ada was free, then asked her for the drinks. She rolled her eyes at me and asked why we couldn't just order something easy. I immediately went to apologise, before she laughed and said she was only kidding, then started making our drinks. Those sorts of interactions always made me feel uneasy – I never knew what the other person was going to say or how I'd be expected to react. Even just going and paying for something at the grocery store made me feel uncomfortable.

But I survived and made my way back out to Astrid with our drinks, putting them down on the table, then sitting down and cheersing her. After we'd talked excitedly about the tattoos for a while and where we wanted them, her phone vibrated on the table.

'Oh!' She squealed, as she picked it up and read the message. 'He said to head over! You ready for this my darling?'

'I.. Yes. I am. Let's do it!'

'Let's bloody do it!'

She put her hands out and clasped mine and we shook hands on it. We both finished our drinks, and then when we got up, she hugged me. The whole mood had changed. There was no more anger. The world felt full of possibilities again. We left the bar, saying bye to Ada, and Astrid made us do the follow-the-yellow-brick-road skip across the blocks to the tattoo parlour. By the time we got there, we were feeling giggly.

Fabien met us with huge hugs when we arrived. He was short and stocky and covered in tattoos. I was fairly certain

Astrid hadn't slept with him. Their vibe was definitely just friendly, and he wasn't her type.

'So nice to see you guys!' he said. 'How have you been, Jess?'

'Oh yeah, good thanks,' I said, smiling in a way that I hoped was one of more familiarity than I was feeling. I recognised him at least. 'How about you?'

'Pretty good, I ended up staying in Paris for six months instead of just the two, so I've been busy slotting back into things here. Your boyfriend is back from America now, right?'

I tried to hide my surprise of how well this guy seemed to remember me when I had such little recollection of him. Maybe Astrid had told him, or maybe I had, but couldn't remember the conversation... those nights were often a bit of a blur.

'Yeah, yeah, he's here now. It's... wonderful.'

Astrid was watching me with raised eyebrows.

'Ah great, I'm so glad to hear it! Ok well, let's get started! Where do you girls want them? And who's going first?' he asked.

'I'll go first,' Astrid said, looking at me with a nod that asked if that was what I wanted. I smiled and nodded quickly in return. She turned back to Fabien and held out her wrist, pulling up her lace sleeve to expose the white underside of her forearm. 'I want it front and centre!'

That was a very obvious spot. I felt my tummy tighten at the thought of getting it there. There was no way I could get away with it.

'For both of you?' he asked, looking at me.

'Um... I think I might need to get mine somewhere else. Maybe on my ankle?'

I saw Astrid's face fall slightly when I said it, but I hoped she'd understand. There was no way I'd be able to hide it from you for long, but at least on my ankle I could hide it from my parents. It was exhilarating to know I was doing this without you or them knowing. It felt dangerous, I felt like a rebel.

Rebel Rebel.

Like on the jacket I was wearing that night.

So Astrid went first. And after only really a few minutes, she was gazing down at her finished lightning bolt tattoo. It was a simple black outline, with beautiful thin lines. It looked amazing and my skin tingled at the thought that I would soon have one too. Before I knew it, I was in the chair and Fab was bringing the gun down onto my ankle. It hurt, quite a lot, and I'm sure it took much longer than Astrid's seemed to. I clenched my eyes shut as he did it. Fab told me that it was a much less painful place than Astrid's had been, and I felt grateful for my decision.

Astrid held my hand the whole time. In a weird way, I kind of enjoyed the pain. It felt grounding. This was my rebirth. Things would be different now.

We slept in her bed that night, like old times. We'd stayed up chatting by fairy light, comparing our tattoos that were now wrapped in plastic, and drinking straight from a bottle of red wine in her bed.

'Astrid,' I said, taking a swig of the wine before passing it back to her. 'Tell me about Paris.'

'What do you want to know?' she asked.

'Everything.'

'Well... there's nowhere really quite like it. Everything feels different in Paris. There's such a feeling of expanse – the streets are so wide, plus there are so many parks and gardens. The sunlight looks different as it falls upon the rows of buildings. It feels like you're constantly in a movie – no matter where you go, it's just so cinematic. Almost unbelievably so. It's not like there are just some opportune spots that have that Parisian vibe, it's literally everywhere. There are whole streets lined with crêperies, plus street vendors always ready to whip up some fresh ones on the spot.'

'I love crêpes,' I said.

'Me too. Breton crêpes are famously served with a bowl of cider too.'

'Yes please.'

'Creativity also never feels far away in Paris. The French government actually supports its creatives, so there's a lot more of it around. There's even a whole street up near Montmartre that's filled with guitar shops, which always makes me feel sad for Denmark Street in London.'

'Denmark Street? What's that?'

'It's where all the music shops and recording studios used to be back in the day. But they're slowly closing. The internet hasn't exactly helped I don't think.'

'Oh, that's sad.'

'Yeah, but as for Paris, it feels like every time you step outside, there's an adventure waiting to be had. There are so many restaurants and cafés to choose from. Sometimes it feels like too many; it's impossible to decide where to go. But the classic Parisian thing is to sit at a table on the street, all the chairs facing out, drinking a glass of red and having a cigarette.'

She painted such a beautiful picture of Paris; it really made me want to go. I felt so excited at the prospect of one day being able to travel to all these wonderful places. There was so much laughter that night and I felt so light. She'd helped me remember that side of me, and I wanted to hold onto it.

Chapter 44

I always got so swept up in the romance of every situation when I was with Astrid that I often forgot about the consequences until later. I didn't regret getting the tattoo, but when the sparkle of that night and that moment in time started to dissipate, I had to face the reality – it was likely to cause a confrontation with you. While I was with Astrid, I didn't seem to care about that. I didn't care what you would think or what you would say. But as reality set in, so did fear. I hated confrontations. I usually did whatever I could to avoid them.

I figured the best course of action was just to come out with it and tell you. I knew you weren't going to like it; you weren't a fan of tattoos at all. But this way you could at least see that I respected you enough to tell you directly. Astrid had once said it was easier to justify something after doing it, than to ask for permission before. The next time I saw you was at The Den. Although we usually spent most of our time together at your place, I wanted to break this to you in the safety of my own space. So I invited you over for dinner.

'You know how I love Bowie?' I said, in a tone that I hoped was light. We were sitting in the living room together having finished our meal. I'd cooked us steak, knowing it was your favourite. I wasn't much of a fan, but I knew it would have the best chance of putting you in a good mood.

'Ummm, yeah.'

'You know how I've loved him for so long and how important he is to me?'

'Sure.'

'Well... I wanted to do something special to signify that.'

You looked up at me. You had been flicking through a newspaper you'd brought.

'What are you talking about?'

'Well – please don't get mad – but I just got a really tiny thing. For Bowie.'

'What do you mean you got a thing What are you talking about?'

'A... tattoo. I got a tattoo.' I watched as confusion, realisation, then anger spread across your face.

'But it's only tiny, I promise.' I continued, quickly. 'You'll hardly even see it. It'll be covered most of the time. It's just for me. Look, you'll hardly even know it's there! See?'

I took a deep breath and pulled the bottom of my jeans up to get under my sock and show it to you. You immediately had a look of disgust on your face.

'For fuck's sake, Jess. What were you thinking? You weren't thinking, were you. You never do. And I guess she made you do this.'

'What, Astrid? No, of course she didn't make me—'

'I can't believe you just went and did that without even mentioning it to me first! I'm the one who'll have to see it!' You'd raised your voice. 'You never think about anyone other than yourself! Did you just do it on a whim? Or have you been secretly plotting this out? You realise you're going be stuck with this for the rest of your life, right? *We're* going to be stuck with it... I actually can't believe you right now.'

'I'm sorry,' I replied, quietly.

'You're what?' you shouted.

'I'm sorry!' I said louder.

I started crying, of course. First because I had let you down, then because I felt that I had let Astrid down by not standing up for our friendship more. But I don't know what I would have said anyway. Arguments with you were always a waste of time. The lawyer voice would come out and I'd just end up saying whatever I had to so that I didn't make you even more angry. Somehow, I always ended up apologising, even if I didn't feel at fault. It was just easier that way. I couldn't count the times you'd said that you can't be expected to deal with me when I was being 'like this'. You would disappear for hours, not talking to me for a day, sometimes more. You needed space, I totally understood that, but nothing hurt me more than you just cutting off from me. I knew it was my fault, though, so I couldn't really complain. You were putting up with a lot, and you didn't even know the half of it. I had always kept a mental list of the things that bothered or upset you, little things I said, or big things like the tattoo. I figured I'd crack how to make you happy eventually; it would just take time to work out how to stop disappointing you.

Of course I knew I shouldn't have got the tattoo without telling you first. But I knew if I'd had time to mention it first, you'd have convinced me not to get it at all. And really, even in the short period of time I'd had it, I had grown to love it. I couldn't imagine ever not having it. Part of me wanted to lash out at you, angry that you thought you had any say on what I did with my body. But the logical side of my brain knew it wasn't like that, you were right – you were going to have to live with it too.

While you were shouting and I was crying, Astrid happened to come home, walking through the front door and into the living room. She clocked the situation immediately and stood there in the doorway, all nearly-six-feet of her casting an almost threatening presence, looking at us with her arms crossed.

'Everything ok in here?' she said, her voice strong.

You looked from me to her, then back to me.

'You two deserve each other,' you said, then got up and grabbed your coat. I tried to tell you to calm down. I asked you to stay, I begged you not to walk out. But you just kept going until you slammed the front door behind you.

I went back to the couch and just sat there crying. I don't know what I had been expecting, but I should have seen it coming. I guess I'd hoped you'd be ok with it, that you'd think it was different on me; that you'd see how lovely and fine it was. I'd hoped you'd support my decision with what I wanted to do with my body.

'You shouldn't let him talk to you like that,' Astrid said, making me look up. She'd gone and made us tea while I was crying, which she was pouring out of the new light blue teapot she'd picked up at a charity shop, filling two mugs for us – our special matching mugs with the A & J on them.

'I'm guessing you told him about the tattoo...' she said.

I sniffed and nodded, wiping the last of my tears on a tissue from the box Astrid was holding out to me. 'Do you ever worry that you've done something that will make someone hate you? Like really hate you? Like you've pushed them too far?' I asked her.

'Sometimes people will love me and sometimes they'll hate me. But either way, I know I'm me, and they can't take that away. I'll never sacrifice myself for anyone, so I don't need to waste my time feeling bad about things. It's just not worth spending too much time worrying about how other people will react. You can't control them. Might as well just be you and they can take it or leave it. You'll only suffocate yourself otherwise.'

Like I had many times before, I wondered how she had so much confidence in herself. Then I realised as I always did, that given how perfect and loved she was, it all made sense.

'I always feel like I've done something wrong. That everyone will hate me for whatever I've done... Or someone will find out that I don't belong.'

'Sounds like a song,' she said.

It took me a moment to realise that what I'd said sounded like it could be a lyric, and then I actually started to laugh. Astrid laughed too, and neither of us could stop. Soon the tears were from laughing and no longer from crying.

'See, Mouse, you're always the writer, even when you're not thinking about it,' she said as she smiled and rubbed my back. 'You know, sometimes you can do things just for you, not just because you think it's what you *should* do, or what someone else would want you to do. You are allowed to do things just because you enjoy them. That is enough. You can't control what other people think of you. The closest you can get is continually holding yourself back for someone else's benefit and that never ends well. Just do what you love and ignore the rest.'

I smiled and nodded. What she said sounded great in theory, but I had to remind myself of how different we were, how different our lives and dreams were. She didn't have anyone she had to try and keep happy, and she seemed to like it that way – for her, being alone didn't mean loneliness because she was so easily surrounded by people. She didn't have a boyfriend she had to consider, or parents with huge expectations. She could just live on her own terms. It was different for me, I couldn't. The thought of being alone filled me with more dread than all the tattoos and subsequent conversations in the world.

It took a few days for you to recover from the tattoo incident. I hated those days. I couldn't think straight, I was just waiting for the moment when you calmed down. I went to work but my mind couldn't keep on any one task. I put books in the wrong place, I struggled to answer customers' questions. I felt overwhelmed by the sorrow that sat in the pit of my stomach.

On those days I felt the most alone, I wanted to message Chris. A manic little voice from somewhere inside me wanted to tell him about the tattoo, but I stopped myself, even though the thought threatened to tear me apart at times. I knew I shouldn't message him on principle, but I think I was also scared of what he would say. I was scared that he would like it, or think it was cool and ask to see it. And I just couldn't take the possibility that he would think it was a good thing. I think it might have broken me. No, I needed to concentrate on building things back up with you. I needed to make amends, not go chasing a stupid past fling. I really couldn't work out what was wrong with my brain sometimes.

I was terrified you would say it was the end, that you couldn't be expected to deal with me 'at all'. But it didn't happen. You eventually told me that although you didn't like it, I could just cover it up when we were around anyone else.

It seemed like a decent compromise. I was so relieved and grateful that you could find a way to forgive me.

Chapter 45

Things between us were back on track and I remember feeling so happy because of it. A few days later I was over at your place. That night, Astrid and I were heading off to a gig I was reviewing. As well as writing for *The Relativity Cadenza*, I'd started writing for a local online culture publication as their music correspondent. It didn't pay cash, but it got me free tickets to gigs, with a plus-one, which I thought was pretty cool. I'd put my favourite black notebook in my bag ready for the gig; I always took notes, lest I forget some detail that might be important. I was about to head out to meet Astrid, who was picking me up from yours, when you called to me.

'Hey, where are you going?' you asked.

'I told you... I'm working tonight.'

'You have a shift starting this late?'

'No, I'm reviewing a gig.'

'Oh, are you still doing that?'

'Of course I am... You know I am.'

'I'm not sure I'd properly realised.'

I sat down on the chair next to you for a minute, confused.

'I thought you'd wanted me to start all this. You pushed me to start working for the paper.'

'Well, yes, of course, I thought it would be good for you to have a hobby but I thought you would have moved on now you've got a proper job. You're not getting paid for the review thing, are you? Why are you wasting your energy on it?'

I suddenly felt ashamed. I suppose I'd convinced myself it was real and that I actually was a music journalist. Sometimes at parties when people asked me what I did, instead of talking about the bookshop or mentioning my degree and plans for future work, I'd say I was a music journalist. It still gave me such a rush every time I plucked up the courage to do it. Astrid called me 'the writer' but I wasn't, was I? I'd written pages and pages of notes in my notebook about things we'd done, but the only things I wrote that saw the light of day were boring recounts of gigs we'd been to. I suppose I'd got caught up in the excitement of it all and convinced myself it was more than it is.

'I guess you're right. Maybe I'll stop after this one.'

You leaned over and kissed me on the forehead. 'It's up to you. I just don't want to see you wasting your time. Maybe think about focusing on the things that pay you. Your time is worth money.'

My mind was all over the place as I waited outside your flat for Astrid to arrive – she was driving us to the gig, because we didn't usually drink on the nights I was reviewing. Just soda and fresh lime – Astrid's idea – and I was chuffed to find they were generally free. At the gig, I mentioned that I might call it a day and not do any more reviews.

She looked at me with confused eyes.

'What are you talking about?' She asked.

'Well, it's not exactly a productive thing to be doing, is it?'

'What do you mean "productive"? You're writing! That's

productive! And why does doing something you enjoy need to be productive anyway? Wait... This has come from him, hasn't it? Did he say something to you?'

'No, I just—'

She always knew when I was lying, she looked at me with that face. That knowing, disappointed face.

'He might have mentioned it,' I admitted, 'But it's kind of true... They don't pay me and it's not going to be my career in the future. What's the point of doing it?'

'The point? The point is that you're writing! And that we're out seeing music and enjoying ourselves! What is this stupid idea people have that creative exploits are a waste of time! It makes me so angry! *He* makes me so angry!'

Jumping to your defence was becoming a more common occurrence; it was becoming a habit.

'No, it's not him. Come on, don't be mean, it's just... I don't know. I've had a good run of it, and we had some fun, but I should probably put my energy into the bookshop. That actually pays me.'

'What, so I'm *being mean* because I'm standing up for you?'

'No, no. I'm sorry. That was the wrong thing to say.'

She rolled her eyes and shook her head. I'd made her angry. I hated that. I wanted to make her happy again.

'We'll see. It's just a thought. Want a drink? I'll go get them.' I turned around and wove my way to the bar to get us two sodas and fresh lime.

I wanted to enjoy the gig, but I was distracted all night. In the car on the way home, we talked about some inconsequential things and recapped on the gig, but it felt like there was something hanging between us. It hung there getting heavier and heavier until Astrid finally came out with it.

'Why do you worry so much about what he thinks all the time? Why do you keep thinking what he wants is more important than what you want? Than what you need?'

'I don't *need* anything.'

There was that face again. 'You're an idiot if you think that.'

'Relationships are about compromise! If you want to be with someone you need to make compromises. That's life! That's growing up! That's just what it's got to be like.'

'Only if you make it that way. I'm never going to compromise myself for anyone. If making someone happy means I have to make less of myself, then they're not the person for me.'

'It doesn't work like that in real life though.'

'He's not the one doing the compromising though, is he? It's only *you* who can't do what you want anymore. He can do whatever he wants. God, it's always the same. You're a square peg trying to fit in a round hole.'

'It's not that I *can't* keep writing. He hasn't told me I'm not allowed to or anything... He would never say that. And he's made compromises too.'

'Maybe you should just spend some time thinking whether that's actually true or if it's just something you tell yourself in order to sleep at night. If being with someone means I can't be myself and means taking up less space in the world, especially because of some man, you can count me out!'

I didn't like the way she saw my relationship with you. I wanted to argue, I wanted to tell her she was wrong, but I've never been good at thinking on the spot.

'Ugh,' she exclaimed, hitting her palms against the steering wheel. 'Some people do not deserve to be loved by the people they're loved by.'

I didn't know what to say. We sat in silence, both staring at the road ahead, a chasm opening between us. Eventually the anger in me fizzled out and she calmed down too and by the time we got home, we were ok again. I was sure she had just said those things in the heat of the moment.

The next day she came into the bookstore where I was working and bought a book I had never heard of. It was called *Mating in Captivity* by someone called Esther Perel. I thought it sounded interesting as I put it through the system before handing it to her. As soon as I got home, I noticed a package on the dining table with my name on it. It was the book she had bought. That was such an Astrid thing to do, always thinking of others. She was only angry because she cared so much about me, but as always, she didn't understand that our realities were so different. And I don't know if I would ever be able to make her understand that fact.

Chapter 46

I was just drifting off to sleep when I heard her voice; it was loud and angry, coming up the stairs and through my open bedroom door. Then I heard yours, also angry. You'd been over at mine for dinner, and Astrid had been out. We'd gone to bed, but I guess you'd got up again to go get some water from the kitchen or something. And she must have just come home. You were talking about me.

'I've helped build her into the person she's become,' I heard Astrid say. 'How do you think she survived when you went away? I looked after her. You can't keep treating her like this. You've made her think so little of herself, she thinks she doesn't deserve anything better. She doesn't think anyone will ever like her for who she really is.'

'That's just her own insecurities. You can't blame me for that.'

'I don't believe that at all. You're not good for her. You're just filling a hole in her life.'

'And you?'

'Yeah, I probably am too. But at least I make her life better. I do everything for her. I take her out, I make her tea, I drive her around, I comfort her when she's down – usually about you, might I add – I support her in her dreams, I encourage her, I buy her wine – I can't actually remember when she's ever offered to pay something, she just stands there looking dumb until someone else gets it.'

'Don't be so harsh, she just gets overwhelmed. Anyway, I do those things too.'

'And treat her like shit.'

'So all these things you apparently do for her, what does she do for you?'

'She supports me. She's there for me. She loves me. And she's always up for adventure.'

'So she's of *use* to you. You use her.'

'Isn't that what we all do, really? If we didn't use other people for our own needs, then we wouldn't ever interact with anyone. Everything we do comes from within ourselves.'

'But she follows you. She worships you.'

'Perhaps.'

'And you think that's better than me? I take care of her. She needs me.'

'You control her. And keep her small.'

'I'm controlling?' you shouted back. 'Who was the one who forced her to get that terrible tattoo?'

'It's not terrible! And I didn't force her, she wanted it! Give her some agency – she is a person, you know. You do realise that, right? She can make her own decisions. You're the one telling her she should stop writing.'

'Well, she's not getting paid for it, is she? And it just takes up her time. I wouldn't expect you to understand – someone who gets handouts from Daddy and doesn't have to work.'

'Are you fucking serious? I bet my father has given me far less than yours has, I've had to work to be able to afford any of this! Why do you think I started uni so late? I'm constantly working. Just because you don't see me doing shifts somewhere or going into an office doesn't mean I don't need to earn money just like everyone else...'

'Well, how then?'

'I don't need to justify myself to you! God, your views are so toxic!'

'I bet you've never had any struggles in your life at all, have you?'

'You are so damn condescending. The things I could tell you, like how I can't even listen to the Everly Brothers anymore because of all the times I played them on my discman, putting the headphones over my sister's ears so she didn't have to hear our parents shouting, all the terrible things they said about us and how we'd ruined their lives. That's just the start of it. You know nothing about me.'

I suddenly remembered the time I'd put on the Everly Brothers album, and she'd abruptly told me to change it. I'd assumed I just chose the wrong music, but it was more than that. I'd never realised how difficult that time had been for her, I'd never thought to ask.

'Whatever,' I heard you say, and I tuned back into your argument. 'Anyway, you don't know her like I do. I was there long before you ever came into her life. And I know she's not acting like herself anymore. What makes you think you can tell her what to do?'

'What makes you think *you* can!'

'I'm her boyfriend.'

'I'm her best friend!'

'Since when? You didn't even know her back in high school. You would have completely ignored her.'

'Don't pretend you know anything about what I was like at

school – you're just making a fool of yourself assuming that you do. You've made some pretty strong assumptions of me, and you have really missed the mark so far.'

'What do you even want with her?'

'Want with her? What does that even mean?'

'Well, we've established that you're just using her... And what's with you calling her Mouse all the time? It's sick. She's not an animal.'

'That's got nothing to do with you, you can't own everything about her, that's between us. And if anyone is using her, it's you.'

'How am I using her? For what purpose?'

'You like to have your nice girlfriend sitting on your arm. Knowing she'll follow you around when you need her, but not cramp your style too much. She won't pull you up on any of your shit because she's too scared you'll leave her. She just gets quieter and quieter, being the nice little future wife you want, not believing she deserves anything more. You really pulled the wool over her eyes. You don't even know who she is now. You haven't even been here.'

'You're just angry because she'll eventually get on with her life and leave you behind. And you'll be all alone – you'll have to find someone else to follow you around and do whatever you want.'

'I don't care if she leaves. I certainly don't need her. I don't even know if I can be bothered to be friends with her anymore if it's going to be like this – it just isn't worth it.'

It just isn't worth it.

I felt that deep in my heart. It felt so real, like actual, physical pain. Surely, she didn't mean that. It must have just been the alcohol talking and tensions running high. It had to just be a flippant comment, she couldn't have meant it... though I had to admit she didn't tend to say things she didn't mean.

I'd heard enough. I closed the bedroom door. You were arguing over me like I was property. All that stuff about you both doing everything for me... Did I really just take and not give anything back? How many times had I made Astrid tea? Not as many times as she had for me, and sure, I guess she did tend to supply the wine and would often comfort me... But you both were my boyfriend and my best friend – that's what you're meant to do, isn't it? Look after me? I curled up in a ball and tried to sleep but sleep felt so far away. I cried until I felt like I couldn't cry any more. I don't know how your argument ended, but you came to bed a little while later. I pretended to be asleep, curled up on my side facing away from you. I hardly slept at all.

The next morning, you left early, and I didn't have it in me to try and stop you. When I finally made it downstairs after having a long shower, Astrid was making us coffee as usual, like nothing had happened. She greeted me with her usual sunny 'good morning, my love' and we drank our coffees in the living room together. Then we went out to brunch, and later, sat in the garden under blankets, reading together.

It was like nothing had happened. I didn't want to let on that I'd heard you both arguing. In the night it seemed like the world had been ending. But in the light of day, I was certain neither of you meant it. Surely it was more about you two than it was about me, I was just caught in the middle. That *had* to be it. I couldn't comprehend any other possibility.

Chapter 47

Then I did something stupid.

I was over at yours, sitting on the sofa reading while you were doing some studying. Or at least I thought you were.

'What's this?' you called over to me, your voice sounded different.

'What's what?'

'This message.'

'What message?'

'The one I just saw flash up on your phone.'

My phone? How had you got my phone? I'd left it sitting on the table, but I looked over to see it was now in your hand. What had you seen?

'It says "I miss you. I want to see you." It's from Chris.'

I froze. My heart started racing.

'It's... A university friend. I think he needs help with study.' That seemed like a believable enough lie.

'Chris? Chris who was at that party? You said he was from Astrid's club crew.'

Of course I did. There had been no reason to lie about that.

'Seems like a weird message. What else has he sent you?'

'Oh, nothing of interest,' I said, hoping desperately that

you might leave it alone.

'Why don't you show me?'

I didn't know what to do once you passed me the phone, so I just stared at it. I knew showing you would mean derailing my carefully constructed life. All my greatest fears were about to become real.

'Show me,' you repeated as I felt my heart beating faster. I wondered if you could hear it. With a shaky hand, I unlocked my phone and passed it to you.

I'd deleted most of the incriminating messages, but not all of them. There were a few I couldn't bring myself to get rid of, I needed the reminder that it had been real.

You were quiet as you read through the messages Chris had sent me.

'How long has this been going on?'

'It's not. It's nothing—'

'You're sleeping with him.'

'I'm... no, I... It... It only happened once, I swear,' I lied. 'You were away. I know that's no excuse, but you had left. And I was drunk. I didn't know what I was doing. It was just one time. It meant nothing. I immediately regretted it.'

The lies came so quick, and I was surprised at how easily they appeared.

You were quiet. So quiet. I wanted you to say something. Anything. The discomfort grew between us – a drawn out moment of tension that seemed to stretch forever.

Eventually you spoke, but you didn't look at me. You stared ahead of you into the middle of the room. Your voice was quiet and steady.

'Get out. We're done. You are nothing to me.'

I started to cry. You continued. 'You are less than nothing.

I regret I ever met you.'

Your words hurt more than I could have imagined. I could only sob and beg you to listen to me, to the lies that were becoming real in my head the more I said them.

'Do you love him?' you eventually asked.

'What?'

You looked up and your eyes met mine.

'Do you love him?'

'No,' I answered quickly, my voice small and shaky.

You shook your head, then went and opened the front door, standing there until I went through it, then slamming it behind me. I walked to the bus stop. I had no idea where I was going – you had always driven me back to The Den. I did the only thing I could think to do. I called my parents.

Mum picked up. She knew immediately that I was crying.

'What is it, Jess?' The concern in her voice felt like a dagger in my heart, knowing I was seeking comfort from her for something terrible I had done. I didn't deserve that concern; I didn't deserve anything.

'I... it's nothing.' I couldn't tell her. 'I just... I...'

'Has something happened with Robert?'

I could only cry, tears streaming down my face as I stood on the street.

'What's happened? What have you done?' She asked.

I couldn't speak. I didn't know how to answer that question. How do you admit to your own mother the horrible things you've done and the mess you've created?

'Whatever you did, just apologise. He'll forgive you.'

I felt annoyance from somewhere inside me that she had jumped to the conclusion it was my fault, but I could hardly be mad considering she was right.

'What if...' my voice sounded so small. 'What if I don't want to be forgiven?'

'Come on, don't be like that. I know it's hard, but this is your life we're talking about. Don't ruin it all by doing something silly.'

I'd already done something silly.

She was right, of course. I knew realistically that life couldn't always be easy, I just needed to find a way to survive. I hadn't been working hard enough – I'd been so caught up in myself that I had let things slip. I hadn't even thought to guard my phone, I'd left it right there for you to see. That was madness. I thanked her, then hung up and sat on the seat at the bus stop, staring at my feet.

It started to rain, and I decided to go back to your house, hoping that maybe you'd cooled off a bit and would change your mind. I knew I had to try. You weren't there and Ethan wasn't home either, so I sat on the step outside and waited.

Ethan came back first and let me in. He clearly hadn't heard what had happened, as he thought it was weird that I was waiting outside. Eventually you came back too. You shook your head as soon as you saw me sitting on your sofa. You looked so angry. I stood up and walked towards you, but you pushed right past me and went to the kitchen to get a glass of water. I followed you.

'Robert... I'm sorry... Please believe me.'

'Don't you dare say my name. I don't want to hear it.'

'I'm sorr— '

'I don't even know who you are anymore. You're not the person I loved!' you shouted.

'I am, I swear!'

'You've changed so much. You never would have done this

before. You hold onto this idea of what life should be like but it's all a lie. You are toxic.'

All I could do was apologise. Over and over again. I lined up my words and kept rolling them out. I wondered how long we could go over the same thing.

'At least now I see you for what you really are. I suppose in a way you've done me a favour,' you said to me as we stood in the kitchen.

'It didn't mean anything.'

'You wanted to hurt me.'

Something snapped in me, I was getting tired of the cyclic nature of our arguments, and so I shouted back at you.

'Yes, of course. I wanted to hurt you. That's all there is to it. That's the whole reason behind any of it.'

I was being facetious. You roared with frustration and pushed past me to leave the room. I lost my balance and crashed to the ground. You continued on to your bedroom and I lay on the floor where I'd fallen by the fridge. I rested my head on its cool flat surface. It buzzed quietly. After a few of minutes you came back. I was still on the ground. I wasn't hurt, I was just in shock. I hadn't expected it to end there. You gathered me up and took me to your room so we could close the door so as not to disturb Ethan, and for the first time that day, we talked in a slightly more measured way.

You blamed it all on her, of course. And that ended up an easy route for us both to take, I think.

'You were never like this before she came along,' you said.

I couldn't deny it. Since I'd met her, I'd glimpsed another life – one that was much more exciting than the one I'd been living. I had been seduced by it. And while I wished it was a world I could be part of, I knew it wasn't mine. It never really could be. I wasn't special enough for it.

'What do you even want?' you'd asked me.

What did I want? I didn't know why it felt like such a difficult question to answer. I wanted the life I was supposed to have. I wanted to be protected, looked after, to not be alone. I wanted to be forgiven so that maybe one day I could believe I wasn't as horrible as I felt. And I wanted things to go back to the way they were. We'd been happy once, I was sure of it.

'I want you. I love you.' If I could fix this, then it would all be ok.

We had sex that night – urgent, frantic sex. Like it was our first time. Or might be our last. I clung to you after, desperate for the closeness, desperate to feel real. For a moment it felt like we might be ok. But you went to sleep on the couch, leaving me in your bed. I felt so alone, so unlovable. I felt like the person I always knew I was.

Chapter 48

Eventually I went home. Thankfully Astrid was there. She was still my best friend. She was always there for me. And now I needed her more than ever.

I collapsed into her arms and sobbed. It was a while before I could speak.

She rubbed my back. 'What's wrong, my Little Mouse?'

'He knows.'

'Who knows? Knows what?'

I just looked back at her with my red eyes through more tears.

'Oh,' she said softly.

She held me for what felt like ages as I cried. Eventually it felt like there were no more tears to cry and I seemed to stop. I was so tired. She kissed me on the head and whispered 'Tea' before getting up and going to the kitchen. She soon came back with the teapot and our two mugs.

'You want to talk about it?'

'I think so.'

I filled her in, between sobs and at times, more tears. She listened patiently and let me take my time.

'What do I do?' I asked her when I got to the end, hoping that she would have the answers for me, that she would tell me how to fix it.

'Isn't it obvious?' she said.

I shook my head.

'Get the fuck out?'

Even just hearing that made me cry more, my shoulders and body moving along with my unstoppable sobs, as I shook my head.

'Ok, well. Really, you have two options. Give him all the power and wait for him to decide your fate, or you take charge. You tell him you want out and you leave him before he can leave you.'

'I can't leave him. It's not up to me to choose what happens next.'

'Why?'

'Because I'm the one who's messed up.'

'So? You think you've lost all your rights because of that? That you don't get a say in any of it? You think *all* fault lies with you?'

'Well, yes. Of course it does. Obviously, it's my fault. I need to pay for what I've done. He gets to choose whether to forgive me or—'

'Can you hear yourself? What the hell, Jess?'

It felt strange hearing her call me Jess.

'Do you actually want to stay with him?' She asked.

I opened my mouth to say 'yes', but the word just didn't come out. I knew I had to make you forgive me. There was no other option. But her question was one that had threatened to enter my mind, just a brief thought during those nights spent in Chris's arms... I hadn't dared give into it, who knew where that would lead. But in the safety of Astrid's presence, I finally spoke out loud, for the first time, the thought I'd been trying to ignore:

'I don't know.'

'You don't know?'

'I mean... I think so. Yeah. I want to be with him. I don't want to throw it all away. I'd be nothing without him.'

'What are you talking about! You're still you – even when you're not with Robert. And so much more! What even is this future with him that you're so set on? Lay it out for me – what's it supposed to look like?'

'Well... I guess... If he somehow finds a way to forgive me, then we get to finally start our lives together – we have our jobs already planned; we'll move to London together. I won't have to be alone. Then once we're stable and established, we'll get married and eventually have some children. It's what we've always wanted. What *I've* always wanted – a family, a home. Somewhere I'm safe and loved.' Even in my upset state, I felt comfort when I said it, but also a strange tightness clenching in my stomach.

She threw her hands up in the air.

'I won't even get into all this 'starting your life' business. I have no idea what you think you've been doing all this time if not life... But more importantly, you want to bring a child into this? This fucked-up relationship where you're so unhappy? Let me tell you from experience, damaged adults do not make good parents. You can't care for someone else if you can't even care for yourselves!'

I wanted to say it wasn't like that, to somehow prove her wrong, but I wasn't sure I could. I didn't *think* I felt unhappy in the relationship, but I also couldn't remember the last time I'd felt really happy. But we would work it out. We had to.

'Well, if you are dead set on careering off this cliff,' she continued, 'at least promise me you'll go to therapy. Both of you. Together. You need to work all this shit out. Anyway, come on. It's bedtime. You've had enough for today. Sleep is all that will help right now.' She got up and went to her bedroom, leaving me alone on the sofa.

Therapy? Were we that damaged and broken? I suppose after what I'd done, we were. I'd broken us. And it was up to me to fix it, to get us back to where we were. Maybe it sounded like a good idea. I wondered if you would go for it. I was willing to try anything.

When Astrid had finished brushing her teeth, I made my way to bed too, suddenly feeling so exhausted and desperate to get some sleep, but I couldn't. I couldn't stop going over and over in my head all the terrible things I'd done and how I'd messed everything up.

I opened my door after an hour or so of tossing and turning, and looked out, but Astrid's door was closed.

I couldn't face going back to bed, just to lie there staring at the ceiling, so I went to the bathroom, got in the shower and turned the tap on hot. As the water poured over me, I slid down the wall, my legs folding up in front of me until I was sitting on the floor, with the water falling on my back and over my head. And I cried. I cried and I cried.

I don't know how long I'd been there, when suddenly there were arms around me. I opened my eyes and Astrid was right there next to me, still in her pyjamas. She wrapped me up against her chest and I sobbed into her as the water kept falling over us both.

'You're so much better than this. Leave him, my love. You deserve so much more,' she whispered.

I found myself nodding and wanting to lean into her, into

the safety of her arms.

'Ok,' I said. 'You're right. I will. I will.' Her arms were around my shoulders, her hands resting on my chest. It felt like there was nothing and no one else in the whole world, just us.

'Then you'll be free,' she said. 'I'll look after you. And I promise that no one is ever going to break your heart again. Not on my watch.'

Could she promise that? Could she? If anyone could, it would be her. And I thought maybe, maybe she could protect me. Maybe it didn't have to be like this. Maybe there was another way...

Eventually, Astrid turned off the shower and we got out. She bundled me into a towel, before stripping off her sodden pyjamas and getting a towel for herself. Then she led me by the hand into her room and pulled out two big t-shirt of hers for us each to put on. And, once again that night, like we had so many times, we went to bed together in her room. The fairy lights around her bedpost twinkled on through the dark hours as she stroked my wet hair and entwined her fingers in mine. And I slept, wrapped in the safety of her presence.

When I woke up, I felt uneasy in the pit of my stomach as I was hit by the weight of everything that had happened, and remembered what I'd said to her, what I'd agreed to. Astrid was still sleeping when I woke, lying so serenely next to me and breathing softly. I eased myself out of her bed quietly and made my way across the hall to my room. I hoped she had forgotten I'd said anything at all. It was just a throwaway emotional comment; I was being ridiculous. Surely, she would realise that. I got so carried away in fantasy when I was with her. But I knew what my priorities needed to be.

And indeed, she didn't mention it. Not that morning as she made our coffee, nor that afternoon as we sat on the sofa reading our books, her legs in my lap. She never mentioned it again.

Chapter 49

You thought going to therapy together was a ridiculous idea when I eventually brought it up. You told me I was the problem, and it was something I needed to fix, not you. You were right, of course. I felt ridiculous for having suggested it.

We were stuck in limbo. One day it felt like we would move forward, the next we went backwards. I couldn't concentrate on anything else as I did anything I could to make you forgive me. Then, when I didn't know how I would bear it any longer, you said the words I'd been so desperate to hear: 'I think we can get past this.'

I rushed to hug you – to thank you – but you put your hand up to stop me.

'But,' you continued, 'I have a few conditions.'

'Of course. Anything.'

'Firstly, you are never seeing him again. I would hope that'd go without me saying, but...' You stopped to look me up and down, making me feel as worthless as I knew I was. 'You don't go anywhere he even might be. You block his number. As far as you're concerned, he's dead.'

I flinched slightly at your use of the word 'dead' in a figurative context but told my stupid oversensitive, overthinking mind to shut up.

'Secondly, *you're* going to therapy. You're got some serious issues that you need to get fixed.'

I nodded.

'And thirdly, you're moving in with me. I'm not telling you never to see her again, but there's no way you're going to keep living with her. I'll finish my exams in a few months, and we'll go to London as planned. And we can finally be free from all this madness you've got yourself mixed up in.'

I felt like I'd been punched in the gut. I hadn't even considered that being with you would mean the end of The Den; of nights in her bed by fairy light, of tea and wine and whisky and watching sunrises after dancing all night, of seeing her first thing when I woke up in the morning. The end of knowing that if I'd had a bad day, she'd be there to make it better. How could I go back to only seeing her occasionally, when she had become so much part of my life that she felt like an extension of myself?

But I couldn't say anything – I didn't deserve to be happy. I just needed to make penance. This was the price to pay for my actions, it was what I had to do to keep my life. I'd had my fun. It was time to grow up. It would all have to end.

I nodded again.

'Go tell Astrid. Now.'

Your tone sounded lighter than it had in weeks, and I swear I saw a hint of a smile on your face.

'And don't expect her to be reasonable,' you added.

My heart sank as I made my way back to the house. You didn't drive me over. I had to make my own way. But you said you would pick me and my things up later that evening. It didn't give me long to talk to her at all, and as I took the two buses to get between our houses, I tied knots in my stomach wondering how I was going to tell her. Astrid had always been so patient with me – always there to comfort me, to make me feel ok. Surely, she would understand that I had to do this too. Or had I already asked too much of her?

I had no idea what to expect when I got home. Walking up to the front door, it truly hit me – the door I'd walked through so many times with a smile on my face, knowing Astrid would be behind it... But it wouldn't be my home for much longer. I had tears rolling down my face before I even finished opening the door.

'He's decided,' I said as I walked in and sat down on the sofa next to where Astrid was painting her toenails black.

'Let me guess. He blamed me,' she said without looking up. I just looked at her. I didn't need to say anything. 'And he doesn't want you to see me anymore.'

'No, he wouldn't do that, he's not controlling like that...' She interrupted me with a scoff, which I ignored and continued. 'It's just... I'm not allowed to live with you.'

She looked up at me then, staring at me for a moment. I couldn't read her face. I think she was angry, but she seemed so calm.

'And you think that's him *not* being controlling...?'

I wanted to defend you but knew it wouldn't get me anywhere. She put the nail polish down on the table with a thud that made me jump, then walked quickly over to the window, where she looked out for a moment before going over to her record collection, putting on Nick Cave's *Murder Ballads*. She stood there for what felt like forever with her arms crossed, staring at the floor. I didn't know what to say, I had no idea how to make this better. Eventually she broke the silence.

'So, what did he say?'

'I have to move in with him until the end of uni. Then we'll go to London. Just like we'd always planned.'

'And when are you leaving?'

'He's coming to get me tonight.'

'And what about me?'

'I'll keep covering the rent here for the last couple of months of the lease. Or I can help you find someone else to move in.'

'And you're ok with this?'

'I have to be. It's what I need to do.'

'Need?'

I put my head in my hands. It felt suddenly heavy. The distance across the room between us seemed to stretch across miles and I wanted more than anything to tell her it wasn't real, that nothing had changed, that we could still be Astrid and Jess.

'Please don't make this harder than it needs to be,' I said, then immediately regretted it.

'Sorry, are you saying that *I'm* the one making this hard? Am I getting the blame for that too?'

'No, no of course not. Sorry, I didn't mean it like that. It's just... what are you going to do at the end of the year anyway?' I said, looking up at her. 'You'll probably go somewhere spectacular, end up doing something that changes the world, in some place I could only dream of. And then what becomes of me?'

'I don't know. Come with me. Go somewhere else. What does it matter? How about *anything* other than trying to appease that controlling psychopath?'

'He's not—'

'He is. I don't know why you're so blind, why everything

you do is about *him*. I'll never understand why you think he's worth so much more than your happiness. You know, you gave me so much hope that you had grown, that you had moved forward – but you're throwing it all away.'

'I'm not! This is what I want! I... wouldn't survive on my own. I can't even bear to think about it.'

'Survive? What about living?' she raised her voice.

'Not everyone's like you, Astrid!' I raised mine too. 'Not everyone is as beautiful and confident. Life isn't that easy for people like me.'

'People like you? What does that even mean?'

'Just *normal* people. Ordinary living people.'

'Sometimes I wonder if you actually realise that I'm a normal, living person, just like you. I have to work hard for things I want, to be where I want to be, and I've been through my fair share of hard times too, believe me – I've got demons when I need them. You can have whatever life you want. This is all just a prison you've built to keep yourself small. How do you *still* think so little of yourself? It's pathetic.'

She didn't get it, she never would. I would never be her. She was different. I would always just be in her shadow, scrambling to pick up whatever I could in her wake. It wasn't my life I'd been immersed in over our time together; I'd merely borrowed it momentarily.

'Maybe one day you'll understand,' she said, her hands on her hips. 'Life is what you make of it. All this is in your head. I hope one day you'll give it up and actually live. Live for yourself. Not in this strange half-state trying to carry the expectations of your parents. You don't have to do everything to make them happy just because your sister died. It's not a burden you need to carry and frankly, I don't think you're particularly doing her justice by taking it on. You don't have to make me happy either, for that matter. Or bend yourself over backwards to make Robert happy. Or Chris. Or any other bloody human on this planet. You owe them nothing. You can just be you and make yourself happy!'

That hurt. I couldn't believe she said that, using Emily to make a point. I wanted to object, to yell at her, but I couldn't get the words out.

'This ends here, Jess. You've made your choice. This is goodbye.'

'But I love you,' I said, looking up at her through teary eyes.

'I loved you too,' she replied. Then, after staring into me for a moment, those beautiful blue eyes holding so much anger, she went to her room.

I cried and cried. Her past tense seared through me like I'd been stabbed. I don't know what I'd expected, but I knew it was what I deserved.

As I packed up my things, I played the whole scene over and over in my head. I remembered how much she hated being disrespected. I don't know why I thought she'd be ok with just meeting up for the occasional coffee or whatever would have been suitable while I paid my dues... Of course she was angry. It must have seemed like I was throwing us away. I suppose I was. I'd seen her react like this before. I wasn't the first. I'd let her down.

By the time I'd finished packing up my things, it felt like the world was ending. There was no going back. There was a heaviness hanging in the air when you arrived to get me. She'd hardly left her room while I packed and cried.

I wanted to say goodbye. I wanted her to hold me, to tell me that we'd see each other again, that it was ok. But it wasn't.

As I made the final trip to the car, my legs felt as heavy as my heart.

Chapter 50

I'd like to say those last few months after I moved in with you were good and that I settled quickly back into my old life. But I mostly just felt empty and lost. Everything was grey. I stopped writing. There was no joy in it anymore and nothing to write about. The words just wouldn't come.

We sort of slipped into a routine together. We would get up every morning and have breakfast together. You would often read the paper and I'd either read a book or just sit there. I took solace in the fact that the domestic scene we'd created in those mornings sometimes made me smile. You would go off to class, I'd head to the bookshop, then we came home, had dinner, and went to bed. I knew it would be hard getting back what we had, so I just put my head down and got on with it. I held out hope that things would get better once we started our lives in London. A new beginning, a chance to reset.

Occasionally we would go out for brunch on the weekends, or you would take me out for dinner which was a nice break in the monotony but mostly I just felt like a ghost – I was only half there. I felt like a ghost of you and a ghost of myself, of my former life. I kept looking for Astrid and would see her everywhere, but when I got closer, it never was her.

If I ever ran into anyone who knew her, I would ask how she

was and what she was up to. One day someone who had come to a few of our parties came by the bookstore and after the requisite amount of small talk, I asked them about her.

'I thought you would know,' they said, which felt like a dagger in my heart. 'I think she's going to Paris...'

I momentarily played with the thought that she was leaving because there was nothing left for her now. But I guess she would have always left anyway. In the back of my mind, I still hoped things could somehow go back to what they were. But I knew they couldn't. Nothing could last forever, and those days certainly couldn't. Mum had always said that university would be the best time of my life and I think she was probably right.

Ethan had started dating a girl named Gemma. She was short and quiet, with straight dark hair, and she wore a lot of yellow. She would come around to the flat quite often and we'd all sit and watch TV shows like *Friends* (which did occasionally make me laugh out loud) and *Seinfeld* (which I hated). As the two girlfriends, she and I were expected to hang out together, and we did, but the conversation never flowed easily. We just didn't have anything in common and I felt strangely awkward around her. It was a familiar feeling; one I'd had with your other friends. I'd never felt that way around Astrid and her friends. With them, I seemed to have interesting things to say, and people wanted to listen to me. I felt like I mattered, like I was cool. But not anymore. I could never think of the right thing to add to a conversation.

Finally, you finished your exams and there was nothing left to do but pack up and move. I still miss that city, even now. I left a big part of me there. I'd made more memories than I ever thought I could, and they would last me a lifetime. But I was never going to stay there forever anyway. I was hopeful about moving forward. I was back on my own path and putting in the work to pay for what I'd done. There was comfort in knowing that.

My parents were excited for us to move to London. I was excited too. Things would be better there. Every time I spoke to Mum she asked when we were going to get engaged. I always said the same thing: 'Maybe soon.' We never again spoke about that call we'd had that night I called her from the bus stop in tears.

I knew even when we got to London that things weren't immediately going to be easy. Love wasn't supposed to be easy, and neither was moving somewhere new. We found a tiny flat out east of the city, near the Bow underground station. It had a canal running nearby which was nice. London felt so different. It was so big and loud. I kept waiting to adjust to it.

I started the job in the finance team of your parent's law firm. You began working as a paralegal while continuing your next round of studies. It was what we'd always planned, where adulthood and the life I had wanted for so long really started.

But I couldn't ignore the feeling of emptiness inside me. I would stare at myself in the mirror each morning, trying desperately to find something familiar in what I saw. The more I looked at my own face, the less it looked like me. It was a stranger who looked back. I put the office attire on, fitting my body into the cheap clothes I had ordered online. I made sure I smiled at everyone, but I often felt dizzy and lightheaded. I hoped it would start to feel easier.

And not a day passed when I didn't think of Astrid and wonder where she was and what she was doing. I played memories of our times together over and over in my mind. I wondered if she ever thought of me. I wanted my love for her to fade, I wanted to think about her less, but I wasn't sure I ever would.

I tried to make friends at work. Sometimes they'd invite me to join them for lunch at the trendy street food market near work, but we just ended up talking about our jobs and other people in the office. Some of them would tell me about their kids and always made sure to say that one day I would have some too, and then my whole life would get more meaning. They also loved asking when you were going to 'pop the question' to me. I don't know how I was supposed to know the answer to that, but I wished that I did. Occasionally we would all go out for a drink on a Friday night and a tiny bit of the old excitement crept back into me. But everyone had to get home to their families. I don't think you would have liked me going out anyway.

I tried to stay upbeat. I had given away too much to allow my negativity to ruin it all now. I had fought for you – to be with you – and that's what was going to happen. I endeavoured to do better.

I did feel closer to you, though. You were the constant in my life. After everything I'd done, you'd forgiven me and stayed with me, which was so much more than I deserved. It was you and me, together forever, making our way in the world, and something about that felt special.

Not long after we moved to London, it was my birthday. I told you I didn't want to do anything that year, I just wanted to forget it. The hole left by Astrid felt immeasurably big around that time of year. Not that I told you that, of course. You said that was fine – that we should be focussing on more important things anyway. And I really did mean it; I didn't want a fuss. But you didn't do anything at all. You didn't make a nice meal or bring me home some flowers. The day itself came and went, and you didn't even say anything about it. I tried to be ok with that – you were respecting my wishes, after all. I got it; it was thoughtful in its own way. When I started to wonder if you'd forgotten it entirely, I chased the thought away. I remembered the bunch of flowers you had sent me when you were off in America – how sweet you had been even when oceans divided us, and I immediately felt like an ungrateful fool.

I just wish you'd said, 'Happy birthday'.

Chapter 51

A few months after moving to London, we got an ornate yellow envelope in the post. I picked it up and turned it over and over in my hands. I already knew what it was, but I hesitated to open it. Ethan had called you to say that he'd proposed to Gemma, and they were getting married. They certainly didn't waste any time about it. They'd only met just over a year before, and were still living in the rented place we'd all shared. The wedding was back in the city we'd left behind.

We went back for the wedding – back to the city where I'd known her and where I'd once existed so boldly. I almost couldn't believe that person had been me. She must have still been deep inside me somewhere, but I couldn't reach her.

It was beautiful, the wedding. And it felt like a tiny snapshot back into the lives we'd left. Ethan had asked you to be a groomsman, so you sat at a table with the wedding party, while I sat with your old friends – the ones from our dorm in first year, the ones we'd lived with in our first share house, all the people I thought I'd escaped.

My mum had been so excited about the idea of us going to a wedding and she kept saying that it would be us next. She told me to make sure I caught the bouquet. But when it came down to it, I felt paralysed and couldn't bring myself to join all the desperate girls on the dancefloor, jostling each other to catch a bunch of flowers. Instead, I stood at the side clutching another glass of red wine and watched as a tall blonde (who wasn't Astrid) caught it.

As I drank more wine, I couldn't help myself – I started searching the reception for anyone who might know where Astrid was. It was a very different group of people to those who surrounded her, but circles often had a habit of intersecting. We had, after all, found ourselves at that first party, the day my life had changed. After asking a few people, I eventually got an answer.

'Last I heard she was playing in a band in Berlin.'

Of course she was.

Ethan and Gemma's first dance was to 'Every Breath You Take' by The Police. I watched them sway like they were teenagers at a disco, and I wondered how they'd missed the creepy meaning of that song. It wasn't a love song; it was a song about obsession and control. And it made me angry because they clearly hadn't taken the time to really listen to it. It wasn't what a first dance song was supposed to be.

I just kept drinking more and more, feeling the calming buzz it gave me. You were drinking a lot too and we were both drunk when we got back to our hotel after the party. I was ready to go to sleep, but for some reason, you were angry with me.

'What was wrong with you tonight?' you asked. 'You've been like a zombie!'

'Nothing was wrong. I was just enjoying the wedding.'

'Who was that guy you were talking to?'

'What? What guy? What are you talking about?'

'Well, if it's not another guy, then what the fuck is wrong, Jess?'

I thought I'd been playing my role so well. I didn't know what to say, which must have made you angry.

'WHAT THE FUCK IS WRONG WITH YOU!' you shouted so loudly at me before kicking over a chair. Then you went to my suitcase and started throwing clothes at me as you spoke, punctuating each word with a floating shirt.

'What is wrong with you, Jess? What do you even want?'

I didn't know how to answer you. All I could do was start crying. As Astrid would have said, I was always crying. It was the only response I could ever find. I couldn't work out how to speak. You made this horrible roaring sound that I don't think was even human and then knocked the kettle off the bench onto the ground, where it fell with a clatter. Thankfully, it was empty.

We both stared at each other.

And then I fell to the ground, my knees just buckled under me. It reminded me of the night when you found out about Chris, when I lay where I fell by the coolness of the fridge.

I was so tired. Tired of all this.

Eventually you calmed down and came over to me. You stood above me and quietly, you asked again, 'What do you want?'

'Where are we going?' I said through sobs. 'What is the point of all this?'

'Of what?' You were still standing over me, and I wanted you to feel menacing. I wanted to feel *something*, but I was just so tired.

'Of this. Of us.'

'What the hell are you talking about?'

'What are we doing?'

'Doing? What do you mean? We're living. We're living our lives. This is what real life is like, Jess. What else is there? Is it that you want to get married?'

Marriage. That was the thing we were supposed to do, wasn't it? Maybe that would fix things. I looked up at you.

'Do you want that?' I asked quietly.

'Yes, sure. That's what's next, right? And maybe then you'll finally be happy.'

'What about you?'

'Of course. I'm happy with anything.'

You started looking around, I wasn't sure what for. Eventually you came back with a small black hair tie of mine. You knelt next to me.

'All right then. Jess, will you marry me?'

I looked up at you and your eyes looked so soft, like I could belong in them.

'Yes, yes of course,' I said, smiling through my tears. And then you grabbed me and pulled me to my feet, and we kissed. We kissed and kissed. You put the hair tie on my finger and then you picked me up and carried me to the bed and we made love like we hadn't since before you left for America. With the exception, of course, of the night after the party where you'd met Chris...

You want to bring a kid into this?

I woke up to her words echoing in my ears. I tried to get my bearings as I looked around at the mess in our hotel room; an overturned chair, a kettle on the floor, my clothes strewn about the place... The previous night was a blur. I got up and rubbed my eyes. I noticed a black band on my finger. Black.

That was Astrid's favourite colour. It started coming back to me. You'd proposed, we'd got engaged. You started to stir next to me.

'I'll get you a proper one when we get back home,' you mumbled in your quiet, gentle morning voice.

Home. There was that word. *Home.* We really were making a home. My year of indiscretions was so far behind us now. You must have forgiven me if you wanted to be with me forever.

And despite myself, despite how empty I'd been feeling, I couldn't stop smiling. This was it.

On the drive back we chattered happily about plans, and the things we did and didn't like about Ethan and Gemma's wedding. 'Not that song,' I'd said emphatically, and you'd laughed. It felt so good to make you laugh. You leaned over and kissed me at every red traffic light as we left the city, and my heart jumped in my chest.

And then, a few days after we got back, you got me the ring. A simple silver band and a little diamond. It wasn't flashy – we couldn't afford flashy anyway – but I loved it.

I showed it off to everyone, finally feeling like I had something in common with my colleagues. Even if I didn't draw attention to it, people seemed to just notice. Engagement rings weren't the sort of thing I'd ever noticed on others, but even women I didn't know very well seemed to fawn over it, and me. It made me feel like I had some sort of status and place in the world. You were now my fiancé. It was a word I loved saying.

But for some reason, I had a feeling of uneasiness that seemed to keep bubbling up. I was starting to feel panicked at strange small things, like the coffee pot being in the wrong place or the zipper on my coat getting stuck. I told myself it was probably just nerves and excitement; it would all be ok now. I would be safe. I would finally be safe.

Chapter 52

We decided to tell our parents in person, so we drove down for the weekend. Mum saw the ring straight away and clasped her hands over mouth, making a squealing sound. Then she ordered Dad to go out and get champagne. He got a bottle of Moët and my breath caught in my throat when I saw it. They kept calling it 'Moway'. I quietly pointed out that it was pronounced 'Mowett', but you all laughed at me and told me to stop being silly.

After we'd all clinked our glasses together and taken a sip, Mum ran off somewhere and came back holding my grandmother's wedding ring. She told me she'd never been so proud of me and that we must use grandma's ring when the time came. That felt nice.

'What are you going to have for your first dance?' she asked.

'I was thinking maybe 'Heroes' by David Bowie,' I said. That had always been the song I'd dreamed of having for my first dance.

You made this groaning sound, then said, 'Do we have to?'

Yes. We did have to. Of course we had to. I couldn't imagine getting married without Bowie's music being part of it.

'I'd really like to,' I said, trying to be firm. You'd told me that you didn't really want to get involved with organising the details of the day, so I was surprised when you had an opinion on this.

'But Bowie? He's so outdated and boring.'

I looked up at Emily's ballet shoes hanging on the wall and I felt like I was about to start crying, so I excused myself and left the room. Mum and Dad still had such big smiles on their faces, and I didn't want to spoil their happiness or let them down. I wished I could stop crying all the bloody time.

Always with the crying.

I was sure you'd change your mind once you understood how important it was to me. Surely. I was just a bit surprised that you didn't already know.

Instead of going to the bathroom like I said I would, I instead found myself standing in my old bedroom. I looked around and wondered who I had been when I'd lived there. I'd once shared that room, but it had only one bed in it now – the bed I'd slept in every night since they'd got rid of our bunk beds. The bunk beds with princess and horse stickers on them. Who even was I now? I'd made it out. I was the one still here... I had the job, and I was getting married. I'd almost done everything I was meant to do. But why did I feel so empty? And then I really did start to cry.

I guess I had been gone for a while because Mum came to see where I was. I wiped my eyes quickly when I saw her and tried to smile.

'Oh, honey, what is it? Feeling overwhelmed with all the excitement?'

I took a big breath in, then out, trying to collect myself.

'Mum, how did you know you wanted to marry Dad?'

'Pardon?'

'I just... Is it something you always knew you wanted?'

She reached out to touch my arm and directed me to the bed, where the two of us sat down.

'Of course I wanted to marry your father. I was delighted when he finally asked me. We'd already been dating for two years by then – he certainly took his time with it. Why are you asking?'

'I don't know, I guess I just wondered if there was ever a moment when you weren't sure if it was really what you wanted. Or if there was something else, maybe.'

'Darling, there's no point in thinking that way. We deserve this; having a supportive husband, and a safe home that we can bring children—' she straightened slightly '—or a child into. Life is about finding someone that you can have a partnership with, then building a life together. You wouldn't want to end up being my age and all on your own, would you? You're so lucky to have Robert. Your father and I are very glad that things are finally working out for you. That's all I've ever wanted: to know you're safe and have someone to provide for you and look after you.'

She hugged me. She so rarely hugged me of her own volition. I relaxed into it. I felt like a little girl again, like I was protected.

'Come on now. Let's not leave the men on their own for too long. Why don't you go out and give your future husband a kiss?'

I nodded and blew my nose.

We went back out, and I sat next to you and smiled. You put your arm around me, and I leaned into your side, laying my head against your chest where I could feel your heart beating. The heart that loved me. Things would be fine. Things would be good.

Chapter 53

I never told you this, but I started writing her letters. I couldn't send them of course, partly because I didn't know where to send them to, but I also don't think I wanted her to read them anyway. Writing to her made it feel like she was still around me, somehow. It felt like the only way I could remind myself of the person I had been.

I still thought about her all the time. She existed as a voice inside my head, the memory of her words accompanied me. I did actually send her a few messages and occasionally she replied, but her responses were always just something short and unemotional.

In a brave, careless moment I emailed her on her birthday. I went back and forth as to whether I should or not. I probably shouldn't have, but after having finished a bottle of wine on my own while you were still at work late, it seemed like the right thing to do.

I wanted it to be poignant.

I missed her.

Dear Astrid,

Happiest of birthdays.

Not a day goes by that I don't think about you and wonder how you are. I am wishing – hoping – you're thriving, as I know you must be. I can't begin to imagine the adventures you must be having out there in the world. This whole year has been marked by your absence and everything has felt a lot more difficult without you. I'll never forget any of our time together.

Yours still,

Little Maus

And then to conclude, stupid idiot me thought it would mean something to add the lyrics of The Kinks song 'Days' – a happy song, but one that always brought tears to my eyes, thinking how grateful I was for my time with her, for everything she'd given and done for me. And how much I missed her. Then I pressed send.

I read it the next day when the sober light of morning was upon me. It was too much. It was way too much. I thought the Kinks song would perfectly frame what I was trying to say, but in the daylight it seemed tacky. *I* was tacky. I spent most of the following days making myself sick with worry at the thought of her reading it and wondering if she would respond. I felt like the most ridiculous, useless person in the world.

I got a reply a few days later. It merely said:

Thanks. I had a good day.

That was all.

Chapter 54

I'd started thinking about the wedding a lot, it was something nice to focus on. We'd set a date for the following year. I knew you didn't really want to get involved in all the details of planning the wedding which suited me fine. I was happy to organise it.

'All I want is to see you walking down that aisle towards me,' you'd said, your arms around me. 'The rest,' you shrugged and waved your hand in the air, 'whatever you want.'

Whatever I want.

That made me smile. I just had to figure out what it was I wanted.

I'd also started thinking about the honeymoon. I was so desperate to travel. I still remembered so vividly that first night I met Astrid, her telling me about Budapest. She'd said I *must* go. So I wanted to go there, and maybe Berlin and Paris... All the places she had so vibrantly described. I loved the idea of going around to a few places in Europe while we were there, turning it into a proper adventure. I imagined us getting the train together, sitting across from each other and marvelling at the countryside as it flew past.

I asked you over breakfast one day, 'What do you think about Budapest?'

'What about it?'

'For our honeymoon. I thought maybe we could start there and go to a few different cities in Europe.'

'Budapest? Isn't it a bit... far away?'

'I hear it has cool bars set up in the ruins of old buildings. Not to mention the baths. They're meant to be great too. Sometimes they even put on dance parties in them - imagine that! It could be a lot of fun.'

'Can't we just go somewhere easy? Maybe the Cotswolds.'

'But that's just up the road.'

'Great. Let's do that.'

'Can't we go somewhere in Europe? Maybe even just Paris? It's the city of love after all, and we can get there on the train.'

'I don't know how you think we'll be able to afford a big holiday as well a wedding right now. Europe is pretty expensive.'

'So is England. And probably even more expensive, for that matter! What about Prague then? I don't think it's too expensive to go there.'

'I don't really want to discuss this right now. I've got other things on my mind. You said you'd do the organising.'

'So you'd be happy if I chose somewhere in Europe?'

You sighed. 'Come on. We don't need to go traipsing around too far. Let's be reasonable. If you're really set on going abroad, maybe we could go to Tenerife? Pete from work went there for his honeymoon and said it was quite affordable. We could spend a few days at the beach. That might be nice.'

A few days at the beach? That wasn't what I'd been thinking at all. I couldn't understand why you didn't want to go out and explore the world a bit. Our honeymoon seemed like the perfect opportunity. But I could hardly make you do something you didn't want to do.

You were in such a good mood after we'd got engaged, but it was only a few weeks before you started to get irritable again. I couldn't work out what I'd done wrong. Maybe it was the honeymoon talk. I knew you were stressed at work too. I tried to support you; I made sure dinner was ready when you came home, and that I didn't bother you when you were studying, other than to bring you occasional cups of tea. But it felt like the more I gave you, the less I had to give. I was empty. I realised there was still something wrong with me. I had a problem and I needed to get it sorted out.

It was time to hold up my end of the bargain that we'd made when you took me back, that I had been avoiding. I thought I could fix myself, but I realised I needed help. It was time to start therapy.

I'd also been avoiding it because of the cost, but when I mentioned to you that I wanted to do it, you seemed glad. You'd mentioned it a few times since we'd moved, usually when I'd made you angry. But I was finally ready to give it a go. It turned out that psychology sessions were available through work's Employee Support Scheme, which meant I would get help paying for it. Though as a result, I had to admit to them that I needed therapy, which made me feel like a failure. I know Astrid had always said there was no shame in going to therapy, that it was totally normal, and everyone should do it. But it didn't feel like that; I felt embarrassed that everyone knew I was broken and needed fixing.

I went to see a therapist named Frances Lloyd, who was suggested through the work scheme. On the day of my first session, it had hardly stopped raining all morning. The pavement that began patterned with raindrops had turned to rivers as I walked towards her office, on a backstreet in central London. I had to ring a buzzer to be let in. I'd been instructed to arrive five minutes early and buzz no earlier than that. There was no reply at first, and I almost turned and walked away. Maybe she wasn't there. Maybe I'd got the wrong place... There was a café on the corner I had walked past, and I thought maybe I could just go and get coffee instead. A nice warm cup of coffee was surely good for my mental health. But I took a deep breath and pressed it again. That time, the door buzzed and I pushed against it and walked down a flight of steep steps.

The room was below the street level, with a window that looked out onto a wall, and only a small sliver of natural light came down from above. That meant that there were those fluorescent lights on the ceiling, like the ones we had at work, which hurt my eyes. There were two lime green chairs sitting across from each other, a small table in between with a box of tissues on it, and a computer on a desk in the corner. She was sitting at the desk when I went in. She looked at me when I opened the door, peering down through her glasses. She smiled, took her glasses off and indicated for me to sit in one of the chairs. I didn't know which chair I was supposed to sit in. I decided to sit in the one closest to the door, facing the view-less window. I hoped that would be ok. There was a bottle of water and two glasses on the table. I was thirsty, but I wasn't sure of the etiquette, so I left it.

After a few minutes she came and sat down across from me, and I immediately regretted persevering with the doorbell.

'Jess,' she said. Her voice was soft but firm.

'Hi...' my voice sounded small in comparison to hers. I wondered if she noticed that my hands were shaking.

She smiled a thin smile.

'Nice to meet you. I'm Frances. What has brought you here today?'

That felt like such a huge question to start with. I thought there might be some general chat or something first. I didn't really know how to answer it.

'I... Well, my boyfriend wanted... I...'

I couldn't think of what to say, how to appropriately answer her question. So, of course, I did the only thing I knew how to do: I started crying. I hadn't even been there five minutes and I was already crying.

Always with the crying.

She leant forward and nudged the box of tissues over to me.

'Would you like me to start by telling you a bit about me and what we do here?'

I grabbed a tissue, wiped my nose, and nodded.

She told me a bit about her specialty, which she said was 'talk therapy' as opposed to 'behaviour therapy'. That didn't mean a lot to me, but I nodded as if I knew it was a good thing. By the time she repeated her question of what had brought me to her office, I was feeling a bit less overwhelmed.

'My boyfriend – fiancé – wanted me to come, we've had some problems... *I've* had some problems. I did something stupid. I... There was... someone else.'

Saying it out loud felt too much. It's not that I didn't think it was real before, but it felt so immediate having to say it. I did my best to explain my situation to her, with as few details as possible.

But she pushed me to talk about it in more detail. She told me shame couldn't survive being spoken, but I knew I *should* feel shameful for everything I'd done. I had been such a horrible person.

At her insistence, I told her about Chris, about the long, heady nights of reckless abandon, about how we'd had sex – not just the one time, as I'd told you, but that it had happened more times than I could remember. I told her about how you'd found out, how my world had come crashing down, and how I'd almost ruined everything for the sake of some silly fantasy. I said I didn't know how you had forgiven me, that I certainly didn't deserve it, but how grateful I was that you did.

I tried to recount the whole thing, but I'm sure there were bits I'd forgotten, and there would be bits, she said, that I had probably buried deep because I felt so ashamed, but that it was ok, and we would work through them.

I wasn't sure if any of it was a good idea. Surely it would be better if I could just try to forget it. But she told me that wouldn't work if I wanted our relationship to survive. She asked me if I did in fact want the relationship to survive. I nodded. Of course I did. I knew I just needed to be fixed before our relationship could be what it was.

'What do you do for work, Jess?' She asked me, and I wondered why it was relevant to fixing me... but figured she knew best.

'I work in the finance department of a law firm.'

'I see. And did you always want to do that?'

'Well, yes. I guess. It's what I studied...'

She didn't say anything, just nodded and looked at me. The silence felt uncomfortable, and I wanted it to end.

'Go on,' she said, and I hated her for it. I didn't know what she wanted me to say.

'That's it really. I used to write a bit, back at uni, but nothing serious.'

'Can you tell me a bit about that?'

'Oh, it was silly. I just wrote some articles here and there. It was this dream I used to have but it wasn't anything serious.'

'And do you still write?'

'No, not anymore.' I felt a strange aching feeling in my heart when I said it but tried to brush it aside. It wasn't a sustainable hobby, I had other things to concentrate on.

'I wonder if it might be helpful for you to start writing some things down. Maybe you could start this week, from the beginning.'

'What, from when I met Chris?'

She shook her head. 'Before that. Go as far back as you can. Just see what comes up. We can talk about it in your next session.'

Write it all down? That task seemed huge and insurmountable. I thanked her and left. I felt deflated as I made my way home. I think I'd hoped she would tell me how to fix things and all I'd done was tell her everything and not got any solutions. I guess it would take longer than that. I tried to sit and write when I got back to the flat but as soon as I went to start, I felt overwhelmed, dizzy and ill and I had to close my book and walk away.

Chapter 55

I didn't want to go to therapy again. It had been exhausting and had made me feel weird for days. I hadn't written anything down and I was certain Frances would be angry at me. Every time I thought about starting, my chest felt tight, I got very tired and could think only of everything else I should be doing instead. But I knew I wasn't any better yet. I was still making you irritated and I wasn't feeling right about things, so begrudgingly, I took myself to my next appointment. At least I knew what to expect.

The session started with talking a bit more about you. I told her that we'd got engaged and that it was great, but I was struggling to make you happy.

'Why do you think it's your job to make him happy?' she asked when I had finished.

I thought it was a strange question.

'Isn't that just what you're meant to do in a relationship? I certainly don't want to make him annoyed or angry... that's not nice for anyone.'

'Are *you* happy?'

My happiness was not something I had really thought about.

'I... I don't know.'

'Ok, but you think it's your role to make sure he's happy,

even if it's not something you're seeking for yourself?'

'Oh... um...'

'Do you feel like Robert's happiness is more important than yours?'

'It's more that... I know I'll find a way to get over things eventually. I can deal with not always being happy, but I'm not sure I'll survive if he doesn't want me anymore. If I push him too far, he might leave. And I just... I can't...' I leaned forward to grab a tissue to wipe the tears that inevitably came.

She nodded as I blew my nose. 'That's ok. It's fairly common for women to feel it's their responsibility to keep the relationship emotionally stable. The fear of being alone is also very real for a lot of people. I wonder if you can remember another time in your life, maybe an earlier memory of being left and feeling alone?'

'Not like that. Not intentionally... Nothing that's relevant to this.'

'You might be surprised... What comes to mind?'

'I mean... it's not related at all, but my sister died when I was seven. We were twins. But I didn't have to make her happy, and I wasn't scared of her leaving me. I was too young to think about any of that anyway.'

'How did you feel growing up without her?'

'Pretty lonely, I guess. I didn't have a lot of friends until I met Robert.'

She nodded. 'And you don't want to go back to that.'

'Well... No, of course not. But I'm not just with him because of that.'

'No, of course.' She was quiet for a moment before she spoke again. 'What about friends? Who's Astrid? You've mentioned her a few times. You two seem to be close.'

I had mentioned her, but I'd tried to avoid talking about her too much. Partly because I didn't think it was relevant, but also because it hurt to speak about her. I hadn't mentioned that she'd left me too in the end, that she'd completely cut me out of her life. My voice came out so small when I replied: 'She's gone. And there's no one else.'

It was getting dark as I walked out of her office, but I knew you'd be working late, so I decided to walk home across London to our flat. I pulled out my iPod to keep me entertained as I walked. I had it on shuffle, which I so rarely did as I usually put a specific album on. A song came on that stopped me in my tracks – it was Above and Beyond's song 'Stealing Time'. I hadn't allowed myself to listen to them. I didn't realise I had them on my iPod, then I realised it was from the playlist Astrid had put on it all that time ago. It was named 'Out Into The Night'. I listened to it as I made my way across London, and I finally got what she meant about walking at night with the right music, nowhere to go, no one expecting me. It really did feel freeing. And London looked so beautiful in the dark. I'd never realised it before, but it didn't properly get dark due to all the light pollution, and that just made it feel safer somehow. I felt alive walking home listening to her playlist.

When I got back to the flat, I wanted to start writing, but it was so hard. I tried to find some inspiration, something to put into words. Perhaps creativity was never a part of me at all. I spent the next few days attempting to write some poems as they seemed only a small commitment, but nothing I wrote made any sense. Sometimes I would write, and my brain couldn't keep up. Sometimes I would think, and my words couldn't keep up. My mind was a mess.

I was avoiding facing the inevitable; doing what Frances

had asked me to. It felt too silly to write my boring story out. But beneath it all was also the fact that readdressing it all felt too raw, too scary.

'Start at the beginning' Frances had said. So eventually, after many failed attempts at poetry, I wrote one sentence:

I noticed her the moment she arrived.

Chapter 56

I noticed her the moment she arrived.

The words cascaded out of me onto my page. I wrote and wrote, after thinking I might never write again. I wrote about the person I was when I first met her. As I wrote, I saw it plainly – Astrid changed my life. My time with her was so beautiful and magic, almost unrealistic, as if it had all been a dream. I felt full writing about our first meetings, how our friendship had grown, our wine nights, dancing into the morning light, listening to Bowie together... I felt fuller, remembering it all, than I had in a long time.

I wrote about how you and I had met – that I followed you to university, not really considering whether it was the direction I wanted to go. I wrote about how you'd told me you were going away for a year to America. I tried to write it as it happened and how I'd felt at the time – the thoughts and fears that had filled my mind – but as I wrote, a growing feeling of uneasiness came over me. You'd told me I was just overreacting, and I'd believed you. But looking back on it, I wasn't so sure. Astrid had said you were being unreasonable, but I didn't want to hear it. For the first time, as I let the words come out, I allowed myself to really feel it rather than trying to brush it aside. Then I remembered your reaction to me getting the tattoo. I knew you didn't like them, but I couldn't understand why you'd got so angry at me for getting one without consulting you, when it was exactly what you had done with America. I was expected to just be ok with your decision, while you were allowed to get angry at me for mine. It just didn't add up.

I lost myself writing about the parties, the nights out, the raves during my year with Astrid. I felt like I was writing about someone else's life, someone else's story. And it was. It was Astrid's— no, it wasn't just Astrid's, it was mine, too. It was ours. I'd always thought of myself as being on the outside, but going back through it all, that no longer felt quite right. I had been there; it was my life too. I don't know why I hadn't realised it at the time. *I'd* been given Ben and James's card and written articles for their magazine. *I'd* climbed that wall and spray painted the roof. *I'd* been invited by Freddie to go to his art exhibition, he'd thanked *me* for the article I wrote. *I'd* written the poem, got the applause, and everyone had gone out to the coast for *my* birthday. How could I not have realised how much I was part of it all?

It hurt me to get to the part where I left her. And it was *me* who left her. I finally had to admit it. I made my choice. She might have sealed it, but I left her no option. Or, should I say, *you* left us no other option. I'd thought you were so gracious, so kind, allowing me to still see her even though I couldn't live with her. I'd accepted it all as necessary, given what I had done. But you'd forced her hand. And mine. I couldn't gloss over it anymore. And what was it all for? For this? Why was it only when looking back that I could see how perfect my time with her had been? And I had spent most of that time thinking about you, worrying about you, and thinking that I wasn't good enough.

What the hell, Jess!

I suddenly remembered all the pages of notes I had written over the time I was living with Astrid, about our conversations, our nights out, the things we'd done. And Chris. Maybe we weren't meant for each other, but he had made me feel so alive, so desired, so seen, so real. So much more than you ever had. My notebooks were still packed away in one of the boxes we still hadn't yet emptied from the move. I'd almost forgotten they were still sitting there. It's funny how things can fade into the background and stop being noticed.

I found my notebooks along with the copy of the book 'Mating in Captivity' that Astrid had bought me. I turned it over in my hands, looking at the blurb, flicking through the pages. It appeared to be about the dynamics of love and desire in long term relationships. There was even a chapter on rethinking fidelity, which caught my eye. It looked interesting – why had I never read it? In my heart, I knew why: she'd been trying to tell me something about our relationship and I just wasn't ready to hear it.

Inside, there was a note I hadn't seen, written in her unmistakable handwriting. The handwriting that had written the names under the pictures she drew for our Greek party invites, the letters that were in her signature, the ones she'd spraypainted on the roof, the same J's, E's and S's she had used whenever she wrote my name.

My Dearest Little Maus, my love, my heart,

Always remember that you are you, and you are valid. You are enough, just as you are. This life is for you as much as anyone else and you are capable of so much.

Live fast. Say yes. Say no. Travel alone. Write like your life depends on it. Chase the sun. Relax. Make plans. Drink water. Drink champagne. Wear white. Make friends. Create moments. Move on. Wear black. Try new things. Spend time alone. Meditate. Make connections. Gaze at the moon. Seize opportunities. Wear nothing. Spend your money. Drink wine. Write notes. Write poetry. Get lost. Love deeply. Stay up talking all night. Watch the sun rise. Never be afraid to change. In fact, change constantly. Hug lots. Take risks. Write letters. Drink more champagne. Count the stars. Play music. Read books. Make decisions. Be spontaneous. Be significant. Be perfect. Make mistakes. Make plans. Drink coffee. Draw lines. Break plans. Be imperfect. Take up space. Play in the autumn leaves. Give things away. Take photos. Kiss passionately. Buy presents. Cross lines. Paint walls. Cause havoc. Play games. Get caught in the rain. Test yourself. Let things go. Drink tea. Dance on tables. Make art. Go on picnics. Spoil yourself. Collect things. Climb trees. Be you. And promise me, no matter what, you will ALWAYS LIVE. And do it as loudly as you can.

A xxx

I paced the length of our flat before walking into your office, where you were working. I wasn't supposed to bother you when you were in there, but there was something that had been bothering me, and I decided I needed to find out.

'You know my birthday,' I said, as I opened the door, startling you and making you look up.

'Yes, I know it. We all have one.'

'You didn't mention it because you were respecting my wishes, right? Because I said I didn't want to do anything?'

'Oh, I probably just forgot. I never remember those sorts of things.'

I figured you must be joking. 'Don't be silly. You sent me

those lovely flowers the year you were away.'

'Oh, that – Astrid messaged me and told me to. It's just not something I consider particularly important. I don't force people to make a big fuss of mine, it's only a birthday. What's the point of making a big deal? We're not children.'

You turned back to your computer, dismissing me so easily, as if nothing was wrong. But I couldn't believe what I was hearing.

I'd made so many damn excuses for you, reassured myself there was kindness in your heart, it just took some coaxing.

But it had been Astrid all along.

I left the room, shaking slightly, closing the door behind me.

All the sacrifices I made; leaving Astrid, giving up that perfect life we'd had...

What was it all for? For this?

Then something in me broke. The veil lifted.

I opened the book she'd got me and started reading.

Chapter 57

By now you'll know I'm gone. That I disappeared on one of those evenings you were out late. The money for two months' rent left on the dining table. I had enough holiday leave saved up at work to be able to just walk away. Holidays I was saving for our honeymoon. It feels almost a poetic ending, using that to leave you. I picture you wondering what happened before you realise I'm gone, and I'm not coming back.

I can see it now, so plainly in my words; all the excuses I made for your behaviour, all the times I silenced myself.

Astrid was so real. The things she said about me that night were right; the night you thought I didn't hear you two arguing. The things I didn't want to hear then, the things no one ever wants to hear about themselves, but I'm ready for it now. She did more for me than I ever did for her. You kept telling me that she was taking advantage of me but if anything, I think it was the other way around. You just wanted to make her the enemy. And you almost did. And I let you.

I always thought it was about you. Life was about getting that perfect dream, the husband, the family, the corporate job, then eventually the children, giving my parents the grandchildren they so wanted. Maybe someday I will, but not like this. That's not how I should honour Emily. From now on I'll do that by staying true to myself, whatever that means. I'm excited to find out.

You can make me the villain if you want, to your family and friends. I thought I would care more about that, but I don't. I've always cared so much about what other people think of me and I lost myself amongst it all. I don't want to live like that anymore. I can't.

I thought I would feel regret for leaving, that I'd think I made a terrible mistake. But what I feel now is relief, and I know it was the right choice. I no longer need to take responsibility for anything except myself. Why is this something I had to learn? Why are women made to feel we need to always take responsibility for everything and everyone?

I know now that what we had wasn't real love.

Real love is in the way she looked at me in the mornings when we'd just woken up. It's in holding hands on the walk home, singing at the top of our lungs. It's debriefing on our nights out once we've found our way back to each other again. It's supporting each other constantly. It's spontaneous pitchers of margaritas on Sundays and afternoons in the park.

I did go to Berlin. I got the train from Potsdamer Platz. I never thought I could make my way around on my own. I listened to Bowie as a constant soundtrack; he was my solace, my guide. So were the memories of Astrid. I felt her all around me.

I'm writing down the last of all this from a café in East Berlin. There's a post office just down the street, where it will start its journey back to you. It makes my neck tingle to think of you opening it; a thick envelope addressed to you, no idea what's inside...

I thought I couldn't do it – be out here in the world on my own – but I've surprised myself. I stare in the mirror still, trying to connect with the person on the other side. I could have done so many things differently. But even if I could go back, I'm not sure if I'd have known how. I could have ended it all earlier, sure. I could have stayed with Astrid... I play out different versions of the story, imagining what would have happened if I'd acted differently. In the version where we're still friends, I ask her about her Dad, about the box under her bed, about her upbringing, about the boys and girls she's loved, about what makes her cry when she's alone. All the things I never thought to ask.

There are still nightmares. When I try to sleep, the dark thoughts engulf me. But I'm learning how to save myself. Astrid always valued being self-sufficient. It took losing you both to realise that I wasn't self-sufficient at all. And that's not what I want to be, not anymore.

I'm terrified I won't feel happy now either. But I will concentrate on being creative. I will allow myself that. I will sit alone in cafes. I will pour myself a glass of red wine on a Friday night, even if I don't have anyone to drink it with. I will get a job in a bookshop again. I will put myself first and I will try not to give to anyone else until my reserves are full. I will try not to rely so much on other people. I will finally travel.

And I will write, write, write. For the pure love of it, for the burning need to get my thoughts down.

This is goodbye.

Don't try to find me.

Like Bowie said, I don't know where I'm going from here, but I promise it won't be boring.

Not this time.

Playlist

Music is such a huge part of this story, so of course, there had to be a playlist.

It has been lovingly curated to be listened to in order. Not as background music, but as an added bonus to follow alongside the book.

So to hear the music that accompanies Jess and Astrid through their adventures (and accompanied me as I immersed myself in their world) please check out the link, or scan the code.

https://jenevetaylor.com/playlist

Acknowledgments

What do they say about it taking a city? It amazes me how many wonderful people lent me their time, their energy, their minds, their eyes, all in the name of helping me to get this novel finished and out there in the world – into your hands. All the cliches exist because it's true – this has certainly been a labour of love. So, where to start...

To Katie, thanks for sitting on the rooftop of the Blues Point Hotel in early 2020, listening to me introduce you to Jess and Astrid and their (strong) personalities and the adventures they were starting to go on. Thanks for helping me to talk through their motivations, their deepest secrets. Thanks for every second since I met you 20 years ago, for all the support, for all the chats, for the early draft read, for being my colleague, sounding board, partner, bestie, soulmate.

Mum and Dad, my biggest supporters, thank you for reading this over, and over, and over again. For picking up typos, for asking what on earth I'm trying to say, for pointing out that the phones we had in 2008 probably weren't big enough to snort drugs off... Thanks for not being weird about reading scenes your daughter wrote about sex, drugs, and rock'n'roll. We were all young once, eh?

To Rosa, for the double read, and all the love and support. For the days of sitting in my flat, working on our own projects, for talking it all through and for both loving and hating these characters at the appropriate times, and accepting them into your world. Thanks for just being my muse in life. I can't imagine how I ever existed without you.

To Louise, another hugely appreciated double read through of this beast. All your thoughts and assistance along the way have been invaluable. Thanks for chats about jacket jackets, and for enabling some of the big pushes through this to have taken place in Paris. Paris!! Your generosity is so wonderful, and you've really helped me to believe I know what I'm doing, and that it's worth keeping going.

To Joce, Sarah and Mairéad, for reads at times I needed to hear someone outside of my head tell me that I know how to write a sentence (when editing tries to convince me I don't). Having you all know these characters too, was essential to them coming properly into existence. Mairéad, thanks also for being a good sport when I made you read the first two chapters out to me in a small cocktail bar after a long day of adventuring around East London.

'Just one more chapter?'

'Jen, I think it's time to go home...'

To Jules, my brilliant big brother whale. Having you read this and relate to it, was one of my favourite parts of the whole process. Knowing that it had reach beyond its pages and specific demographic made me realise how important it is for me to share the things I create. You gave me such a boost to keep going and reminded me of how much doing all this means to me.

To Lina, who agreed over coffee to read this through for me, after years of trying to read my words. You won this round. Though I think perhaps, I did, really.

To Megan, for your kindness in offering your and time and

energy to go methodically through the manuscript when I was terrified of how many mistakes had crept in during the editing process (a lot, it seems, but that's a story for another day). The formatting gods are particularly grateful for your input.

To Natali, for your belief in me and wonderful guidance, for being there to answer questions, and step in with a cavalcade of wonderful people to help and support at different stages.

And to all these people who pushed through reading this as a pdf/word doc on a laptop... it's really not the greatest reading experience, I appreciate it.

To Kerry, without your support and life changing 'Write Like A Grrrl' courses, I'm not sure this novel would exist, and I would certainly have fewer people to thank in these acknowledgments. Your encouragement to call myself a writer, and just write, felt revolutionary at the time. Now, it feels like the only option.

And for a last minute situation I hadn't prepared for, thanks to Mum and Sarah, for stepping in and taking over as my hands and eyes, when I went suddenly blind (yes, completely, totally blind), in the final moments of trying to get this finished and published. In a very scary time, your willingness and dedication to helping me to get this done, really blew me away.

To all the Jesses, and all the fellow Astrids of the world. To friendships, enduring and lost. To the girls who didn't leave, for without them, I wouldn't have had the drive to write a different narrative.

Note from the Author

This book is not autobiographical. It is not a thinly veiled memoir. It is not about me. But of course, I am in all of the characters (maybe not Robert... But then again, maybe... I did do debating for years...). And yes, bits and pieces of my life crop up here and there, as do anecdotes I have collected over the years.

As Lauren Groff said, 'I have held every human I've ever met upside down by the ankles, and shaken every last detail that I can steal out of their pockets.'

As authors, we have to borrow from reality at times. For all intents and purposes, these characters *are* real. But they're their own people.

So if you see yourself in any of the characters or an event feels familiar, maybe it's a coincidence, or maybe I did commandeer it (singing Zombie together while walking home drunk... carrying around an emergency apple, maybe...), in which case, thank you.

If you liked the book, I would be so grateful if you could rate and review it for me! On Amazon and/or Goodreads.

About the Author

Jen is originally from Sydney, Australia, but now lives in London - her life's one great love story.

She has been writing forever - does a writer ever not write? She's dabbled in most formats, but her most prolific forum is her blog, *The Cancer Chronicles* (www.thecancerchronicles.blog), where she writes about her adventures with a pesky bit of bone cancer (osteosarcoma) that seems to be intent on hanging around. Thus far it's claimed her eye, her top jaw, teeth, and cheekbone, and most recently, her remaining eyesight, plunging her into complete darkness.

Aside from writing, music is her life (if you didn't pick that up from the many music references spinning their way through this novel). Her album, *Dreams of the Lights* by Jen Eve, can be found on all your favourite music streaming platforms.

You can connect with me on:

- https://jenevetaylor.com
- https://twitter.com/jen_evetaylor
- https://facebook.com/profile.php?id=61552060522536
- https://thecancerchronicles.blog
- https://www.instagram.com/jen_eve